Lia Mills

Another Alice

POOLBEG

*All characters in this publication are fictitious
and any resemblance to real persons, living or
dead, is purely coincidental.*

First published 1996
by Poolbeg Press Ltd
123 Baldoyle Industrial Estate
Dublin 13, Ireland
This edition published 1997

© Lia Mills 1996

The moral right of the author has been asserted.

The Publishers gratefully acknowledge the support of
The Arts Council.

A catalogue record for this book is available from the British Library.

ISBN 1 85371 674 X

Photograph of sea by Robert Vance
Photograph of woman by Mark Nixon
Cover design by Poolbeg Group Services Ltd
Set by Poolbeg Group Services Ltd in Garamond
Printed by The Guernsey Press Ltd,
Vale, Guernsey, Channel Islands.

ACKNOWLEDGEMENTS

One of the first things people say about writing is that it's a solitary activity. And so it is. But every time I lifted my head from this manuscript and looked for help, whether with practical information, or a critical reading of a draft, or reassurance that I wasn't mad for trying to write this novel, I got what I needed. I often got more. The writing community in Ireland is incredibly generous and welcoming to new writers, while my family and friends have been unfailingly supportive. If I were to thank everyone individually for their contribution, whether practical or emotional, to the writing of the novel, the list might well be as long as the book. But, besides a general acknowledgement of the help of my family, friends, and colleagues, there are a few people whose help I must recognise individually, because without it the experience of writing the novel would have been entirely different, and it may never have reached completion.

First of all, special thanks are due to Rosemary Liddy, who encouraged me to begin this novel, and to Kate Cruise O'Brien, who helped me to finish it. Simon, Zita, Emma and Vanessa Robinson gave me the benefit of their patience, tolerance, humour, endless cups of tea and, most of all, their love and belief in me through years of writing. (It's *really* finished, this time!) Thanks also to Jackie Mills, David Collins, Pam and Frank Robinson, Clair Callan and Gael Blair.

For their critical readings of early drafts or sections of the novel when it was in progress, I'd like to thank: Gerry

Beirne, Pat Boran, Evelyn Conlon, Susan Connolly, Sherie de Burgh, Anne Enright, Felicity Hogan, Ann Marie Hourihane, Aisling Kearney, Colm Keena, Jim McAulay, and Zita Reihill. Thanks also to participants in the EWU Workshop (1994) at the Irish Writers' Centre, and particularly to my co-conspirators in the New Writing Workshop in the summer of 1994: Jeanette Boyne, Louise C Callaghan, Susan Connolly and Colette Connor.

For specific technical insights in different areas, I am indebted to Maeve Lewis, Rosie Liddy, Robert Vance, Brigitte Walley, Denise Weinberg. The synthesis and representation of the information they have given me are, however, my own responsibility.

I have been particularly lucky in the generosity and support of Paula Meehan, Ronit Lentin, and Jeanne Wells. I have also been sustained in many ways by Ailbhe Smyth, and by my colleagues, the staff, students and associates of the Women's Education Research and Resource Centre at University College Dublin. In particular, for their encouragement of and interest in the novel, thanks to Bernie Dwyer, Fidelma Farley and Joan McBreen.

I will never forget the first reading I gave of some of the more difficult passages of the novel. To the group that listened and applauded and encouraged me to go on writing, I owe more than I can say. Mary, Caroline, Nicola, Paula, Dorothy, Catherine, Celine, Suzanne, Shay, Rosie, Maeve, thank you. I hope it was worth waiting for.

Parts of this novel were written at the Tyrone Guthrie Centre (Annaghmakerrig). Thanks to Bernard and Mary Loughlin, and to the Arts Council/An Chomhairle Ealaíon, who also made it possible for me to attend the Eastern Washington University Workshop in the Irish Writers' Centre (1994).

Finally, thanks to Philip MacDermott and everyone at Poolbeg, especially Nicole Hodson for her patience.

For Rosie
and
For Simon, Zita, Emma and Vanessa
with love and thanks

PROLOGUE

This is not me, Alice thought, the first time she found herself sitting in Ruth's office. It can't be. What am I doing here?

She studied the door, her mind racing.

Ruth sat across the room, waiting for Alice to speak. The question she'd asked a while ago still hung, unanswered, in the air.

"I don't know," Alice said eventually.

Outside, dark was gathering, even though it was only five o'clock. Ruth's office was dim but lights blazed out in the hall. The closed door hung crooked on the jamb, and Alice could see a triangle of yellow light through the gap in the wood. Beside her, in a small brass grate, a low fire was burning.

"Don't you remember *anything*?" Ruth rephrased her original question.

"It's too . . . ordinary, to remember. You know? I grew up. Like everyone else."

Alice shifted in her chair uneasily.

You've got to say something, she urged herself. Otherwise, what's the point?

But her mind was empty. Drifting. She let it drift and slowly it began to rock. Lift and fall. Like water.

"I remember the sea," she said.

PART ONE

CHAPTER ONE

The waves were winning. They rolled Alice over and over. She tried to stand when the water fell, but it came surging back and pounded against her, knocking her into the foam. If only she was stronger. Taller, so she could lift her head over the water and breathe. The sea sucked at her legs, dragging her backwards.

She tried to stand again. Her eyes were salt, her chest burned. There was a roaring in her ears. Her mother lay up there on the beach, solid and dark like a log on the sand. If only she'd look, surely she'd see that Alice was in trouble and come and lift her out of the hungry water.

She didn't come.

Alice made one last effort to throw herself towards the beach. At first she didn't understand that the next wave that broke was behind her. Its foam swirled up around her shoulders, but not over her head. Then the extra breathing space gave her the strength she needed and she pulled herself clear of the sea at last, coughing, fighting to pull air into her burning lungs.

She sat at the edge of the water, panting. Harmless wavelets washed around her ankles and rivers of sand flowed away from her legs. A calm blue sky stretched over her head. You couldn't tell, from here, how strong that single line of breakers was.

She drew up her legs and wrapped her arms around them, holding on to herself. She rested her face on her knees and her hair fell around her like seaweed, darkened by the water it trailed into. She shivered. Her breathing had eased but now her teeth had begun to chatter and her swimsuit, the bright red one with the frilly skirt and the sailboat pattern that had been an early birthday present, clung coldly to her skin. Her seventh birthday! If she'd drowned, it could never come.

Alice looked back at the water, her mind floating and blank. An oystercatcher ran in and out of the wavelets on its long bright legs, its head bobbing. Gulls wheeled over her head. Down where the water rolled in to meet the sand at the headland there were rock pools, the water clear and calm. She liked to lie on her stomach and stare into their strange, silent depths, the underwater plants like a forest on some other planet. You had to look for a long time before you could see the tiny creatures that swam there, but once you'd found their movement you could see hundreds of them. Her father had told her the names of things that clung to the rock. Barnacles, mussels, winkles. Bladderwrack and kelp.

She looked away towards the high dunes at the back of the beach. Her mother hadn't moved. Alice got to her feet and walked towards her, her legs weak and wobbly. She sank up to her ankles in the soft hot sand, its dryness sticking to her, making her skin prickle. When she reached the beach blanket she flopped down onto it beside her mother, who sat up abruptly.

"You're all wet!"

"I've been in the water."

Her mother brushed at the sand that had fallen from Alice onto the blanket. "You're cold, too. Wrap yourself in this," she said, throwing a yellow beach towel towards her. "Not here, you're showering me with sand! Stand over there to do it."

Alice shivered as she moved off the blanket. She wrapped the towel around herself. "I was stuck out there," she said.

"Where?"

"In the water."

"Oh?" Her mother pulled her sunglasses down her nose with her index finger. Her pale blue eyes studied Alice. She hated any kind of fuss.

They both looked down at the sea. From where they sat the waves appeared to roll over each other in soft white frills, making an even sound like breathing. Alice couldn't blame her mother for being so casual when she said, "Well, you're all right now, aren't you?"

"Yes," Alice said, fighting tears.

There were goosepimples on her arms and legs. Her knees folded under her and she knelt at the edge of the blanket, shivering. Her mother pushed her sunglasses up again and inched away from Alice's cold, damp, sandy body.

"You look frozen," her mother said. "You'd better go back to the caravan and get some clothes on, before you catch your death."

Alice stood up again. She let her shadow stretch out beside her mother's body until they were the same length.

"Don't block my sun, Alice!" her mother said, but lazily, not crossly.

She didn't open her eyes as she turned over to lie on her stomach, pushing her grey hair away from her face. She wore a plain black bathing suit. It was odd to see so much of her skin exposed. Her shoulders were covered in big, flat freckles like the ones on Alice's nose and forehead, which were peeling from the sun. Every day more and bigger freckles appeared on her mother's shoulders, all running together, turning her the colour of tea. Alice's pale skin just burned and peeled and burned again.

They were on their holidays. It was the first time in her life that Alice had spent a night anywhere except in their house and she loved it. She loved the sound of the wind rushing through the ferns that grew in the dunes around the caravan they had rented. She loved the way her bare feet sank into cool fine sand when she jumped down from the door in the early morning. By lunchtime the sand was burning hot and she had to run across it, moving quickly away from the pain before she felt it. She had to watch out for the spiteful marram grass, waiting to spike her feet if she wasn't careful. The sand got into everything. It stung her eyes. It got into the webs between her fingers and toes and into her mouth.

In the evenings, when the air cooled, they walked up the lane to sit in the pub where the smoke stung her eyes all over again. She sat quietly with her parents and listened to other people shout and laugh and bang glasses together, until it was time to go back to the caravan and fall asleep with the sound of the sea moving in her ears.

She walked slowly across the dunes towards the caravan, still shaky and sore, as if she'd been beaten. There was a sudden rustling behind her and Max appeared out of the ferns, wagging his strong dark tail.

He barked once when he saw her and pushed his body against her legs. He was panting. His tongue slid, pink, over his teeth as he smiled at her. Alice wrapped her arms around his neck and buried her face in his fur. His solid body reassured her. She was safe. Her knees folded up again and she let herself fall against him, breathing him in like air.

"There you are!" Her father came up behind her. "Did you have a good swim?" He touched her head. "You'd better brush the salt out of your hair."

He'd told her that her hair was like money because of its bright, almost silvery colour. Her mother twisted it into long plaits every night and he liked to wind them round her neck and tickle her ears with the ends. Rapunzel, he sometimes called her.

Her father was always telling stories. Everything that happened reminded him of something and he'd be off, a faraway look in his eye, his voice pulling Alice after him. He called her different names, depending on the mood he was in, what character she put him in mind of at the time.

Now he twisted her hair in his hands and squeezed it. Drops of water fell from it and darkened the sand at her feet.

"You remind me of the Little Mermaid," he said. "Look at you, you've never been on land before." His voice deepened. "You don't know how to walk yet, on your brand-new legs."

He picked her up, laughing, his mouth open. She could see his teeth, the salt stains on his glasses above his smiling mouth.

"You've never worn clothes before," he went on. "Never mind, we'll find you something." He carried her the rest of the way to the caravan.

Alice had moved in and out of his stories for as long as she could remember. Her mother gave out to him sometimes.

"It's no wonder the child gets nightmares, Michael," she said, making a tsking noise with her tongue against her teeth. "She's confused."

Down here he told her water stories. About a place across another sea, where the heroes lived and no one ever got old or died. About the children of Lír, changed into swans for nine hundred years. It made her shiver. She felt exposed, out there on the beach, surrounded by sea and sky and waving ferns. She could see nothing familiar. It made her dizzy, so much emptiness. They could have been anywhere. Anything could happen.

They lived near the sea in the city, but the beaches there were different. There were always other people around, boats sailing in and out of the bay. Yachts in the summer-time, the car ferry, trawlers. Behind the beach was the railway line and the road, always busy. There were round stone towers, like sandcastles with flat tops, along the coast. The one nearest their street was sometimes open in the summer, dark and airless. You could buy ice cream there, but Alice hated going into it. The cold darkness pressed on her skin and gave her goose-bumps, crept through her nostrils to the back of her throat. The light and heat of the sun seemed far enough away to be lost forever.

Narrow jetties, like baby piers, stretched into the sea beside this tower and the waves broke over them at high tide. People swam off them, but not Alice. She crouched in the water and moved around, staying well clear of the edge, afraid of being swept into water out of her depth. She preferred low tide when the water was calm and warm and far from where her father waited, back on the wall, watching. Thinking she was swimming. He even told her mother she could swim. How could she tell them it was a lie? That she stayed within her depth and walked along the sand, her feet hidden by the sea?

Down here in Brittas, she sat for hours at the edge of the sea, felt the sand run away from under her while the water curled around her, and wasn't afraid. After days of this, she thought that she could overcome her fear and walk through the surf, start swimming on the other side. But the waves grew as she tried to pass them. She panicked and swallowed water, lost her bearings, went out too far. She should have known better. She should have stayed on dry land.

On the last morning of their holiday, Alice's birthday, they picked blackberries. She'd already had her presents.

The bathing suit. A bucket and spade for the beach. They'd given her a book of legends that morning.

While her parents packed everything up and cleaned the caravan, they sent Alice down to the water to wash out her two beach buckets, the bowl they'd used for washing dishes and an extra metal bucket her mother had brought along, just in case. Alice rinsed them all at the edge of the sea and then carried them back across the sand to the caravan, where her parents waited.

They walked along the quiet lanes and filled their containers with plump purple berries.

"We'll bring them home and make jam," her mother said. "These are beauties."

Alice got absorbed by the hunt. Every berry that she picked drew her eye towards another one, glossier and more darkly bright than the one before it. Her fingers were stained purple and juice spilled down her chin onto her clothes, but even her mother smiled at her and said it didn't matter.

"You'll be growing out of that old shirt soon anyway. We'll throw it away when we get home."

Alice couldn't believe her ears. They never threw anything away. Old clothes were torn into strips and used as rags. The kitchen drawers were crammed with folded brown paper, odd buttons, lengths of string. They used newspapers to spread on the floor after they'd washed it. She wished they were in a story, in a place where time stopped and nothing ever changed. She wanted them to be like this, always. Her mother smiling and relaxed, her father lifting her so she could reach any berries that she wanted.

But when all the buckets were full they had to pack up and go home. Her mother's smile faded as they loaded the boot of the car, an old Alvis her father had been working on for weeks before they'd left.

"I still think we shouldn't have used this car." Her mother touched the chrome doorhandle nervously. "Mr Kennedy's already paid for it. What if it gets damaged?"

"Then I'll fix it up again." Her father sighed heavily. This was a conversation they'd had before, many times. They'd fought about it on the way down. Alice could tell the holiday was over by the tone of her father's voice. "We're doing him a favour, running it in for him. May as well find out if there's any problems before he collects it. Isn't that right, Alice?"

Alice wished he'd leave her out of it. She pretended not to hear, and fussed over the blackberries on the floor behind the driver's seat instead. She covered them with a beach towel, as her mother had told her earlier, so that they wouldn't spill on the drive home.

"Well, drive carefully," her mother pleaded, sitting into the front of the car. Max jumped in beside Alice, his tail wagging.

"Don't let the dog sit on the seat, Alice!" her mother went on.

"But the berries . . ."

Her mother got out of the car again, cross. "All right, then! I'll take the berries in front, with me. Under my legs." She sighed loudly. "All that distance, and no leg room. I suppose it can't be helped." Her glare was hot on Alice's face for a second, then she lifted out the buckets and struggled into the front with them.

"Are you quite ready? Can we go now?" Alice's father's voice was heavy and rude. He got into the car and slammed his door. Her mother winced.

Alice rested her face in Max's warm fur and then pushed him gently down off the seat. He stretched across the narrow space at her feet and put his head on his paws. She slipped off her shoes and curled her toes into his thick coat.

Her father drove fast along the narrow roads back to the city, making her mother nervous in the front. His window was open all the way, funnelling the early September air back into Alice's mouth, making it hard to breathe. But she liked the taste of the moving air and let it fill her up until she had to turn away. His elbow rested on the open edge and he leaned back into the seat, comfortable.

When her mother drove she sat bolt upright, her back not touching the seat, both hands locked on the wheel, staring straight ahead of her. She never let Alice sit in the front.

"It's too dangerous," she warned.

But he did. When there was just the two of them in the car, he let her sit between him and the steering wheel, holding her hands under his. She ignored how cramped she was between him and the wheel as she looked under its rim at the road ahead and pretended she was driving. As soon as her legs were long enough to reach the pedals he'd teach her how to drive. He'd said so.

She knelt on the back seat and leaned her head on her bent elbow, watching all the places they'd left behind slip away into the distance. The road was like a ribbon, twisting back between hills and trees. They drove through a steep valley of loose-looking rock and she held her breath, wondering if the boulders would fall on top of the car. When they were safely through it she began to bounce up and down on the seat, relieved.

"Stop doing that. You'll scratch the leather," her mother complained. Alice turned around so she was facing the front. She sat on the edge of the seat, leaning forwards, still bouncing. She couldn't help it. Below her, Max's tail began to move in sympathy.

"Come on, Daddy!" she cheered, the way he did at the radio when the races were on. Her mother's silent back grew more and more rigid. Her grip tightened on the strap in the front of the car.

Alice and her father sang out *Ten Men Went To Mow* and *She'll Be Coming Round The Mountain* as he rushed across hills and dips in the road making the car leave the earth for a second, scattering sparks and the long ash from his cigarette. In a sickening, delicious rush, Alice's stomach flew up to her throat. It felt as if she might never touch ground again. It made her squeal.

"Faster, Daddy, go faster," she urged him, eager to pass every other car in sight, hungry for speed, wanting flight.

"Be quiet!" snapped her mother. She glared at Alice as she said, "For God's sake, Michael, slow down! You'll kill us all!"

His glasses gleamed when he turned around to look at Alice in the back, not watching the road at all, and said, "What do you say, Alice? Do you think we'll be killed?"

She stared back at him, mesmerised.

"I want you to go faster."

He smiled at her. "That's the girl."

He turned again to look where he was going. But Alice shrank back, then, down into the seat, because her mother's ears had gone a funny colour and she knew she was in trouble, that she would pay for this later.

Words like *show-off*, *notice-box*, *brat*, icy and sharp as broken glass, hung in the air of the car. Alice couldn't be sure her mother had spoken because her face was turned away. He went back to humming, but Alice didn't join in this time.

She stared instead at passing hedges and trees and telegraph poles and wondered what it would be like to live beside those roads, to be still and solid while the whole world rushed past you in a blur of dust and exhaust fumes and noise. They passed the rigid red body of a fox and she stared so hard that her eyes watered. She put herself into a trance of stillness and didn't notice the time or the countryside passing, coming back to herself only as they turned into their lane, slowing, home again.

Then she began to feel how stiff she was. When she saw the house waiting at the end of the narrow terrace, its windows blank and empty, her own weight crept over her again. It was hard to move her legs and arms, to get out of the car and step through the back door into the cold blue kitchen. Walking into the house felt like a defeat. But at least Max was there, happy to be out of the car, barking and chasing his tail, breaking up the cold air with the fuss he was making.

CHAPTER TWO

Alice hated the house. It was tall and thin, like a person. She wished they weren't at the end of the terrace, with the naked side of the house exposed. It was always cold. She thought there was something sly about the way its net-curtained windows veiled the light. She could feel the broad chilly glass of the windows behind her whenever she went out. Watching her go. Knowing she'd be back. They never had visitors, except for the priest who called round for a sherry sometimes, on Sunday afternoons. If the other children on the street called for Alice, they were left standing on the doorstep until she came out to play.

It was a quiet house. Her parents' talk seemed to circle above her head not reaching down to touch her. Down at her level, darkness crouched in the corners and stretched in pools between the furniture. Sometimes she could hear it breathe and knew that it was alive. It was a monster that had swallowed her and she lived inside it. Captive. Everything was set up to look like an ordinary house, the ones that other people lived in, with rooms and windows and furniture. This fooled most people, but not Alice. She knew it was an other-worldly place, enchanted, like the ones her father told her about in his stories. It revealed itself at night, in dreams of looming figures and muffled sounds.

She felt better when he played music on his record player in the daytime. The sound filled the air and filled her, so that she didn't know if it was inside her or out. The darker, heavier music meant danger and when she heard it she stayed well away from him, but at least she knew where he was, what to avoid.

When he played lighter music she sat with him and listened to the sound spill into the air, like water. She liked to let it wash over her leaving her empty when it was finished. They could sit for hours by the record player as it sang out symphonies and oratorios and operettas, the louder the better. He had the scores for most of them and followed the music on paper as well as in his head. She liked, but didn't understand, the symbols that flowed across the page in front of him. Sometimes he conducted with his cigarette, leaving trails of fire and smoke in the air.

When he played songs she sang along with him. *The Student Prince* was their favourite, they shouted it out together in loud exaggerated voices and Alice stamped around on the pocked wooden floor in time to the music: "Drink, drink, drink, to eyes that are bright . . ." She rolled her rrrs and nodded her head and stamped her feet. Even if she made the needle jump on the record, for once he didn't seem to mind, his glasses shone at her, benign.

When he was in a bad mood he listened alone and in the dark, very still, with the curtains drawn, smoking one cigarette after another. His Adam's apple bulging in his neck. He hated to be interrupted then. If Alice disturbed him he would rage and roar and cough, his face purple and swollen, until she ran from the room, shaking.

Even her mother stayed well clear when he was like that. If she needed to tell him something she sent Alice instead. "Tell your father he's wanted on the phone."

Alice would deliver the message, fast, from the doorway, and leave without waiting to see if he'd heard or not.

The night they came back from Brittas, Alice fell asleep quickly, worn out by a whole week of sunshine and sand and the sound of the sea.

"You'll sleep well tonight," her mother told her.

But the house creaked and settled around her, stirring, coming alive.

She was caught in a sack, like a drowning kitten. The hungry sea was rising, coming for her. Her throat closed in panic. Mounting waves crashed around her and the thing that lay coiled at the bottom of her bed twisted around her ankles and held her down, sweating with fear and fighting for air.

Then she was under the water, down on the sea-bed, trapped in oozing slime. A dark figure leaned towards her, murmuring. She tried to call her mother but her mouth was caught in the sack . . .

"Alice." Her mother's voice called her back to the surface.

She was in her own room, the room with no lock.

Her mother must have turned the light on. Alice could see the heavy red curtains that covered one wall, the chest of drawers, with the crooked top drawer jammed slightly open, the tall grey wardrobe with painted sheep peeling in the corner. Her mother's face furrowed as she bent over her, squinting. Her hair in curlers.

"I'll bring you a drink," she said, and pulled the covers up over Alice's shoulders.

Alice could hear the keys falling against each other as her mother unlocked the doors downstairs, on her way to the kitchen. At night, her mother locked all the doors carefully. Rooms, cupboards, everything was locked. Alice never asked why. It was something they didn't talk about. She thought it might be to stop the house coming too alive, but she was afraid to ask in case her mother laughed at her. Her mother had a round metal key ring, heavy enough to knock someone senseless if she wanted to. It jangled while she tried out the different keys, sighing with impatience until she found the right one.

The only doors that had no keys were Alice's bedroom and the bathroom. The bathroom door had a heavy black bolt on the inside, but Alice was forbidden to use it until she was much older.

"Something might happen," her mother warned. Alice wondered what she meant. It was all part of being a prisoner in the house, trapped, while the dreams came and went as they pleased.

She breathed carefully and waited until she heard

the keys again, signalling her mother's return, up the narrow stairs.

"Here you are." Her mother handed her a steaming mug full of hot milk and whiskey, sweetened with sugar, the way Alice liked it. "Drink that up and go back to sleep."

"Can Max sleep in here with me? Please? Just this once?"

"Don't be silly. Max can't stop you having nightmares. You know as well as I do, they're not real."

Alice stared at the puckering skin on top of the milk and shuddered. She hated it. She reached into the hot liquid. The skin clung to her finger as she lifted it out again and scraped it on the side of the mug.

"Please?"

"You heard what your mother said. Max sleeps downstairs and that's that. Stop being such a baby. Go back to sleep." Her father had come in behind her mother, crowding the room. He looked different without his glasses. Like someone else. Alice squeezed her eyes tightly shut.

When she opened them again the light was off and her parents had gone. She knew her mother would be tired and cross the next day because of her. She knew, because this had happened before. Her mother sometimes said that she hadn't had one decent night's sleep since Alice was born.

Alice curled up into a tight ball and pressed herself against the headboard and tucked her nightie close around her feet. She woke in the morning stiff and cold, her ear aching as it often did.

Her mother put cotton wool soaked in warm oil in her ear. "Stop whining," she said, irritable from lack of sleep.

"But it hurts!" Alice complained.

"Of course it does, if you dwell on it. Think about something else. I'm going to make jam with the blackberries after Mass, Sunday or not. I won't have time tomorrow after work. Do you want to help? We can check for worms and then you could weigh the sugar."

Alice nodded, taking her cupped hand away from her ear.

"Stay well clear of the pot, though. I'm warning you, now. I don't want to have to keep saying it. Jam gets really hot, Alice. Hotter than anything. You'll be scalded if you're not careful."

Alice weighed the sugar while her mother watched. Then her mother stirred it into two big aluminium pots, where the berries were already simmering. Alice couldn't see the jam, but she could see and smell the delicious steam rising from it. The smell was thick and sweet, like toffee. It made her mouth water and her stomach began to growl.

"Stand well clear," her mother reminded her as she went over to the sink, where dirty bowls were stacked high in the soapy water.

But Alice couldn't resist that smell. She stood on tiptoe and leaned towards the cooker, felt heat on her face as she tried to see inside the pot. "Alice!" her mother called out sharply. "Be careful! How many times do I have to tell you . . ."

Alice jumped with fright. Suddenly she felt her wrist gripped hard, from behind. She tried to pull it away, to move back from the cooker, but her father's body blocked her own, trapping her. He took her wrist and pulled it forwards, over the top of the cooker. Something hot and red ran through her fingers and down the inside of her arm straight to her heart and squeezed it. The room fell away from her.

"Ah, Michael," she thought she heard her mother say, from very far away.

The next thing she knew she was sitting on her mother's lap at the table. Her mother held her reddened hand into a bowl of milk. Her father stood beside them, talking very fast, wheezing.

"She's got to learn. You've got to learn, Alice. Do you hear me? Now you know never to reach up there again, or something worse might happen to you. This is for your own good. Do you understand? Do you?" He shook Alice's shoulder. "Answer me!" He coughed, deep down in his stomach.

Alice couldn't see him properly. Her face was hot, everything was hot and there were sparks inside her head. There was a red cloud around everything she saw. The inside of her ears was burning too, all the way down into her neck. She felt sick in her stomach and struggled against it.

Don't, oh don't be sick.

Her eyes were watery and her nose was running and still she heard his voice above her head.

"It was the best thing to do, Elaine. Sometimes you've got to be cruel to be kind. She won't ever forget to be careful around the cooker again. Will you, Alice? You've learned your lesson. Haven't you? Haven't you?"

He shook her again, harder. The milk spilled out

over the sides of the Brer Rabbit bowl, the one her mother was holding her hand in. The pads of her fingers were flaming and swollen, the tops of them beginning to lift in white bubbles.

His voice went on. "This is all your own fault. If it hadn't been for you, we wouldn't even have picked those bloody berries in the first place . . . You won't forget this, will you? That it's for your own good." His glasses loomed in front of her face.

"No," Alice said, looking at the bubbles.

But she did forget. When her fingertips throbbed she put them into her mouth to soothe them without knowing why. When she read about the Salmon of Knowledge in the book they'd given her for her birthday, she believed that she had been chosen, that she could have magic powers if only she could prove herself worthy. She pressed her fingers to her lips and waited.

Her mother was exasperated by this habit. "Only babies suck their fingers," she said, painting a foul-tasting ointment around Alice's nails to stop her putting her hand in her mouth. "It's disgusting."

In rage, Alice chewed the ointment off her fingers, taking layers of skin with it. The sockets of her nails became inflamed as she tore at them, making small craters in the skin around them. After a bath, softened by hot water, her hands looked bizarre, her fingers honeycombed, uneven. The more ointment her mother applied, the more skin she chewed away. It amazed her that it grew back so quickly. No matter how red and disfigured her fingers were at night, they usually healed by morning.

Then she had to start all over again.

CHAPTER THREE

At the back of their yard, behind the shed where her father kept his tools and spare engine parts, a cluster of nettles and dock leaves grew wild and uncontrolled.

"If ever you get stung by a nettle," her father told her, "look around you. There'll be a dock leaf growing nearby. Nature's like that."

Alice didn't like to think what else might be in there, lurking in the undergrowth, hidden, unseen.

That autumn she found the body of a kitten lying stiff and twisted right there in the wet grass, stretched out as if she had been running for shelter from the rain. There were tooth marks in her neck, the soft orange fur matted.

"Rats," her father said when she called him over to look. He bent to pick the kitten up.

"What are you going to do?" Alice asked him.

"Throw it over the wall into the lane."

"Don't!"

"Well, you deal with it then. I'm busy."

He went back to work outside the gate. Alice stared at the kitten, wondering what to do. She'd never touched a dead thing before. She reached for the body, cautiously. Her fingers recoiled from the rigid cold beneath the limp fur. The kitten looked nearly perfect, except for those two red marks in her neck. As if the rats had killed her just for the sake of it. To show how easy it was. For fun.

Alice shuddered. She decided to bury the kitten, even though she'd never seen her before. She went inside and got her facecloth from the bathroom and wrapped the kitten in it, so that the spirits would know someone had cared about her. Then she put it in a green Clark's shoebox and carried the box across the lane and into the field behind the house.

The lane beside the house curved at the back and ran behind all the houses on their street. The lane was full of weeds and junk. Bits of rusted metal, an old bath with the enamel stained and peeling, a set of tyres. This was where Alice's father worked, rebuilding engines. On the other side of the lane was a crumbling brick wall separating the lane from the field, which was part of the garden of a big old house that nobody lived in and everyone said was haunted. Alice liked to climb over the wall and play in the field, staying well clear of the house.

There was a ditch out there where the ground was mucky and soft after the rain. She scooped out a pile of cold, soggy leaves. Then she got her spade and dug a big hole. She put the box carefully into the hole and threw a handful of dandelions on top of it. The leaves were useless, all their colours washed out. She covered the box with earth and then cried, a little.

She didn't usually cry and she wasn't squeamish. She liked to cut up worms and watch the pieces wriggle away in different directions. But finding the

kitten like that upset her. She had been bright, like the
sun. The rats were dark and secret and Alice hated
them. She knew that the kitten would never come out
of that box. Out of the hole in the ground where Alice
had put her.

Max jumped down off the wall, his tail waving. He
had come looking for her, his tongue out over his bottom
teeth, his breath warm and smelly against her face.

"Lie down, Max," she told him. Then she lay on top
of him and rested her head on his side.

In the field Max could be anything. He was Merlin to
her Arthur, A wolfhound to her Maeve. He was a
shapeshifter, like her. When other people looked at him
they saw a big German Shepherd and usually backed
away. His torn ear made him look like a fighter.
Mothers took their children by the hand and crossed
the street to avoid him. Only Alice knew that he was
something wonderful in disguise. Once when she had
done something wrong and her father put her across his
knee and began to spank her, Max growled at him. It
made her father laugh and he let her go.

"Your guard dog has saved you," he told her.

In their games, Alice and Max were heroes from an
ancient world. Alice dreamed that she was a secret
survivor of the Fianna. She believed it was up to her to
re-learn the old traditions, to bring them back to life.
She had a hide-out in a ruined tower against the far
wall of the field and a cedar tree she called her own.

Now she slid in between its lower branches and sat at
the base of its rough trunk, shrouded in green, shut away

from everything except Max. Max was the only person who came to the tree with her, although her friend Kate played in the field too and everyone knew about the tower. There was always litter scattered around on the ground up there: sweet papers and cigarette butts, broken bottles and metal bottle tops. Alice liked to sit in the tree and feel its rough bark at her back, the fallen needles in heaps under her feet, reading. From the outside, no one could tell she was there.

She loved reading. She'd learned early, when she was three. Her father liked to show off her skill and made her read paragraphs from the newspaper to the priest on Sundays.

"I taught her myself," he boasted. "They're never too young to learn. Have another drop, Father."

Alice stumbled over some of the words in the newspaper. Her father taught her how to say them properly. He told her she'd find out what they meant soon enough. What mattered was to sound as if she knew. She preferred comics. The drama of the pictures, the difference between what the characters said and what they thought. The words were enclosed in bubbles over people's heads, a solid line for when they were talking, a wavy, cloudy one when they were thinking. Sometimes the wavy ones and the solid ones were side by side and Alice played with swopping them around.

In the first book she'd ever read there was a fairy tale about two sisters. When one of them spoke, she scattered riches. Pearls, rubies and sapphires fell from her mouth. But the other sister uttered loathsome creatures, toads and worms and creepy crawlies. It was Alice's biggest fear, that one day she'd open her mouth and nothing but slime would come out of it. Once she drank old milk and it made her sick. For hours she fought against vomiting while her stomach cramped and twisted, but she won in the end. She kept it down.

Her mother didn't approve of comics. "Penny Dreadfuls!" she sniffed, when Alice begged if she could have one. She didn't approve of sweets either. So when Alice found a penny or two lying around the house, on her mother's dressing-table or in someone's pocket, she took the money and bought things to share with Kate.

Kate's dad owned Kenny's, the sweet shop down the road, and he gave them great value on penny assortments. Alice loved sweet things: fizzbags, aniseed balls, liquorice allsorts, hot dogs and dolly mixtures, the names tasted nearly as good as the sweets, rolling around on her tongue. Bullseyes and rum and butters and, best of all, turkish delight, leaving soft trails of powdered sugar on her fingers.

Alice went down there to do messages for her parents, to get the paper, or packets of cigarettes for her father, singles for her mother. The Kennys didn't mind when she sat on the floor behind the counter with Kate, the two of them reading, sweets making a bulge in their cheeks, talking about the stories and swopping over when they'd finished. When Kate's dad got sick of them being in his way he said, "All right now girls, that's enough. Get lost, will ye?" and they ran off to Kate's house, or to the field.

All kinds of berries grew in the field. Gooseberries, blackberries, loganberries. At this time of year there were hazelnuts and beechnuts and she and Kate filled their pockets with shining conkers after school and played with them like marbles. There were three old apple trees, too. Bare now. Every year they tasted the apples too early and every year they were disappointed by their stubborn tartness, the rough wall of skin. Then, overnight, there would be the windfall and the slow rot in the autumn grass.

Alice liked to lie in the grass when she was alone, the green stalks high around her like a forest. She liked listening to the grasshoppers ticking. She would stare at the sky until she saw it tilt, felt the earth begin to move beneath her, a long slow spin as if it was all about to flip over. She got dizzy then, and scared, certain the sky was falling. She jumped to her feet and ran like mad for the trees, scaring up blackbirds and magpies all around her. One for sorrow, two for joy, three for a girl . . .

When her mother saw a magpie by itself, she tugged at Alice's sleeve, saying "Look, look, do you see it?" Because a single magpie brought bad luck if only one person saw it.

Alice knew that if you curtsied three times you cancelled the bad luck, like throwing salt over your left shoulder into the eyes of the devil. But the tilting of the earth was too big a thing to cancel. She knew that one day it would turn right over, upside down, and they would all fall off. Only the houses would be left, silent and empty.

Thinking about this made her nervous.

"Come on, Max," she said. "Let's go and find Kate."

The shop was busy. Four people waited to be served. Mr Geoghegan, the lawyer, was one of them. He passed their house every morning at the exact same time on his way to the bus. When she saw him go by, Alice's mother would put her cup down and stand up from the table, knowing it was time for her to clear away the dishes before she, too, went to work. He always wore the same dark clothes and walked with his head tilted back. He carried an umbrella, even in the summer. Alice's father once said this was because someone had told him that no one would know he was a lawyer if he left it at home. Her mother laughed herself stupid.

"It's not that funny," he told her, frowning. She stopped laughing at once, her face red, her eyes wet, pressing her hands to her chest to flatten her breathing.

Mrs O'Flaherty was there too, a little old woman, narrow like a bird, with a beaked face. She lived next door to the shop and often came in, in her slippers and her flowery apron, her thick stockings rolled down around her ankles. Alice didn't know who the other people were, she'd never seen them before.

Mr Kenny smiled when he saw her. "Kate's in the back, Alice," he told her, handing change to Mr Geoghegan.

She ducked under the flap of the counter and went through to the storeroom behind the shop. Kate sat on a kitchen chair, swinging her plump legs and reading. There were crisp crumbs on the bare concrete floor and all over the bright red cardigan that clashed with her hair.

"Hiya," she said when she saw Alice. Her big brother, Dermot, was stacking crates against the wall. The whole family helped their parents out in the shop. Dermot and Kate's sister Susan, who was twelve, were in there often. Even Kate stocked shelves, swept the floor and rinsed jars. Only Karen, who was the baby, did nothing. Yet.

"You're in my way, Carrot," Dermot said, to Kate. "If you're not going to help, go away." He ignored Alice. He usually did. She was beneath his notice because he was fifteen.

Kate stuck her tongue out at him and stood up. "Come on," she said to Alice. They went and sat on the big shelf under the counter and listened to Kate's dad talking to the customers, guessing who each one was. Sooner or later everyone who lived around there came into the shop.

Alice didn't understand why the Kennys didn't live here, but in a house around the corner. When she grew up she wanted to have a shop just like this, with shiny glass jars of coloured sweets in rows on the wooden counter and piles of papers and magazines, the shelves at the mysterious back of the shop where you could find anything if you looked hard enough: shoelaces, copy-books, lightbulbs, skipping ropes. But Alice would live over her shop, and then she'd always be able to eat and read whatever she liked.

"Why don't you live here?" she asked Kate now, as if she'd only just thought of it.

"We wouldn't all fit. I wish I had my own room, like you. I hate sharing with Karen." Kate scowled. "She's such a baby. I have to be quiet when she's asleep. You're lucky."

Lucky.

Alice rubbed the wooden shelf with her fingers, feeling for splinters. "I found a kitten today," she said.

"Where? Can I see it? Are you keeping it?"

"She was dead. She's gone, now." She was sorry she'd said anything. "I buried her. In the field."

"Show me where."

But Mr Kenny stopped them at the door and said, "It's too late to go out now, Katie. You'd better go on home for your tea. You go on home too, Alice. I saw your Ma going by a few minutes ago, on her way home from work. She'll be looking for you."

When Alice's mother got ready to go to her office in the mornings, Alice sat on the bottom stair and watched her back as she patted powder onto her cheeks. Then she pulled on her coat and fixed the belt in place. Last of all she tied her navy-blue scarf under her chin, covering her grey hair. Then she turned around to say goodbye. When she did, Alice held onto her tightly, every morning, as if, this time, she could make her stay. Every morning her mother pulled away.

"Let me *go*, Alice. I'll be late." She hurried out the back door and up the lane to the street, the straight seams of her stockings dividing the backs of her legs neatly in two.

Alice's mother worked in an insurance office. In the evenings and at weekends she brought papers home with her and sat at the kitchen table sorting them long after Alice went up to bed. She did sums on a piece of paper, squinting at the small print and yawning, the shadows under her eyes deepening. Once Alice found her asleep, bent over the papers, her arms under her head, the inkstains on her fingers showing beneath her hair.

She scoured her hands with pumice to get the stains off but they were never clean enough to suit her. On Saturday mornings she wore rubber gloves when she took out the scrubbing brush and bucket and knelt down to wash the kitchen floor, kneeling on an old rag. When she'd finished and spread newspapers across the floor to help it dry, she sat at the table again, sorting mounds of paper into buff coloured folders. Rubbing her eyes and frowning.

"I work in Risks," Alice heard her tell the priest once. Her father shouted with laughter.

"Risk it for a biscuit!" he said, slapping his knee. "That's a good one. Have you met my wife, Mrs Risk? And this," he pointed to Alice, "is our little Risk."

The priest looked as if he wasn't sure whether to laugh or not. He smiled a little smile that left his face quickly, leaving no trace of itself.

It was true that her mother always looked for disaster. Whatever they did, she was sure to point out what could go wrong. She warned Alice not to get her feet wet, not to sit on stone, always to wear a vest, never to talk to strangers. She pointed out the danger of walking under ladders. The deep creases in the skin between her eyebrows got deeper as she listed the things Alice should avoid.

Alice didn't talk to strangers, but she watched them. Sometimes she followed them. They never paid any attention to her, because they didn't know she was a spy.

School was her cover. She had to be on her guard, of course. All the time. Not to give anything away. She was an expert at blending in. She jumped up to offer to clean the blackboard, held doors open for the nuns, said please and thank you. She was bold, but quick to admit whatever she'd done wrong. That way she won the support of friends and teachers alike and avoided further questioning. It was excellent training for a double agent like her.

She was like the French singer in the comics who smuggled secrets to the Resistance, the one everyone despised for being a collaborator. When the war was over and they found out the truth they'd be sorry. Alice set up her headquarters in the ruined tower in the field and organised her resistance from there. Hers was a secret war. Everyone else pretended nothing out of the ordinary was going on and that made it harder to fight. She gathered information to smuggle to the outside world and waited for someone to come for it. She climbed to the top of the tower. In the distance, she could see the sea. Gulls flew in, crying, over her head. They carried messages, of secret sailings and impending storms.

Alice knew that no one would ever guess she was an agent. She didn't tell Kate because Kate couldn't keep a secret, she told her mother everything. Alice decided that Kate's father was a spy, too, but he could never let on. Never even hint at what they were really

talking about, especially not in front of Kate. He didn't
want to put her in danger.

He passed messages to Alice, hidden in sweets, and
spoke to her in code. If she went into the shop and he
said, "Hello, darlin', what's the weather like today?"
he really meant to ask whether or not there was any
danger, if the enemy suspected anything.

"Anything strange?" he'd ask.

Sometimes he smiled and said, "I have something
for you," and passed a lollipop across the counter,
winking at her. Then she ran straight to the tower to
unwrap it, certain there was a clue hidden inside the
wrapping paper.

She used special hand signals and codes which no
one understood but her. If she thought someone looked
suspicious, she followed them. If she thought she was
being followed, she went out of her way to shake the
enemy off. It was a strain.

"But, why do you want to go the long way?" Kate often
complained. "I'm tired. I don't want to walk any more!"

"Come on, she said fiercely, I'll explain later," said
Alice.

"What did you say?"

"I said, come on. I'll explain later."

"No, you didn't. You said, 'come on she said
fiercely.' Why did you say that?"

"Did I?"

"Yes."

"It was a joke."

"Oh."

One day she got a splinter of bark stuck in her foot.

She sat in the lane and howled while Max barked beside her, until her father came to see what was wrong. He picked her up in his big hands and carried her in to the kitchen and put her sitting on the table. Her mother looked up from a column of figures.

"For heaven's sake, stop roaring while we have a look and see what's wrong," she said.

Her father rolled up his sleeves and pressed the skin on her foot. She shouted with pain.

"There's a sliver of wood in there. We'll have to get it out," he said to her mother. "We'll need a sewing needle."

"Better boil it first. It might go septic."

Alice fought them but her mother held her hard while he prodded the raw flesh of her sole with two scalding needles. She tried to jerk her foot away. He circled her ankle with the thumb and finger of one hand, pinching her skin.

"Be still," her mother hissed in her ear. "Can't you see that you're only making everything worse? If you just stop fighting, it'll be over sooner."

Alice heard her and stilled. She drew herself into a tiny space and watched what he did from a great, hollow distance, not even breathing. She listened to the sudden quiet, saw the skin of a foot raw and open beneath her, the brown shavings of wood lifted out from it. She saw the peroxide fall from a brown bottle over that foot into a waiting bowl, saw the sudden white foam around the cut. She felt nothing.

When she saw that it was over she let go of the tight ball she had made of herself and grew quietly back down into her body. There was a dull ache in her foot but she couldn't remember how it got there. Her father's hand was still squeezing her ankle. Her foot below his yellowed fingers was an ugly purple colour. She saw the splinter on the table beside her in three jagged pieces.

When her father lifted his hand from around her ankle there were round marks where he had held her, the same colour as his fingers. Her toes began to tingle as the blood came back into them.

"Now go and put a clean sock on. And your shoes, so you don't make that cut dirty," said her mother. "I'd like to know what you were doing out in your bare feet in the first place. That's what you get. Silly girl. You'll catch your death one of these days."

After that, Alice practised pain. Not reacting when something hurt. She stood deliberately in the cold and rain, went to bed with wet hair. She climbed barefoot on the rocks down by the sea to harden the soles of her feet, clutched at nettles, engraved patterns on her palms with needles. She did it so that she would never give in to torture.

She stalked imaginary prey in the field, taught herself silence, stillness, invisibility. The undersides of leaves, the holding of a breath, the freezing of time. She tried to learn the secret of making things move or stay still at her command. She tested what was possible, stretched everything beyond its previous limit: the reach of her arm, the length of a step, the height of a jump, the space of stillness. The power of her stare to create openings. She looked for signs and omens. She practised forgetting what she knew, because if she didn't know, she couldn't tell.

CHAPTER FOUR

She perched on the edge of the rocks, looking wildly around her for a place to hide. Far behind her she could hear the sounds of the hunters, beating their way through the jungle towards the edge of the world where she crouched, in danger of slipping off the treacherous rocks and falling into the sea.

Then she saw a shadow, halfway up the cliff. It might, or might not, be a cave. Dare she risk the climb? What if there were no hiding place? She would have lost precious time and the hunters would surely catch up with her.

A dark shape came gliding through the water rocking and slapping at her feet. She caught her breath, willing herself not to scream and alert the monster to her presence. He was her sworn enemy. She had vowed that if he ever caught her she would give him no easy victory.

She backed carefully away from the ledge. She would risk the climb up the glass-encrusted cliff face. She had no choice.

Carefully, hand over cautious hand, she climbed towards the beckoning shadow. If it was not the cave she hoped for, she would throw herself off the cliff. She would never give her pursuers the satisfaction of bringing her into captivity, enslaving her. Never. Because she was the last survivor of an ancient and noble people . . .

"What on earth do you think you're doing?"

Her mother's horror broke into her own. There was a split second of confusion when Alice was trapped between two worlds, not knowing who or where she was, where to go. They had caught up with her, she was doomed. No, THEY were lost. It was her mother who had caught her.

"Get down from there this minute! How dare you?"

"All right, all right, I'm sorry," she mumbled, as she edged off the sideboard onto the dining table, moving two crystal decanters cautiously out of her way.

"You'll destroy the furniture!" her mother went on furiously. She gestured around the room. Alice had arranged the chairs and table to represent rocks, hills and islands, in the middle of an ocean of floor.

"I took my shoes off," Alice muttered, "so I wouldn't scratch . . ."

"No cheek out of you!" her mother snapped. She reached an impatient arm and pulled at Alice roughly, making her lose her balance and fall with a crash to the floor. The clawed brass feet of the heavy table dug a jagged hole in the skin above her knee and the two of them stared at the brightly welling blood in horror.

"Oh, my God," her mother said.

Alice screamed. She screamed because she recognised the marks of the Tyrant, it was his cruel talons that had ripped her flesh. He had marked her now, he would find her wherever she went. He would never rest until he had her in his fiery clutches, she was doomed . . .

"Now look what you've done," her mother said, producing a handkerchief and pushing in vain at the spreading blood.

"I didn't do it! You . . ."

"Be quiet! If you hadn't been clambering around playing your ridiculous games this would never have happened." The force of her mother's voice silenced Alice as her father appeared at the door.

"What's going on?" he asked.

"It's nothing," her mother said. "She was fooling around and she fell. She needs some ice, maybe. That's all."

"Do you think it might need stitches?" He said nothing to Alice. This was between her parents now. It had nothing to do with her.

"Of course not. Just ice. And a bandage. Get one, will you?"

"You're lucky you didn't smash those decanters," she went on, to Alice, when he'd left. "There'd have been hell to pay."

There were two cut glass decanters and four glasses on the sideboard in the good room. They were a set. They'd been a wedding present from her mother's favourite aunt, who'd left to go and live in America. Her mother often took them down and polished them with a piece of soft leather until they split the light in the room into flashes of colour. Alice was not allowed to touch them.

There used to be six glasses, until one day when her parents had been shouting at each other in the kitchen. Alice was sitting on the stairs, hidden by the bannister so that when her father came out he didn't see her before he slammed in to the good room.

When he'd gone she slipped quickly through the open kitchen door and saw her mother staring out the window with her arms wrapped tightly around her waist. Holding herself as if she was afraid to let go. Alice went and stood beside her.

It was the way his silence made them feel that made them both turn to look at him when he came back in. He had a glass in each hand and his mouth was twisted into a half smile. As they looked at him he held the glasses out towards them and then slowly opened his fingers so that they fell straight to the floor and smashed with a sound like music.

Her mother's face crumpled, as if the bones behind it had fallen in on themselves, but she said nothing. She stared at the floor until he'd gone, banging the door behind him. Then she got down on her knees and picked up every little shard of glass, not seeming to notice the beads of blood that sprang up on the tips of her fingers. She made a humming noise, tuneless, as she did it.

When Alice hunkered down beside her with the dustpan she saw that her mother's eyes had gone away. She promised herself that, when she was grown up, she'd never care about anything so fragile.

Remembering that day, she was glad she hadn't knocked

over a glass when she fell. If she'd remembered it sooner, she would have stayed clear of the sideboard.

"You've no one to blame for this but yourself," her mother said. Then her mouth snapped into a thin silence as she pressed on her handkerchief. Red, now. Ruined.

"I was careful," Alice protested. "If you hadn't . . . ouch! You're hurting me!"

The pressure on her knee tightened. "Don't start that." Her mother's voice was low, hoarse, full of menace. "Just don't start. Do you hear me?"

Alice looked away. There was no point in arguing.

During the school holidays, she hung around her father while he worked in the lane. She passed him spanners and wrenches when he asked for them. She knew about spark plugs and piston rings and fuel filters. When he forgot about her she slipped off to the field. Sometimes in the evenings he took her down to the harbour although the boats were in dry dock for the winter. Sailing in the winter was called frostbiting, he said. The thought of it made her shiver. Looking at the sea in its restless grey surges against the harbour wall made even her eyeballs cold. He knew the names of all the boats. They were called *mermaids*, and *dragons*. Other names were painted on their sides. The Lady Helen. Beloved Albatross. He snorted at that one. No real sailor would call a boat after an omen of doom, he said.

He told her he'd built a boat once, himself. With his own hands.

"Where is it now?" she asked.

"I sold it," he said, his hands deep in his pockets, staring across the sea. "Things change, you know." And he told her the story about Oisín, who sailed away for hundreds of years and came back on a fairy horse. How he was warned not to set foot on land or he would die. But he stopped to help some men in a field and fell off his horse and aged by hundreds of years in front of their eyes.

"Dust," her father said in a hollow voice. "He turned to dust."

He took a packet of Sweet Aftons out of his cardigan pocket. "It comes to all of us," he said, staring out to sea. "Sooner or later."

He pulled out a cigarette and lit it, cupping his hands around the flame of the match. The smoke must have gone down the wrong way because he started to cough then, doubled up, his breath shuddering.

A man walking past with a small brown dog on a lead turned to look at them and Alice stared back. She didn't care if it was rude. She knew her father didn't like anyone to notice when he coughed like this. They all had to pretend it wasn't happening. If her mother was talking and he was taken over by a coughing spell, she stopped in the middle of her sentence and waited until he'd finished. Then she carried on, right where she'd left off.

Max was interested in the man's dog and ran off after them, wagging his tail. The man walked faster to get away from him and Max loped back to Alice, his eyes bright.

"Good boy, Max." Alice made a fuss of him, pulling at his ears. She looked out across the smooth, quiet water. There was a misty twilight and lights shone like jewels across the bay.

"Is that Tír na nÓg, Daddy?" she asked when he'd straightened up and wiped his mouth, breathing again instead of coughing.

"That's Howth, you eejit." He sounded cross.

"Oh. Sorry." She pushed her hands deep into her pockets and balanced one foot on top of the other, hunching down into her jacket.

"Come on," he said. "It's getting late."

The tide was low, the sand mirrored and calm. They walked home beside the railway line. A train passed them, its windows lit, making the ground shake under Alice's feet. She waved, and people in the train waved back. Max ran off into the water and came bounding back after them, shaking himself heavily, spraying them with cold salt.

All through the winter she lay awake at night and listened. She loved the sound of the wind sweeping across the field and the foghorns sounding on the water, signs of life beyond the house. She searched the sky for flares but never saw any. She listened to her father's cough and held herself away from sleep because of the nightmares. The thing coiled at the foot of her bed, the hungry sea rising, her throat closing in panic. Sometimes she woke up screaming and sweating, fighting for breath. Her ears burned down deep in her neck. Her mother brought her hot milk and whiskey to calm her down and make her sleep.

"It's this recurring throat infection that's making her ear ache," Dr Roche told her mother when he came to the house near the end of spring. "Referred pain."

"But she doesn't complain about her throat."

"I don't understand why not. It looks sore to me. I'll give you a prescription for it. Now, how's your husband today?"

They left her room without looking back, their heads close together, muttering. Alice couldn't hear what they said. Her father's cough was worse. On and on into the night she heard him in his room, hacking and retching and spitting.

She hated the sound of his cough, as if his stomach was trying to tear its way up through his chest. There was no way to block it out. She hid her head under the pillow but her ears throbbed. Sometime in February he stopped working altogether and stayed in bed. Tall black oxygen cylinders with metal taps and rubber tubing stood beside his bed.

"You'll have to stop smoking now, Michael," her mother said, trying to make a joke of it. "You could blow us all to smithereens."

He growled at her, his face grey over his striped pyjamas. "Don't you tell me what to do," he wheezed.

She shut her mouth into a tight line and turned away, shaking her head. She went into her own room and shut the door.

"It can't go on like this," Alice heard her say to the doctor later, in the hall.

"I'm afraid it will get even worse, before it's over," he warned.

It didn't go on. Her father got better. But the new cloud that had settled over the house with the doctor's warning still lingered over the spare oxygen cylinder that stood in the far corner of his room, waiting for the next time. Alice would have known there was going to be a next time even if she hadn't heard what the doctor said. It was in her mother's eyes, the anxiety in her voice. It was in the way her father got smaller, how he sat huddled into his cardigan at night, one hand to his mouth, the other clamped on a cigarette. The fact that he no longer crossed the railway line at the tall footbridge because the steps were too much for him.

His face was as yellow now as his fingers, and cords of skin stood out in his neck when he coughed.

"I won't put up with it!" he yelled at Alice once, when she had done nothing but walk into the room where he sat. "I won't!" And he pulled himself up out of the chair and stormed out past her. As if it was her he couldn't put up with.

One day he called her into his room. He was sitting on the bed. She stood at the door and looked at him, wary, but he smiled at her. "I've something to show you," he said. "Come here."

She walked cautiously towards his beckoning fingers.

"There's a box under the bed," he said in a low voice. He was wheezing. His breath smelled sharp and sour. "Lift it out for me, will you?"

It was a plain cardboard box with numbers on the outside. Alice straightened up and handed it to him.

"Sit down," he dipped his head, looking at the eiderdown, "until I show you this." He lifted the lid off the box and unfolded some sheets of tissue paper the colour of skin, crinkled and rustling. He reached in to the paper and lifted out something rounded and yellow with two great big holes in it. Alice stared.

"Do you know what this is?"

Her feet clenched under her. She could feel every hair on her head tightening. She shook her head.

"It's a skull. Do you remember the stories I told you? Remember I told you that the heroes used to wear the heads of their enemies tied around their waists? 'Course, those ones would still have bits of skin and hair stuck to them. Blackened, probably. Rotting. Here, hold it."

But she jumped away from him and stood out of reach, her hands clenched behind her back, breathing hard.

"You must respect the dead, Alice," he said thoughtfully.

Then he laughed. He worked the jaws. The teeth clacked off each other.

"He's laughing at you, see?"

But Alice knew it was her father laughing as she ran away from him, crying.

"What's the matter with you?" her mother asked, putting out an arm to stop her at the top of the stairs. Alice pushed past her and ran away, crying harder than ever.

That night she lay awake and listened to them fighting. She knew it was about her. It was all her fault. She pressed her face against the wall.

Now, oh *now*, let me through.

But nothing happened. The voices went on and on. Outside in the lane cats were fighting and crying like babies abandoned in the night.

CHAPTER FIVE

The next day her mother didn't go to work. She spent a long time on the phone in the hall. Then she came to find Alice.

"How would you like to go down to the country for a while, Alice? School is about to stop for Easter and I think you need a holiday."

"You mean, like when we went to Brittas?"

"A bit like that."

"Where?"

"Do you remember my friend, Sheila, from the country?"

Alice shook her head.

"She and I were girls together. She sends us the Christmas cake every year."

"Oh." Alice hated Christmas cake.

"Well, you're going to stay with her."

"Does she live on a farm?"

"Not exactly. They've a house outside a small town, a couple of acres, some cattle. Sheila's husband, Conor, has a shop."

"Like the Kennys?"

"No. He sells tools and bridles, things like that."

"Are you coming?"

"No."

"I don't want to go."

"Of course you do. You'll like it. They have a daughter, called Nell."

"How old is she?" Alice asked.

"She's fourteen. Twice your age. Now stop asking questions and go and get yourself ready. Hurry up, we've a long drive ahead of us, almost to the Border. We're leaving after lunch."

The Border. Alice brightened. She knew all about borders, but she'd never seen a real one. She wondered what it took to make people admit it was there. Something extraordinary, she knew.

There was barely time to pack some clothes in her satchel and kiss Max goodbye before they left. "Why isn't Daddy coming?" Alice asked, looking around for him as she got into the back of the car.

"He's resting."

"Can I sit in the front?"

"May I," said her mother automatically. "No. It's not safe. I'm sick and tired of telling you that."

They drove off slowly. Her mother stayed close to the pavement as long as they were in the city, but as soon as they'd left it behind she drove down the centre of the road, staying well clear of the dusty hedges.

"Tell me about Nell," Alice said. "What's she like?"

"She has seven brothers, but they're all much older than she is. They've all gone to England except Joe. The cattle are his."

"But what's she like?"

"She rides horses, that's all I know."

Horses. Perfect. It could be part of her secret training. She would be a fearless horsewoman, galloping away from her enemies, racing for the Border, for freedom . . .

"You behave yourself down here, Alice. I'm warning you. Mind your manners."

"I will."

Alice recited the names over and over in her mind so she wouldn't forget them and make a mistake when she got there. Sheila, Conor, Nell. She liked the sound of Nell, it was a soft name, round and friendly. She wondered if Nell would like her. She wondered what the country would be like. Like the field, probably, only bigger. She asked her mother what kind of animals there'd be besides horses and cows.

"Oh, sheep maybe. Lambs. We're coming up to Easter, after all. Don't distract me, Alice. I'm driving."

Alice stared out the window. She had butterflies in her stomach. She'd never been on a drive this long before. Even when they took the caravan in Brittas for the week it had been a shorter drive than this. The countryside was different, too. The ground was flatter, the hedges high. Trees leaned untidily towards each other across the road. Alice made herself dizzy by concentrating on the hedges, waiting for a sudden flash of vision through a gate, of fields, mud, cows.

The houses were sparse and different. They were big and square and grey, or else squat, low bungalows with odd coloured bricks. At first she tried to keep count of the ruined towers like her secret headquarters that they passed, but she soon gave up.

She'd come back later on her horse, and gather her followers around her . . .

Gorse blazed at the side of the road. There were young animals everywhere: lambs, calves, foals. Alice's stomach jumped. She was excited and scared at the same time.

They stopped once at a square white hotel with bright blue and red flowers in pots on the window sills. Her mother drank tea and Alice had a coca-cola with two cubes of ice in it and a wedge of lemon.

"A special treat." Her mother smiled at her.

Alice took the lemon out of her glass and dropped it in the ashtray. She sucked her fingers dry and shuddered at the sour taste. "I want to come home with you."

The smile went away. "Don't be silly. Drink that quickly and come on. I have to drive all the way back again and I don't want to have to do it in the dark."

Alice felt sick with nerves by the time they arrived. When they turned off the road there was a sudden loud metallic noise and she nearly jumped out of her skin.

"What was that?"

"Only a cattle grid."

"What's that?"

"Bars in the ground to stop animals wandering in and out." Her mother looked over her shoulder at Alice. "There are lots of new things here, Alice. It'll be an adventure for you."

"I don't want to stay. I want to come back with you."

"Don't start all that again. This is for your own

good. You'll enjoy yourself. It's only for a fortnight. I'll come and get you before school starts again."

"But . . ."

"Here we are." Her mother stopped the car outside a stone house. A narrow river ran down one side of it. The house was square and grey, with five windows at the front. The frames and the front door, which stood open, were painted a dark green colour. Daffodils lined the grass in front of the house. Ivy grew up the walls. Her mother tsked in its direction.

"They'd want to watch that," she said. "It'll destroy the house."

There was a long green field in front of the house with cows in it. A black horse stood with his neck bent to the ground, his tail waving slowly. Alice's heart beat faster as she looked at him. On the far side of the house there was a tall barred metal gate in front of a stone building with a corrugated iron roof.

Alice looked across a stretch of green towards the horizon. "Does all this belong to them?" she asked.

"No. Just the long field, the house and the yard. It's not a proper farm, Alice. I already told you."

"But, the cows . . ."

Her mother laughed. "They belong to Joe, all right, but that doesn't make it a farm. Conor's shop is the main thing. I grew up on a farm, you know. A real farm. More than a hundred head . . . We lost everything."

She took her hands off the steering wheel, lifted the keys from the ignition. "Then I married your father."

Alice's mind filled with questions. Her mother had

never mentioned growing up before. There were so many things to ask, all of a sudden. She wished she could wind back time and have the drive all over again. She would ask her mother everything she hadn't known to ask the first time.

It was too late now. The door of the house swung open and her mother got out of the car. A dark-haired woman wearing men's trousers and a flowered apron crossed the gravel towards them.

"Elaine!"

"Hello, Sheila. How are you?"

The two women shook hands and smiled into each other's faces. Alice's mother turned and put a hand on her shoulder, pulling her forwards. "Here's Alice, Sheila. Thank you for taking her."

"Not at all. It's the least I could do. How are things? How's Michael?"

Her voice was heavy and slow and musical, every word on a different note. She sounded different to anyone Alice had ever heard before. Alice's mother opened her mouth to speak, but then closed it again as a big man came through the yard gate. He had a cloth cap on his head and an oily looking green jacket. His trousers were tucked into boots that had straw stuck to the bottom of them.

"How are you, Elaine?" he said, stretching out his hand to Alice's mother, who took it, nodding at him. "And who is this fine young lady?"

He took his hand back and stroked a thick, reddish beard. His voice was like Sheila's, fast and lilting.

"Hello, Conor. This is Alice."

Alice's mother nudged her forward towards the man, whose smile was wide as he looked at her.

"Call me Uncle Conor," he said. "You may as well."

Alice studied him. "Are you my uncle?" she asked.

"No. But it's more friendly than Mister, now, isn't it?"

Sheila was looking at Alice too, her head tilted to one side.

"She's the image of you, Elaine," she finally said.

Alice was astonished. She stopped looking at Conor and turned to her mother instead. Her grey wool coat, the navy blue scarf tied around her steel coloured hair, her dark eyebrows, her lipstick. Alice knew she was nothing like her mother. What could Sheila mean? There was treachery in the air. She could feel it.

Her mother laughed. "You couldn't be more wrong," she said. "She's a real daddy's girl."

"Is that so?" said Conor. He winked at Alice. "Tar anseo," he said. "Come here to me, girl. Reach your hand in there and see what you find."

He held out the pocket of his jacket. Alice stood close to him and put her hand carefully into the pocket. The two women watched. He smelled of smoke, like her father, and something sweet and unfamiliar. Her fingers touched cellophane and she lifted out a boiled sweet.

"There you are now, that's for you. You're very welcome. Go on inside with your mother. I'll see you later."

Alice followed the women into the house, through a

long dark room with a fireplace against one wall and two doors opening out of it. A glass case over the fireplace held a dead bird with a long neck and brightly coloured feathers, stretched as if in flight.

"Here is where we sit in the evenings, Alice," Sheila told her. "And this is the kitchen, through here."

The kitchen was a large square room with windows along two walls. A third wall was taken up by a big yellow Aga with clothes drying on a rack which hung over it. The floor was tiled red and a table covered with a blue and white checked cloth stretched the length of the room in front of the windows. A half door swung open to the yard. There was a tall press with shining glass doors near the Aga and Alice could see plates and cups behind the glass. There was a delicious smell of baking.

"You'll have a cup of tea?" Sheila asked Alice's mother. "There are scones just ready to come out of the oven."

"All right, thanks. A quick one."

"Nell will be along in a minute to show you upstairs, Alice. Oh, here she is."

When Nell appeared on the outer doorstep she looked very tall. Her hair swung around her head in dark curls. She wore jeans tucked into her wellingtons the way Conor's had been. Suddenly Alice wished she had boots too.

"Hello, Mrs Morrissey," Nell said, her voice following a now familiar pattern, rising and falling and rising again. She shook Alice's mother's hand.

"Aunt Elaine," Alice's mother sounded awkward.

"It's your father's idea," she said as her hand fell to her side again.

"Right-o. Auntie Elaine." Nell smiled at everyone. "Can I take Alice upstairs now?" she asked. She tilted her head to one side and winked at Alice. "Come on," she said, walking quickly across the kitchen.

Alice followed her out of the room through the opposite door, the one that led back through the house.

"Take off those boots, Nell!" Sheila called after them. "Don't be tracking mud all over my hall!"

"I've no boots," was the first thing Alice said to Nell, in a whisper, at the bottom of the stairs.

Nell smiled and took her hand. "Don't worry, I'll give you an old pair of mine," she whispered back.

Alice got used to being in the country. She got used to the smells and the noises, the feeling of manure squelching under her boots in the yard. She liked the big teas Sheila made, hot scones with butter melting through them and jam every day.

In the evenings, back from the shop, Conor sat her on his knee, pretended he was a horse, and bounced her up and down until she was breathless and laughing. He hid sweets and coins in the pockets of his trousers for her to find.

"Try harder," he encouraged her, his ruddy face laughing down at her. "Look further, see what you find." He pushed her hand down deep, moved it around in search of money.

"No luck? Here." He gave her heavy round coins with a harp engraved on one side. On the other there were animals. The rabbit, the pig, the salmon. The horse was her favourite. Half-a-crown.

Sheila didn't seem to mind much what Alice did or where she went. "There are three rules," she told Alice at breakfast on the first morning. "Always close a gate behind you if you open it. That's the most important one. Don't get underfoot. And don't go further than the cattle grid on your own. I don't want you getting lost on the road. If you remember all of that, you'll be grand."

When Nell wasn't around, Alice played in the cobbled yard and in the barn, brought carrots filched from Sheila's kitchen to Nell's horse, O'Hara, if he was in his stall. She offered them nervously, jerking her fingers quickly back from the velvet of his nose.

Once Sheila brought her into town to do the messages and they called in to Conor's shop. It was dark and dusty and it smelled of oats and saddlesoap and leather. Bridles hung from hooks attached to the ceiling and a large saddle shone on a trestle inside the door. When Alice touched it it creaked like a loose floorboard. Conor leaned against the counter, a newspaper open in front of him. Two men stood in front of him. They were talking about the racing odds in the paper. Alice hung back, shy, near the door while Sheila spoke to Conor. They all ignored her, as if she didn't exist. She was relieved to get back outside, even though there was a fine drizzle and by the time they'd walked back to the house she was soaked through and shivering.

"It's like winter, back again," Sheila said. "Go and get a towel and dry your hair. I'll put the kettle on and light the fire."

Apart from that time, Alice didn't go far from the house. She got used to the smell of wet straw and animals, and the thick clotted smell of butter churning in the dairy. She liked to climb the bales of straw in the barn and sit up in the cool dark under the roof listening to the wind.

She was afraid of the cows, large slow animals. Everyone laughed at her for it. There were about twenty of them, but when they were all massed together there seemed to be hundreds. She was shocked by how big they were, close up. Their loud breath. She didn't mind them when they were penned in, or at a distance. But when she met them in the lane on the way to be milked, lowing, her pulse raced. She backed up, turned away, pretended to herself that she had changed her mind about going that way, or had forgotten something back at the house.

She hung over the half door of the stalls when the cows were being milked, wrinkling her nose at their dirt.

"Come on, girl, and earn your keep," Conor called out to her. "Come and milk this cow."

"Try it," said Sheila, encouraging. Joe said nothing. He'd barely spoken to her since she'd arrived. Nell leant against the cow she was milking, her hands working rhythmically, milk falling into the metal bucket in regular spurts. Alice could hear it drumming, like rain on a roof.

She went cautiously over to the stool and sat down nervously.

"It's easy, once you get the hang of it," Conor told her.

She reached under the belly of the cow, but her fingers squirmed away from the big rubbery teat. The feel of it in her hand revolted her and she got up quickly.

"I can't," she said and walked away, leaving Sheila and Conor laughing behind her. She didn't care. She didn't want the spray of warm milk on her skin.

She watched Nell ride with an ache of envy in her throat as she flew around the field, jumping the narrow stream and the exercise jumps she and Alice set up for O'Hara. Nell explained to Alice that O'Hara was not a pony and that the difference had everything to do with size and power and speed. Nell hunted and rode in point-to-points, her bedroom was full of rosettes and small trophies.

"Have you ever been to the Horse Show?" she asked Alice. "It's brilliant. When I leave school I'm going to join the army. I know girls aren't meant to be soldiers, but they'll let me. I know they will. And I'll be on the show-jumping team."

Alice believed Nell could do anything she wanted to. She was afraid of nothing. Alice hadn't known that she was afraid of anything before she came here. Her fearless exploits as leader of the Fianna in her own field had convinced her she was brave. She was wrong. She was afraid of the cows, horses made her nervous. Only the neighbours' sheep, small and distant behind barbed wire, didn't bother her, although their crying, or something, kept her awake at night.

Once Nell managed to coax her up onto O'Hara, and led her round the paddock in a circle. Alice held on to O'Hara's black mane as well as the reins and closed her eyes because she didn't want to see how far away the ground was. Nell laughed at her and called her a baby, but kindly, as she helped her down. She offered to lead her like that as often as she liked, until she stopped feeling so scared. But Alice shook her head and said she didn't like it, the sensation of bumping and swaying along so far off the ground made her feel sick. Like being on a boat.

"You don't mean you're afraid of boats, too?" asked Nell, who had never been on a boat in her life. Alice, who had been on the ferry once, on a day trip to Holyhead, nodded.

"I should call you Mouse from now on. Is there anything you're not afraid of?"

Alice stared at her feet and thought hard. She didn't know what to say. She couldn't think of anything, but luckily Nell was distracted as O'Hara jerked the reins in her hand, wanting to sample a clump of weeds beside the gate.

"Come on, Mouse," said Nell. "Time to put O'Hara in his stall."

Alice held the gate open and then closed it behind them. She made sure to shoot the bolt completely home. Every time she did this she felt proud, as if she had a right to be here in the country because she knew how important it was about gates.

Nell quickly got used to having Alice shadow her around, asking questions, hurrying to open and close gates, carrying buckets, listening to every word she said as if it carried weight. No one had ever taken Nell, the youngest in her family by years, and a girl besides, so seriously. She decided that she liked Alice.

"We have to stick together, Mouse," she said.

Alice nodded, delighted.

"I've always wanted a sister." Nell looked doubtfully at Alice. "More my own age, though."

"We could be blood-sisters," Alice said eagerly. She had read about this ceremony in a book. She'd thought about doing it with Kate, but Kate hated blood and always made such a fuss over the slightest scratch that you'd think she was dying. And there were things she'd never tell Kate. She knew, for example, that Kate wouldn't understand about the Fianna. She'd laugh. Kate didn't care about heroes, she read books about girls in boarding schools. And she had a habit of going home when Alice got too bossy. You couldn't have secret agents who went home when they felt like it.

"I don't know," Nell said, doubtfully. "You mean where we cut ourselves and mix our blood together?"

"Just a little cut. On our fingers."

"Wouldn't you be scared?"

Alice shook her head and smiled. Here was something she knew she could do. "I don't mind," she said.

After they'd found Conor's razor and brought it out to the barn, it was Nell who hesitated before cutting herself. Alice pushed the pointed tip of the blade straight under her skin and then sliced upwards, as if she had been practising. She didn't flinch. She didn't even shut her eyes.

"Well done, Alice," said Nell, impressed.

They sat with their fingers touching, embarrassed.

"What do we do now?" Nell asked. "This is your game."

"It's not a game. We make a vow. I swear I'll always be your sister. Em, in sickness and in health. For better or worse."

"That's a wedding, you eejit. All right. My turn. I swear, too." Nell shrugged. "That's it, I suppose." She changed her voice, made her eyes bigger. "Now we'll be sisters, for ever and ever, amen," she announced in dramatic tones. Then she said, in her normal voice, "We'd better go in for supper."

Sheila was in a temper about something, banging around in the kitchen. There was a smell of burning. "Do you want any help?" Nell asked her as they walked through the kitchen.

"Just stay out of my way," Sheila warned. "Supper's going to be late."

Nell rolled her eyes at Alice. "I'll go for a ride, so," she said. "I won't be long." She slipped quickly out the door.

Alice went through to the sitting-room where a fire was blazing. Conor was sitting in the big armchair near the fire, reading the paper. She wondered if she should offer to set the table, but when she heard Sheila crashing plates around, she decided not to. Conor looked up and caught her eye and winked, like he always did, smiling.

"It sounds stormy in there," he said.

Alice smiled back at him and went over to stand beside his chair. He was reading the newspaper. She leaned against the arm of the chair and looked over his shoulder at the picture on the front page, trying to read what it said underneath.

Conor didn't move.

Suddenly the air of the room hummed, as if it was alive. Heavy.

Alice's skin prickled, warning her.

Slowly, cautiously, she began to straighten up but his arm was already around her and he pulled her forward, towards him. She was falling into him, and he pulled her face to his.

"You're a sexy little thing, aren't you?" he said, before his rough, hairy mouth fastened on to hers. As if in a dream, she saw it happen. She felt the air slowly flow out of her body through her mouth. He sucked it out of her, crushed her between his two hands, pulled her down into him. The room behind him darkened.

Suddenly he let her go. And laughed.

Alice lurched against the chair. She pushed herself away from it and looked around at the place where he was looking. There, in the doorway, stood Sheila. A dishcloth was crumpled up in her hands, as if she was drying them. Her face was flushed. She stared hard at Alice, but she said nothing. Then she turned around and went back into the kitchen, letting the door slam behind her. Without a word.

Sheila didn't come to dinner. Her empty place accused Alice, the knife pointed blame directly at her.

You see how bad you are? You can't go anywhere without causing trouble.

Conor read his paper. Joe, as usual, said nothing at all. Nell talked enough for all of them, about a point-to-point she was riding in the next weekend.

"You can help me clean the tack, Alice," she said.

Alice nodded and went on staring at her plate. There was a fine crack in the glaze and her eye studied its length, out over the edge of the plate then back to its starting point again. She reached out and poured pepper on her mashed potato, then put the pepper pot between her and Sheila's knife.

"I thought you hated pepper," said Nell.

"I've changed my mind," Alice said. Then she sneezed. "I'm not hungry," she told Nell's elbow, on the table beside her plate.

After they'd done the dishes she stayed close to Nell for the rest of the night. She sat beside her and read over her shoulder in the firelight. She followed her out of the room and waited in the cold dark hall while Nell went to the toilet, then trailed back into the sitting-room behind her. At last she followed her upstairs.

"Are we going to bed now?" she asked, looking longingly at Nell's bed. It was piled high with clothes, magazines, a riding crop.

"I suppose so. We may as well." Nell sounded cross. "All you're doing is following me around. Like a baby."

Alice took off her shoes and jumped quickly into bed with her clothes still on, hoping Nell wouldn't notice. That night she lay awake, rigid, listening to the wind rush around the house and to Nell's loud, nasal breathing. She was waiting, but she didn't know what she was waiting for. The only thing that came was the morning.

She got out of bed and put her shoes on as slowly as possible before going downstairs. She didn't know how to walk into a room that had Sheila in it, what would happen when Sheila saw her again, but she knew she couldn't put it off forever. She walked quietly into the kitchen behind Nell, as if this would somehow make her invisible.

All that happened was that Sheila gave her a long look. It wasn't the look Alice had expected.

"I have news for you," she said. "Your mother phoned last night. She's coming to pick you up tomorrow."

CHAPTER SIX

It was already dark when Alice's mother came to collect her. Nell and Alice were polishing harness leathers outside the kitchen door when they saw the lights of the car move slowly up the drive and then blink out in front of the house.

"You'd better go on inside and get your stuff," Nell said. "I'll finish this."

Alice stood up and let the bridle she had been holding fall to the step. She worked each boot off with the toes of one foot pushing against the heel of the other, then put them side by side against the wall. She pushed the bottom half of the door open and walked quickly across the tiled floor of the kitchen, letting herself slide the last few feet to the other door. It opened just as she got to it, giving her a fright.

"He's not well," her mother was in the middle of saying. "Not well at all."

"Oh, Alice, you startled me!" Sheila was flustered as she and Alice collided at the door. "Look, your mother's here."

"Hello." Alice felt suddenly shy. All the adults were looking at her and each look meant something different. She went and hid her face against her mother's front.

Her mother patted her shoulder kindly. "Hello, Alice. Have you a kiss for me?"

Alice lifted her face quickly and kissed her mother on the cheek. She could smell the face powder her mother wore. It smelled the way it looked, soft and pink. "I'm going to get my bags," she said.

"Good girl."

The adults filed past her into the kitchen.

She pulled the door after her, but stood there a little longer, listening. She could hear Conor go on through the outside door and say something to Nell before he closed it behind him, leaving the two women alone in the kitchen.

"You were saying?" This was Sheila's voice, low and urgent.

"Dr Roche says it's a matter of time before . . . Michael makes a bad invalid. He hates being helpless. And now, with Alice coming back . . . he's worse when she's around. Every little thing seems to annoy him lately. He was so bad today after Dr Roche had been, that he went out for a walk. It's a long time since he did that. He gets breathless, you see." Her mother's voice trailed off. "He still wasn't back when I left, but I couldn't wait any longer. I don't know what to do. Between the two of them . . ."

"We could keep . . ."

"Not at all, I wouldn't dream of asking. No, school starts again on Monday, it'll be all right." Her mother's voice was stronger now. Sure of itself. "You're very good, Sheila. Thanks for having her for so long."

Alice crept away from the door. Her feet whispered

against the floor in their socks, but the blood roared in her ears, terrifying her. Surely they would hear it?

She brought her satchel down and sat waiting on the bottom step while her mother drank tea with Sheila and Conor in the kitchen, all of them solemn and whispering. Alice knew they were talking about her. She could feel trouble in the thickening atmosphere of the house, the way her breath was sticking in her throat. As their talk rose and fell in the other room and her pulse stabbed deeply into her neck, her ear began to ache. A sure sign. She sat on her hands, her satchel in front of her, and waited for her mother's anger to break over her head as soon as they'd said their goodbyes and left.

But Elaine said little in the car on the drive home. It was a car Alice hadn't seen before, a grey Morris.

"Whose is the car?" Alice asked when they'd crossed the grid, hoping to distract her mother.

"We're going to keep this one."

"You mean, for ourselves?" Alice looked at the car more critically. The leather on the back seat was split, showing a dull foam underneath. There was a tartan rug folded on the back window, with big squares in different shades of red and green blending in to each other. Alice spread it on the seat beside her and played with the braided ends of the wool.

"Did you behave?" her mother asked. Alice wondered if it was a trick question.

"Mmmm," she said vaguely, wondering what Sheila had said. She didn't even think about Conor.

She settled back against the seat and stared at the passing dark.

"I never went to the Border," she said after a while. "I never got to see it."

"The Border isn't something you can see, Alice. Except on maps."

She might have known. Her ear, woken up by her raging pulse earlier on, still throbbed. She covered it with her hand, making a warm cup for the pain, but it kept building up. She lay hunched against the seat, staring at the solid colours of the rug, trying to slip between them to a place where nothing hurt, but she couldn't do it. The throbbing in her ear kept pulling her back. Noises began to come from her throat. She buried her head in the blanket to stifle them, hoping her mother wouldn't notice, but finally she did.

"Are you all right?"

Alice lifted her head and saw her mother's blue eyes dark in the driving mirror, watching her. They looked scary like that, a pair of eyes suspended in space. Like God's. Able to see Alice without turning to look directly at her. But seeing everything. Backwards.

"My ear hurts."

Her mother sighed.

"I'm sorry, Mummy. I can't help it." Now that she'd started, the tears fell down her face in globs and her voice wobbled out of control. A hot stab in the side of her neck made her cry out as if she'd been hit. "Ouch!"

"We still have a long way to go." Her mother's eyes swung towards and away from Alice as she checked her daughter, then the road in front of her. "Do you want to come into the front?"

Alice was shocked. She climbed quickly over the back of the seat into the front before her mother could change her mind. She pulled the blanket with her, wrapping it around her as she lay down with her head close to her mother's body, feeling the car rock under her. But after a while the novelty was not enough of a distraction and she began to moan quietly again, clutching at her ear.

"Sit up," her mother said. "Pass me my bag."

Her big square leather handbag was on the floor of the car. Alice picked it up with two hands and put it beside her mother, who opened the clasp with her left hand, still looking at the road. She reached into the bag without looking and pulled out a flat leather hipflask. "I thought you might need this," she said, passing it to Alice. "Here, drink it."

"What is it?"

"It's whiskey."

Alice opened the lid and sniffed. The strong smell of whiskey, unsoftened by milk and sugar as she was used to it, caught at the back of her mouth. She wrinkled up her face and coughed.

"Drink it." Her mother's voice held a warning. "It'll make you feel better. It'll help you sleep."

Alice forced herself to swallow a little. The drink burned the back of her neck on the way down and she gagged, but her mother told her to swallow some more and she did. Her eyes watered and her throat stung. The singing started in her brain.

"I can't drink any more," she said when she'd caught her breath.

"Look, I didn't have time to mix it the way you like it. And if I had, it would have cooled by now. There'd be skin on it. You always make such a fuss about that. Stop being difficult and do as I say. Hold your nose and drink it quickly, that will help it go down."

Elaine's hands gripped the steering wheel hard. Her knuckles whitened and seemed to grow as Alice stared at them, poking out of her skin. She blinked and did as she was told. Then she fastened the lid on the bottle, put it back in her mother's bag and lay down again. She covered her head with the woolly rug, determined that her mother wouldn't notice if she cried again. The sound of the darkness they were passing through was a current of air in her brain.

The next thing she knew, she was being led out of the car and upstairs to her bed. She felt her shoes being taken off, heard them fall to the floor as if it was a long way down, then felt the familiar weight of her own blankets pulled up around her shoulders and settling around her.

In the morning her head was heavy and it ached, but the pain in her ear was gone.

She got cautiously out of bed and looked for her shoes. She found them neatly placed side by side under the bed. She pulled them on and went downstairs to look for Max. She could hear his tail wagging against something in the kitchen before she went in. Just as she opened the door he let out a "Woof!" as if he couldn't restrain himself any longer. He jumped at her, grinning, and they got into a mess of arms and paws and hair and fur and she pressed her face against his neck and smelt the warm soft Max smell she loved.

"Hello, Max," she whispered, breathing his smell deep into her stomach.

"Don't kiss the dog, Alice. How many times do I have to tell you . . ." Her mother had to shout over the sound of Max's tail thumping against the table.

Alice kissed him one more time before she stood up, her fingers still twined into the warm muff of hair around his neck. She slid into the nearest chair at the table and looked at her mother.

"Good morning, Alice."

"Morning, Mummy."

She reached for the cornflakes and filled her bowl. "Can I have the milk?"

"Please. May I. Stop touching the dog." It would have sounded as if she'd never been away except that her mother's heart didn't seem to be in it. Alice waited to be told to go and wash her hands but it didn't happen. The cold city milk splashed over her cornflakes, whiter than the milk at Nell's had been. It tasted different too. Thinner. Cleaner.

"I like our milk better than Nell's," she said.

"Good," said her mother.

"Where's Daddy?"

Her mother frowned, as if she was thinking. "He's not here. He hasn't come back from his walk."

Since yesterday? Alice wondered.

"But he's left his glasses," she said instead. She pointed to the windowsill.

"So he has." Her mother stared at them, then rubbed her own eyes as if they were tired. "Well, he'll be back soon, I'm sure. You've got school tomorrow, Alice. You'd better get your things ready. I left a new copybook and some pencils on the sideboard inside."

When her satchel was restored to itself, with pencils and ruler and jotter, Alice slipped off with Max to the field. It seemed smaller, somehow, the old house standing sadly to one side, with gaps in the plaster. An upstairs window had broken while she was away and gaped blackly against the sun. Birds flew in and out of the chimneys. The grass hummed with life. Winter was definitely over.

Her father never came back. After three days Kate showed her a page she'd torn out of the newspaper. "Swear you won't tell anyone I showed it to you," she said. "I'd be killed."

Alice snatched the piece of paper from her. *Local Man Missing*, said the headline. Underneath there was more, in smaller print. Michael Morrissey, a married man, had gone missing on Saturday afternoon, it said. His clothes had been found folded neatly on a rock near the Forty Foot. His watch and some loose change were wrapped in a handkerchief in his pocket. It was believed he had gone swimming.

"Swimming?" Alice asked, disbelieving.

Kate shrugged, but didn't look at her. "I wish I hadn't shown it to you," she said. "Da will be livid."

"I won't tell that it was you," Alice promised. She read the article again.

"It doesn't say anything about me," she said.

"What?"

"It says he's married. But there's nothing about me."

"Why would there be? Give it back."

"Here." Alice handed over the newspaper and went home.

Her mother was at the table, watching tea leaves spin on the surface of a cup of tea, when Alice burst in through the back door. She hadn't been to work for days. Not since Alice came home. All she did was sit, unless she was talking on the telephone in the hall. Alice was not allowed to stay in the hall during these conversations, so she didn't know what was going on. Now, her mother would have to tell her.

"Daddy never went swimming. Never." She slammed the door behind her. "He always said the water was too cold for his lungs."

Her mother looked up. "What? Why do you say that?"

"I saw a paper . . ."

"That Kate! I wish people would mind their own business!" her mother snapped.

"It wasn't Kate. I just saw it, that's all."

"What else did you see?"

"Nothing."

Her mother stood up, then.

"They say he went swimming." Her hand rested on Alice's hair. "Alice, he may have drowned."

Alice pulled away from her.

"Why? He never went in the water."

Her mother's hand shot out and gripped her wrist. "He loved swimming! You know he did."

"No, he . . ."

"I'm telling you, he did. He always took you swimming. Remember? All those times the two of you went off together to the beach. He taught you how to swim." Her voice was low, insistent. "Remember."

The story of her swimming lessons grew over the next two weeks. How her father had loved to swim and wanted her to learn, had brought her to the water ever since she was a baby. It worried Alice. Something was wrong. She waited to be found out.

"You must be like a fish, Alice," Kate's mother said warmly one day, when her own mother had finished telling the story yet again.

Alice shuddered. "I can't . . ." she began.

"Poor mite. Of course you can't," Kate's mother soothed. "It must have put you off, all this . . ."

It was like a weight lifting off her. A way out. "I'll never go in the water again!" she said loudly. "Never."

A few days later, her mother called her into the kitchen. Alice went reluctantly. She'd been chasing Max around in the lane. She was breathless and the back of her neck was sweaty. It was a hot day. She stood, one foot on top of the other, and looked back through the window at Max who was smelling something in the grass, his tail waving. The table was cluttered with her mother's buff folders, piles of papers. She had been trying to catch up on some work, she said. All pushed to one side.

"Alice. Look at me. I have to tell you something. Sit down." Her voice sounded slow and heavy, as if she was speaking underwater. Alice knew she didn't want to hear whatever was coming next.

She sat down opposite her mother. A fly buzzed at the window, trying to get through the hot glass to the air outside. The small top window was open, but the fly didn't know this. He buzzed and buzzed at the glass, angry, getting nowhere. Alice watched him intently.

"Move up, the window's open!" she said, but the fly ignored her and continued to press angrily against the glass as if he could force his way out.

"Alice! I'm talking to you."

She looked around, at last. Reluctant.

Her mother cleared her throat.

"They've found your father."

Alice stopped breathing. She stared at her mother. "Where? Where is he?"

"I mean, they've found his body. He's gone, Alice. He's dead. He's gone to heaven."

"For how long?"

"He's not ever coming back. I'm sorry. Come here," Elaine reached her hand out across the table towards Alice, who stayed as if stuck to her chair and went on staring at her.

She's lying. That's not him they found.

Alice watched herself sit and look at her mother. She watched her mother's hand reach out for her.

You're supposed to cry, she told herself.

Instead she stood up suddenly and opened the side window. The loud buzzing stopped abruptly as the fly followed the current of fresh air out into the open. Alice banged the window shut and turned and ran out of the kitchen, out the back door of the house, down through the garden past the bank of dock leaves to the gate, across the lane and out into the field.

She ran towards the trees, pushing the long heavy grass out of her way with her hands, frantic, as if something was chasing her, knowing she had to hide. She had to get away. When she was inside her cedar tree, she stopped, fighting for breath, her heart pounding. She listened to the stillness of the early summer morning, the faint hum of heat. She wondered where her father was hiding. He could be anywhere. He might even be in her tree. The branches rustled and sighed around her. Her skin prickled. Slowly, so he wouldn't know that she knew he was there, she edged her way back out into the light. Everything was different now. She knew he was waiting for his chance to come back and get her. But this time no one would see him coming. Not even her.

"Why did you think that?" Ruth asked.

Alice considered the question, then shook her head, puzzled.

"I don't know how I knew it, I just did. It was like, I belonged to him. He was my father, he owned me.

We had some sort of secret pact and this was part of it. I wasn't surprised that they all thought he'd gone, but I knew I had to be careful."

She tucked each hand inside the opposite cuff of her jumper and slid them up under her elbows. It was an easy movement. Practised.

"I knew he'd be back. He'd take me away and no one would ever look for me."

"Did you want him to?"

Alice shrugged. "It's just the way things were. The way they'd always been in the dream."

"The sea dream?"

"There was more to it than that. I haven't told you . . . it's so sordid."

"Go on, Alice."

"There was a man." She coughed, hard, and smiled weakly at Ruth. "One of these days I'll have to stop smoking."

"A man?" Ruth pressed, not rising to this.

"I was his slave. I thought of him as the slavemaster. He controlled . . . everything."

She scratched her forearms violently as her hands re-emerged from her cuffs. "That's it."

"What did he control?"

"Oh, you know . . . dream-stuff. Madness. Me. I could never get away from him. And now that my father was gone, they were the same, somehow . . . they had extra power. And they could see right through me, right to the evil depths . . . Like God. They"d always been allies, but now they were all in the same place. Watching me. What was scary was not knowing where they'd come from, or when. It was terrifying. Max was my only hope, because he could sense things that I couldn't see."

"Did you tell your mother what you felt? Did you tell her about Conor?"

"No." Alice's mouth twisted.

"Why not?"

"It never occurred to me. What was there to tell? What difference would it make? Anyway, I never thought about it. I didn't forget, exactly. It was just a part of me I stayed away from."

"That's interesting, that you say it was part of you, rather than something that happened to you."

"Why is that strange? It's like . . . I knew there was something horrible about me that made things like that happen."

"Things?"

Alice looked at her blankly.

"You said 'things'."

"Did I?"

Alice wished the silence was a blanket she could pull around her and rest in. She smelled scorching and wondered idly if her chair was too close to the fire.

"What about your father, Alice?" Ruth prompted.

"Oh. Well," Alice kneaded the skin on her forearms. "I hated being alone after that. I stopped going to the field."

CHAPTER SEVEN

Now that the field had turned against her, Alice read more than ever. One word pulled her towards the next, leading her out of herself. It was as if they made a curtain she could slip through, any time she wanted. It put her beyond her mother's reach.

"Alice!"

Startled, Alice lifted her head, marking the page with her finger.

"Why are you ignoring me?"

"What?"

"I'm hoarse, calling you! Hurry up, we have to go out. We'll be late! Why didn't you answer me?"

"Where are we going?"

"I've been looking everywhere for you."

"I didn't hear you."

Her mother sighed heavily. "We'll soon sort that out. We're going to get your hearing checked, at the hospital. I'm sick to death of having to repeat myself, over and over again. Now come on. You're so slow."

They walked down to the clinic at the hospital. There was a big waiting-room with a marble floor and walls that smelled green. Doors with round windows set into them like portholes led out of it. People waited on rows of wooden benches, like a church. Alice looked at the portholes and imagined herself at sea. Outside the big window gulls wheeled in the white sky.

She had a premonition. Storm coming, watch out for rocks, this ship is headed for destruction. If only she could find the Captain, make him listen to her . . .

"Alice Morrissey?" A large woman in a white uniform, with what looked like a huge serviette folded on her head, called out her name.

Her mother dug her elbow into Alice's side. "Here!" she called and got up, pulling Alice after her towards the nurse. "Here she is."

Alice could hear the nurse's nylons brush against each other as she followed her to an open door. It was a busy sound. It made Alice feel sick.

The doctor's room was small and just as smelly as the waiting-room had been. His desk was crowded with papers and metal trays full of shining steel and rubber tubing. Alice checked for needles but she couldn't see any. She sat down in the chair he pointed to, relieved.

"Dr Roche sent us," her mother explained. "I'm at my wit's end with this child, she's in a constant dream. Sometimes I have to call her four or five times before she hears me. She's had a string of earaches over the years. He said to come down here, that you'd check her hearing for me."

She sat back and folded her hands through the strap of her big black handbag, her ankles crossed under the chair.

The doctor smiled at Alice over the square tops of his glasses. His hands were linked in front of him on the desk. His fingers waved at her while he talked.

"How do you get on in school, Alice?" he asked her.

"Not as well as she could," said her mother. "That's what the nuns say. She doesn't try. Always daydreaming. They say she could do much better, if she tried."

"I'm going to look inside your ears with this light, Alice. It won't hurt you, it's like a torch, see?" He showed her a metal cylinder, one end bent at an angle. He screwed a black tip on to the end and switched it on. A tiny dot of light glowed behind the tip. Dr Roche had one just like it, but she'd never had a good look at it. The light was tiny, like a star.

The doctor looked at her, waiting. "Well?"

She realized that he was waiting for permission to look inside her ears.

"Oh. Yes, all right," she said.

He got up and walked around the desk and shone his light into her ears. "Can you wiggle your ears?" he asked her.

She blinked, confused. Was this part of the test? She looked up at him. His ears were moving backwards and forwards on the side of his head. She laughed and he beamed at her.

"Good girl. Now we're going to do a little test. I'm going to put these ear-phones on and I want you to tell me when you hear a sound and then tell me when you stop hearing it. All right?"

She nodded. The test went on. High-pitched sounds opened and closed right inside her head. She frowned and concentrated, wanting to please this doctor who was so friendly. When it was finished he smiled at her and asked her to wait outside while he talked to her mother.

While she waited, Alice wondered if she should have told him about the ship sinking.

The ship's doctor. The captain would listen to him, surely. Maybe they could still turn back, maybe it wasn't too late. . .

But then Elaine stood in front of her and said in a clear, clipped voice, "Come on, it's time to go."

On the way home, Alice had to run every couple of steps to keep up with her mother who walked fast and didn't relent until they were inside their kitchen. Alice ran to rub Max's ears but her mother opened the door again.

"Outside, Max!" she snapped. "You need a run."

She turned back and filled the kettle noisily and banged it down, hard, on the cooker. Then she pulled off her coat and scarf and brushed past Alice to go and hang them up in the hall. Alice stood in the kitchen and waited. Her mother was already talking when she came back into the room.

"There's not a thing wrong with you. Not one, single, solitary thing. Your hearing is perfect. You hear what you want to hear, is that it? It's only me, apparently, that you choose to ignore?"

"No, Mummy." Alice was bewildered. "What do you mean?"

"Oh, you don't understand what I'm talking about, is that it? Well, you can always pretend you don't hear me then, can't you? Little brat." She slammed the teapot open beside the kettle and poured some hot water into it, then stood there, swilling the water around in the metal pot, glaring at Alice.

"Mortified," she said. "I was absolutely mortified."

Max scratched at the back door and whined to be let in. The window was clouding over with steam from the kettle. Suddenly Elaine moved forwards and Alice dodged out of her way. She emptied the water down the sink and went back to the cooker. Alice opened the door for Max and stroked his head as she watched her mother put three spoons of tealeaves into the pot and then fill it with steaming water.

"You've made a holy show of me. Do you know what that doctor had the nerve, the gall, to say to me? Do you?"

Alice shook her head.

"He said there could be other reasons that you couldn't hear me. That there were other avenues to explore. That's how he put it. Avenues to explore. As if I have the time to be wandering up and down avenues, sitting around in waiting-rooms. No, I told him straight. I said, I know that girl and you don't. It's laziness, that's what it is, pure and simple. Laziness and defiance. I knew it all along. You could hear me perfectly well if it suited you, isn't that the truth?"

"No..."

"Don't you dare lie to me. Don't you dare! You can hear me now, can't you?" She was shouting.

Alice thought the neighbours could probably hear her, with no trouble at all.

"Yes," she said.

"Well, I'm warning you. You'd better watch yourself. Don't think you can make a fool of me. Now put that dog outside. And get out of my sight."

CHAPTER EIGHT

One Friday, when Alice was eleven, she and Kate walked home from school as usual. It was the last day of term, the end of the school year.

"What'll we do next week?" Alice said, listlessly. She was sweating. Her school-bag, full of extra end-of-term junk, was heavy.

"I'll help out in the shop, what else? Some of the time, anyway. And we're going to Wexford, but not until July," Kate said, rubbing her neck where the shoulder strap of her bag chafed against her skin.

"You could come over to my house when you're not busy, but you know how my mother is about having you there when she's at work."

"You come to me, then."

"Right. See you on Monday, so."

Alice trudged on up the road towards her own house. When she opened the door, the house felt cold and musty as if it had been empty for a long time.

"Max?" she called, her skin prickling. She hated coming home when he wasn't there. He was her radar. He could sense things that she couldn't. He'd been getting slower on his feet and he didn't go out as often as he used to, but his big, cone-shaped ears were still as alert as they'd ever been.

"He's getting old," her mother had warned her. "He's older than you, remember."

That morning he'd been asleep when she left for school, his plate still full from the night before. "Max hasn't eaten," she'd told her mother, unnecessarily.

"I'll call the vet before I go to work," her mother had promised. "Now hurry up or you'll be late."

To her surprise, her mother was home before her. She walked into the room as Alice stood looking around, wondering what was missing.

"Hang up your coat," she said.

"I want to keep it on for a while," said Alice, pulling it closer around her and walking over to the kettle. "It's cold in here. Where's Max?"

"There's bad news about Max, Alice. I'm sorry. The vet came this morning and said he had a cancer. He said it wouldn't be fair to keep him alive."

Alice stared at her, stunned. "Do you mean, he's dead?"

"The vet put him to sleep."

"He's dead. Why didn't you tell me?"

"I didn't know."

Alice wrapped her arms tightly around herself. She could hardly see her mother because her eyes were clouding over. "I wish you'd waited."

"That would have been cruel to Max. I'm just as upset as you are. I had to make a decision and you weren't here to tell. I'm sorry," her mother repeated.

Alice began to rock on her feet. She wanted to

scream, I didn't get to say goodbye! But her mother's tightly folded arms, the angle of her chin, warned her not to say anything. She turned away.

"Put the kettle on, would you? I'd like some tea," her mother said.

Alice filled the kettle and put it on. Then she walked out of the kitchen and slammed the door.

Make your own tea.

She went up to her room and lay down, staring at the ceiling. There was a weight in her throat that pressed all the way down to her stomach. A collar of pain stretched around her head. She held herself rigid.

Oh God, don't be sick.

She pressed her hands over her mouth. If she got sick, she knew she would die.

Over the next week she was jumpy. She looked over her shoulder everywhere she went. She startled at sudden noises. Her temperature rose and she burned at night and shouted, disturbing her mother in the other room. She walked in her sleep. She cried and shook for no reason. She saw things that weren't there, shadows. Just beyond her field of vision something shimmered. The glass of water she took to bed with her spilled when she was nowhere near it. She couldn't control the trembling of her hands.

Her mother called Dr Roche. As usual, they stood over her and talked about her as if she wasn't there. Alice tried to explain what was happening in her head, that her brain was swept by strange currents, that a monstrous storm was brewing. They didn't listen. They talked across her, about glands and medicines and rest.

Alice could tell that it was inconvenient. Her mother's lips were pressed tightly together and her face had that rigid look that Alice knew so well.

"This is a very busy time for me at work," she said, after Dr Roche had gone. "I don't know what to do with you. I'll have to see if I can find someone to help."

Alice wasn't listening. She felt as if she was burning with a dry heat, the waves in her brain folding whitely over each other like sea foam, stirring. Dredging up whitened bones, skulls with empty eye sockets tumbling over each other in the sand, jaws gaping. And then, in the distance, the horror started. A tall wave rose up out of a sea she hadn't known was there, right there in the corner of her room, and rushed towards her, gathering force and height every second. She could never hope to outrun it. As it licked around her bed she could make out her father's face below the surface of the water.

The room buckled and heaved and her bed rocked. She cried out as the wall of water struck her and raged through her, through and between every cell in her body.

Then, as abruptly, the water was gone, leaving her stunned and shaken and dispersed, shocked to find herself coming together again. Like the mercury she'd found on the floor in the school lab once. She'd wrapped it in her hankie and carried it around for days, convinced it was alive.

She was terrified. She knew the wave would come

back. The sensation in her brain that warned her it was coming was familiar, but she didn't know where from. It swept over her again and again, the rising wall of water right behind it. When she felt it coming, she tossed and moaned and pleaded, Oh no, no. Please, not again. Go away.

She was exhausted.

Dr Roche said it was glandular fever.

Her mother was impatient with her fear. She had never had much time for things she couldn't see or explain.

"I've told you, Alice," she said, again and again, "there's nothing there." As if her saying it wasn't happening was enough to cancel the terror Alice was living through.

And then, miraculously, Nell was there.

"It really looks as if she sees something, Auntie Elaine," Alice heard her say. She saw Nell looking over her shoulder, as if to check. "It's real to her."

Alice's brain was folding up again in warning and she pulled away from Nell, pressing herself against the headboard, curled as tight and small as could be, waiting for the storm to pass.

When it was over and she lifted her head Nell was stroking her hair, smiling at her.

"Has it gone?" asked Alice, and Nell nodded.

"Did you see it, Nell?"

"No. But I know you did."

Alice lay back, exhausted and relieved. Nell believed her! It wasn't enough, but it was something.

She let Nell rub her head and then her mother came in with a mug of hot milk and whiskey and Alice drank it and fell asleep.

Nell had come to help. She stayed until Alice was better. She played games of Scrabble with Alice, watched television with her mother in the evenings. Alice's mother was more relaxed while she was around. They liked each other.

They liked each other so much that when Nell came up to Dublin that autumn to go to college, she went to live with Alice and her mother. Her parents didn't want her to live in a flat, where they suspected she'd get up to no good.

Alice was glad. But Nell had changed. She was older, more serious than she used to be. She had come to study commerce, so that she could go home and help her father to expand his business.

"It was Mam's idea," she explained on her first night, when they'd gone into the good room to sit, the first time Alice could remember doing so for years. "Daddy thought I could just do book-keeping, but Mam said I may as well do it right, so long as I could stay with you."

Alice asked her about O'Hara.

"We sold him years ago," Nell said, in a casual way, as if it didn't matter.

"Are you still going to join the army?" Alice asked, puzzled.

Nell looked at Elaine and they both laughed, as if it

was a stupid question. Alice's chest tightened and the tips of her ears burned. She felt betrayed.

"That was ages ago, Alice," Nell said, twisting a curl through her fingers. "I've outgrown all that."

Nell did all the cooking. That was her side of the bargain, she said. She said she liked it. Alice couldn't understand. What had happened to her?

Before their first meal together was over Nell made it clear that she expected Alice to do the washing-up. Alice was used to that from her mother, but Nell?

At first she hung around in the kitchen, offering to help, but Nell only gave her the dullest of jobs to do. Washing the pots, or peeling potatoes, a job Alice loathed. Nell did it in the old way. The way Sheila did it. With sheets of newspaper spread on the kitchen table, masses of potatoes in a big bowl, a pot of water to put them in, a fat-handled peeler with a sharp tip for scouring out the eyes. Alice preferred to do it at the sink, to rinse her hands as she went along, to use a sharp knife and slice off the skin quickly.

Nell was appalled. "It's such a waste! Look at all the food you're throwing away! It's not even as if there's pigs to feed."

In school Alice mocked her, imitated her to amuse her friends. "Not even pigs to feed!" she echoed, in revenge, letting her voice rise and fall through the words the way Nell's did.

She hated the scum of the potatoes on her hands, the sharp sweet smell released when the skin came off and fell onto the paper, the rotting bruises and lumpy eyes. The crevices around her fingernails from where she chewed the skin filled up quickly with dirt, with muddy ridges that tasted horrible no matter how well she rinsed her hands when she'd finished.

Nell liked to experiment with desserts: flans and pies and even soufflés. Alice and her mother had never eaten so well. When Alice offered to help with the baking she was put in front of a sink full of soapy water and set to washing mountains of mixing bowls, or else she was asked to grease the baking tins. She hated the slippy sensation of butter on her fingers. She soon learned to stay away, drifting in to the kitchen just in time to lick the bowl.

They arrived at a cautious sort of truce. Nell was an easy target with her piety and her soft country voice. Her speech was littered with God-phrases that Alice had fun with in school: godbless and godforbid and pleasegod. When Nell complained, Alice laughed and told her to offer it up.

"You shouldn't treat Nell like that," Alice's mother warned her. "As if she was stupid."

"I don't know what you mean," Alice said. She didn't really think Nell was stupid. Just treacherous.

In the mornings Nell sat at the breakfast table peering into the blade of her knife as if it was a mirror, inspecting her face for damage. The bathroom filled with multi-coloured balls of cotton-wool and things Alice had never seen before. Q-tips, tweezers, mascara brushes, bottles of lotion.

Nell paid a lot of attention to her skin, which was cratered and rough. She squeezed her blackheads with enthusiasm and interest. Alice thought it was revolting. Once she saw her mother squeezing a blackhead in Nell's ear, using matchsticks, her face screwed up in concentration just as Nell's was when she did this to herself on some more accessible surface, like her chin. It was disgusting. They deserved each other.

But Nell could be her ally too. One day she came home early from college and caught Alice, smoking, in her room. They stared at each other.

"What are you doing in here?" Nell asked.

"What does it look like?" Alice tried to brazen it out.

"But why are you in my room?"

"Well, she doesn't care if you smoke, does she? So if she smells it in your room there won't be any trouble, will there?" Alice didn't know what to call her mother any more. She'd told Nell to drop the "Auntie" and call her Elaine. It put them on an equal footing that excluded Alice. She didn't know why she was so angry, as if Nell was the person caught doing something wrong, and herself the injured party. Her heart pounded as she took another drag from her cigarette to show that she didn't care.

"I see," Nell said, thoughtfully. "You have a point, there." She took her own red and white packet of cigarettes out of her shoulder-bag and put a cigarette between her lips. Then she rummaged through the bag again.

"Want a match?" Alice passed her a yellow box from her pocket, the rough strip down the side darkened, nearly worn away. Red lettering on the top said *Friendly*.

"Thanks." Nell took the box and opened it. "Ah, now, that's a terrible habit."

"What?"

Nell turned the box so Alice could see all the burnt out matches. She shook the box and picked through them until she found one with a fresh red tip. "There. You've only two left." She shook the box again. "And anyone'd think it was full. I hate that."

Alice took the box back. "I hate it too," she said.

They smiled at each other. Nell turned on her transistor and began to hum. Alice leaned against the chest of drawers and Nell sat on the bed and they both drew on their cigarettes, not speaking, until Alice stubbed hers out in the cracked ashtray.

"Elaine would go mad if she saw you," Nell said, watching her.

"I know."

"You're better off not smoking in the house at all. But, I suppose, if you're going to, you may as well come in here to do it. But don't get caught, mind."

"I won't."

"If you are, I'll say I knew nothing about it."

Going to Nell's room to smoke and listen to pirate

radio stations gave Alice a new refuge. Nell smoked like a train. She sang along with the radio, completely out of tune. She taught Alice how to rock'n'roll, how to do the twist and keep going even when she had a stitch in her side.

"It's a great dance," she sighed. "Great for the figure. Pity no one does it any more."

She taught her how to slow-dance and how to kiss.

"You've got to know what you're doing, Alice," she said, very serious and matter-of-fact. "Don't get caught out."

Alice pretended to know what she meant.

Nell never opened a book, so far as Alice could see. On Friday nights she went out with a group of girls from the college to the pictures and on Saturdays she went to the library.

One weekend Elaine went away to a conference. "I'm glad you're here to keep an eye on things, Nell," she said.

I suppose she means me.

Alice stared hard at the back of her mother's neck, indignant. She was practising how to make people feel uncomfortable from a distance. It often worked with teachers, who would become oddly restless at the blackboard, fiddle with their hair or surreptitiously check their hemline, under the pressure of Alice's focused stare. Sometimes they swung around, as if looking for the source of their discomfort, but they never caught her staring.

It didn't work with her mother, who went on talking to Nell, oblivious. "Are you sure you can manage, now?"

"Of course I can. Don't you worry about a thing," Nell reassured her, as she carried her overnight bag out to the car. "You just enjoy yourself."

"This is business, Nell."

"I know. But there's no harm in enjoying yourself at the same time, now is there?"

Alice's stomach turned, hearing this.

"Why do you have to suck up to her so much?" she demanded as the car drove out of the lane.

Nell turned a blank face towards her. "Suck up, is it? You really don't have a clue, Alice, do you?" She shook her head and went back inside. "Come on and we'll have a cup of tea and a fag."

Alice brightened as the possibilities of this weekend dawned on her. The freedom. To play music as loud as they liked, smoke wherever they felt like it, stay up all night if they wanted to. She followed Nell through to the kitchen.

"It will be great, not having her here all weekend," she said.

Nell turned on her.

"Don't talk about her like that!"

"Why not?" Alice was startled by the strength of Nell's reaction.

"She's your mother. I know she can be hard on you sometimes, but you don't make it easy for her, either. Not ever. Why do you fight her all the time? Can't you allow her to at least *think* she's winning?"

"No!" Alice's breath was sour. She filled a glass with water and drank it. She stood with her back to Nell as she rinsed the glass under hot water. Her fingers reddened.

"What will we do?" she said, trying to sound casual. She knew the weekend would be a disaster if she and Nell were fighting.

Nell seemed fascinated by the strip of silver paper she was folding and re-folding on the table, smoothing down its edges with her thumbnail. "I have a friend coming to dinner. You can go out if you like."

"What friend?"

Nell studied Alice. "Can I trust you?"

"Nell!" Alice was hurt.

"All right. Look, it's a man, Alice. His name is Brendan. We've been going together for ages."

Alice tried not to look shocked. Her mind raced. She'd had no idea. Nell had been living here for two years, except for the holidays, and apart from her Friday night outings with "the girls", had never shown any interest in going out. With anyone.

"You never said."

"No. Daddy and Mam would have a canary if they knew. It seemed easier to keep it quiet."

"But you're going to be twenty-one next month. You can do what you like."

"Why rock the boat? Why have everyone make a fuss and spy on me? Why do you think they made me come and live here in the first place?"

"I thought you wanted to . . ."

"Oh don't be such a baby! Look, in a few more months I'll have my degree and then I'll tell them. We're going to get married in the summer."

"Married?"

"As you say, I'll be twenty-one. They can't stop me. Brendan's getting a job near Galway, in the bank. We'll move out there. It's all arranged. Unless someone," she glared at Alice, "opens her big mouth and wrecks it all."

"I won't say a word," Alice promised.

A whole new era began then. When Alice got up the next morning and found Brendan sitting in the kitchen she made a point of looking straight at him, as if it was the most normal thing in the world to find a man she barely knew spending the night at her house, with Nell. Brendan was a quiet, brown man. His face was weathered, his eyes were dark and he wore a brown tweed jacket over corduroy trousers. His hair was curly and light. He had a soft country voice and a slow, wide smile.

"I like him," she told Nell after he'd gone. "I don't blame you . . ."

"Don't get any ideas, Alice," Nell warned. "We didn't do anything. We're going to wait."

"Oh yeah?"

"I mean it."

Alice didn't believe her, but she pretended that she did.

She liked having a hold on Nell. It evened things out between them. Now that she was in on the secret they included her in what they did. They brought her to see films she couldn't have got into on her own. Once they took her out to dinner at a restaurant, with candles on the tables and waiters wearing striped waistcoats and starched white shirts. In return she was their alibi, lying as easily on Nell's behalf as she ever had on her own.

When Nell got her degree she went home. Things went exactly as she'd predicted. There was uproar when she first told her parents that she was going to marry Brendan. Alice heard her mother on the phone to Sheila, swearing ignorance. She could tell by her mother's protests that Sheila didn't believe her.

"She thinks I was in on it all along," Elaine said when she'd hung up and saw Alice standing there, leaning against the bannister.

"I suppose you knew?" she asked.

Alice said nothing, but she smiled a little, so that her mother would know.

"I don't think I've ever known anyone as vindictive as you can be, Alice," her mother said wearily. "I'm going up to bed now."

"But it's only eight o'clock."

"I feel sick," Elaine said. She looked right at Alice then. "In my stomach."

Alice stood back to let her pass, pulling herself right against the wall so that her mother's body would not touch hers. She willed the aching muscles of her face to hold her mouth in that same half smile until her mother had passed her. Elaine's back going up the stairs was like another door between them, closing.

CHAPTER NINE

The house fell silent again when Nell left. She left her transistor behind for Alice, a half-used packet of cotton wool balls in the bathroom and a pile of magazines on the floor beside her bed. But now that she'd gone there was nothing to soften the air between Alice and her mother. Alice looked for excuses to stay away from home.

The music teacher in school, Miss Sweetman, was one of Alice's favourite people. She was completely different from the nuns in their dusty black habits and the older teachers in their tweed skirts and flat shoes. Her chestnut coloured hair fell loose around her shoulders and she dressed in brightly coloured clothes. She moved with a smile on her face and sang to herself in the corridors. The girls tapped their foreheads after she'd passed them but they liked her. She taught them folk songs and hymns and talked to them about musicians and foreign cities: Vienna, Leipzig, Paris, Milan. She'd been to all of them.

One day she brought some sheet music into class.

"Today we're going to learn the *Ave Verum*," she

told them. "See how you get on with sightreading. Please try not to massacre this, girls."

She sat at the piano and played the opening bars. Alice, looking at the score in front of her, felt a tug of memory. A clear ribbon of sound lifting high over her head. A recorded voice, a boy-soprano, a darkened room. She began to sing along with the others, her voice becoming that other voice in her head and flowing out of her, steady and sure, following the pattern of notes in front of her.

After the opening bars there were a few beats of silence. She waited. Around her, hesitant voices took up the "Cujus latus" too soon and faltered when the piano stopped. Miss Sweetman opened her mouth to speak. Alice's pulse measured the silence. When it had stretched out to its precise and proper length, she lifted her chin and a pure, unearthly sound soared out of her throat. That other voice. She closed her eyes and listened, entranced. The sound continued. She realized that no one else was singing and opened her eyes. Everyone was staring at her, including Kate. Miss Sweetman's eyes were shining.

"Thank you, Alice," she said. "That was lovely. I wish you people would learn to *count*. Let's try it again."

They went back to the beginning. Alice was more careful this time. She was shaking.

"Wow," Kate whispered to her when they'd stumbled through the piece to the end. "I didn't know you could do that."

Alice ignored her, embarrassed.

After class Miss Sweetman asked her to stay behind.

"Do you play any instrument, Alice?" she asked.

"No."

"Would you like to?"

"I never thought about it." Alice shook her head. "I don't think so."

"What about voice lessons?"

Alice shook her head.

"You have a fine voice. You've kept it well hidden. What about the piano? Do you think your mother would agree to lessons?"

"I don't know." Alice bent and pulled up the fawn coloured uniform socks that constantly fell around her ankles. She didn't know what to say.

"Would you like to come to theory classes?"

Alice shrugged. "I don't mind."

"You don't mind." Miss Sweetman studied Alice for a minute, then went and sat at the piano and began to play. "You don't know and you don't mind," she said conversationally. "I've heard them talk about you in the staffroom. They say you're clever but you couldn't be bothered trying."

Alice found it hard to think while the notes the woman was playing reached inside her head, disturbing her peace.

"Is that true?"

"I don't know." Alice smiled, then, hearing herself say it again.

"Well, I'll tell you what I think. I think you have a musical soul and that's something money can't buy. If you decide you want to join my theory class, you let me know. You'd have to stay late after school on Wednesdays. And I will speak to your mother about piano lessons. Now go back to class."

"Thank you." Alice felt awkward. She was being offered something and she wasn't sure what. She didn't even know if she wanted it, but before she'd left the music room she knew she'd take it. Extra time in school meant less time at home. Every time she walked into the cold emptiness of the house she could feel Max's absence, Nell's departure.

Sometimes she walked home with Kate and did her homework in the Kennys' kitchen which was always warm and brightly lit and full of people talking. It was hard to concentrate on school work, but Alice didn't care. She liked being there. Kate's mother usually came home from the shop at around the same time as they got in. She sat and had a cup of tea with them, listening to their news and adding stories of her own, her smile including Alice. Then she got up to cook, still ready to listen, to answer a question.

She was as likely to ask Alice to set the table as Kate, whether she was staying for tea or not. It made Alice feel welcome, somehow. She offered to do things for Mrs Kenny that she only did with bad grace for her own mother, like emptying the bin or ironing shirts. At the Kennys', it was an excuse to stay longer. At home it was the price she paid for living.

Her mother agreed to send her to Miss Sweetman for

piano lessons. "But we've no piano," she pointed out. "How will she practise?"

"In school," said Miss Sweetman briskly, as if this was no problem at all.

The piano made Alice feel awkward. The simple pieces Miss Sweetman started her on humiliated her because her fingers were clumsy on the keys, leaden. They fell heavily and out of time, making Miss Sweetman throw her hands into the air and shake her head.

"You must practise, Alice!" she insisted. "If you had the discipline, you could be very competent indeed."

Alice didn't want to be competent. She wanted to shine. She wanted her fingers to recreate the drama that she felt surging through her veins with music, but they were useless. There was no connection between what she felt and the sounds she made, as if her body was a rigid block, an obstacle.

She loved theory classes, when she stayed after school to listen to music and learned how to trace patterns in the sound. It was a small group and Miss Sweetman asked them questions as if she really wanted to know what they thought. She said that Alice had a gift for harmony and made her sing descant in the school choir. Alice tried to explain her enjoyment to Kate who was in the choir as well, but only because the extra practice got her out of class.

"All these words are so weird," said Kate, looking over Alice's shoulder at her manuscript book. "*Dominant, sub-dominant, tonic.* How do you remember it all? They just look like notes and chords to me."

"It's not that simple," Alice said seriously. "I'm trying to figure something out for myself as well. It's not just the notes, you see. When you think of a chord, you think of the notes, right?"

"Right."

"But it's not that at all. It's the silence that matters. The notes are the outside, but it's the shape they make, what's inside, that makes the sound . . . I can't explain it."

"I haven't a clue what you're talking about. Listen to this." Kate had discovered Led Zeppelin.

They practised hard for the end of the year performance of *Messiah* with a local boys' school. The presence of the boys made everyone restless. There was a lot of nudging and giggling behind the stage curtains. Miss Sweetman's patience vanished. She was tense and harsh, pushing their voices beyond any limit they had reached before.

"Handel had no pity," she told them, two weeks before the performance, when some of the seniors begged for mercy. "He treated the human voice as an instrument. You people are all instruments! This is a demanding piece of music. It would be a crime to take it on and not do it justice. Anyone who wants to leave, leave now." She tossed her head, folded her arms and waited.

A few people tittered, but no one moved. Alice's heart pounded until Miss Sweetman lifted her baton again and said, "All right. Senior sopranos only. *I Know* . . . Again, please."

The actual performance stunned them all. The power of all their voices coming together seemed to infect each one of them. Strange to themselves in stiff new clothes, white shirts and long black skirts or creased black trousers, they rose to the occasion, giggling and complaint forgotten. No longer entirely human, they soared above themselves in a wave of sound.

When it was over, Kate slipped an arm through Alice's. "Wasn't that something?" she said.

"I feel so weird," Alice told her. "As if everything inside me is shaking."

"You girls were wonderful." Mr Kenny came up to them, beaming. "I was proud of you both."

"So was I." Kate's mother smiled. "What did you think, Elaine? Weren't they great?"

"Great." Alice's mother looked rattled. The line between her eyes was more pronounced than usual. She looked older than the other mothers. She had worn the same two business suits for as long as Alice could remember. Tonight she wore the charcoal grey with the narrow white vertical lines like chalk. A fur hat the same grey as her hair sat firmly on her head and she carried her old square handbag. Miss Sweetman waved at them over the heads of the crowd and began to move towards them, smiling as if she wanted to say something.

"Come on, Alice. Time to go." Her mother pulled her towards the door.

They said goodnight to the Kennys and Alice followed her mother out onto the street. She could still feel the music pouring through her. She had never been so much a part of anything before. It had been profoundly shocking and wonderful.

"That reminded me of your father," her mother said unexpectedly as they walked home.

Alice stared. They never talked about him. She couldn't remember one single time since he had died that her mother had so much as mentioned him.

"Why?" she asked.

"He would have enjoyed it."

Alice had never felt as raw as she felt that summer. One day a strange thing happened. She looked out the window and knew she couldn't go out of the house alone. It was far too dangerous out there. Overnight the house changed from being a place she only ever wanted to escape from, to being something she couldn't leave. Fear made a barrier across the door, something she couldn't push her way past unless someone, even her mother, was with her to hold it at bay.

She stayed in her room. When her mother went out to work she got up and wandered around downstairs, aimlessly, turning the dials on the radio but not really listening. She soon went back upstairs, uneasy. She lay in bed and stared at the wall.

She got up when her mother was due in from work and hurried downstairs to start the dinner and avoid a row. She went straight back up to bed again when she'd cleared away. And lay staring at the ceiling, out the window, into space.

She slept little and ate less.

"Why are you pushing your food around your plate like that? You've eaten nothing," her mother commented.

"I've been picking at things all day. I'm not hungry."

"It's a waste of food, it's a disgrace," said her mother. "Don't you know there are people starving out there? Do you have any idea how lucky you are?" She turned back to her newspaper.

Alice's clothes didn't fit her any more. She'd always been thin, but now her sweaters hung loosely from her shoulders. When Kate came back from camping with her family, she was taken aback.

"You've got so thin! Lucky you!" She was envious. She'd taken to moaning about her figure, her skin, her glasses. "Did you do it on purpose?"

"No," Alice said.

Kate, weight and all, had a new boyfriend, and spent most of her time with him. She brought Alice out to meet him.

"Do you know what Eddie said?" Kate asked, later. "He said, 'who could fancy Alice? If she turned sideways, you could mark her absent.'"

"Thanks for telling me."

"It's a compliment, Alice."

"Oh yeah?"

Alice didn't care what Eddie, or anyone else, thought. She was secretly, savagely, glad that she was thin. She began to stay away from the windows. The pressure inside her built up until she thought she would burst. Every time she opened her mouth to talk to her mother her throat closed and her stomach moved up into her neck the way it did when there was food in front of her. Soon just walking up or down the stairs became too much of an effort.

One day she didn't even bother to get out of bed. When Elaine came home to an unlit house with no sign of dinner underway, she came up the stairs to find out what was going on. Alice listened to her steps, slow and heavy. For some reason, it occurred to her that her mother was tired and getting old. So that when Elaine stood over her and asked, "Are you ill?", she answered her as truthfully as she could.

"There's something wrong with me. I want to see someone."

"Do you have a pain? Is it your stomach? Your head?"

"No. I don't know. There's something . . . I'm afraid." She fought tears.

"Afraid of what?"

"I don't know."

There was a long silence. Alice sat up and leaned against the headboard, twisting the sheet in her fingers as she spoke. "And I'm too thin. Everyone says so."

"I see. And who is 'everyone'?"

Alice knew she'd made a mistake.

"No one. I only mean, people tease me. At school.

Look, there's something wrong with me and I don't know what it is but I want to go and see someone about it."

"And who, exactly, did you have in mind?"

"I'm not sure. A psychologist?" She wasn't sure what a psychologist was, but it was the only thing she could think of.

Her mother flew into a rage.

"No!" she said loudly. "I'm not spending good money on that nonsense. People interfering in our private affairs. God only knows what you'd say to them!"

"This has nothing to do with you! It's me, can't you see?"

But her mother wouldn't listen. "Mental illness is a luxury we can't afford, young lady," she stormed. "What would people say? What you don't understand is that families are supposed to be loyal to each other, and not go discussing private matters with outsiders. You and those friends of yours! I suppose they put you up to this. It's pure self-indulgence, if you ask me!" She refused to be drawn any further.

Alice lay down, under the covers, turned over and stared at the wall. She refused to get out of bed the next day. Or the next. At last her mother gave in.

"But I will choose," she warned, "who you talk to. I will find out who is the right person for this sort of thing."

What she thought "this sort of thing" was, Alice didn't know, but the person who turned up in her bedroom the next day did nothing to reassure her. He was a tall, elderly, ugly man she had never seen before, with a whiny insistent voice and hair growing from his nostrils. He peered at Alice under the bedclothes.

"I see," he said. "We've gone on strike, have we?"

Alice hated him at once. She pulled the covers more tightly around herself and held them there, watching him, wishing he'd go away. He was, he explained, a psychiatrist.

"We can begin," he said, "by you telling me all the dirty thoughts you had when you were little. The ones you're most ashamed of." He pulled a chair up beside her bed, sat down, folded his arms and waited.

Alice wondered if she could have heard him right, but that's what he'd said. She clamped her mouth shut, afraid of what might slip out. She didn't take her eyes off him for a second until he'd gone.

He complained to her mother that she was unco-operative. He seemed offended. He mentioned taking her "in" for observation.

When her mother told her that, Alice thought about what it would mean, to be observed by him and people like him. To have him in charge of her welfare. She decided to get out of bed.

"You see?" her mother gloated. "There's nothing wrong with you at all."

CHAPTER TEN

Kate tried everything to lose weight, that summer, even pills.

"You're not fat, Kate!" Alice said. "I don't know why you go on about it all the time. Who cares?"

"That's easy for you to say. I want to lose at least a stone before September."

"What's in September? Only school." Alice shook her head. "You're mad."

"It's worth a try. I even got some diet pills. But I don't like the way they make me feel. I took one yesterday. It was weird."

"Let's have a look?"

Alice was sitting on the back step. It was a perfect blue day and the sun struck chips of mica in the garden wall, made the granite sparkle. Kate had brought a bottle of red lemonade up from the shop when she'd finished working and they were drinking from tall tumblers full of ice. Now she pulled a packet out of her bag and handed it over to Alice. Then she lay back on the grass, cupping her head in her hands. She looked exhausted.

She was spending a lot of time at the shop. Dermot had stunned everyone the year before by announcing that he was going to be a pilot. He had moved into a flat on the north side with some other trainees to be closer to the airport. Mr Kenny's face had turned bright red, and stayed that way. A few weeks later Susan had got married, at nineteen. Alice knew this was young, but she was surprised by Kate's mother's reaction. She had cried a lot and then gone very quiet, smoking heavily and spending a lot of time staring into space and sighing.

"Our parents," Kate announced, "are having their mid-life crisis. Just our luck, that they should have a joint one."

"Well, at least we'll only have to go through it once," said Karen, philosophically. With all the drama, she and Kate had become allies.

Then it turned out that Susan was having twins. Alice thought that was far more shocking than an early marriage, but for some strange reason, it cheered everyone up again. It was as if all the moods and arguments and tears and slammed doors of the previous winter and spring had never happened. Except that Kate had to work at the shop more than ever. She didn't seem to mind, but Alice did. Her mother wouldn't hear of her getting a job, the one time that Alice had suggested it.

Kate was still talking about diets. "Maybe I'll try the grapefruit diet instead," she said. "Have you heard of it? You eat nothing but grapefruit for days."

Alice made a face. "Yuk." She turned the flat foil packet in her hands. Hard bubbles of plastic cradled baby pills. "They're tiny!"

"They make me dizzy. I'm not going to take them any more. Eddie asked me to give them to him."

"What for? Surely Eddie's not going on a diet?" Alice still hadn't forgiven the "sideways" remark.

"He thinks they're great. But my mother says they're really bad for you if you take them without a prescription. I think I'll just throw them away."

"I'll put them in the bin for you if you like," Alice suggested. "I'm going in anyway, to get some more ice. Do you want some?"

"OK."

Alice went inside. She slipped the packet quickly under the pedal bin behind the door and then went to the fridge. "Do you want more lemonade as well, Kate?" she called. "I'll bring the bottle."

After Kate had left, Alice took one of the pills. She sat on her bed and waited to see what would happen. She swung her legs while she waited, until restlessness drove her to her feet and she began to pace around the room.

"Hurry up," she muttered. "Hurry up. Something has to happen."

She was hot. Too hot. She fanned herself with a magazine, then went downstairs to get a drink. Her mouth was as dry as sandpaper. She drained two mugs of water in one long gulp, or so it seemed. Some of the water spilled over onto her neck and shoulders and she began to laugh. Coolness rippled over and through her. It was delicious.

She went and got the radio from beside her bed. She turned it on, loud and then louder, up to the top of the dial. Her pulse pounded with the music and she began to sing and sway through every room in the house, dancing as she hadn't danced since Nell left. But the house wasn't big enough. Its smallness pressed against her nerves. She'd have to go out, find somewhere to go, something to do.

She'd found what she needed. A way to make herself leave the house, to overcome the terror she felt. It was like filling herself with adrenaline, shocking her system just enough to get out the door and keep her moving on down the street.

When the pills she'd taken from Kate were finished, she went to a local chemist's shop. The chemist was a man past retirement age who couldn't bear to stop working. She'd heard that if you went in during the assistant's lunch break, you could talk the old man into giving you anything.

The first time she tried it she was nervous. She put on extra layers of clothes to pad herself out and on top of that a heavy man's overcoat that she'd bought at a second-hand clothes stall in the market in town. She prepared a whole speech about her weight problem, drawn largely from conversations with Kate, but she needn't have bothered.

When she walked in the shop was deserted. The air was stale. The chemist had jowls and big, sad eyes with thick white eybrows jutting over them. Alice was already ashamed of herself before she asked for the pills by name. She drew in her breath, ready to launch into her explanation.

"How many packets do you want?" he asked.

"What? Oh, um, two. Please." She wasn't sure she had enough money, and if she asked for more, would he get suspicious? She smiled her best smile at him and asked for a tube of toothpaste as well, to avoid suspicion.

He put it all into a plain brown paper bag and counted out her change with bony fingers. His hands were covered in large freckles and they shook. They beamed at each other, relieved and mutually delighted, when he'd finished.

"Thank you," Alice said, with absolute sincerity.

Then she hurried back out into the busy street. God, she thought, that was horrible. That poor, poor man. I'll never do this again. Never.

But of course she did. More and more often. One day, as she came out of the chemist's, she recognised someone she'd once seen with Eddie. His hair was long and pale and tied into a pony-tail. He was dressed exactly the same way that she was: jeans, desert boots, army coat. His jumper was grey and hers was black. They could have been in uniform. He winked at her. His light eyes were on a level with hers.

"Come for the rush-hour, have you?" he asked, nodding at the bag in her hand.

She laughed when she got the joke. "Rush-hour. That's not bad. Mind you, it's the first time I've met anyone else coming in here," she said.

"That's because we have a rota. Had. Until you spoilt it."

"Really?" For a minute she believed him. "Who's 'we'?"

"Come on and I'll show you."

He brought her to the field. Someone had bought it and demolished the old house. Now they were building a new estate. A group of teenagers she half-knew sat on stacks of sewer pipes, drinking Woodpecker's cider out of brown bottles. They nodded to her, unsurprised by her arrival.

"Hi, Kevin," a girl with long blonde hair and a fringed waistcoat said. "Did you bring any skins with you?"

"I brought Alice," he said, sliding his arm along her shoulders. He looked around at her, slyly, as if waiting to see how she'd react. His arm felt comfortable on her neck. Besides, she wanted to stay and see what happened here. She let herself lean into him a little.

"And I brought skins as well." He took his arm away from Alice, but his eyes looked steadily at her face. She knew that his arm would be back before very long. She sat on the grass beside the girl who'd spoken and watched him roll a joint. She'd never seen it done before. It made her nervous and she looked around to make sure no one was watching them. She caught the other girl's eye.

"Hi," Alice said. "I'm Alice."

"Yeah. I'm Christine. Chrissie. Are you with Kevin? I'm his sister."

Alice shrugged, not knowing what to say.

"That depends what you mean, 'with'," she said, trying to sound casual. "Is Eddie here?"

"Eddie? Jesus, no. Eddie's all talk. Too much talk. He's dangerous. Don't tell him anything. He's not a friend of yours, is he?"

"No." It was true. Kate was her friend, but that was different. She didn't think Kate would fit in here.

"Good. Here, have a drink." Chrissie held out the long brown bottle that was passing around the group.

Alice took it and tilted it against her mouth. The sharp, sweet taste of cider slid over her tongue. It was that easy. It was like coming home.

Now she had somewhere to go, people to be with. She began to play a mad form of chemical roulette. She begged, borrowed and stole pills of every kind. She stole money from her mother, or traded Elaine's sleeping pills for more exciting things, like acid. She haunted the building site with Kevin and Chrissie and the others, taking shelter from the wind and rain in the unused sewer pipes as if they were caves.

When the pipes were laid, and all the mud was smothered by tarmacadam and people began to drive up in cars to look at the bare new houses, Alice and her friends moved on. They hung out at local beaches, drinking and smoking in the concrete storm shelters.

By now she was seriously thin, almost two dimensional. The amphetamines she was taking meant that she ate even less than she'd eaten before. She weighed under six stone, and she was as tall as she was ever going to be. Five foot nine.

One day, late in August, she was in town, alone,

striding around in her big black overcoat. She walked quickly, as if she had somewhere to go but in fact her eyes were scanning the crowds, looking for a familiar face, someone to connect with. She walked from the quays across the river and up past Trinity, avoiding the students who streamed in and out through the iron gates. They had nothing to do with her, although she sometimes liked to go in under the stone arch and onto the cobbled square. She liked the look of it, the solemn buildings, the stone, the trees, the sudden quiet.

Today she kept going. But the pressure of the crowds made her heart pound. She fought to lift the weight from her chest so she could breathe. There was too much blood in her veins. They would burst any minute. She had to get off the street. She'd find a toilet somewhere and go and get herself together. She had two amphetamines in her pocket, not enough, but they'd take care of it until she got to a chemist's and bought some more.

The last time she'd walked in to their friendly local chemist's the old man hadn't been there. The assistant had given her such a hard stare that she'd lost her nerve. She'd picked up a packet of throat lozenges, paid for them and hurried out without asking for what she really wanted.

She turned into Brown Thomas. There was a toilet in there that anyone could use, in the far corner of the shop, upstairs behind the women's underwear. You didn't have to pay, but there was a saucer on the counter for tips for the lavatory attendant, a large woman in a blue shiny uniform who smelled of steam and chlorine and had big red hands. She had a way of looking at people, as if she saw right through them, that made Alice nervous. In fact this whole shop made her nervous, but it was better than the street.

She thought there was something unreal about the place, it was like a film set with smells. From the instant when she stepped throught the door into the sudden blast of heat she was overwhelmed by the sickening haze of a hundred different kinds of perfume. Expensive trinkets hung from racks on glass counters. Expensive-looking women wandered around looking at make-up, fingering scarves. Even the women who worked there looked expensive, to Alice. They watched her closely from under false eyelashes as she made her way from the door to the stairs.

She could feel the store detectives gathering, watching her. She knew it stood out a mile that she had no business being in there. She took her hands out of her pockets and let them hang in front of her, so that they could see that they were empty and would leave her alone. As if she'd nick anything from there.

She walked up the deeply carpeted stairs, knowing she was being watched in the mirrored wall beside her. She was sweating. Her skin felt prickly under the heavy material of her sweater, the woollen weight of her coat. It was as bad in here as it had been outside. But she had to keep moving. If she stopped now, wavered, she knew she'd be lost.

At the top of the stairs she began to hurry, desperate to reach the small cubicle, lock the door, reach into her pocket for the two small tablets waiting for her. She put her left hand deep into her coat. To hell with the watchers. Her fingers closed around the hard plastic wrapping. Still there. Good.

Then she saw someone walking towards her. She looked familiar. Alice knew she knew her from somewhere.

She's one of us.

As the other girl looked at Alice, she began to smile, a little uncertainly, as if she wasn't quite sure that she knew her. Alice smiled slowly too.

Where do I know her from?

She felt relieved to find someone she knew in this unlikely place.

She walked right up to the other girl and said, "Hi. What are you doing here?"

She froze, horrified, as the girl mouthed back at her.

The person she had said hello to was herself. Her own reflection in a free-standing shop mirror. She had seen herself walking towards herself and said hello. She had thought she was someone else. She looked around quickly, wondering if anyone had seen.

∞

"Ah, God," Ruth broke in.

It wasn't like her to interrupt. Alice looked at her. Something deep inside her cracked. Opened. Just a fraction.

"Can you imagine," she asked carefully, not trusting her voice, "what that's like? To meet yourself and not know who you are?"

"How does it make you feel now?"

"Sorry." She cleared her throat. "I feel sorry for her."

"For who?"

Alice gestured vaguely. "You know."

"Who?"

"Her. That poor, scrawny little bitch in the big coat."

"You mean yourself."

"I suppose so."

But now she felt angry instead. Angry with Ruth. Angry with her own younger self for being so pathetic.

Alice looked back at her stricken reflection.

"Stupid," she said, out loud and with venom.

She put her head down and hurried past the mirror towards the toilet. There was no queue and she ran into a cubicle, slammed the door and bolted it. She dropped the lid and sat on it, sweating under her heavy coat. Her pulse raced. Her mother's frequent warnings about public lavatories floated through her brain. She took brief, vicious pleasure in ignoring them.

Her hands shook as she prised the small pearled tablets loose from their foil covering and pushed them into her mouth. When she had swallowed them she began to breathe more easily. After a while she stood up and flushed the toilet, even though she hadn't used it. She washed her hands at the pink enamel sink and dried them on the roller towel. Then she left the room and strode straight out of the store, not slowing for the watchers. She was afraid they'd stop her before she reached the door. Afraid they might find something in her pockets even though she knew that she hadn't taken anything.

It was like when she was little and her father would come into the room and say "Come on, own up now and you won't be in trouble." She used to rack her brains, wondering what she'd done. Knowing there had to be something, if only she could remember what it was. Something terrible, his face reddening and his hand resting on his belt, waiting . . .

But she made it safely through the doors of the shop and smiled to herself. She could feel a rhythm build in her walk. Power flooded through her. Her steps got longer and stronger as she strode up the street. There was a definite knack to getting around this city. You had to flow along, not hesitating. Swoop around people who moved too slowly, move on and off the pavement in an unbroken rhythm.

It was like a dance. The numbers and slowness of people on the pavement began to irritate her so she stepped down into the street and moved along with the traffic. A horn blew behind her and she turned and waved, grinning at the driver of a bright silver car who shook his fist at her. She enjoyed his useless anger, laughed to herself at the obvious irritation of some of the pedestrians hemmed in by the crowds. Why didn't they do what she did? She felt a surge of pride, of identification. This was her city. She knew how to move around it, freely and with ease. She knew its secrets. It was hers.

Then she was at the chemist's. She walked quickly through the glass door and straight up to the cash register, without hesitating. She said what she wanted in a clear voice.

"Two packets," she added firmly.

The woman behind the counter had narrow eyes, the lids darkened. She peered at Alice. "Do you have a prescription?" she asked.

Alice's face began to burn. "Prescription?"

"Yes. Do you have a prescription?"

"No. I . . . they're for my mother."

"Well, does she have a prescription?"

"Yes, yes she does."

"May I see it?"

"No. I left it at home. I didn't know I needed one. I've never . . . I mean, I got them for her once before and you didn't ask me for one then."

"Not in here, you didn't."

Alice could feel her blood begin to fizz and boil. She stepped backwards, began to retreat.

"No, it wasn't here," she said, "but I did get them. I did."

"You have to have a prescription," the woman called after her as she reached the door of the shop. Alice looked back through the window and saw the woman talking to a man in a white coat who had come out of the woodwork. They both stared at Alice and she turned and hurried away.

The feeling of power left her. She hurried along as if she was being chased, bumping into people as she went. All her pavement skill had deserted her. What would she do now? She could have tried another chemist's, but she didn't have the nerve.

Two days later there was a sudden storm. Large, foreign boats anchored in the bay, taking shelter. Alice and Kevin walked to the end of the pier and sat at the end under the lighthouse, watching the waves rush towards them, foaming and furious. Alice's heart was pounding, whether from fear or excitement she couldn't tell.

"Let's go back," she shouted, even though Kevin was right beside her.

They leaned into the wind and held onto each other, laughing, as they fought their way back. The sky hung low and black over them.

Behind the pier there was an old bathing place where no one swam anymore. It was hard to believe that anyone ever had. The stone jetties were cracked and low tide uncovered a mass of rock and seaweed, inhospitable. Now it was like a scene from a film, with water racing over stone and sending spray up towards the road.

Kevin took Alice's hand and pulled her through a gap in the wall and they ran to the shelter. He took out a small lacquered box and crouched with his back to the wind.

"What are you doing?" Alice shouted.

"Cutting some lines of speed," he called back. She couldn't see what he was doing so she looked out over the heaving sea instead. She shivered.

"Ready! Come here."

She stood beside him. "You first," she said.

He leaned over the lid of the box. She watched him close his left nostril with a finger and then inhale deeply through a straw. One of two short columns of white powder shifted like sand and disappeared into his nose. He sniffed twice, loudly.

"Now you." He held out the straw.

She took it from him, bent over, and did exactly what she'd seen him do. To her relief, it worked. As if she'd been doing it all her life.

They sat in the shelter and watched the storm and waited. Sometimes they touched and sometimes they didn't, because that's the way it was with them.

Alice began to fidget, restless. She jumped to her feet.

"Come on!" she called, to Kevin, to the sea, to herself, and she was off. She raced the waves from one shelter to the next, with Kevin right behind her. She emptied her lungs, screaming challenges to the water. It fell back, only to come rushing after them again, roaring. Angry.

It went on like that for a long time. Alice yelled at the sea and then ran across its path. The sea clamoured right back at her and chased her feet.

"You're mad," Kevin said eventually. "It's like you're playing chicken with the sea. What are you doing?"

She was soaked through and panting. Her eyes stung and her voice was gone. "I don't know," she whispered. She squeezed her hair and began to climb the steps to the road. "I want to go home," she said, in a voice she didn't recognise. Already she was coming down. She knew because when she touched herself, on the face and on the arms, she could feel the touch through her skin and not just through her fingertips. It was the worst feeling in the world.

When school started again she didn't go to choir any more. She had a heavy cough which she used as an excuse. Her voice was cracked and hoarse from smoking, her fingers stained brown to the knuckles the way her father's had been.

"I don't want to play the piano any more," she told Miss Sweetman in the first week of term when the teacher came looking for her to arrange classes.

"Why not?"

"I can't do it. It's not worth the effort." She couldn't meet Miss Sweetman's eye.

"Do you realise what you're doing, Alice?"

"Yes."

"I don't think you do. You're giving up so easily."

"It's none of your business!" Alice blazed at her.

Miss Sweetman stepped back, her face frozen. "I suppose you're right," she said stiffly.

Alice watched her walk away down the long corridor, heels clicking on the tiles, her hair falling out of its soft bun. She wanted to run after her and take it all back, but she didn't. Instead she went down to the beach and got stoned.

Eventually she stopped going to theory classes too, not able to stand the memory of Miss Sweetman moving quickly away from her, the new chill in her voice when she asked Alice a question.

She hates me, Alice thought, staring at her reflection in the bathroom mirror. She thinks I'm useless. She scowled deliberately, exaggerating the hollows under her eyes, pinching her mouth.

Look at you, you ugly, stupid bitch, she said to herself. She's right. You're useless. A useless heap of shit.

CHAPTER ELEVEN

"This is boring," Alice said. "I'm really sick of it."

Ruth raised her eyebrows. "I'm not bored at all."

"Well, I am. It's such a dreary rendering of your average teenage alienation and self-pity. I don't want to go on. Every day was the same as the day before it and the day after it. All I cared about was speed. And hatred."

"Who did you hate?"

"My mother. And myself."

"Why?"

Alice thought for a minute before answering.

"Do you know what it was like? Did you ever see those documentaries about space flight?"

Ruth nodded.

"That whole thing was so weird. I must have been about nine when men first landed on the moon. Everyone thought it was so great, so exciting. Except me. I thought it was an outrage. I loved the moon. I watched it for hours on clear nights through my window. Its light was so . . . clean. And the different shapes, its phases. Sometimes it seemed suspended, heavy and huge, and you could make out shadows on its surface and wonder about the other side, the side

131

you couldn't see. And other times it was a pure sliver of light hung in the sky. And now they'd been up there, clumping all over it as if it was something ordinary. How dare they?" She caught her breath. "Try to make it less than it was, walking all over it like that?

"Anyway. I saw a documentary about it all and they showed footage of different landings. Those giant heaps of metal hurtling into the sea . . . or wherever it was, I'm not sure. Water, anyway. And I wondered how the astronauts could bear coming back. It must have been magnificent out there. All that infinite space and silence and beauty. To have drifted through space where none of the rules apply, not even gravity. To float free like that, weightless. As if you had no body at all. And then to have gravity take hold of you again and pull you into itself. As if to say, you can't escape, there's no way out after all. I'll get you in the end. After they'd been fished out, how could they stand feeling their own weight again? Every step an effort, their feet like lead weights, their bodies pinning them down to earth. Do you see what I mean?"

"I'm not sure . . ."

Alice gestured impatiently. "That's what it was like, coming down. I hated it more than anything, that moment of re-entering myself, where it got darker and heavier and more lonely every time. So I promised myself I'd stop. Every time was going to be the last time. I'd do just one more line and then I'd stop. But it was a trap. Because the only way to stop feeling what I felt when I came down was to do it again."

She laughed. "Always, just one more line."

"How did you? Stop, I mean?"

∞

One day Elaine came in from work with a newspaper rolled up in her hand. She waved it at Alice and threw it down on the table in front of her, on top of her history notes.

"Have you seen this?" she demanded.

"What is it?"

"Read it yourself and see."

Alice could feel her mother's eyes hard on her face as she read an article about the growing local drugs problem among teenagers, around the park and the beaches. Local gardaí were intensifying their efforts to track down the dealers responsible for bringing drugs into the area, it said.

As if no one who lived there could be responsible. She made herself shrug and look innocent.

"So?"

"So? You go to beach all the time, don't you?"

"Everyone does. It doesn't mean anything."

"Do you know any of these people?"

"Which people?"

"Drug-dealers. People who take drugs. Any of them. Do you?"

"No."

"Are you sure?"

"Very sure."

So that when Chrissie was in the paper the next week

because she'd taken an overdose and was lying in a coma in the hospital, Alice had to pretend ignorance.

"Do you know this girl?"

"No."

Her mother squinted down at the print. "Pass over your father's glasses," she said. "This print gets smaller and harder to read all the time."

"You should get your eyes tested, it can't be good for you to wear someone else's glasses." Alice shivered, as if someone had just walked across her grave.

"I can see perfectly." Her mother frowned over the print. "That name is familiar. Doesn't she go to your school?"

"Yes, but she's not in my class. Is she going to be all right?"

"They don't say."

Alice slipped out later and ran around to their house. Kevin answered the door.

"You'd better not come in," he said awkwardly. "There's war."

"How is she?"

"She's come round. They think she'll be OK. If she survives the homecoming, that is." He laughed, bitter. "The parents are raging. You'd swear she'd done something to them, not to herself. I'll have to stay cool for a while too." He leaned against the door-jamb and smiled with half of his mouth. Framed by the doorway, he didn't look like Kevin. She'd never thought of him in a house before.

"What's wrong?" he asked.

She stood with her weight on one foot, hands deep in her pockets. "You seem different."

"How, different?"

She shrugged. How could she say, I never thought of you with parents. In a family. With limits. Like me.

Behind him she could hear a television turned on loud, proclaiming the amazing merits of a brand of washing powder. "It's biological," the television boasted, as if this settled everything.

She backed away. "I'd better go."

"Yeah, well. Thanks for coming."

"Give Chrissie my love when you see her."

"Will do. See ya."

Soon after Chrissie came out of hospital, her parents decided to move to London.

"Da has a new job," Kevin told Alice. "They say it'll be a new start for all of us."

"Do you mind?" she asked when her pulse had settled and she could see him clearly.

"I mind leaving you. But London's a blast, and it's not that far away. Will you come over and see us?"

"Maybe." She knew she wouldn't. She was detaching herself from him, cell by cell. She knew that she would never go over there, because the only way to get right out of Ireland is by boat or by plane, and she was terrified of both. That meant she was stuck here forever. But how could she say that?

After they'd gone, she settled into a fog of despair. It was a bleak, cold winter. It stretched on and on.

Everything was whitish grey and pinched-looking, as if there'd never been a summer and never would be again. She welcomed the lengthening dark. It suited her mood. When she came home, still buzzing from speed, she sat on her bed, holding her elbows and rocking backwards and forwards or tracing patterns on the wall with her bitten fingers.

At Christmas her mother noticed her pallor and commented on it. At the end of January the school sent a note home. Alice's performance had dropped below its usual disappointing level and she was no longer participating in sports, the note said, polite but determined. Were there problems at home, of which they should be aware?

Elaine bristled at that, but she looked at Alice again and brought her to Dr Roche.

Dr Roche was now a white-haired, stooped old man, but kindly. He peered at Alice's tongue and the whites of her eyes and shook his head.

"I'm taking a blood sample," he told Alice's mother, sinking a needle into Alice's exposed arm.

When he'd taken it out and folded her elbow to stop her bleeding she crossed both arms across her concave chest to protect it from the cold or her mother's look, she wasn't sure which. Her stomach knotted as they discussed her, the way they had when she was a child. As if she wasn't even there.

She stared at the clutter of pens and prescription pads and free medical samples of this and that on his desk. She was too exhausted to care about what they were, what they might do. Whether they'd be worth stealing, if she got the chance.

"I'd say she has a bad case of anaemia. It's normal enough in teenage girls, but I'm concerned about the severity of the symptoms. I'll know more when I get the lab results. But she's very pale and she has no energy. She looks run down. I know you have to work, Elaine. I think a short stay in hospital might be a good idea."

Alice shivered. "Can I get dressed now?"

"Of course, my dear."

He turned back to her mother. "I'll organise a bed and let you know when to take her in. I'd say tomorrow at the latest."

So Alice went into hospital. Elaine seemed content with anaemia as a diagnosis. It was reassuringly physical. Alice lay in a corner bed with her back turned to the rest of the ward and cried all day long. When the nurses asked her what was wrong she said that she was so tired she couldn't help it. They brought her egg flips and a tonic that tasted of rubber.

The woman in the bed beside her took her teeth out noisily every time she ate, and placed them carefully on her bedside locker. She grinned over at Alice, prepared to be friendly, but Alice couldn't bear to look at her. She asked the nurses to close the curtains around her bed.

The smells of the hospital made her insides stick together, a mixture of overcooked vegetables and disinfectant, with something sweeter underlying it. She said she couldn't eat, but they insisted. One of the student nurses felt sorry for her and brought her bowls of runny white ice cream, unwanted by the older patients, as a bribe.

For the first few days she went into the ward toilet when she couldn't bear it anymore. She sat sideways on the black plastic seat with her knees pressed against the wall and leaned her burning forehead on the cool green wall, rolling her head from side to side. The rough plaster made marks on her skin which were easily covered by her fringe. Her skin crawled as if it was something alive and separate from her. No amount of scratching under the long sleeves of her flannel nightie could relieve it. She felt as if each vein in her body was collapsing for lack of the chemical rush that had held them open. Her throat locked against some loud, betraying sound that her stomach wanted to make.

When her forehead began to bleed she stopped, afraid that someone would notice. And yet, she pushed her hair off her face when the friendly student nurse brought her in some magazines to read. As if she wanted her to see.

But the nurse noticed nothing. "I'm in a dreadful hurry, Alice," she said. "We're really short-staffed today. Have a look at these. Maybe I'll have time for a chat later."

Alice brushed her hair back down over her forehead with her fingers. Stupid, she thought, hating the feeling she had inside as if she was a huge well filling up with emptiness.

Then she was glad the nurse hadn't noticed. Just as well, she reasoned. Soon you'll be out of here.

She instructed herself to brighten up. She began to help with the trays, fixed pillows for women who lay back like stranded whales after unnamed operations, pale and unable to move. She learned how to arrange her own plate so that it looked as if she'd eaten more than she had, and to help clear away so that no one could be sure how much she'd eaten anyway.

"That's better," the nurses beamed at her. "You're looking so much better. You'll be going home soon."

"I was there for ten days. No one came to visit me except my mother."

"What about Kate?"

"All my old friends were avoiding me then. I thought their parents had warned them off. Kate told me later that it was me, that I scared her because I didn't seem to care about anything. It was true, too."

"And Nell?"

"She had just had Shane, her first baby. He was only a couple of months old. She couldn't get away. I went to stay with her for the school holidays that Easter and again in the summer. I loved it down there. They have this square white house with big windows and a field that goes all the way down to the lake. It was quiet. No one expected anything of me. I slept and read and ate. Nell fed me really well. I suppose," she sounded surprised, "it was like a convalescence. I hadn't thought of that before. But it was like being given a second chance."

She sighed and was silent for a while, remembering.

Then she straightened in her chair. "I stayed away from everything and everyone connected with speed after that. I knew if I went back to it I'd be lost. It's like, I always had some instinct that saved me at the last minute. I'd push things to their limit, the extreme edge of what was safe, and then pull back."

"Why do you make that sound like a crime?"

"Do I? I suppose it's because it's like having been a lemming who cheated. I rushed to the edge and then stopped and watched my friends pass me and fall, one by one, over the cliff. All through that spring and summer my mother kept pushing newspaper articles and bits of gossip under my nose. Did I know this person who'd been arrested, or that one who'd gone into a clinic. In the end I ignored her."

"What did you do instead?"

"Well, there were books. I'd discovered these writers who just knew all about what I felt. I could tell. They saved me, really. Because if they could write about it, that meant I wasn't the only one. Or something. It meant there was hope. That there might be a life for me if only I could find it. Reading was like another kind of drug. It was just like when I was little. I could be sitting there in an armchair, all curled up and innocent looking, not taking up very much space, and in my head I was off in another world, with people who were every bit as bitter and twisted as I was, as full of hate and despair. I could go there whenever I wanted to." She laughed. "And it fooled my mother, completely. As far as she was concerned, I was less threatening that way. Quiet. Behaving myself. She thought she knew where I was. She thought she knew who I was with."

"Well, didn't she?"

"No! I just told you . . ."

"Maybe you thought it was an escape, Alice. But in fact, in reality, you were doing what was expected of you. Behaving yourself. Not rebelling."

Alice could feel her face twist in a murderous rage.

"You don't understand anything! Who cares about reality?"

"I thought you did. Isn't that why you're here?"

Alice chewed her fingers, furious.

"What about sex?" asked Ruth, after a pause.

"What about it?"

Ruth waited.

"At first," Alice said when she couldn't stand the waiting any more, "I was really cautious with boys. You know. Even with Kevin. I held him off. Later I changed." She laughed. "It didn't seem to matter any more. Then I wished I *had* slept with him, after all. A lot of things might have been different if I had." She shrugged. "But that's just wishful thinking. The truth is, I couldn't see what all the fuss was about. Put me in the right circumstances and I'd sleep with anyone. Anyone at all." She looked quickly at Ruth. "Are you shocked?"

"Why should I be shocked?"

Alice shrugged.

"What were the right circumstances, Alice?"

Alice shifted uneasily in the chair. She pulled her feet up under her. She considered. "If it was possible, I suppose. You know. The right degree of insistence and that was it. I couldn't be bothered . . ."

"What?"

"You know. It wasn't worth the effort . . . there was no point, it just didn't seem worth it."

"What didn't seem worth it?"

"Saying no. I mean, it didn't matter anyway. Did it. It was as easy to go through with it as not. I can't explain it any better than that. There seemed to be no point. It made no difference in the end."

Her hands pulled at each other in her lap, twisting. Otherwise she was completely still.

After a while, Ruth said, "You were in trouble all along, weren't you?"

"What do you mean?"

"Well, look at what you've told me. You were in trouble with drinking. Drugs. Not eating. And now it sounds as if you were in trouble with sex as well."

"Why? Because you don't approve?"

Ruth laughed. "No. Not because I approve or disapprove. Because you don't seem to be very happy about it yourself."

Alice shrugged, sullen.

"I told you. I don't care. I didn't care then. Why should I care now? It didn't matter."

"What if you'd got pregnant?

"After the first time, I went on the pill."

"How old were you then?"

"Sixteen."

∞

When Alice and Kate left school the Kennys took them both down the country for a week, to celebrate. When she came back, Alice found Elaine tight-lipped and angry and knew she was in trouble. She had no idea why. For a minute she thought that her results had come in early, that she'd failed her exam, but she dismissed the thought at once. It was too early.

Maybe the nuns had been talking to Elaine, yet again, about the waste of Alice's mind. It was still their favourite topic. They didn't seem to notice that she had worked hard all year because it gave her somewhere to hide. They seemed to take it personally that she was "throwing her life away." If only they knew the extent of it. She almost wished they did. That someone did.

And then, what? She sneered at herself.

She brought her bags up to her room and dropped them on her bed, then went down to the kitchen to make tea. Her father's old glasses were on the table beside the teapot, the lenses yellowing and dusty.

"Do you want some tea?" she asked her mother. She pushed the glasses to the other side of the table to make room for the teapot.

No answer. Alice shrugged and poured out a cup for herself. She sat at the kitchen table, reading, and waited. After pacing the kitchen for a while, sighing, Elaine sat down, heavily, across from Alice, but didn't look at her. She picked up the glasses, then put them down again. Agitated. She folded and unfolded the stems. Finally she put them on.

"I don't know what to make of you," she said. As if it was Alice who was behaving strangely.

"While you were away," she went on, "I was looking for some notepaper in your room . . ."

Alice stiffened, alert.

"Can you guess what I'm going to say?"

"I could, but I won't," said Alice thickly. A violent pulse beat in her throat. She felt cornered. What horrible evidence had she left behind?

"It was in your desk."

"What was?"

Elaine sighed. Her face was scarlet. Her hand held her cardigan bunched together at her neck. "The pill. I found it. Three months supply. How could you? How could you? You don't even have a steady boyfriend!"

Alice stared at her mother. She couldn't understand why she felt relieved. Excuses raced through her mind, but she said nothing.

"What do you have to say for yourself?"

"Nothing."

"What do you mean, 'nothing'? How could you be so . . . brazen? Have you an explanation?"

Alice considered. Then she shook her head. "I wish you hadn't gone through my things," she said. A week with the Kennys had made her brave.

"What? How dare you! I'm your mother . . . I have a right . . ."

"No. Do you know what? I don't think you do."

They stared at each other. The colour on Elaine's face deepened and she breathed fast. She looked stricken. Alice saw this. With every second that passed she felt her own pulse calming, her blood cooling, a great weight lifting.

She reached into her pocket for a packet of cigarettes, pulled them out and lit one, blowing the smoke carelessly into the air between them.

"I'm sorry," she said eventually. "Not about the pill, but that you're upset about it."

"What? Alice, I don't understand you, I've never understood you. What do you mean, you're not sorry?"

"No. Would you prefer if I'd come home pregnant?" She stubbed her cigarette carefully on the edge of the ashtray, watching the glowing ash disintegrate. Then she pulled on it again to keep it going.

"Alice!" Elaine crossed her arms in front of her and rubbed her upper arms roughly. All the colour left her face. She looked as if she might get sick right there at the table.

"Would you?"

Elaine stood up. She was shaking. "I don't know what I've done to deserve this," she said. "I've never known what I did, to deserve you. You are . . . you've always been . . . I don't even know what you are. Dirty."

She began to cry and shout at the same time. "I don't want you living here any more. I don't want to share this house with you. I don't want . . . you. Do you hear me? I don't want you eating off my plates, using my . . ." she gasped, pounded the table with both fists, making Alice's mug jump, ". . . towels. The same towels as me. Diseased. I don't want to be contaminated by you. I want you out of here. Pack your bag and go, go back to your precious Kennys, I don't care what happens to you! You're a monster!

You're going straight to hell! Do you hear me? You'll be sorry. You just wait and see. You'll be sorry. You'll pay for this!"

She was almost incoherent. Alice got up and walked past her. Some old instinct made her flash past the point of contact and breathe more easily on the other side. She went upstairs and picked up the bag she'd carried in and set on her bed a short while before. Everything had changed. She wondered why it had been so easy, why she felt so little. She watched herself pick up the bag and cross the room. She told herself to turn at the door and look back, but the room meant nothing to her. As if she'd never lived in it.

She didn't bother to close the door behind her. She walked slowly down the stairs.

This is the last time I'll ever do this, she thought.

She saw her mother, slumped at the kitchen table. She hesitated. She didn't want to walk past her to the back door.

"Goodbye," she called from the hall.

"Alice. Please."

"What?"

"Come here."

Warily, Alice walked towards her mother. Elaine lifted her head as she got close to her and to Alice's absolute horror she saw that her mother was crying.

"Don't do this."

"You've asked me to go. I'm going."

"Don't . . . please . . ." Elaine's face was distorted. Alice looked at her. She watched herself, looking at her mother, crying at the kitchen table.

If you stay now, she told herself, you will never, ever, get away from her. At this minute you are stronger than she is. This is the one and only chance you'll ever get.

"I'm sorry," she said carefully. "Really, I am. But I think this is best. I'll be all right. I'll let you know where I am. I'm old enough to go, I have friends . . . don't worry. What did you say?"

"I said," Elaine glared at her through her swollen, reddened eyes, "I said, what about *me*? What about me?"

"Oh."

Get out, get out.

Alice shrugged, helplessly. "I'm sorry. I'll ring you."

She turned, walked quickly to the front door and pulled it open. It was heavy and stiff. There was the street, waiting for her.

Do it now, she urged herself. Don't stop.

She stepped through the front door and pulled it shut behind her.

❧

"So she didn't have to be contaminated by me after all," she told Ruth.

"Is that what she said, that she didn't want to be contaminated?"

"Something like that. I don't remember exactly. More likely, she didn't want to catch something off me. Yeah, I think that was it."

Alice's face and voice were tight. Her eyes burned, the way they often did when she was with Ruth. She rubbed them, angrily, making the room blur. "I didn't care what she thought of me," she said. "I hated her."

"I'm sure you did."

"No, I mean I really hated her. Enough to kill her. I thought the only way things could ever be settled between us was for one of us to die. I used to lie awake at night plotting how I'd do it."

"How would you have done it?"

"Easy. A pillow to the face while she was asleep. It would have been so easy."

"But you didn't do it."

"No. I didn't do it."

Alice's face was working, she couldn't control it. She felt it contort and twist and was powerless to stop it. She couldn't look at Ruth, but felt her steady look take in what was happening.

"What is it, Alice?"

Alice shook her head. She couldn't speak.

"Tell me. What's going on?"

Alice took a deep, shuddering breath. Then another. She wrapped her arms tightly round herself as she said, "It's what I wanted to do with Holly."

"With Holly?"

Alice nodded.

"You wanted to cover Holly's face with a pillow while she was asleep?" Ruth's voice was the same as it always was. Alice risked a quick look and saw nothing but concern in Ruth's face. No shock, horror, or blame. She looked, simply, worried.

"When she was a baby," Alice said, tentatively.

148

PART TWO

CHAPTER TWELVE

When Alice conceived Holly, she knew at once. She felt a deep shock of fusion, electric. She called out and the call spun away from her, then echoed back again, bringing Holly with it.

Of course, when the vibrations stopped and she came back to herself and her surroundings and breathed normally again, she told herself this was all nonsense. But she knew, all the same.

She knew because the hollow cavity that had opened up inside her when her mother died was filling up. She had never imagined that Elaine's death would create such hunger in her, an emptiness that no amount of drinking could fill. She grew obsessed with the lack she felt, the need to draw something into herself to fill the vacuum.

The last time she saw her mother, Elaine was lying motionless beneath a hospital sheet, her skin translucent. Her arms lay on top of the sheet, stretched out straight beside her body as if she had already been laid out. She looked small and defenceless. Much too small to carry the weight of Alice's hatred.

Seeing her like that made Alice wonder how she had ever believed that Elaine was strong and powerful. That had been someone else, not this woman who was waiting to die.

When she first got sick and Alice went to visit her, Elaine had looked at her with empty eyes and said "Why have you come?"

She turned to the nurse fussing around her bed. "Why has she come?" she asked petulantly. "I don't want her here."

"Nonsense, Elaine," the nurse replied briskly, straightening the sheet. "That's nonsense, and you know it."

She followed Alice to the end of the ward and touched her arm sympathetically. "She doesn't mean it, you know," she said kindly. "She doesn't know what she's saying. It's the tumour and the drugs. Don't let it upset you."

Alice nodded, but said nothing. Her throat was cramped. She knew her mother was going to die. If she wasn't, the nurse wouldn't be calling her by her first name. She wouldn't dare. There was distance in the way her eyes swept across the ceiling and back again in a slow, steady curve. But she had meant what she said, all the same.

All during the slow weeks of her mother's dying, Alice stayed away. Nell and Sheila drove up to visit her at the weekends, but Alice couldn't bring herself to go. "She doesn't want me there, Nell," she explained once when Nell, exasperated, had rung to tell her to pull herself together and go.

"You know that's not true, Alice!"

"It is true. She said it."

"Oh, grow up!" It was unlike Nell to raise her voice, but she was shouting now. "She'll be dead soon, and then you'll be sorry and it will be too late. Do you understand that, Alice? Too late!"

It's already too late, Alice thought, feeling sorry for herself. It's always been too late. She hung up on Nell and poured herself a large glass of gin.

One Saturday a nurse called from the hospital to say that her mother had taken a turn for the worse. If Alice wanted to see her, she should go now, the nurse advised. She warned Alice that her mother was extremely withdrawn.

"She may not respond to you. She may seem like a stranger," she said.

She always was, Alice thought, still bitter. Her heart beat hard and fast as she climbed the stairs to the ward where Elaine lay. It all felt unreal, as if she was watching something on film. Something scripted.

But when she saw Elaine, something in her settled. She sat in the plastic chair beside the bed for a long time without moving. Without speaking. She was hungover and her head throbbed. When she looked at her mother she felt a pressure in her throat. She watched her breath rise and fall in short, shallow bursts, her moving eyes, her still hands small and pale against the whiteness of the sheet.

For the first time that she could remember, Alice

felt an urge to touch her mother without violence. They had the same hands, the same irregular nails, the same crooked joints at the end of the fingers, the same large knuckles. Neither of them could wear rings. The skin on Alice's fingers was split and torn. Elaine's were smooth and young-looking. Her skin was translucent. Thin blue veins strained against it.

Alice wanted to take Elaine's hand into hers and hold it. She wanted to compare their hands, length for length. She wanted to memorise the comparison and carry it away with her.

She didn't do it. Her own hands felt like lead in her lap, held in place as if weighted. It seemed too great an imposition, to reach across and touch Elaine without permission. Alice sat on in the chair and looked at her until her eyes burned and she had to look away. She swallowed air. Her throat was dry. She needed a drink. There was a pub just down the street from the hospital.

"Do you think it would be all right if I slipped out for an hour or so?" she asked the nurse, who nodded.

"You may as well. She's comfortable, there's nothing you can do. She could go on like this for a long time."

When she touched her mother, lightly, on the forehead, Elaine's skin felt cool. Later, Alice wondered why she never paid attention to what she knew. Because when she came back two hours later and saw Nell and Sheila standing outside the door of the ward, Sheila looking hunched and small and old in her blue coat, she knew immediately what had happened.

With hindsight she believed the coolness of Elaine's

skin was her temperature sinking towards death. She'd felt it. It had snagged at her attention. She should have stayed.

All the things it was too late for suddenly burst in on her. Now she could never go back, never meet Elaine's eyes or pick up her hand, tell her not to be afraid. Tell her she was sorry.

A great hunger came and curled at the root of her spine, demanding to be fed. Over the next few months it pulsed and grew until she could think of nothing else. It made no sense to her. In the end she could think of only one way to satisfy her need.

❦

"It was a problem," she told Ruth. "I wanted to be pregnant. But I wasn't involved with anyone, hadn't been for ages. If I'd stopped to think about any of it, about money, the future, I'd never have done it. But then, there was nothing rational about this feeling. It was an obsession. It felt like a life-and-death kind of hunger."

"So what did you do?"

"Well, I had two different jobs then, to keep me going. I did a few nights a week in a restaurant, washing dishes, and I'd started to work for Brian about a year earlier. Photographer's assistant. It was the first job I ever really liked. I thought it might take me somewhere. I'd done just about every kind of job you can think of in the six years since I'd left home. I'd been a receptionist, worked in shops, tried waitressing . . . that was a disaster. I got all the orders confused. Kate's brother Dermot even taught me to drive for a job I wanted in a car-rental company. I got the job but they went out of business a month later."

She drew her knees up towards her on the chair and tucked her feet under her. "I'd got into the habit of going out with anyone who asked. They bought me drinks and dinner and I went to bed with them. It seemed a fair enough exchange. But I hated it, and them, more and more as time went on. At last, I had a brainwave. I became a dishwasher! I could eat in the restaurant, but food wasn't really the issue. Often at the end of the night there were bottles left over with dregs in them and we'd sit around and drink until they were empty. Other than that, I learned to drink alone, in my flat. I got into less trouble that way. I kept the habit even after I stopped working there."

She sighed, tightened her grip around her knees. "But I'd have to get sociable now, wouldn't I? In the end, it was easy enough. Like I said, I was already working for Brian."

"How did that come about?"

"I worked in a framing warehouse and I got really interested in photographs. Especially old black-and-whites. So I took a night class and began to restore prints I bought cheap in junk shops in town. I met Brian at the warehouse and he was really encouraging. He lent me one of his old cameras to get started. Then, when he saw I was serious, he began to give me bits of work here and there. Taught me the darkroom, straightforward stuff at first. I did a bit of everything. He had a shop and he did portraits, Holy Communions, special visa requirements for embassies, you know, the correct amount of earlobe showing for the Americans. That kind of thing. Gradually I took over the shop and the simpler work. It was straightforward, mechanical. He pretty well left me to it after a few months while he took on more arty kind of work and assignments for this glossy magazine his wife worked for. Flattering head shots of famous people. Politicians at home with their families. I avoided all that. I preferred the shop. It was more anonymous."

She cleared her throat. "Anyway. He had a friend who was visiting, from Hungary. He was gorgeous. He had these hypnotic eyes. I could look at him forever. He was a pianist, with the most amazing hands. I used to think his bones were like a bird's. You know, hollow. Weightless. He was perfect for what I wanted. We spent a weekend together in a hotel down the country and then he left. Does this strike you as cold? Calculating?"

Ruth's silence was making Alice nervous. She straightened her legs and sat up straight, waiting for the verdict.

"Why do you care what I think? You got what you wanted."

"Yeah, I did. Didn't I?"

❧

When her period was late, she counted the days until

she could buy a home-testing kit and find out for certain. On the first possible day, she did the test, excited, under the sloping ceiling of her bathroom.

She lived in an attic flat, two rooms shaped like cones, square floor rising to a pointed ceiling in the centre of each. There was a tiny bathroom. The flat was cheap because it was so small. Claustrophobic, Nell said when she saw it, but Alice pointed out sourly that not everyone could rise to a country house on the Corrib. The flat suited her very well and she loved it. She liked the way the walls folded around her, leaving room for little else. It made her feel protected, especially now.

She wondered who else was doing the same test that morning, pouring fluid into test tubes, standing them carefully where they could look for the telltale ring without disturbing the liquid. She put hers on the broad windowsill and looked out the window, over the rooftops. The trees in the square were beginning to lighten, the leaves ready for their fall. She wondered how those other women felt. Some excited and nervous, like her. Others desperate. Some filled with dread.

The test result was negative. She was shocked. She had been so sure. She felt as if she'd been hit, a jolt deep inside her belly. No, she thought. It's wrong. It must be wrong. I must have done it wrong. She wondered if she was going mad. She waited three days and then went to the Family Planning Clinic for an official test.

When she rang for the result the woman who told

her it was negative obviously expected her to be pleased.

"Are you sure?" demanded Alice.

"Well, there's always a margin of error. If your period hasn't started in a week you could do the test again."

Alice hung up the phone, miserable.

Why can't they see?

She was obsessed by now. Wild.

"It's just as well it was negative," Kate said when Alice told her, not able to keep it to herself another second. "What do you want a baby for anyway?"

Kate had a three-year old son, Jake, and her marriage was falling apart. She was weighing up her options. The thought of leaving and looking after Jake alone, the responsibility and loneliness of it, terrified her. She thought Alice was mad to even consider it.

Alice couldn't answer. She didn't, in any case, want a baby. She wanted *this*. Even though she didn't know what *this* was, who it was, stirring inside her, spreading roots into every cell of her body. That's how it felt. Holly had taken root in her, twined herself around every fibre of Alice's being, taken hold and settled in. Made herself at home. Alice knew she was there, all right, but where was the evidence? Her restlessness built to a pitch where she could hardly contain herself. She went down to visit Nell.

"You're mad, Alice," Nell said. "Children need two parents and a stable home . . . "

Nell often talked in clichés. When Alice was

younger, trailing around after Nell, full of admiration, she hadn't noticed this. The things Nell said had always seemed to carry weight, to matter.

"That's why they're clichés," said Nell comfortably, one time when Alice, exasperated, had challenged her. "Because they're true."

Alice stopped talking about her dream pregnancy. But she talked, inwardly, to Holly. Constantly. A running commentary in her mind.

Don't you listen to them. You stay right where you are. I know you're there.

Don't leave me.

When the third test confirmed Holly's presence, Alice felt triumph, a fierce joy.

You see? I knew you were there and no one else could see it. We won!

Her centre of gravity shifted, deep inside her, to include her pregnancy. It gave her substance. Holly had been her ally from the start. Her ally and her only confidante. That feeling was so strong in her that it never occurred to her to wonder whether it was a good idea or not, or worry about how she was going to manage to raise a child all on her own.

She forgot that she didn't like children and never had. It hardly seemed to matter. She didn't think in terms of having a baby who, in turn, would grow into a child. This was different. Holly was, would be, completely different from everything Alice had ever known. She loved her for it already.

CHAPTER THIRTEEN

It was amazing how many people managed to convey, without actually saying so, that they were surprised that Alice was going ahead with her pregnancy. She got sick of hearing people ask what she was going to do.

Even Nell, staunch conservative, asked her, "Have you thought it all out? I don't think you realise what you're letting yourself in for."

"I think you're mad," Kate said, more bluntly. "But you've always been one of the most stubborn people I know, so I don't know why I'm even surprised. Where will you live?"

"I'll stay right here." They were sitting in Alice's attic flat. Kate was drinking tea. Alice held a tall glass full of gin, with lots of ice. The ice was a concession to pregnancy.

"Alice, how will you carry a baby up and down all those stairs? And your shopping? And everything? You're mad." Kate said again. Then she added, "I have all Jake's baby stuff still, in a cupboard somewhere. I'll give it to you, if you like."

"Don't you mean, lend?"

"No, I'll give it to you. I won't be needing it again."

"You'd better stay out of the darkroom," Brian said when she told him at work the next day. "All those chemicals can't be good for you."

She made a face at him. She loved the darkroom, the dull red safelight, the peace of knowing no one would disturb her when the warning sign was up. She liked the silence when she developed the films manually, the images vulnerable until she fixed them, rinsed them and clipped them up to dry. But it was true that her stomach was uneasy in the fumes.

Because they were coming up to Christmas, people were bringing their children into the studio for portraits to hang on their walls, or send to relatives abroad.

"I don't know why they bother," Alice grumbled. "Everyone knows the little darlings only look like this for five seconds out of every year, while they're having the photo taken, and only because of some bribe or other."

"Don't complain, it keeps us going," Brian reminded her. "It might be different if the magazines paid better. Or paid on time. But at least, since we're so busy, we can afford to train someone in to help. We'll need someone to take over when you have your baby."

"Are you telling me to leave?"

"That's not what I said." He shook his head. "Don't be so defensive. I'm just being practical, Alice. You'll probably want to work part-time for a while. Haven't you thought that far ahead?"

"How will you manage?" Nell asked, on the phone.

"I'll be fine," Alice said lightly. "At least at first, it won't be a problem to bring the baby to work, Brian says. Then I'll find a babysitter, work shorter hours. He's suggested I do some freelance work as well."

"It sounds complicated. But I'm glad you've quit the restaurant, at least."

"I had to. I was too tired. I was falling asleep into the suds."

"What about the money your mother left? Can't you use that?"

Alice reached for a cigarette before she remembered that she'd stopped smoking because the taste of cigarettes made her sick. The money was a sore point. Elaine had left her some, but stipulated that she wasn't to touch it until her twenty-fifth birthday. As if, even dead, she didn't trust Alice.

"I'll get it a few months after the baby's born," she said. "I think it will be enough to buy somewhere small to live."

"Are you taking advice? Shouldn't you invest it or something?"

"You make me sound like a millionaire, Nell! I've talked to Brendan about it. I told him what I wanted to do and he seemed to think it was a good idea."

"Oh? He never said anything to me."

"He probably forgot. I figure once I have a place to live that no one can take away from me, I'll always get by somehow. I always have."

"I suppose so."

This was a sore point with Nell, because she had never had a paid job in her life. Alice felt mean, but Nell had backed her into a corner. What business was it of hers, anyway?

"I'm only thinking of you, Alice."

"I know. Look, Nell, I'm really tired. I'd better go. Why did no one tell me this whole business could be so exhausting?"

"You don't know the half of it, my dear." Nell's voice softened as she evened the score. "You go and get some rest. I'll talk to you soon."

Every crevice inside Alice seemed to fill up and then go right on filling until she thought she would burst. Although her back ached and her feet swelled up and throbbed, she liked to walk through the city holding her distended belly in front of her with defiant pride. For the first time, she felt no fear. She felt that only her pregnancy was visible. Not her.

She had a craving for meat, salt, blood. She bought small joints of that season's lamb, roasted them lightly and ate them, almost rare, from the bone. But it was blood she wanted, not the meat itself. She soaked it up with wedges of bread. It made her feel stronger, ruthless, predatory.

At night she lay awake reading and felt Holly's early vague movements gather strength and determination. From her eighth month on, she began to resent these sudden intrusions. The movements were sometimes painful. There was a spot at the top of her bladder which Holly especially liked to rub against, giving Alice a sharp, sickening sensation like the nerve of a tooth exposed. Once, when she was startled by a particularly violent kick under her ribs, she shocked herself by hitting back, savagely, and winding herself.

Fool, she told herself, when she'd recovered. What did you hope to achieve by *that*?

Her ankles and her neck thickened, the skin of her fingers grew puffy. Her skin stretched taut everywhere. She wondered how long it would hold together. She was swollen and heavy, drooping like the laburnum that flowered below her window. Every few days she had to go to the clinic to have her blood pressure checked. The nurses told her that she should be careful, but when she asked them what she should look out for they grew vague, as if they didn't trust her with the information.

"Ask the doctor," they said, then hurried on to the patient in the next cubicle. But the doctor was even more abstracted and Alice hadn't the heart to hold him up with questions. She could see he was busy.

"You'll be grand, Alice," Kate reassured her. "Do you want to know the best advice I got from anyone? My mother told me a story about when she had Dermot. She was all uptight, afraid of making a mess on those clean hospital sheets, of making too much noise, of causing a fuss. So she was whimpering away, with her knees locked and getting nowhere. Then the midwife suddenly barked at her, 'For God's sake, Missus, push! Push, like you was constipated!' And she got such a shock she heaved Dermot out one split second later. It's funny the things that go through your head when you're in labour, but I remembered that when I had Jake. It really helped. Do you want me to come with you?"

"No. Thanks, but no."

In the end, Holly's birth was stormy. Intense and urgent. Alice was gripped by pain and held there. She felt herself stretch immeasurably and open, become a channel. She felt life flaming through her, powerful and determined, and she abandoned herself to the energy that swept through her. It was a hypnotic rhythm and she lost herself in it willingly.

But she panicked when they told her to push. Her mind came back to the surface, briefly, and struggled against it. Her muscles locked. "I can't. I can't do it!" she wailed. "Make it stop now."

The midwife, a stout, older woman with a square and kindly face, sat down on the bed and took her hand.

"You're nearly there, lovey," she said. "You're doing a great job. Don't give up now."

Alice, panting and struggling to escape her body, her eyes squeezed tightly shut, barely heard her.

"This is no time to be fighting your body. It knows what to do, if you'll only let it."

Alice's eyes opened and focused on the midwife's

face. Their eyes met and held. The fireball inside Alice swelled and grew again, wrenching her open. She moved outside herself, towards the calm eyes in front of her. Below her, her body loosened.

"Work with that, Alice. Push hard, now."

Kate's story came back to her. She saw herself, red and straining on the hospital bed. She started to laugh and all her muscles relaxed. She poured all her energy into an enormous effort to bring Holly with her to the surface.

She was still laughing when the nurse beamed up at her: "That's it, good girl, the head is out. One more big push, now, and you're there. Just one more."

And the baby slid wetly out of her. "I did it!" Alice shouted. She began to cry and laugh at the same time.

I really did it.

But when she first heard the baby cry, she was shocked. A baby! She'd forgotten, somehow, that this was what it was all about. She stared at the hospital blanket they'd wrapped her in, the black fuzz on the top of her daughter's head, and panicked when the nurse brought the baby over to her.

"I don't know how to hold her," Alice said and felt instantly ashamed. Stupid.

But the nurse just laughed. "You'll soon learn," she said and arranged the blanket along Alice's arm.

Holly's name slid quietly into her mind. *Holly*. Alice liked it at once. A sturdy name that meant nothing but itself. Names were important. No one knew that better than Alice did. Her own was deceptive. It seemed innocent enough, but Alice knew what it really meant. It meant someone stuck in a nightmare, trapped in a world of shape shifters. A world full of menace. And then the polite fiction that the madness had been a dream, the lie that demanded that she wash her hands and go demurely in for tea.

"Hello, Holly," Alice said, trying out the sound of it. But at the same time she was thinking, this wasn't what I meant.

Somehow, despite the deep sense of connection she'd felt with Holly from the very beginning, despite the books on pregnancy, the childbirth classes, the advice from her friends, she had managed to avoid knowing that the end of it all would be this: a real baby.

They stared at each other. The books all said that infants couldn't see properly at birth, but Alice felt the power of Holly's ancient look and knew that the books were wrong. She seemed strange and familiar all at once. Alice had talked to her often over the last few months, felt her stir and grow inside her, felt Holly's spirit touching her own. Light. Something feathered.

But the being she had recognised and welcomed had little to do with this wrinkled, slippery baby now blinking and sucking her fist, wetly, against Alice's breast.

"Try feeding her," the nurse in the ward suggested, and showed Alice how to shape her nipple and stroke

Holly's cheek with it so that she would turn and take it in her mouth.

"Don't try and push it into her mouth," the nurse warned. "Or use your hand to turn her face. That will confuse her. She has an instinct to turn towards you if you only do it like this, gently. Don't force it."

Holly's face creased up when she sucked, which she did fiercely, as if ravenous, or angry, for a few minutes. Then, abruptly, she fell asleep. Alice laughed out loud. She couldn't help it. "She's so funny!" she said, looking up, but the nurse had left the cubicle.

Alice looked back down at Holly. "You're so funny," she whispered, and something inside her dislodged, loosened, began to flow.

Her body was still cramping, but she felt euphoric, powerful. It was as if a sudden rush of speed flooded her system. She knew in that instant there was nothing in the whole world that she couldn't do. She leaned back against the pillows and felt the extraordinary new lightness of her body, the weight of her baby against her arm, and her spirit lifted. She felt shattered and exhilarated all at once. She still tingled with residual electricity. If blue lightning had streamed from her fingertips right then, she wouldn't have been at all surprised.

The nurses took Holly away so that Alice could rest and she slept for a while. She woke suddenly in the unfamiliar ward, startled by the smell of antiseptic. She was aware that she was sore, now. Battered. She remembered Holly and stretched, but carefully. I'm a mother, she thought, astonished. She felt as if her body had been given back to her. She touched the skin of her belly, folding in on itself now that it was no longer taut and distended. It had become soft and spongy, alien. She looked around her at the two rows of beds, a woman resting in each of them, some sitting, some sleeping. One, holding a baby, smiled over encouragingly at Alice.

"What did you have, love?" she asked as Alice pulled herself up to sit, wincing.

"A girl," Alice answered, filled with a wild current of joy and relief. A girl. She looked down at her swollen breasts, tingling now as she remembered the tight fierce pull of Holly's mouth.

God, she thought, it works. This body really works. It's amazing.

For the first time, ever, she felt something like tenderness and respect for her body. It had survived her own best efforts to destroy it. Survived and become miraculous. She looked back over the months of growth, all the time that the intricate, complex structure that had now become Holly was evolving; the extraordinary process of birth. She was stunned.

I did that, she thought. I lived through it. And now there's Holly.

She was filled with wonder. She thought of all the women walking around the city, outwardly calm and ordinary. Each concealing this explosive secret potential. She thought of all the women she knew who were mothers, who had gone through this and never let on. Women she liked and those she didn't like. Teachers she had had in school. The neighbours of her childhood. Kate, for God's sake. Her own . . .

All of them, capable of this. It was like a universal secret that had been kept from her.

A slow rage began to burn in her. She felt cheated. She wished that she had known. She didn't know what difference it would have made to her, but she knew that it would have changed something.

The euphoria didn't last. It ebbed away from her like the strange tide that had brought it, leaving her scared and uncertain about the future.

What have I done? she asked herself. What have I done?

Nell invited her down to stay, but Alice refused. "I'll come in a few weeks," she said. "When we've got used to each other."

She didn't want Nell to witness her mistakes with Holly. She was afraid that Nell would gloat, fuss, sort everything out. She'd cluck all the time about the choices Alice had made and how difficult her life would be.

She knew Nell would say none of this to her, but would discuss it all with Brendan when Alice and the children were in bed. Alice wanted to live up to her independent image. She would go down to visit Nell and Brendan when she was confident of herself as a mother and not before, so that she could carry off the impression of capability she desperately wanted to feel. If the image was undermined, she was afraid that she would fall apart and never recover. Afraid she'd end up handing Holly over to Nell, bleating, "You were right! I can't do it on my own. You take her."

Alice had a nasty suspicion that that was what Nell secretly wanted to happen. Every now and again, strange ideas like that floated into Alice's mind and then quickly floated away again. She wondered if she was entirely sane.

When Nell drove up to town to visit her, bringing all kinds of gifts, she felt ashamed. Nell brought baby clothes, her old buggy, a baby car-seat.

"You'll need it when you bring her down to us. Not that I think you should drive her anywhere in that old banger of yours. Why don't you let Brendan find you a decent car? He has a friend in Galway who owns a garage."

"I'm quite capable of finding my own car, thanks," said Alice. "Besides, I'm happy with the one I've got."

She drove a battered old Alfa. It was bright red and erratic and Alice loved it. She loved to drive, full stop. She drove fast and well. She loved the power, the speed, the precision of it. It made her feel strong, the tension of balancing gears between her feet, the weight of her hands on the wheel. She lay back deep against the bucket seat of the Alfa and felt enclosed, cradled, as she sped along.

City traffic was a dance to her, weaving in and out

of lanes, knowing the precise heft and weight of each hill and corner of familiar streets. She enjoyed the intricate grace of roundabouts, judging the exact moment to release the car into the stream of traffic, relishing the sense of split second timing, of being part of the city's movement. She was in tune with the engine of her car, alert to the slightest shift in tone, in rhythm, and adjusting to it. There was a degree of trust about it that scared and exhilarated her. Trust in the car, in herself, in the goodwill of other drivers.

She loved the road to Nell's as well, open, familiar. Rushing across the country she took possession of it, she felt herself full of power and speed, a creature in flight. She became herself. She thrilled to the knowledge of a ton of metal enclosing her, in her control, under the direction of her hands and legs. She knew that speed and sudden death were in her gift. She watched the countryside and small towns flash past her, the list of towns a litany in her mind, marking her route to Nell. Maynooth, Kinnegad, Loughrea, Oranmore. Then the Headford road, winding towards the house. The motion of the car soothed her, her own passage through space and time soothed her. It was the only time she felt completely alive.

When Dermot had taught her to drive, he'd taught her shortcuts through neighbourhoods she knew she'd never live in: broad streets with leafy gardens and houses set well back from the road. Dermot would drive an extra mile to avoid stopping at a traffic light. Alice kept the habit because she loved the intimacy of leaving the main road, of knowing her way around. There was one particular route she always took, down a curving street from the top road towards the sea. There was a bend in the road like an elbow, and an old chestnut tree grew there, solid and impassive. More than once when she drove past it, stoned or drunk, or both, the thought that she could just neglect to steer into the bend crossed her mind. She could slam into that tree and end everything in a matter of seconds. She liked the idea. It was a safety net. The imaginary cyanide pill of her secret-agent childhood. She liked knowing it was there, that she could come back to it whenever she wanted. She thought of it as her death-tree, but in a strange, twisted way, she knew that it kept her alive.

The most expensive thing she owned, after her cameras, was the sound system in her car. It made a massive sound that Alice could feel rising through her body in waves. Its rhythm fed her blood, made her heart beat faster. She could feel her personality change, relax and open under the combined influence of speed and sound. She wondered now if having Holly would change all that. She doubted it.

"Thanks for the car-seat," she said to Nell. "I hadn't thought of it."

"I wish," Nell said wistfully, "you'd let me drive you home."

"I'm fine, Nell," Alice insisted, guiltily. She had decided to get a taxi home from the hospital. She wanted to be as independent as possible, to do everything herself. She didn't want help. She didn't want to share Holly with anyone. She was going to manage this on her own. She'd show them all. She knew what they thought: that she was selfish and irresponsible and had bitten off more than she could chew (Nell); that she would need help and support (Kate), that she had made a mistake. All she had to set against that was Holly, with the shock of dark fuzzy hair that stretched from her eyebrows all the way down to her shoulders, her cross face.

"All that stuff about mothering instinct is a lie," she told Ruth. "I knew nothing about babies. Or children. Just what I'd seen Nell do with her kids, and Kate with her son, Jake. I'd never changed a nappy in my life before I had Holly."

"Didn't you ever help Nell?"

"Oh, Nell's the type who likes to do all that for herself. You know. She loves the whole mother-thing. My job down there is to take over the kitchen. Especially the dishes, since I've been a professional. Ha. It suited me, too, though, I must admit. Babies made me nervous. I stayed away from them as much as I could. I'd stay up half the night, sleep away the morning . . . one way and another, I managed to avoid it all.

"Anyway, it was just as well I was breastfeeding. All the paraphernalia of bottles and sterilisers would have defeated me completely. I was far too lazy for that. But I had to make it all up as I went along. It was horrible. How did I know I was doing it right?"

CHAPTER FOURTEEN

As soon as they got home, Holly began to fuss and complain. She cried easily and couldn't be soothed. She was a restless baby, always wriggling and fretting. Alice couldn't figure out why.

When Alice tried to feed her she roared even louder, her face red, wrinkled and angry. Her limbs went into spasm and she pulled back, rigid, from the nipple. She screamed when she was put into the cot Kate had given them. Alice would check her nappy and find it dry, but as soon as the baby was all buttoned up again, she would suddenly flood it.

Alice was terrified of the black curling stump at Holly's navel, no one had ever told her about that. There were so many things she had never known before. The extent of her ignorance shocked her because Holly was so dependent on her for everything. If Alice couldn't get it right, Holly had to suffer. She wondered if it would always be like this.

Both of them were half-crazed from lack of sleep. When Holly did eventually doze off on the bed beside her, Alice would lie awake, tense and anxious, watching her breath rise and fall, her tiny fingers curled up against her sallow face. In her sleep, smiles spread across her face and Alice watched them until the knot inside her softened and she could lie down and close her eyes at last.

But never for long. Holly slept in short snatches. No one had told her that she was meant to sleep at night and be sweet and accommodating during the day. Alice had no energy, there was nothing left in her to give, but still Holly kept asking.

One night Alice was pacing around the living-room, only now feeling the limitations of its angular walls as they leaned towards her. She fought the urge to throw Holly against the looming surface. Her arms mimed the act, propelling outwards and then falling back against her, rocking Holly violently.

She began to sing, loudly, to drown the sound of Holly's crying, fighting it with noise of her own. The words of a Beatles' song she used to love came back to her. "Blackbird singing in the dead of night . . ." Her voice calmed and settled to the song and she began to sway, the movement of her arms slowing, rhythmic. "Take these broken wings and learn to fly . . ."

Holly stopped crying.

"Do you like dancing?" Alice asked her, amazed.

Holly stared back at her gravely.

"You do, don't you?" Alice bent and kissed her and Holly blinked. Her eyes crossed, as if the effort of focusing was too much for her. She looked demented.

"You're a sweetie," Alice told her, smiling.

After that she reeled and swooped around the flat, day or night, singing, holding Holly against her shoulder. And Holly would stop crying and stare at her in wonder.

As they swayed together in those early nights, dancing their peculiar ritual behind closed curtains, worn out from lack of sleep and the strange hauntings of her own mind, Alice felt the weight of a terrible grief. Her body was lonely for the intimate enfolding of pregnancy. As Holly taught her the dreadful need of babies that cannot be postponed, the unbearable, constant, demands for touch, for comfort, for sustenance, she ached with the knowledge that no one had ever done this for her. She knew, with certainty, that Elaine had never held her like this, or fed her from her own body. The intimacy would have revolted her. Yet, against her will, she felt a stirring of sympathy for Elaine.

Is this what it was like for you? she wondered. Were you empty too?

One night, she was sitting in the armchair in the corner of the living-room, feeding Holly. Through the window she could see moonlight edging the clouds. Holly's steady sucking had lulled her into a trance. Suddenly she felt something move against her skin, under her T-shirt, and she started.

"God!" she shouted out. "What's that?" She jumped to her feet, still holding Holly against her.

Holly let go of the nipple and stared at her, amazed.

"I'm sorry, Holly. I think it's a spider or something." Alice shuddered. Her heart pounded. She looked down at her side but there was nothing there. Except Holly's right hand. Alice sat down again slowly and Holly settled against her, the way she had been before. Her left arm crooked against Alice's T-shirt, her right falling loosely beneath her against Alice's side. Alice held her breath and waited as Holly latched on and began to suck again, her eyes open and wary. There it was again, that light tickling sensation. It was Holly, touching her.

"It's you!" Alice said softly. "It was you, all along."

When Holly was a week old, Alice took her out for a walk. It was a soft June day and big fluffy clouds hung low in a sky which stretched far and blue above them. After two attempts to carry both Holly and Nell's buggy down the stairs, Alice abandoned the buggy and took out a soft yellow baby sling she'd bought when she was pregnant. The only other thing she had bought was a soft, shapeless brown stuffed dog which now lived in the cot that Holly refused to sleep in. It looked nothing like Max, but that's what Alice called it all the same.

It took her a long time to figure out how to fasten Holly into the sling and then tie it to her chest, but she managed. She liked the feel of Holly's weight against her, held her right hand protectively over the sling, lightly cupping the baby's head under the yellow corduroy. Worn out with all the fuss, Holly fell asleep before they got outside.

"Hello, my dear," Mrs Harrington, an old woman who lived in the house next door, called out as Alice emerged, blinking, into the sunlight. Mrs Harrington was sitting, as always, at her open front door. She liked to watch the comings and goings on the street. A rust-coloured shawl was wrapped around her shoulders despite the sunshine.

"Come over here, dear, and let me see the baby." She gestured towards Holly, her face forming a question.

"She's a girl," said Alice, smiling, as she climbed the stone steps towards the old woman.

"Let me see," repeated Mrs Harrington.

Alice bent down, still holding Holly's head. "You can't really see her properly because of the sling," she apologised. "Except for her hair!" Just then Holly sighed and turned her face around so that it was no longer pressed against Alice's shirt, but turned towards Mrs Harrington. For an instant her slate-grey eyes opened, then they slid shut again. The small hollow beside her mouth deepened.

"Oh, my dear, she's precious!" Mrs Harrington's old eyes fastened greedily on Holly, then lifted to Alice. "You'd better watch out," she said, "or someone will steal her away from you."

Alice's heart began to pound. Silly, vicious old bat, she thought. She straightened up, the smile frozen on her face. She brought her other arm up across Holly's body as if to protect her from this woman's thoughts.

The bad fairy at the christening.

Mrs Harrington went on smiling as if nothing unusual had happened.

Alice shivered. "It's colder than I thought it was," she said stupidly. "I'd better go back and put more clothes on the baby."

181

"What's her name, dearie?" Mrs Harrington called, but Alice moved quickly away as if she hadn't heard.

Don't tell her anything, she thought frantically, fumbling in her pocket for her key.

Holly's weight was suddenly an obstacle. Alice couldn't see around her properly, couldn't sort her keys with only one hand, couldn't reach the lock.

Hurry up!

As soon as they were inside, with the front door closed behind them, Alice remembered to breathe again.

Don't be mad, she told herself, slowly climbing the stairs, feeling her heart beat wildly against Holly's sleeping weight. It's only daft old Mrs Harrington. She didn't mean any harm.

But the image of the woman stooped, crone-like, her crooked finger resting against Holly's cheek, stayed with her.

O God, she touched her. I should have stopped her.

"I won't let them get you," she said aloud, to herself as much as to Holly. "Don't you worry. I'll be more careful in future."

As the days went by, Alice fell into a depression so deep it seemed infinite. It was so paralysing that she didn't even understand what was happening to her. This feeling had nothing to do with the fits of crying she had dimly imagined post-natal depression to be, or not having the energy to get dressed and go out, although that was part of it. The worst of it was the constant fear she felt. It was an obsession. There was an idea trapped in her head like a moth inside a lamp.

What have you done? You've had this baby and the world is out there, just waiting to destroy her. To brutalise her. She doesn't stand a chance. How could you have been so stupid, so selfish?

She paced the floors at night with Holly, holding her while she cried through the wakeful small hours of the morning. Alice cried right along with her, while the future stalked them. She couldn't bear to think of Holly growing up in the world she knew. But she knew she couldn't keep her shut away in this attic forever. She paced and paced, furious, trying to escape the visions that haunted her.

When the doorbell rang she ignored it. If the phone was for her, and the other people in the house called up to her, she pretended she was out or asleep. Once someone came to knock on the door and Alice froze on the bed where she was feeding Holly.

"Ssh," she whispered to the baby, who stopped sucking and stared at her, wide-eyed.

"Don't make a sound," whispered Alice. "They'll go away." She held her hand against Holly's cheek, waiting to cover her mouth if she gurgled or whimpered. Then an idea, half-remembered, floated into her mind.

The pillow. It would be quick and gentle . . . She'd never know.

Alice fought herself. The desire to cover Holly's face while she slept, to end it all, the certainty that this was the kindest, the best thing for her, struggled with something else, something outside Alice. Something stronger, that saw Holly's breath, her skin, her sudden smiles, and said, *wait*.

She paced the floor with Holly behind closed curtains, desperate for sleep and relief from this nightmare of terror and exhaustion. She was sure that if she opened the door and stepped outside she would fall straight into the mouth of hell, bringing Holly with her. There was a war being fought in her head. When the urge to smother Holly came over her, she'd turn the stereo on, loud, not caring whether anyone else was in the house or not, urgent rock music drowning out the chaos inside her, the voices in her mind. Then she'd pick Holly up, so that she wouldn't be lying down and vulnerable, and dance around the room, holding onto her and talking to her loud and fast, singing. Days and nights blurred into each other.

She never sang lullabies. She had forgotten every song she ever knew except old Beatles' tracks, but Holly didn't seem to mind. When Alice sang to her she stared and made noises in her throat and twined her fingers around one of Alice's. Music seemed to be the only thing that could calm her frantic crying spells. Music and dancing with Alice.

Alice had to be careful. One day she looked out the window, in that spacey state when her head was spinning. She was haunted by everything she wanted to protect Holly from and knew she couldn't, because it was all so inevitable. Then she saw, as if for the first time, how far it was from her window to the ground. The window was set vertically into the roof, like a skylight. As she stared down towards the ground, the house seemed to tilt. She felt herself falling, pulled.

I could jump from here, holding her. We'd both smash to pieces on the gravel.

She gripped Holly tighter. She couldn't do it. She had an awful vision that Holly would not die, but would be left broken and battered, crying. And then come insanely together again and follow her, shattered and screaming, through eternity.

Alice stayed away from the window after that. Its pull was strong. Like a voice, calling. Urging her to listen, to do what it said. She drank to ignore it.

The next time her doorbell rang she went unsteadily down to answer it.

It was Kate and Jake.

"Oh good, you're here." Kate marched in past Alice without being asked. "How's the baby?"

"Holly. She's fine. She's asleep."

"Oh, well can we peep at her? We'll be quiet, won't we, Jake?"

Jake's hands were pushed deep into the pockets of his shorts. He nodded earnestly. He seemed strangely, suddenly, grown up to Alice after days of seeing no one but Holly.

Kate was halfway up the stairs already, as if determined to get to the flat before Alice could change her mind and somehow shut them out. "I've come around a few times," she called back over her shoulder, "but no one answered your bell. I rang too."

"I've been sleeping a lot," lied Alice, hurrying to catch up with her.

"Lucky you. When I had Jake I don't think I got enough sleep for six months afterwards. He was a horror. Weren't you, Jake?"

Alice wondered how she could sound so cheerful about it.

"Well," she said as they reached the top of the stairs, "She doesn't sleep much at night. So, when she dozes off during the day, I go to bed too." Thinking to herself that she spent most of her time in bed anyway. She tried to figure out how long it had been since she'd been outside the building in daylight. She hardly counted the twilight slinking to the shop on the corner for basics like milk and gin. It seemed a lifetime since Mrs Harrington had put a curse on Holly. A lifetime, and she had managed not to hurt Holly. Or herself. Yet.

"How old is she now?" Kate asked, going straight to the kitchen and putting on the kettle for tea. "I've brought some goodies," she called over her shoulder. "Some fruit juice and nuts. And," she appeared in the doorway, waving a package, "Carrot cake. Your favourite and mine."

"Lovely. Thanks." Alice tried to remember if she'd eaten that day. "She's three and a half weeks already. It's amazing."

Kate smiled sympathetically. "The years go by fast, too, you know. But I know how hard it is at first. How are you getting on?" She looked around the flat, gloomy with all the curtains closed, the dishes piled in the sink, the garbage bag spilling over.

"I haven't made it out to the bin," said Alice,

following her gaze. "And the curtains are closed because of Holly."

"Is that her I hear?"

"She must have woken up. I'll go and get her."

Kate followed her into the bedroom. "Oh Alice, she's gorgeous. Can I hold her?"

While Kate fussed over the baby, Alice made tea and gave Jake a glass of juice. She had to rinse a plate before she could slice the carrot cake. She set it down on the low table under the window.

"It's dark in here," said Jake.

"I'll open the curtains."

Alice blinked again in the weak light. It was a grey day outside, but the light was stronger than she was used to. It hurt her eyes. When she turned back into the room she was struck by how grubby it looked. Holly's paraphernalia of cloths and powder and vaseline was strewn all over the room. The bucket where her nappies were soaking was visible through the half open bathroom door. Socks and knickers were drying on the side of the bath.

She looked reluctantly at Kate. "It's a bit of a mess," she said.

"Rubbish," said Kate briskly. "This is me you're talking to. And you've been looking after a baby, what do you expect? How are you, really?"

"Not great." The relief of saying it shocked her. She sat down abruptly. "It's awful, Kate. She cries all night. I can't put her down. I'm shattered. I can't seem to do anything else besides look after her, and I don't even feel like I'm doing that right."

"Of course you are. All you have to do is look at her to see that. She's a little dote."

"You don't understand."

"Maybe I understand more than you think I do."

They looked at each other for a long minute, then Alice looked away.

No, don't tell her.

She was afraid that Kate might tell someone else, that Holly would be taken away from her.

Remember Mrs Harrington.

"Can I watch TV?" Jake asked.

"All right. But I'll bring it in to the bedroom. You can sit on the bed, OK?"

"Yeah." Jake was pleased. He liked Alice's bedroom. He said the ceiling was like a hat. Alice unplugged her portable black and white television set and wiped the dust off it before she carried it into the bedroom and set it up for Jake. Then she brought him the whole plate of cake and his juice and left him to it, bouncing on her unmade bed. Kate gestured to her when she came out and Alice closed the door behind her.

"I'm sorry for not coming sooner, Alice. I should have tried harder. But you weren't exactly encouraging. And things have been really weird, for us. Mark's leaving."

"Oh, Kate, I'm sorry."

"So am I. It's funny, I knew it was coming. I thought I'd be relieved. I didn't expect it to hurt." She rubbed her eyes with her hands, as if she was tired.

"What will you do?"

"Well, he's leaving us the house. That's something. It's funny the way things happen. Dad's been talking about retiring. He's offered me the shop."

"Are you going to take it?"

"I have this idea that I'd like to start a health food shop. I've talked to Dad about it and he said he'd help me get started. I've got to try and get a loan from the bank. What do you think?"

"Health food?" Alice said listlessly. She knew she should show more interest, but all she felt was exhaustion. She tried to pull herself together. Kate had been an enthusiastic vegetarian for years. "There's nothing you don't know about food. And the shop's in a good place for it. Where's the nearest one?"

"Miles away. In town," said Kate, straightening up, pleased. "That's the point."

"I think it's a great idea. Does Jake know?"

Kate shook her head. "Not yet. No one knows. I wanted to tell you first." She looked ruefully at Alice. "Old habits die hard." Her mouth twisted and her eyes filled with tears. "I'm going to miss him, the shite."

She put Holly lying on the sofa beside her, fast asleep. Then she pulled a tissue out of her pocket and blew her nose, hard. "Oh, and there's something else I wanted to tell you. I nearly forgot!"

"What?"

"You know the house Dermot's bought? Remember I told you he converted it into two self-contained parts so there'd always be someone to keep an eye on things for him when he's away on transatlantic flights?"

"Dermot, the jet-set pilot." Alice smiled. She was fond of Dermot.

"You could marry him, Alice. It would make the parents happy. He needs someone to look after him."

"Listen to yourself, Kate. What are you saying? That's exactly the way Nell thinks. Next you'll be telling me he has a great salary and a pension."

Kate laughed. "Well, he does. But you're right about Nell. I'm sorry."

"Dermot is the last person to want someone to look after him. You know better than I do, he's as solitary as a monk. And even if he did, I'm not the one to do it. I can barely look after myself."

"And Holly."

"Mmm. Holly."

They both watched Holly stretched out on the sofa, her arm bent so that her fist rested against her cheek.

"Where is the house, exactly?" Alice asked.

"About half way between our house and the harbour. You know that terrace off the main road? The houses are one storey over a basement . . . it's the basement he's selling. It's lovely, Alice. He's done loads of work on it. It's really bright, not a proper basement at all, just slightly below street level. There's a great little garden, all overgrown . . . you'd love it."

"I don't know."

"Didn't you say you'd like a place of your own?" Kate pressed. "And a basement would be an awful lot easier to manage with a baby than this bird's nest."

"Well, *excuse me*," Alice said, mock-indignant.

"Oh, come on, Alice. You know what I mean. I told him you might be interested."

"Did you, now?"

"I did. I'm not trying to run your life or anything, don't get all crabby on me. Look, think about it. But don't leave it too long. He said he'd hold it for you if you want it, but he has to know in the next day or two. Someone else is already interested."

"How much does he want?"

"I'm not sure. You'll have to talk to him about it. But he likes the idea of having you there, not some stranger or other. He knows you'd leave him alone, you see. You know how he is. I don't know how he survives all that exposure to people in foreign countries! When he's here, he's practically a recluse. Is there a word for people who are afraid of meeting new people?"

"I don't know. Is there a word for people who are afraid of people?"

Dermot's introversion was a long-standing joke with them, but secretly Alice understood it. "Is he around at the moment?" she asked. "I'd like to go and see it. But I won't get the money for another couple of months."

"He'll wait," said Kate, as if it was already settled.

As, indeed, in Alice's mind, it was. She remembered the call of the window, the distant gravel. If she was in a basement, there would be nowhere to fall to. The more she thought about it, the better it got. Dermot within calling distance would be a perfect compromise between contact and isolation. "I like the idea," she said. "If I can afford it."

"That's great. It will be like old times. All of us together again."

"Not quite," Alice said ruefully as Holly began to fret. Jake appeared in the door.

"Your baby's crying," he told Alice, accusing. "You'd better pick her up."

CHAPTER FIFTEEN

By the time Holly was four months old, they were settled in the house with Dermot. It had cost Alice every penny that her mother had left her, but she knew she was doing the right thing. She booked Holly into a small crèche nearby because it was impossible to bring her to work any more. She struggled to get out of her baby chair and rolled into corners when Alice left her on her blanket. She got stuck then and yelled furiously to be rescued. Some clients smiled and talked to her, but others frowned disapprovingly at Alice. She decided to leave Holly in the crèche and work until two every day in the shop, try some freelance work on top of that.

Going back to work had made her feel more normal. She was still tired, but the terrible isolation lessened. The shop put structure in her life. The routine reassured her.

The house looked small from the street. A short flight of stone steps led up to Dermot's front door. Alice's door was cut into the side of the steps, slightly below ground level. The main room ran the full length of the house in an L-shape, with windows on three sides and a fireplace set into the inner wall. A small room behind the fireplace was set up for Holly, with Alice's room and a bathroom across the hall. The kitchen was square and small and opened out onto the back garden. The grass was almost knee-high. A dense shrub of rosemary grew at the back door.

Alice touched it the first time she opened the door with her own key and stepped out into the crisp, late September air. She smelled her hand. It was pungent. As if it had gone deep into the earth and had come back to her.

"I'll cut the grass," Dermot called down from his open kitchen window. He was leaning on the sill, blowing smoke rings out into the air. His shirt sleeves were pushed up over his elbows, showing freckled forearms. Alice thought he looked more like a farmer than a pilot. It still amazed her that, when Dermot went to work, hundreds of people put their lives in his hands.

"I suppose that's something we'll have to work out," she said. "Who does what in the garden. But there's no rush, Dermot. I like it like this. It would be . . . naked, if we cut the grass. I'd like to put a tree in, or something. I wonder why the people who used to live here didn't?"

"What kind of tree?"

Alice shrugged. "Oh, I don't know. Willow. Or cedar."

"What about a fruit tree?"

"I didn't think of that. Why not? Oh, hang on a minute, I think I hear Holly. I'll go and see what she wants."

She waved and went back inside. Holly was

grumbling and chewing her fist on the rug where Alice had left her. Alice picked her up and carried her over to the rocking-chair she'd bought at the market and sat with one foot on the fender, pushing herself backwards and forwards.

"There's so much space here, Holly," she said dreamily, "And it's all ours. No one can take it away from us. Ever. We're going to be OK." She stroked Holly's soft hair. "It will be all right," she promised.

Alice felt cocooned and sheltered, living there, almost underground. When winter came, she liked drawing the heavy blue curtains and lighting a peat fire in the sitting room grate. She felt safe and warm and lucky, shut away from the rain and the dark.

It was good to know that Kate was only two streets away and that Dermot was upstairs if she needed him. Sometimes a whole week would go by when they only saw each other in passing, or waved at one another through their windows. But still, Alice knew that they were there.

That year, she loaded the car with cameras, light-meters, brollies and stands, and drove around to people's houses for their Christmas portraits, bringing Holly with her. It was a popular idea and she could hardly keep up with the demand for family portraits in front of Christmas trees.

One day a client showed her a box of old family photographs, all different sizes. Alice could tell by the clothes the people wore that the photos were more than fifty years old.

"I'd love to do something with these," the woman said, "But most of them are faded and look, the surface of this one is split. Have you any ideas? I'd hate to just throw them out."

Alice handed back a large print of a man whose face was broad and freckled under a peaked cap.

"Do you want to give one to me? I could work on it, try to restore it, and bring it back to you. If you like it, you can give me the rest. I could mount some of them in frames for you."

"Would you? I'd love that. Here's one, of my parents."

Alice set up a darkroom in the alcove under Dermot's steps. She brought in a worktable and bought a set of camel hair brushes and some gouache. She made a duplicate print and began to re-touch it carefully. At first she was cautious, but she soon realised it was the same as restoring the old city streets she'd worked on years ago. Her lips blackened as she worked late into the night, absorbed by the intricacy of the task.

"This is good, Alice," Brian said when she showed him what she'd done. "You should do more. I bet there's a demand for this kind of thing. You could put a notice up in the shop. Maybe this is what you need, a business venture of your own. You could keep separate books . . ."

"Do you think it'd work?" Alice was doubtful.

"You've nothing to lose."

"I suppose not. I'll try it."

"Why not?" said Kate, when Alice told her. Kate's new business was thriving. Her shop was fast becoming the centre of an information network. She had a noticeboard full of phone numbers and circulars about alternative medicine and evening classes. She was rushed off her feet.

"Who would have thought we'd both turn out to be business women?" she asked, taking off her shoes and stretching her legs in their jeans towards Alice's fire. Jake was shaking a rattle over Holly's face and talking to her. She stared at his face, wide-eyed, instead of at the toy. Then she suddenly rolled over, sat up, and grinned at everyone. She was thrilled with this new skill of hers. Since Alice couldn't be relied on to cheer each time she did it, as she had in the beginning, Holly applauded herself instead. She clapped her hands, wildly and inaccurately.

"Clever Holly!" Jake laughed at her.

Alice smiled at him before she answered Kate. "I'm not so sure," she said doubtfully. "So long as we can get by, it's all right. But I don't see myself as a business-whizz, somehow."

"What do you see yourself as?"

She shrugged. "God knows."

"Don't you have any ideas?"

"No. I can't see that far ahead. How about you?"

"Well." Kate paused for effect, one hand waving backwards and forwards. "All other things being equal?"

"Yes."

"OK. Don't laugh. A restaurant. Not now, but in a few years."

"That's a great idea, Kate."

"You don't think I'm mad?"

"No. I think it will be a huge amount of work, but why not? If anyone can do it, you can."

Coming back out to live near the harbour made Alice see it differently. It was smaller than she remembered. She put Holly in a sling and went exploring the beaches she'd ignored since she left home. She photographed the boats docked for winter, listened to the halyards clicking in the cold wind, scanned the shifting horizon.

As well as her restoration work, she began to sell single shots of the coastline, rocks and driftwood to a photo library. One day she found a shag, shivering and dishevelled, its beak enmeshed in the plastic rings from a six-pack. She shot a full roll of film before putting the bird into a cardboard box and bringing it to a vet. The picture made the front page of a national newspaper and a local environmental group asked if they could use it for their advertising campaign.

"I hope they paid you for it," Nell said, on the phone.

"They're a small group, Nell. They're broke."

"So are you."

"Well, at least it's good publicity."

"You can't eat publicity."

"I've got to go, Holly's crying," Alice lied and hung up, seething. She picked Holly up and hugged her tightly.

"Why does she still treat me as if I'm a kid?" she asked.

"Ma," Holly said, struggling.

Alice loosened her grip. "You said it, baby."

"Watch yourself," her mother used to say. "You just watch yourself, girl." It had been a warning. Now Alice learned how to do exactly that. Through an imaginary lens, she watched herself mothering Holly. As she watched, she became more like the kind of mother she wanted to be. When she saw herself smiling at Holly, blowing raspberries on her stomach, she approved and encouraged herself to do it for longer, rousing Holly to a dizzy pitch of delight.

But when Holly cried she flooded with an icy rage and hunger for violence. She locked herself into the darkroom and held the door shut against herself, willed herself not to open it. She tuned in to her Walkman and turned the volume up until her head hurt but she could no longer hear Holly cry. She was more tired than she had ever imagined it was possible to be. She lived in a cloud of exhaustion, barely conscious. The months passed in a haze.

Holly was an active, curious baby who moved with lightning speed. Every day Alice had to rearrange something to accommodate her growth, move things out of reach so that she wouldn't hurt herself. She had started smoking again soon after Holly was born, and they had daily battles over the ashtray, boxes of matches, which Holly always tried to suck, and packets of cigarettes.

Holly couldn't bear to be left alone. She refused to

sleep in the small room Alice had set up for her so she slept in Alice's bed. Alice loved the feel of Holly's weight against her in the middle of the night. Their breathing matched, as if one pair of lungs would have been enough to sustain both of them. Their bodies leaned against each other in sleep, as if they were trying to grow back together. Holly's skin felt like an extension of Alice's own.

One evening in early summer, Alice carried Holly into the bathroom on her hip. They'd been digging in the garden all afternoon and Holly's nails were black with grime. There was dirt in the folds of skin at the back of her neck. She clung to Alice's body with her strong, wiry legs, her fingers fisted in the shoulder of Alice's sweater, looking in front of her, smiling, her dark curls falling into her eyes. Alice saw herself walking at that peculiarly maternal angle, hip jutting to support the baby. She saw herself warming a towel on the radiator. It made her feel good. Justified.

You're doing it. You're being a real mother.

She filled the bath with toys and bubbles and then put Holly in to play. Alice sat in the overstuffed armchair under the hot press and read, with her feet up on the side of the bath. Holly sat waist deep in water and smeared bubbles on the small blue and white tiles.

When Holly was finished in the bath, Alice lifted her out of the water in a towel fresh from the radiator. She wrapped the towel around Holly and held her close, smelling her clean pink skin. She slipped outside herself and watched. It looked good.

Holly pulled herself away and ran, giggling, out of the bathroom. The towel unwound itself and fell to the floor. Her legs were still chubby and crooked, but surprisingly strong. She'd been happier since she'd learned to walk and didn't have to count on Alice to carry her everywhere. She was flushed after her bath. Her hair straggled, wet, across her shoulders. Her eyes shone. She stopped at the door and looked back at Alice, giggling.

"You want me to chase you?" Alice made a mock growl, deep in her throat. "I'm going to get you!" she called, and pounced.

Holly shrieked with delight and threw herself towards the bed, burying her face in the quilt. Her legs made climbing motions but they weren't quite long enough to get her up onto the bed.

Alice reached out and caught her, turning her in her hands as she lifted her. She put her mouth against Holly's stomach and blew. The baby skin made a loud rasping noise and Holly squealed happily, her open mouth showing six tiny teeth.

She's so perfect, Alice thought, smiling against Holly's skin. So clean.

Suddenly the air was charged, electric. Alice felt the skin on her face freeze as her heart fell heavily against her ribs and thudded there.

What are you doing? she asked herself. What the hell are you doing?

Slowly, carefully, she put Holly down on the bed. She picked the towel up, off the floor where it had fallen and wrapped Holly tightly in it without looking at her. Her hands shook. Her stomach twisted and pressed against her throat.

Oh no, she thought. No. No. No.

CHAPTER SIXTEEN

"I don't know if I can tell you this," Alice told Ruth. She covered her face with her hands. "I don't think I can do it."

"Go on, Alice. It's OK."

"OK. All right. Umm." She took her hands away from her face and began to twist the sleeve of her sweater instead. "One night this thing happened. It scared me and I didn't understand it, you know? It was late, you see. I was really, really tired. Wrecked.

"It was soon after that night. I was keeping her at a distance. You know. And forcing her to sleep in her own room. After I'd put her into bed I'd plug into my walkman and sit there drinking, waiting for her to fall asleep. It didn't work. She did more crying than sleeping and neither of us was getting any peace. She cried half the night . . . even when she was asleep her breathing was all jerky, as if she was still sobbing. Her face wet. During the day she was cross, she clung to me, we yelled at each other. I couldn't work. We were both strung out. Waking or sleeping, it was a nightmare. Anyway, on this night I was furious with her. I'd had enough. All I wanted was a few minutes of silence. I was desperate. You know?"

Ruth nodded.

❧

Alice wanted Holly to go to bed, but Holly wanted to play instead. She kept running away on unsteady legs and when Alice chased her she squealed that squeal of hers, delighted. Alice was ready to explode.

She could feel the pressure build in her chest, the tight grip around her forehead. "This is ridiculous, Holly!" she snapped. "I'm the one who's meant to be in charge here."

She decided that she'd grab hold of Holly, no messing. She'd change her, get her ready for bed, whether Holly liked it or not. Maybe, if she was determined enough, Holly would sense it and go down without a fight. The way it was meant to be, according to the books.

She caught hold of Holly as she scooted past her on all fours. Alice carried her over to the bed, talking to her.

"I want you to go to bed early tonight, Holly. And no crying. I want some peace and quiet, OK? It's not much to ask. I'm going to change your nappy now and get you into your pyjamas and then I'll read you a story and put you into your bed and you'll go straight to sleep. Right, sweetie, here we go."

She put Holly on the bed, lying on her back. She took her wet nappy off. Holly grinned a gorgeous, dimpled grin and rolled over, ready to escape.

"No," Alice told her. "Come back here. I'm going to change you now, whether you like it or not." She picked up a clean dry nappy and waved it in front of her face. Holly beamed back at her as Alice peeked out over the top of the white cloth: "Boo!"

Holly wriggled with delight and she struggled to sit up. Alice felt the smile fall away from her face. "Lie down," she said. She could hear her own voice, tight and mean. Holly tried to climb off the bed.

Alice's mind darkened. She dropped the nappy and grabbed Holly, yelled at her to lie down. "I *am* going to change your nappy. You won't get away from me. You have to have a nappy on! You have to!"

Holly began to cry and twist her body away, trying to escape Alice's hands. Alice held on tighter. Too tight. Holly cried harder and they began to struggle. Holly's strength, her determination to get away, amazed and angered Alice. She pushed Holly over, onto her back.

Holly contorted her whole body in an effort to get away, arching her back and screaming with rage. But Alice was bigger. She was stronger. Holly couldn't get away from her. In the end, Alice had to win.

She held both of Holly's ankles in one hand, lifted her lower body and pushed the dry nappy under her, then let her down on to it. Holly's body went into spasm, a contortion of fury and resistance, her back arched, her legs rigid and twisted. She screamed with rage, her face purple.

Something suddenly hit Alice. She sat down on the edge of the bed, stunned and sick. She saw Holly's little, baby body all twisted and heard the sounds she was making and knew what it meant.

❦

She was crying, a tight, inward sort of crying, hard dry shuddering breaths, eyes hot but dry. She couldn't see Ruth's face.

"What hit you, Alice?"

"I thought . . . *Rape . . . This is like a rape*. It didn't matter how long or how hard she fought, I'd get her in the end. I was so much bigger and stronger than she was. I had to win. Because I was the adult."

❦

As soon as she saw it, she caught Holly up and held her. She sat on the bed and rocked backwards and forwards, holding Holly, both of them crying.

"Oh I'm sorry, I'm sorry, I'm so sorry," Alice whispered, over and over again, long after Holly had fallen asleep, still shuddering sometimes, against her shoulder.

Alice's mind tried to slam shut. She felt a deep inner shrinking, a revulsion, against what she had seen. She felt herself grow smaller and tighter inside, a core withdrawal even from her own self. In that flash of insight she had become Holly. What she saw and felt had been herself.

No, she told herself, *no*.

She wanted to get up and pour herself a drink but she didn't because she had a stronger need to hold Holly until her sobs had died away. She lay down and pulled the quilt over both of them, Holly's body curling into hers. Alice stared over her daughter's head. She felt sick. Her body heaved and her mind convulsed, resisting a stream of images building up behind her eyes. That baby body, the large hands closing around it.

"No!" she called, out loud, startling Holly awake.

"Go back to sleep, Holly, it's OK." She kissed the damp baby forehead. Holly shoved her thumb into her mouth and began to suck. In seconds she was asleep again.

Alice was flooded with a sense of shame, like a tide, washing over her. She moved away from Holly and went to pour herself a glass of gin. She set the bottle down on the floor near the bed, and then sat down beside it. Where she could see Holly, but wasn't touching her. Her back was against the wall, her knees drawn up tight. She watched Holly sleep.

There was something she couldn't hold back, no matter how hard she tried. Like a wall, falling. She tried everything to keep it in place. But as she shut down the impression of baby skin and large hands, another image took its place. She sat very still. She couldn't push this away because it was as clear as if lit by a Tungsten light.

She reasoned with herself. The thing that was pressing on her mind had nothing to do with what had just happened.

You were sixteen then, she reminded herself. There's no comparison. And that was not rape. You asked for it, remember? It was your own fault.

But she thought of Holly at the same time, and she knew.

No. I didn't deserve that. He knew exactly what he was doing. The bastard.

She drank thirstily and refilled the glass. She told herself that if anyone, ever, laid a finger on Holly she would kill him.

I'll kill you, you shit, you prick, you fucker, she shouted in her mind, or maybe out loud, she wasn't sure. I'll kill you.

She was sixteen. Nell's brother, Joe, was getting married. The girl he was marrying looked young to Alice, but in fact she was nearly twenty. During the speeches at the reception there were the usual jokes about dusty bachelors and young brides, but Joe argued back that twelve years was a decent age gap. "She'll have to mind what I say," he said, to loud roars of approval.

Alice sat with Nell, who was heavily pregnant. Her face was swollen and she looked like someone else, but she smiled sleepily at Alice.

"I can't wait for this baby to come," she said, when Alice asked her how she felt. Brendan joked about going straight to the nearest hospital from the wedding and Nell said that would suit her fine. Then Conor came over, fat and red-faced and unsteady on his feet.

"Sit down, Dad," Nell said.

"I'll sit over here." He landed heavily in the chair beside Alice and pulled it close to her. "How's the girl?" he asked.

"Fine, thank you," she said stiffly, not looking at him.

"We haven't seen you for a long time. But we hear all about you." He leered at her, his eyes unfocused. "Let's have a drink."

"I'll get them." Brendan got up and went over to the bar.

Conor's leg pressed against Alice's under the table. She felt his hand stroke the silky material of her dress along her thigh. She pushed her chair back and stood up just as Brendan came back with their drinks. Conor stared at a plate of half-eaten wedding cake on the table in front of him, half-smiling.

"Dance with me, Brendan?" Alice asked.

When they came back to the table a friend of Joe's had joined them. "Dance?" he said to Alice and she nodded, looking over to the next table where Conor now sat, leaning against the chair of a girl Alice didn't know. The girl blushed scarlet and squirmed away from him. Alice was glad to turn her back on them.

"Do I know you?" Joe's friend asked her from under heavy eyelids when they were dancing.

"I'm a sort of friend of the family," she explained.

"I see. And are you, sort of, from around here? I haven't seen you before."

She shook her head. "I'm from Dublin," she said stiffly, embarrassed. She thought he was sneering at her.

"Oh, a city girl. Bright lights and fast cars, or is it women?"

"That's right," she said sweetly. "Bright women and fast cars."

"Oh very smart, that's a good one. Ha ha."

They sat down again. Two more rounds of drinks had arrived while they were gone. Alice drained hers, one after another, thirsty in the smoky air.

"I'll get you another," he offered. "What are you having?"

"Gin and tonic, thanks." She wished she had some speed with her. The line she'd done before leaving the house had worn off long ago.

"You drink too much," Nell said, her hands folded on her enormous belly.

"It's a wedding, for God's sake."

"You're too young for gin. I'll be glad when the baby is born and I can get back to normal, mind you," said Nell, placating. "I'm drowning in orange juice."

"Surely one drink wouldn't do you much harm?"

"Ah, if it was as easy as that," said Nell. "What do you think of your man?"

Alice looked over to where he was waiting at the bar, talking to another man, laughing. His thick hair fell over his dark face and the suit he wore was elegant, the white shirt byronic and frothy over his cummerbund.

"Weird clothes," she said. "But he's good-looking."

"The dress looks good on you." Nell stroked Alice's arm.

Alice wore a long green silky dress that Nell had given her for her sixteenth birthday, three weeks earlier. She'd never worn anything like it before. She liked the way it felt, cool and smooth against her skin. Her collar bones jutted above the neckline like wings

and the sleeves fell in folds across her wrists, covering
her hands.

"Does it? Thanks a million, Nell."

"You look . . . you're very thin."

"You think everyone's skinny as a rail these days."

"True, I suppose. I feel so bloated." Nell looked
over at the bar again. Joe's friend was heading back
towards them with a tray of drinks in his hands.

"You'd want to watch yourself with him." She
leaned towards Alice. "He has a reputation." She
narrowed her eyes. "Be careful," she hissed and
straightened up again as he put the tray down on the
table.

"Here we are," he announced. "And a double for
yourself," he handed Alice a glass.

"Thanks."

They danced again. Alice thought about what Nell
had said. A reputation? She wondered what she meant.
It sounded like the kind of thing her mother would say.
Why should she take Nell seriously? Nell's life was so
safe, so ordered. Carefully contained. As if she had
jumped straight from her middle teens to middle age.
What did Nell know about real life, about Alice?
Nothing. She let him dance her into a corner and kiss
her. To hell with Nell's warnings. She kissed him back.

"Do you want to go somewhere?" he asked, leaning
against her.

She laughed. "I'm here with my mother," she told
him. "We'll be leaving soon and driving back to town."

"Here with your mother! You're a laugh a minute,
do you know that?"

She glared at him.

"I'm coming up to town next week," he said. "On Friday. There's a party on, in a club. Do you want to come? Or would you have to bring your mother?"

She had to decide quickly. Over his shoulder she could see Nell waving to attract her attention. Elaine stood beside her, frowning in their direction. "Yes, I'll come. Without my mother. I've got to go now. Nell can give you my address."

"I'll pick you up at eight," he called after her.

She half believed he wouldn't turn up, but he did. Her mother was not impressed. "He's far too old for you," she said, cross. "I don't understand why he wants to take you out."

"Thanks a lot," said Alice, drily. "Look, don't worry. Everyone will be there. He's very respectable, you know," placing emphasis on that word, respectable. It carried a lot of weight. Then she clinched it. "He's a friend of Nell's."

When she opened the door she smiled at him and hurried away from the house before her mother had time to change her mind and try to stop her. She'd done it before. Alice had learned to lie and cheat and sneak her way out the door, to climb out her window as a last resort. But tonight she just brazened her way through, all geared up for the night ahead. A line of speed already singed the edges of her brain, she had more carefully wrapped in foil in her bag. Mirror. Blade. Straw. She was all set. She felt lucky. He even had a car. No need to worry about catching the last bus home.

She settled into the passenger seat of his car, eyes tight, mouth dry. "Let's go," she said, "I'm dying for a drink. A long cold gin and tonic."

"A girl after my own heart." He grinned at her and revved his engine, taking off suddenly, like a rocket, up the narrow streets and in towards town.

Alice laughed. "God," she said, "I love speed."

"Is that right?"

The party he brought her to was a blur of noise and faces and movement. All the men wore dickie bows and the women were in long dresses. She was glad she'd worn the dress Nell gave her, even though he'd seen it before. She couldn't have come here in jeans and a sweater, they wouldn't have let her in.

After a few hours she began to falter. The speed was wearing off and none of her friends were there. She had known they wouldn't be, but it had sounded so good when she said it to her mother that she'd ended up half believing it herself.

She excused herself from the table they were sitting at with his friends and went in to the toilet. She locked the door, unwrapped the silver foil from her bag and checked the contents. There was enough for two good lines, maybe more. She funnelled the speed onto the tiny Biba mirror she always carried, not to check her face but for this slow sift and mix with the blade, cutting and crushing the powder until it was as smooth and fine as talc. She shaped two fat lines on its surface.

May as well be generous with yourself tonight.

She leaned over and put the short section of straw into her right nostril, holding the left closed with her finger, and inhaled deeply. A few short sharp snorts, then the same on the other side until there were only tiny particles of fine white powder left on the mirror. She picked them up on the tip of her index finger like grains of sugar, and put it in her mouth, licking it clean. Then she licked the mirror too for good measure.

Waste not, want not.

She was ready for anything now, even going back to the dreary conversation about mortgages she had just left. She knew nothing, and cared less, about mortgages, but they seemed to be a hot topic at this party. She strode out of the toilet, blood singing, and let the door slam behind her. People looked around but she didn't care. Let them look, she was strong, alive, her blood was singing.

"Go to hell," she said chattily to a middle-aged man with a bald head and a hairy face who frowned at her. The combination of hair and hairlessness struck her as ridiculous and she started to laugh. She was still laughing as she dropped into the seat beside the man she'd come with.

"Where have you been?" He sounded annoyed.

"Oh, somewhere. Anywhere. I don't remember." She sniffed, rubbed her nose.

He looked at her more closely. "Do you have any more of that?"

"Sorry, no, I finished it."

He shrugged. "Never mind. You were gone a long time. I bought you these."

Three drinks had accumulated in front of her chair. She licked her lips stiffly as the speed began to kick in.

"You're a lifesaver," she told him. "I really need these."

"Lucky I'm more generous than you." He watched her drain the first clear glass and half of the second. "But I'll get you back. Sometime. Drink up and then dance with me."

On the dance floor she realised she was in trouble. Her arms and legs wouldn't work the way she wanted them to and the floor curved away from her. Her stomach heaved and she fought for breath. She stood still, sweating, while the room swayed around her.

"Are you all right?" He took her arm. He held it too tight, but he'd stopped her falling and she was grateful.

"No, I . . . think I need to sit down."

"Come on." He led her back to the bar, put her unfinished drink in front of her. She didn't want it, but she was thirsty. She took a small mouthful but her stomach heaved again, rejecting the sour taste.

"I can't," she said. Then, with an effort, she lifted her head and looked at him. His face was strangely unfocused. "I think I've overdone it. I'd better go home now. I want to lie down."

"Home? What you need is some strong black coffee. Come back to where I'm staying."

"No. I want to go home."

"Listen, if your mother sees you in this state there'll be trouble. You need to sober up."

"I can't. Please. I want to go now."

"OK." He seemed to make a decision. "Come on, I'll take you home."

In the cold, clean air of the night Alice breathed a

little easier, the heat died from her skin, the sweat dried on her face.

"Better?" he asked and she nodded, not able to speak for breathing.

She got into his car and rolled the window all the way down, leaning gratefully against the door, letting her eyes close. The night rushed over her face, lifting her hair as the car moved along. Nothing else seemed real or important, just the cold moving in and out of her with each breath.

"Here we are."

The car had stopped. Alice opened her eyes. Nothing looked familiar. She was confused. She lifted her head. "Where . . . ?"

"This is where I'm staying. "

"You said you'd bring me home."

She knew she sounded petulant. She felt like crying or throwing up, she wasn't sure which. Her body would explode if she didn't lie down soon. Now.

"I know. But listen, you really need some coffee to make you feel better. Then you'll be able to face your mother. How are you going to explain the state you're in if she sees you like this?"

Alice looked at him doubtfully. "I feel sick," she told him.

"I know you do. Come on inside and we'll fix you up."

It seemed stupid to go on arguing when they were already there and she needed a bathroom, fast. She knew she was going to be violently sick, any minute. It would be a relief. She'd got over her childhood fear of vomiting once she'd started drinking. She'd had to.

She let him take her arm and lead her up the steps to the front door. Her legs still didn't work properly. Inside he showed her the bathroom and she went in and locked the door. When she'd finished retching she splashed water on her face and sat for a long time slumped against the cool wall, not wanting to move. But she couldn't stay in there forever. She dragged herself upright and out towards the kitchen where she could hear him, busy with a kettle.

"I'll just be a minute," he said. "Sit down."

She sank into a big old sofa in the sitting-room. She let her head fall against the armrest. If only the room would stop swaying. If only she could rest. If only.

"Coffee."

She opened her eyes. He stood over her, looking down, two steaming mugs in his hands. He looked much bigger, looming over her like that. She tried to sit up but her legs were caught in her dress. She was stuck.

"Stay where you are," he said. "You look wrecked."

He put the mugs down on a low table beside the sofa and came to sit beside her. She moved to make room for him, still trying to sit, but he leaned over and put his mouth over hers. She lay there and let him. His mouth was harsh and intrusive. He pressed his body against hers. It was big, heavy, stifling. When he took his mouth away she struggled to sit up again. Everything made it awkward for her, her drunkenness, the long dress twisted around her legs, his weight. She didn't want to be there. The walls closed in on her, then receded.

"Let me sit up," she said, pushing at him. "It's time for me to go."

"But I'm not finished with you yet."

The words spun coldly straight to her stomach. His face was flushed and set, his eyes cold and strangely empty. She felt as if she'd been punched. Some echo tried to make itself heard, *get out of here* . . .

"I want to go home," she told him thickly, half sitting now, still trying to stand. "Now. I really must."

She broke free of him and was halfway to her feet when he pulled her back down on top of him. Her body fell across his and she felt his erection like a shock, pushing hard into her stomach. His arms were like iron around her back, pressing her against it. He held her there. She was sprawled, half kneeling across him. She looked up at his face and saw his eyes narrowed and his face flushed. He was breathing hard. He held her there and said nothing, pressing her tighter and harder. She felt very small, looking up at him. Young. Stupid. Defenceless. He controlled everything. Including her.

Suddenly she was absolutely sober. She knew exactly what was happening. What was going to happen. Why he had brought her there. She watched it all from somewhere up on the ceiling.

There's no way out of this, a voice inside her warned. It has gone too far. This is a man, an adult. He's determined. He's not going to let you go.

Still, she tried to lift herself free. He moved, suddenly, forward, still holding her, and they both fell to the floor. Her head knocked against the table and the mugs fell over, spilling hot brown fluid on the carpet.

"Silly bitch," he hissed, "look what you've done."

"I want to go home," she said again, "please." But his weight was on her, crushing her. She could hardly breathe, let alone speak. She felt his penis pressing against her as he struggled with her clothes, breathing hard, determined. Angry.

Don't make him angry, the voice advised, you'll only make it worse.

She stared at the ceiling where part of her had gone. She stared back at herself. She saw everything.

Get it over with. Just get it over.

She was as limp as a rag doll as he pulled at her clothes, tugged her dress impatiently out of the way, pushed himself between her legs, straining against her. He tried to push his way inside her, but her body had tightened against him, gone into spasm. Her body didn't care that the voice was telling her to make it easy, get it over . . .

After a while he stopped. Alice wondered if he would let her go now. But instead he told her to go with him to his bed. He held her arms, tight, above the elbows and pulled her to her feet. He held on to her arm and pulled her along behind him. She followed him, in a trance.

At the door to the bedroom she stopped. She saw the shape of it, dim in the half-light from the street light outside the curtains at the window. Outlines of heavy furniture. The dark looming mass of the bed in the centre of the room. It seemed to fill the whole area as she looked and then quickly looked away. A heavy, half-remembered smell caught at the back of her throat and her stomach stirred. She knew that going into that room was an act she would never be able to undo. The stranger in her body gave in to the pressure of his hands and crossed the threshold, not looking at him. Not speaking.

"Come on," he said, his voice quiet now, almost gentle. She was doing what he wanted, acting the part he wanted her to act and he seemed mollified. "I'm going to make love to you here," he said. He was still holding her arm, tightly. Now, at last, he let go.

"Take off your dress," he said.

She did it. She did what he told her to do. She took off the long green dress Nell had given her and let it fall to the floor, her last friend. In a daze she moved to the bed and sat on it, not looking at him. She couldn't bear to look at him. When he made her lie down on the cold, clammy sheets she shut her eyes, shutting him out. Shutting out the streetlight, the outline of the window behind the curtains, a whole world where people were free to move along the streets, to go wherever they wanted. A world beyond her reach. But part of her kept watch from the ceiling. Saw everything.

He was like a battering ram. She was a puppet. A rag doll with floppy limbs and empty head. She did everything he told her to do and she said nothing. It seemed unreal.

When he finished she gathered herself in, tight, and waited for a chance to slide away from him, off the bed. He lay between her and the closed door. She felt his bulk and his restlessness in the dark. His smell caught in the back of her throat.

He began to talk to her, his words bouncing off the walls, coming at her like an echo, hollow and distant. About how he'd known she was hot for him from the beginning.

"I could tell the kind of girl you were as soon as I saw you," he said. "Wild. Ready for anything. It's easy to see you've been around. I like that. It keeps things simple."

Then he lay on her again. She thought it would never end. She had never had a life outside this room. She'd never get away from him. It would go on forever.

After a while he stopped and gave her a cigarette. She took it, not wanting to make him angry again. Her legs throbbed and itched and stung. She was lying in a mess of sticky oozing fluid. She held herself rigid, careful not to let any part of her body touch his. She didn't want to draw attention to herself in case he started again. She smoked quietly, barely moving, staring away from him, wondering how to ask if she could go home so as not to antagonise him, although he seemed calmer now. Home. She didn't know what the word meant. Any place that was not here. She put out the cigarette and opened her mouth to ask him and he covered it, and her, again. One more time.

When he'd finished she saw a faint square of grey behind the curtain. Morning. The night was over. Soon her mother would wake up and find her bed empty, her sheets cold. She sat up.

"It's morning," she told him, flatly. "I'm going

now." She reached for the dress that no longer felt as if it belonged to her and pulled it over her head. He didn't argue. He offered to drive her.

She said, "I'd rather walk."

"Don't be silly." He looked at her speculatively. She couldn't see what he saw in the growing light, and whatever it was, she didn't care.

"You can't walk home like that," he said. "Your dress is torn."

She wondered what he thought might happen, or why she might care. "You don't owe me anything," she said, meaning she wanted nothing more from him, nothing to do with him, but still afraid to make him angry. She didn't want to sit in his car with him again, but it wasn't worth fighting over. She thought nothing would ever be worth fighting over again.

All she cared about was getting home before her mother woke up and realised she wasn't there. She mustn't find out. She must not, ever, know.

She got to her feet and walked out of that room. He followed her. She went in silence to the sitting-room, stepped over the tumbled cups, the spilled ashtray, found her shoes where they had fallen beside the sofa a million years ago. They didn't seem like hers any more than the dress did. But they fit, so she put them on. He watched her, seeming uneasy, but she ignored him and went straight to the door. She couldn't bear to look at him, to see him. She stared straight ahead, not wanting to see any part of herself either. No part of her felt like her. She had only one thought in her mind and that was *out*.

Get out of here.

Neither of them said anything in the car. But when he pulled up outside her house he suddenly said her name. For the first time since the night before she looked directly at him, at his face. Anxious, sweaty, hair damp and sticking to his head. She wondered why she had ever agreed to go out with him. He fiddled with his keys. He said that he was sorry.

"Sorry?" she asked, as if he was speaking a language she couldn't understand. The word didn't carry any meaning.

"It could have been . . . different. I had too much to drink."

She couldn't be bothered answering him.

She got out of the car and closed the door quietly, not wanting to wake anyone up. She didn't watch him leave. The only thing that mattered was that it was broad daylight and she had to get into the house without her mother seeing her.

All her instincts now were for concealment. In through the night locks, Don't wake her up, and up the creaking stairs, No one must ever know, and across the landing, How could you have been so stupid?

She undressed quickly and pulled on a big T-shirt, not looking at the bruises starting on her breasts, the purple marks encircling her arm, the scratches on her legs. She dropped her clothes in a crumpled heap on the floor, knowing she would never wear them again. She went stealthily to the bathroom. It stung when she peed and for the first time she realised that she was bleeding.

She bled sporadically for three days, using pads because she couldn't bear to touch herself, it was too painful, Serves you right. Sitting and walking made the bleeding break out again and she moved around with cautious stiffness long after it stopped.

It never occurred to her to get help, that she had been hurt. All she wanted to do was blot it out. Forever. It was over now and she was a whole lot wiser. Nothing mattered except that no one must ever know.

She wiped it out of her mind.

It wasn't like that. It never happened.

❧

"Why won't you look at me, Alice?"

She shrugged, staring at the floor, her legs folded under her on the chair, her arms wrapped tightly around herself.

"It's hard," she said, her voice still shaking.

"Why?"

"I'm not usually like this. Avoiding people's eyes, I mean. I think it's the things I tell you."

"Did you tell anyone? Then?"

"No."

"Why not?"

"Don't be stupid!" Alice was raging. Her face burned. After a while she admitted, "I told Nell that I'd slept with him. I don't know why, she was being smug and matronly. She'd just had her baby. I wanted to shock her. I pretended that I'd known all along what would happen. I should have. I should have known. I still can't believe how stupid I was. How naïve."

"And that makes it your fault?"

"Yes! No. I don't know." She looked quickly around the room, as if she was getting her bearings, checking the door. "What do you think?"

"What matters is what you think."

"Jesus!" Alice exploded. "You're no fucking help at all."

She stared out the window, her face working, her body tense, ready to spring. "I don't know what to think," she finally managed to say. "Can't you see that? I want you to tell me. I want you to say what it was."

Ruth waited.

Alice breathed deeply. "I think it was rape," she said, eventually. "But every time I think that I swing right back and say, no, it was your own fault, you asked for it. Rape is something else, something that happens in a dark alley, with a stranger wielding a knife or something. I should have known better. I shouldn't have got so drunk, for a start. I did tell Nell, eventually. After I'd remembered it, that night with Holly. Do you know what she said?"

"What?"

"She said . . . we'd both been drinking. She said that she'd always admired me for being such a free spirit, that I did all the things she never had the nerve to do." Alice gestured angrily. "That was news to me. Then she said that now she was disappointed. I was turning out to be just like everyone else in this country after all. Avoiding responsibility, bleating that it wasn't my fault, it was the drink that did it."

Alice reached for a tissue and blew her nose. "Then she said that she was sure that, in my mind, it was rape.

But she knew him and in his it would be completely different."

Alice looked at Ruth. "You see?" she said. "That's true. I know it's true. Oh God, you look angry. Don't be angry, Ruth."

"I'm not angry with you," Ruth said, leaning forward. "Listen to me, Alice. Yes, he probably does see it differently, but isn't that convenient for him? You're the one who was there. You're the only person who knows whether you wanted to have sex with him or not. No one else can know that. No one. Do you understand?"

"But I did so little to help myself."

"Did he ask you? Did he say, do you want this?"

Alice shook her head. She was suffocating. "No," she shouted. Then she sat back, fighting for breath. "No," she repeated. "I told you. I asked him to bring me home. He said he would. I told him I wanted to leave. But then, when I knew what it was, what was going on, I gave up. He seemed so big. I was looking up at him and I suddenly felt like a child."

"Sixteen is not a child."

"No. But that's how I felt. As if I'd shrunk, somehow. Helpless. I can't explain it. And there was that voice, telling me what to do. Telling me to make it easier for myself, not to make him angry. You mustn't make them angry." Her voice was getting smaller, as if it was slipping away from her through a tunnel of years. She sounded like a little girl, even to herself.

"Why not?"

"Because . . . because if you make them angry they only hurt you more."

When she'd managed to subdue the thing that fought its way out of her, she spoke again, not noticing that she had crossed time.

"I tried running away," she said. "I used to hide in the field. Or walk down to the beach, sit in a bus shelter. I'd go as far as I could, but in the end I always went back. I had nowhere to go. I despised myself for being so small and useless. It was like . . . it proved something. That they were right about me. Once I packed my school satchel and headed up the lane towards the road. I was determined that this time I wouldn't go back, no matter what. Nothing, not hunger, or darkness, or anything else, could make me."

"What had happened?" Ruth asked.

"I don't know. I forget."

Her satchel was crammed to bursting with knickers and pyjamas and her teddy bear. The satchel was heavy and it bumped against her leg with every step. But she wouldn't stop. She knew her father was watching from the window. She knew he was laughing at her. It was a big joke to him, he'd already told her that she'd be back, that she wouldn't get far.

She wouldn't let him see her stop to rest or put the satchel down and rub her fingers, even though that was what she wanted to do more than anything. She tried to walk faster, thinking that once she got to the road she'd be all right. But when she got there, her fingers suddenly failed her. They unwound, bloodless, from the strap she was holding. The satchel fell and burst open and everything spilled out onto the pavement, right in front of a crowd of schoolboys who were passing, in black blazers and grey trousers.

"Would you look at yer wan and the holes in those knickers!" one of them called out, a fat boy with red cheeks. The others stared and laughed. Alice was ashamed. She could feel how red her face was getting, redder even than the boy who'd spoken. She knew then that she'd never get away. The same cruel laughter was waiting for her everywhere. She had nowhere to go. And even if she had, she was too small to get there.

She heard a door open behind her. She picked up what she could off the ground and stuffed it back in to the bag, stretched both her arms around it to stop it bursting again. Her whole body felt as if it was on fire as she made herself walk back to the house. Her father stood at the door smiling, watching her every step. She could feel him looking at her, but she didn't look at him.

"And you have no idea why you wanted to run away?" Ruth asked.

Alice shook her head furiously. "No!"

"I think you do."

"No. I can't say . . . I'm not sure."

"Tell me anyway."

"It's mad. It has nothing to do with anything, it's just . . . mad. And I can't say it." Her arms squeezed her sides.

"Try."

Ruth waited until Alice understood that there was nowhere else for this to go. She'd have to say it.

"It's really stupid," she said at last. "It has something to do with that recurring dream I told you about when I first came. Do you remember? I don't know what it was. I was asleep and I wasn't asleep. I can't explain it. It was like a waking nightmare. It played itself out over and over again, I had no control over it. I never remember a time when it wasn't part of my life. It's disgusting. I can't tell you."

"The slave dream?"

Alice twisted her head as far away from Ruth as she could, straining to look out of the window, over the sea of leaves. "Whatever it was."

She coughed, trying to clear the silt from her throat. In the end she gave up and did the best she could to push the heavy words through it. "The man in the dream, the slavemaster . . . He stripped me naked. He lay on me. He . . . covered me in slime. Smothered me with it."

There you've said it.

"The weird thing is, there were other children there too. But they weren't like me."

"I don't follow . . ."

"They were . . . defeated. Helpless. I despised them for . . . You see how impossible this is? If only I could make him see that I was different . . ."

"Who was he, Alice?"

"What?" Alice dragged her eyes around and looked at Ruth's shoes. They were open-toed. Ruth's toenails were square and pink.

"Who was he?"

"I don't know. I swear to you, I don't."

"Who do you *think* it was, then?"

"He was everywhere. I couldn't get away from him. It was a dream but I was awake. I couldn't stop it."

"Alice, *who was he*?"

"No! I've told you! I don't know! I can't . . ." She was rocking herself wildly, fighting to drag air into her collapsing lungs. "It was only a bad dream." She straightened her back, unfolded her legs so that her feet were square on the floor opposite Ruth's and smiled weakly. "A waking nightmare. It can't be real."

"What did you just do?"

"What do you mean?"

"Just then. You shut something down."

"Did I? I don't remember." She laughed nervously. "Don't be angry. I know I did something. But I don't know what. That's the truth."

"I think you know more than you're saying, Alice," Ruth said quietly. "And I'm getting tired of all this evasion. Try giving me a straight answer."

Alice's heart raced. What would she do now? The finality in Ruth's voice scared her. What if Ruth refused to see her again? She was cornered, and she knew it.

"How can I make you see . . . it's so hard," she answered. She sounded distant, as if part of her had gone away. "Just when I think I can grasp something, it evaporates. It's gone. I can see a shadow in the corner of my mind, but when I look directly at it, it disappears. It's . . . if this was a photograph, the thing I'm trying to see would be what lies just outside the frame. Or, something I can't quite bring into focus. The alignment is wrong. It breaks up into fragments. The only way I can hold it there at all, even as a shadow, is by focusing on something close to it. Trying to put words on it . . . that's impossible. Words mean nothing. They have nothing to do with *me*. Remember when I first came? I told you that I felt I'd been abused, but I couldn't remember it clearly, that I remembered nothing. I keep coming back to it, now. I can't avoid it any more. If I was honest, I'd admit that that's what I think this is all about."

She shivered and pulled at the collar of her shirt. Her voice had started to waver again. "But when I say it, I feel as if I'm lying. Because part of me won't believe it. And I hate that feeling. It reminds me . . . there's nothing worse than being a liar. So I avoid saying it. Is there no easier way of doing this?"

Ruth smiled and shook her head.

"I wish there was proof of some kind. Evidence." Alice sighed. "It's like, 'there were no witnesses, yer honour'. So how will I ever prove it?"

"Aren't you forgetting something?"

"What?"

"There was a witness, Alice. You were there."

"But that's just it, I wasn't. I cut myself off from everything so well that I can't get back to it. It's not fair! I'm no closer to knowing now than I was at the beginning. Will I ever know?"

"You'll know."

"How? How, if I can't make this thing stay still long enough for me to get a good look at it? How, if I don't even believe myself?"

"All right. Let's leave abuse aside for a minute. What else could this be about?"

"You mean the nightmare?"

"If that's what you call it."

"Maybe I'm just plain mad. Did that ever occur to you? I mean, there could be a perfectly logical explanation for it."

"Such as?"

"It could be about evil. Hating myself. One of those biblical things, you know, like Jonah and the whale."

She sat back, and closed her eyes. This argument exhausted her. "Didn't Jonah bring bad luck or something? And they had to destroy him? I was like that. I was the one who made it all happen. It was all my fault."

"What was?"

"Hurting myself, too." Alice went on as if Ruth hadn't spoken. She squeezed her eyes more tightly shut. "I was always at myself, then. I couldn't stop it. I rubbed myself until I was raw and . . . sore. Crying with pain."

"Do you mean masturbation?"

Alice shivered. "Yes. I tried so hard not to. I begged for it to stop, but no amount of pain could satisfy me. I couldn't hurt myself enough. It was all," she shrugged helplessly "too big for me." She caught her breath, as if she felt a sudden sharp stab of pain. "Oh."

"There's nothing wrong with it, Alice. It's natural. Every child does it. But." Ruth waited for Alice to look at her before she went on. "If a child is compulsive about it, especially a very young child, it can be a sign of abuse."

Alice shuddered.

"I said it can be. It doesn't have to be."

"I don't want this," Alice whispered. "I don't want any of it. I don't want it to have anything to do with me."

CHAPTER SEVENTEEN

When Holly was five, Alice's control finally snapped.

It happened when she was driving Holly to school. They were late, because Holly had fussed about what clothes to wear, had lost a shoe, and fought Alice over what she'd bring for lunch. Alice was supposed to open the shop and she'd been late twice already that week. Her head throbbed from the previous night's drinking, her tongue was furred, her stomach uneasy.

As soon as they got into the car, Holly announced that she had to go to the toilet.

"Oh, Holly. Can't you wait?"

"No, Mummy, I'm *bursting*."

Alice got out of the car and let her back into the house. She stood at the door and clenched her fist around the keys. They dug into her palm.

Don't lose your temper, she advised herself. She'll be in school in a few minutes and everything will be all right.

But it was a wet morning and the traffic was heavy. Sullen drivers refused to allow other cars to pull out in front of them and Alice got stuck in a side street. She drummed her fingers on the steering wheel. She bit her lip, tapped her left foot on the floor of the car. She blew her horn angrily at a man who cut into the lane in front of her.

To hell with this, she decided. She pulled out,

suddenly, into the main street, in front of a red van. The driver flashed his lights at her, but she ignored him.

She hated being late, it got everything off to a bad start. This was the kind of morning when things were bound to go wrong. The processor would break down, the shutter would jam on the camera for the most obnoxious, impatient client. She knew it. All she wanted was to go back home and crawl into bed. She hoped she wouldn't forget anything important. She hoped she didn't smell of drink. Lately she'd begun to notice that Holly turned her head away when she kissed her at night. She knew why, although they didn't talk about it.

When she looked, briefly, into her rear view mirror, she saw that Holly had unfastened her safety belt and was standing up on the back seat, looking out the window, waving at the van behind them.

"Holly! What are you doing? Sit down."

"No, I don't want to."

"You must."

Holly ignored her and leaned her elbows on the back window. Alice reached back and tried to grab her, but Holly moved easily out of her reach.

"Holly! Sit down at once!"

Alice reached for her again and Holly bent away from her.

"I don't have time for this, Holly, I'm warning you. Sit down. It's not safe to stand on the seat like that. I've told you a million times."

"No."

"Suit yourself," Alice said, biting her teeth in fury. "You'll see."

She drove right up to the car in front of her and stayed close on its bumper, cursing under her breath. "Get out of my way, I'm in a hurry."

She looked in her mirror. Holly had turned around, was facing forwards, still standing.

"Sit down," Alice warned and swung the car suddenly around a corner, turning left. Holly staggered slightly, fell against the door and laughed.

"Do that again, Mummy. That was fun!"

Right. Now you'll see.

Alice braked, hard.

Holly fell forwards. Her laughing mouth hit off the passenger seat as she crashed between the seats. There was a sudden silence.

Oh, Christ.

Alice tried to find her in the mirror, but couldn't. She pulled over and turned around, afraid of what she might see. "Are you all right?"

Holly began to roar. Alice leaned over the seat and tried to pull her to her feet. Her face was bright red, creased, outraged.

"Are you hurt, Holly?"

Holly went on crying, her face scarlet, tears streaming from her eyes, but Alice could see that she was more shocked than hurt.

"You see? I warned you. Didn't I? Didn't I?"

Holly's eyes accused Alice and made her turn away.

"Now you know what I meant," she said, looking through the windscreen at the traffic and the rain. "Now you see what can happen, if you're not careful. It's up to you. Are you going to sit properly and buckle up, or not?"

Holly, snuffling, sat properly onto the back seat and fastened her safety belt herself.

"Good girl," said Alice, a pulse beating violently in her throat as she moved off from the kerb.

All day her head throbbed.

How could you? she asked herself. What have you done?

She knew it was pure luck that had saved Holly from real injury. She knew that at the moment she'd done it, she hadn't cared. By the time she went to pick Holly up from school, she blamed her hangover for what had happened. For months she'd been telling herself to stop drinking, but so far she hadn't managed it for more than a couple of days at a time.

She drew up a plan of action. She'd tried to stop drinking before, but this time she was determined. If she had managed with speed all those years ago, surely she could do this too.

"We're going to play a game, Holly," she announced that night after they'd eaten an easy dinner, egg and chips. "We're going to pretend we're camping. We'll bring the TV into the bedroom and I'll go to bed straight away and you can sleep in your sleeping bag whenever you're ready."

"Why?" Holly looked doubtful.

"To see what it might be like. If we like it, maybe we can borrow a tent and go camping in the summer." Alice was improvising, but it worked.

"OK," Holly agreed.

Alice took the phone off the hook, had a shower and climbed into bed with a book. She moved the TV into their bedroom so Holly could watch it until she fell asleep. Holly loved TV. Alice brought her a tray with crisps and a cup and a can of coke to keep her amused. Holly couldn't believe her luck.

"Can we do this again tomorrow?" she asked.

"If you like."

Because bed was the only place she did not associate drinking with, Alice knew this would help her break the habit. What she didn't bargain for was being unable to sleep, and the unquenchable thirst she felt. She drank litres of water every night. When she did manage to sleep, she startled awake suddenly, sweating and afraid. Her childhood dream came back to haunt her, the waves chasing her away from some edge she couldn't identify.

Once she was awake, the dream continued playing, as it had when she was a child, as if her mind was a screen condemned to show the same images over and over again, but flickering out when she looked too closely. She lay with her hands bunched into fists, her knees drawn up, sickened by the familiar sequence. She was caught, under the sea bed, her skin coated with slime. A shadowy figure, the slavemaster, loomed over her. She knew there were other children tied beside her, because she could hear them crying, pleading. Babies. She could taste her hatred. And then the storm, the violent tossing, her body crushed and fighting for air . . .

She left the television on until the stations closed, for company. Holly's nightlight still burned in the hall. Holly had grown out of it years before. It was Alice who was afraid of the dark.

For weeks she was irritable, nervous, sleepless. It was a cold day in July when she finally saw how dangerous things were getting. She had just come out of the supermarket. Her hands were weighted with plastic bags. Holly skipped along beside her, holding onto Alice's coat because neither of her hands was free. She was chatting away, telling some interminable story about school.

Alice wasn't listening. She was miles away, although afterwards, when Ruth asked her, she couldn't remember what she was thinking about. Suddenly the cement of the pavement seemed to buckle and heave. The ground swam before her as if in a heat haze, despite the cold. Cracks appeared in the sky. Alice stopped dead, her heart pounding with terror. Panic flooded her body. She couldn't breathe. Something swelled and pressed at her throat, her chest, her diaphragm. Her pulse was so violent that she felt as if it would break loose, that her body would fly into a million separate pieces.

She struggled for air, wondering wildly if there was an earthquake. But no one around her was paying any attention. Breathing hard, she looked more closely at the scene and saw that everything had subsided. The ground no longer heaved, the sky had closed over. She had no idea where she was or how she got there.

Holly tugged at her coat. "Come on, Mummy. I'm cold. Let's go."

Alice looked at the small figure in the bright pink coat, the wiry black hair, the round face tilted up to hers, cross. It took a minute for her to recognise who this child was. Holly tugged again. "Come on."

Alice smiled a tight smile and let her daughter lead her along the street. As they walked she began to remember, to piece together information. Bags. Shopping. Supermarket. Street. The sea was beside her, quiet and distant. Each familiar shop reassured Alice, restored her to a sense of where she was, where she was going.

They passed the station and the yacht club. There was Kate's shop on the corner, and then they turned away from the main road. Alice couldn't face going in to see Kate, making conversation. She still felt raw, shaky and uncertain. She didn't understand what had happened to her, or know if it would happen again.

She was relieved when they got home, down the steps and in through the front door. She felt warmed as they came in and she was able to draw the curtains, light the lamps and the fire. Even though it was July, the air felt like winter.

She gave Holly a packet of crisps and let her watch her favourite video. She lit a cigarette and stood in the kitchen waiting for the kettle to boil so that she could make hot chocolate for Holly, tea for herself. She stared at the wall, wondering what had just happened to her.

"Mummy?" called Holly from the next room.

"Yes?"

"Are you OK?"

"Mmmm."

"Will you come and watch with me?"

"All right."

She finished her cigarette and made the drinks, then curled up on the sofa beside Holly. They leaned into each other and stared at the screen, Holly enraptured. Alice was oblivious to what they were watching. She thought about what had happened. What if it happened again, and she was driving, with Holly in the car? She knew she had to do something. She couldn't ignore this any more.

⚭

"I can be in the most mundane circumstances," she explained to Ruth at their first session, "and suddenly I can't breathe, my heart is racing, I'm afraid I'm going to die. It's weird."

"What you're describing sounds like a panic attack," Ruth told her. "Do you have any idea why it happened, that first time?"

"No."

"Do you remember what you were thinking about?"

"No."

"Well, is there any possible explanation?"

Alice pulled cigarettes and matches out of her pocket.

"It would be better if you didn't smoke," said Ruth.

"Oh. Sorry."

"It's a distraction."

Alice shuffled her feet, then drew her legs up under her in the deep, comfortable armchair across from Ruth. "I recently stopped drinking," she offered, when she'd settled herself to her satisfaction.

"I see. Did you drink a lot?"

Alice laughed.

"Are you an alcoholic?" Ruth asked, as if it was the most natural question in the world, like asking, Do you take sugar in your tea?

"I didn't go to AA or anything like that, if that's what you mean."

"That's not what I asked."

Alice looked at the door. It seemed very far away. She pulled at the baggy sweater she was wearing in spite of the heat. Summer was over, Holly had gone back to school and the sun had, finally, come out. So that even the evenings were warm and clammy.

Alice perched on the edge of the old brown armchair, resisting the urge to fall back into its depths. Ruth sat into an identical chair across the hearth.

Alice's fingers tugged at her sweater, then flew together and locked in her lap. Her knuckles whitened.

"You remind me of a teacher I once had," she said.

"What did she teach?"

"Music. I liked her. She was . . . important to me. For a while." She stopped, knowing she sounded manic.

"How did you come to me?" Ruth asked.

"I heard you on the radio, months ago. It was a chat show, do you remember?"

Ruth nodded.

"They were all going on about damaged people. The difficulties of life. The awfulness of it all. And then you said that you didn't know about that. You had a group of people who were just about to finish, to leave you, and you figured the world had better watch out for them, that it wouldn't know what hit it once they let loose. You said they were dangerous, but you meant it in a good way. That's what I heard, anyway." She looked quickly at Ruth for confirmation and saw her smile, remembering.

"That's what I want. I want you to make me dangerous. I want to be dangerous."

Ruth laughed. Her bracelets fell against each other.
"I see. And are you not?"

"No. God, you must be joking! If I was, do you
think I'd be here?"

"What are you then?"

"I don't know. Nothing much."

"I doubt that, Alice."

"How would you know? You've only just met me."

"Why don't you tell me, then."

"Tell you what?'

"Tell me about yourself. Why you've come."

"Um. I don't know really. Yes, I do. It's just . . .
hard to say, you know? I suppose I should have
thought about what I'd say before I came." She
laughed nervously and looked away, hating herself.
She had thought of little else ever since she had made
this appointment. Rehearsed it over and over again in
different ways. But now that it came down to it she
found herself totally unprepared, blank. All she could
think was: *help*. She made herself look at the woman
who sat over in the other chair, who looked steadily
back at her but said nothing. Alice had to look away.

"Go on," suggested Ruth.

"Don't you want to ask me questions or something?"

"No."

"It would be easier if I'd something to answer."

"You're doing fine."

"What about time? Your next appointment?"

Ruth smiled, not looking at her watch. "You have
plenty of time. But, if you like, you could start by telling
me what your life was like when you were a child."

Alice frowned, puzzled.

"I don't know," she said eventually.

PART THREE

CHAPTER EIGHTEEN

Afterwards, Alice could remember little about that first session except the peculiar, thick quality of the many silences.

She remembered staring at a box of man-size tissues on the floor beside her chair and wondering what she was doing there. The tissues and the silences seemed unbearable. Naked. She remembered wondering what would happen if she suddenly screamed. She imagined her throat opening, the shattered silence, the jangling air, scattered dust. But still, she thought, this woman would sit and watch her. She'd say nothing, do nothing to intervene. And what then? She thought about shards of glass.

"Glass," she said. As much to get it off her mind as for any other reason, because by then she could think of nothing else to say and the silence was embarrassing her.

"I'm sorry?"

"Glass. I feel as if I live behind a thick wall of mirrored glass. A barrier between me and . . . everything. But no one knows it's there except me. I'm like a cylinder. The surface is smooth and hard, it reflects back to people whatever they want to see. But inside . . ."

"Yes?"

"Inside, it's completely hollow. A vacuum." She cleared her throat. "There's no one there."

She stopped talking and stared, unseeing, out the window. She sensed Ruth's look, but she held herself away from it.

That's enough. You've already said too much.

I wish I'd never come.

"There's someone there, Alice."

"How do you know?"

"There's always someone."

"What if there's not? I'm really afraid that there's no one. Nothing."

Alice let her eyes meet Ruth's. They looked at each other.

"What else do you feel?" Ruth asked.

"Nothing. That's part of the problem. I feel nothing. About anything."

"Numb?"

"No. Numbness is a sensation. Isn't it?"

"Is it?"

"Yeah. You know, that horrible . . . disguise. Like when you're at the dentist's. They give you an anaesthetic with that big horse-needle and it hurts like hell. Then they batter away at your mouth doing horrible things they'd never dare do to you if you could feel enough to stop them. They pretend that nothing unusual is happening while they drill into you, and you're bleeding, and it's all chat about the weather. You're supposed to be grateful, even though your mouth is outraged. Then you go home and you can't feel your face properly, it's not that you can't feel at all, but you don't feel it right. So you bite your cheek by mistake and burn yourself and spill coffee down your chin, out of control, making it all worse. And then it all starts to wear off."

She stopped, surprised to see that her hands were shaking. She wrapped her arms around herself and leaned back into the chair. "I hate that feeling."

"Which feeling?"

"When it starts to wear off. Delayed pain. You know. When you begin to realize the extent of the damage."

"Ah, yes."

Alice smiled at her, encouraged. "It's a cover-up, that 'numbness'. But I suppose it makes it easier for them. Just like it made it easier for me. Makes. Makes it easier for me. At the dentist's, I mean."

"Do you know what it's about?"

"I have an idea. But I don't know if I can say it."

"Try."

"I don't think I can."

Ruth tilted her head and looked straight at Alice. When she had Alice's full attention, she said, "We won't get very far with this if you don't tell me what's on your mind, Alice."

"But it's mad." Alice looked away. "And I might be wrong. I *must* be wrong."

"All right. Look, whatever you say to me in here will never go any further. I promise you that. Why don't we agree that you tell me whatever is in your mind, with the understanding that it's only a possibility, and we'll take it from there. If you're wrong, there's no harm done. It's a place to start, nothing more."

"But I'm afraid."

"Of what?"

The sheer impossibility of answering this clogged Alice's brain, thickened her tongue. Of lying. Of telling the truth. Of being wrong. Of being right. Of being exposed. Of being unheard, disbelieved, rejected. Most of all, of the horrible annihilation that would surely come with the words.

"You've done a lot of work with people who've been, you know, abused?"

"Yes."

"That's it." Alice ducked her head and held herself, waiting for the sky to fall.

"You've been abused?"

"I could be wrong, remember?"

Ruth nodded. Alice could read nothing in her face when she said, "Could you be more specific?"

Alice was shocked that Ruth went on talking as if this was a conversation like any other, that the room was calm, the furniture still in place, her body, despite its trembling, still in one piece. She looked at Ruth's hands. She wore no rings, but heavy bangles circled her wrists.

"I think . . . I may have been abused. When I was a child."

"And who do you think it might have been, who abused you?"

Alice stared at the box of tissues beside her chair.

They suggested tears, but she was light years away from emotion now. She spoke slowly.

"My father?"

Her heart lurched.

"I can't believe this," she said. She pulled the collar of her sweater, suddenly too tight, away from her neck with both hands.

"What can't you believe?"

"Any of it. It's just like a dream. That I'm here. That I said that. That it's possible. It feels . . . unreal. Like something I've made up."

"You think you 'made up' that you were abused?"

"No." Alice was surprised when she heard herself say it.

"No," she repeated, very slowly, testing. Then, "I don't know. There's something, but it's really vague, you know? And slippery. Hard to hold on to. I can't explain it. It's like looking for something you absolutely know you have, but haven't seen for a long time. You *know* you have it, you just can't remember where you left it, and when you go back to look for it, you can't find it. It could even be right under your nose, and you don't recognise it. I'm sorry. I'm not making much sense, am I?"

She didn't want to think about it any more. She stared out the tall window behind Ruth, at an old chestnut tree, rich with leaves, in the rusty glow of streetlights. She could hear nothing, but she saw the leaves move, could imagine the rustle and sigh as they lifted and spread and fell back into place in the wind, some drifting loose towards the ground. She must remember to look for conkers on the way out. Holly was collecting them.

"On the contrary, Alice. I think this is an excellent place for us to start."

Over the next few months, images drifted into her mind and settled there, like falling snow, silent and heavy. Her childhood coming back to her. Her father's glasses, her mother's stiff retreating back on the way to work, the sly curtains that faced the street. Little by little she began to see beyond them. When she recalled Max, glimpses of scenes came with him and slowly she rebuilt chains of events, cause and effect.

When she first told Ruth about the dream that had haunted her, and Ruth asked her what she thought it meant, Alice felt herself shut down tight, as if someone had thrown a series of switches and one by one every vital function stopped. Only her heart kept beating, painfully, behind her ribs. Months passed before she could answer the question.

She couldn't talk about it. All her courage had been spent at their first session. She worked her way around the edges of the dream, spinning off on tangents by talking about Holly, or work, or Nell. Some weeks she barely spoke at all, dragging herself into Ruth's office as if it was her only refuge, falling asleep in the chair.

She was still assailed by panic when she least expected it. In the supermarket, on the street. All of a sudden her heart seemed to stop, her breath was caught in a terrible, strangling grip, her skin thickened and threatened to suffocate her.

❧

"What can I do?" she asked Ruth.

"Just keep breathing."

"You make it sound easy."

❧

Time took on a new quality. Throughout that spring and early summer she lived from one session with Ruth to the next. Nothing that happened in between had any meaning for her. She took Holly on long walks, her backpack loaded with cameras, lenses, filters. When panic struck her, she took out her Rolleiflex and flipped the top up, knowing that what she saw in the viewfinder would calm her, change her perspective. She took pictures almost at random, but she was drawn to stone, slate roofs, walls, rock. The texture of shingle.

She worked automatically, unconsciously. In the darkroom she mixed chemicals, immersed film, checked temperatures, not knowing what images would float up to her in the red light, what she'd tried to capture. When she collected transparencies from the lab she had already forgotten what she'd composed so carefully through her lens.

She revived her interest in old photos of the city. She bought them cheaply from junk stalls and restored them, mounted them in new frames, and sold them. Brian had been right, there was a market for old prints. But what she loved most about them was the texture of stone and brick which she still saw all around her. Cobbles and paving stones, granite walls with vivid purple flowers thriving in the cracks, soft-coloured, graceful brickwork. She put her new photographs beside the restorations and wondered idly what to do with them. The contrasts in the coastline were startling, between the present and the past. Land had been reclaimed, the railway line built, jetties added, the pier extended. The only constants were the sea and the rocks.

She was asked to illustrate a book on local history. She knew she should have been thrilled, but she found it difficult to care. The work pulled her out of a deep inertia whose claim seemed stronger.

She began to shout at Holly and lose her temper for the smallest things, like toys scattered around the floor, or just for talking when Alice wanted to be left alone.

"She's invading my space!" she complained to Ruth. "I can't stand it."

She'd always prided herself on the fact that she never hit Holly.

"I don't have to," she explained, when Ruth asked her. "If people only knew, there's no need. Kids are so easy to control. All you have to do is withdraw from them. I pull away from her. I see myself doing it. I empty my eyes and voice, make everything cold and distant. She'd do anything, then, to get me back. Anything at all. I know exactly how to make her do what I want.

"There are times," she went on, "when I could swear my mother has jumped out of my mouth and is standing right there between us. I don't like it, but it's better than hitting her. I'm afraid, you see, that if I started I wouldn't know how to stop."

"So you shut everything down?"

"Yes."

"And where do you think it goes, your anger?"

"What do you mean? I just told you. I don't get angry. I close it down before it starts."

"Why?"

Alice shook her head. "I don't want to be an angry person."

"I think you already are. An extremely angry woman."

"Well, I'm not."

But she was afraid.

Every night she fought sleep as long as she could and then fell into a nightmare where she was reliving an old chase, her father the predator and herself the prey. Although she ran and tried to hide while he stalked her, she always knew the outcome was inevitable, because it had happened already. She ran and ran and then found herself in her old room, back pressed to the wall. Shrinking. Every time he reached for her, she woke up, trembling violently as if every cell in her body wanted to shake itself free through the pores of her skin. As if the effort of will that held her together in one body couldn't hold her for much longer.

❧

"Why can't I let him touch me and see what happens next?" she complained to Ruth.

"You will when you're ready. You're fighting it."

"No. I'm not."

❧

But she knew she was. Once she'd seen a building being demolished, in a film. It was an old, silent film, in black and white. In silence, the heavy black ball swung towards the wall and struck. For a second, nothing happened and then the whole structure of the building gave way at once. That was what she felt like now. Like the building. The ball was swinging. She waited for the moment of impact, the sudden disintegration. Her foundations were quaking.

She felt as if she was on borrowed time, on the edge of panic. Time was running out and she would never be able to recover the ground that was falling away beneath her feet right then, never mind the ground she'd already lost. Every time she left Holly she was afraid that she would die before she could get back to her and make everything all right. But when she did get back to her, nothing was all right. She wondered if it ever would be.

She had expected that when she'd finally managed to talk to Ruth about the rape, she'd feel relieved. She'd been sure that once she brought the dream out into the open she'd feel safe. But she was wrong. Now that she'd done both, she was gripped by a new terror that refused to let her go.

Liar, liar, pants on fire, the chant invaded her head when she was driving home that day. It sickened her. When she stopped the car, she covered her ears with her hands but that only locked it all in. How could she hide from something that was inside her?

She'd been with Ruth for nine whole months. Instead of feeling better, everything seemed worse, infinitely more terrifying than when she'd started. Soon Holly would get her summer holidays, and how would Alice cope with her now? The past threatened to swallow her up, and where would Holly be then?

That night, she dreamed that she was back in her parents' house. God and her father waited in a thick black cloud that surrounded the house. They were waiting for her. They could afford to be patient, they knew they would get her in the end. It was only a matter of time. She stood at the window, small again.

∞

The window ledge is level with my eyes and I have to stand on tiptoe to see the inky cloud. I watch it pulse and grow and try to think of a way to escape. They laugh inside my head and I know that as fast as I think of a way out they will know and beat me to it. My only hope is to set up such chaos in my mind that even I can't be sure what I'm thinking. I stir up a wild riot of ideas and, hiding under it, I move along in every direction at once, hoping they won't figure out which way I'm going. I know that my only chance is to tell the whole world what's happening, that God is a fraud. Tell all the things they've done to me in one big shout, before they can stop me. If he's exposed everywhere at once there's an outside chance that he'll lose his power before he can destroy me. An outside chance. The only one I have. Heart pounding, I creep in widening circles towards the door. Daring myself to burst through it and run, screaming out the truth for the whole world to hear. Wondering if I have the courage to make a break for it.

When she woke in the morning her heart was racing and her sheets were damp with sweat. She got into the shower and turned the water up as hard and as hot as she could stand it. She wanted to steam the sweat off her skin. It smelled bad to her, fishy. Rotten.

She closed her eyes and let the water fall on her, her mind floating loose with the steam, curling upwards. A heavy June rain fell against the window. The day promised to be a dark one. Alice wanted to stay under the stream of hot water forever.

In the end she had to get out because it was time for Holly to go to school and, anyway, she was dizzy from the heat.

"Your skin's all blotchy," Holly told her.

"It's just a heat rash, from the shower."

"Oh. It's really red."

"Leave me alone, Holly. I want to get dressed."

Her skin felt tight across her face as she drove Holly to school.

No amount of work could still the voices raging inside her. What she had told Ruth about the rape replayed itself over and over again in her mind. What she'd said. What Ruth had said to her.

Something bothered her, there was something wrong, something missing. She couldn't bring herself to talk about it again but, between sessions, she struggled to remember over the clamour of the voice that sneered and accused her of lying.

There was something, about size, about being small ...

She chewed her fingers until the skin was blood-red and flowered, like lace.

One day, when she couldn't bear it any more, she rang Ruth. It was the end of July and Ruth was taking the whole month of August off. She did it every year. She was going away. She'd warned Alice weeks ago, but she'd managed to forget, and waste all those sessions with evasions. Now she measured time and knew that she would surely die if she didn't get to see Ruth again before she left.

The nights got worse. She woke suddenly, her heart pounding, convinced something had woken her. A noise at the window. Someone in her room. The doorbell. She got up to check, but there was no one there. She felt better when Dermot was upstairs even though she never called him. Something was pressing on her mind. She had to see Ruth again before she left, to try and let it out. Had to.

She rang. "Please call me," she told the machine. "I have to talk to you before you go."

Then she rang again. "It's urgent," she pleaded.

That night, she dreamed that she was on a blackened stage. The floor and walls were all dark planes that shifted as she walked, like a three-dimensional maze. When she put one foot in front of her, the ground dipped away from her and the walls around her shifted. She woke up cold and clammy with sweat. She thought about Ruth leaving without returning her call and her stomach turned with rage.

Tense and sleepless, she tossed restlessly in bed and muttered angrily, full of the knowledge that Ruth had gone beyond her reach, couldn't hear what it was that Alice wanted to tell her. Alice didn't know, exactly, what she wanted to say. But she believed that if Ruth would listen, would look, she'd see what it was that Alice wanted to show her. Then she could explain it all back to her, taking the terror out of it. Alice raged and fumed. But Ruth was gone. She didn't give a shit. She never had.

In the dim light from the nightlight, she could see the outline of the books beside her bed but she knew they couldn't help her anymore. Her mind had closed, it was in a spasm that not even reading could relax.

She stared at her arm, fist balled and tense on the pillow as if wanting to strike, or holding itself as tightly shut as possible. Her cheek rested on her upper arm. Neither seemed real. She turned her head and opened her mouth, slowly, as if compelled against her will. She took her skin into her mouth, then began to rock and suck, dreamily, like a small child, reality falling away from her as her mouth filled with the taste of salt.

CHAPTER NINETEEN

In the morning she was shocked when she saw her ravaged skin.

She could barely understand that she had done this to herself, but knew that she had. She got up and got dressed, pulling on an extra sweater, her favourite, the one with sleeves long enough to cover her hands, so that Holly wouldn't ask questions. How could she possibly explain the tracks of scratches down her arms as if she had fought her way through brambles, those angry purple rings on the insides of her shoulders?

She could barely hold herself upright. After an hour she said, "I'm going back to bed, Holly, I think I might be getting flu. You can watch videos all day if you like. OK?"

"You mean, even *The Little Mermaid*?" Holly followed her into the bedroom and watched her get into bed, fully dressed.

Alice winced. She'd banned that one for a week, she was so sick of it. "OK." She shut her eyes.

"And *Cinderella*?"

"If you must."

"And can I have crisps?"

"Help yourself." Exhausted, Alice turned her back

on Holly, the quilt pulled high around her neck. "I'm going to sleep now."

But she didn't sleep. She stared at the wall beside her bed. In the corner near the door the plaster was coming loose.

That's a sign of damp, she told herself, looking for something to think about. But she couldn't focus on the problem. She lay there and waited for the phone to ring. When it did, two hours later, she was jolted out of a numb trance that was close to sleep. It was the mother of Holly's friend Mary, wanting to know if she could play the next day.

"Yes," said Alice shortly, not bothering to ask Holly what she wanted. "She'd love to. The whole day? Great. Thanks."

Then she went back to staring at the wall. It seemed to waver. Alice thought she could make out a dim shape moving behind it. She watched, sickened, as the outline shifted.

This is it, she thought. I'm going insane. Why doesn't she ring me?

She dragged her nails along the bruises on her arms. It made her angry that she felt no pain.

When the phone rang again, she startled and her heart pounded.

Her hands shook as she picked up the receiver.

"Hello?"

"Alice? This is Ruth."

"Oh, God."

Now that it came to it, she could say nothing. She had been staring at the wall for so long, oblivious to everything except the obsessive thought of Ruth leaving, that she couldn't think what to say. Her brain froze, numb.

"What's going on?"

"I need to see you."

"Alice, you know that's not possible. I'm going away tomorrow."

"But I have to talk to you."

"Well, talk to me now."

"I can't. Not like this. Why didn't you get back to me sooner? I've been desperate, Ruth." Her voice wavered.

"Has something happened?"

Alice swallowed, hesitated.

"It's about the rape. I want to tell you something."

Then it was as if some barrier in her brain lifted and words came pouring out in an unexpected torrent.

"It's just . . . it's been on my mind and I need to talk to you and you're going away . . ." She could hear her own voice getting smaller and younger as if it was moving into a tunnel, accelerating away from her.

A weight shifted from the centre of her chest and suddenly she was crying. It was a relief. Like the relief of finally letting something that was too heavy to carry slip from her numbed fingers.

"It's like . . . I'm trying to tell you something and you won't listen, you don't want to hear it. You're going to leave me here alone with him, please don't . . ." Her mouth was loose, trembling, she was small and damp and redfaced. She shivered. "Don't leave me with him. Listen to me!"

She stopped, shocked. She crossed a wide stretch of time to say, "I didn't know I was going to say that."

There was wonder in her voice, in her mind. Something had broken down and she was left with this knowledge, of being left, abandoned, despite her pleas, her efforts to tell . . .

"Alice? You do realise you're not saying all of this to me?"

"Yes. I mean, I'm not saying *all* of it to you. But you should have rung me sooner. You don't care!"

"You know that's not true."

Alice struggled for breath. "I wish you'd be there when I need you." Her voice cracked again. "I know this isn't all aimed at you. I mean, I know you can't be there all the time. It's just because you're going . . . I'm scared, Ruth."

She hesitated, then went on: "I feel as if I'm talking to you on about seven different levels, here."

"I can hear all seven of you."

Alice could tell by her voice that Ruth was smiling, and she smiled too.

"Most of us love you, you know. We'll miss you."

"Look, I'll only be gone for four weeks. You'll be fine. You don't need me."

"Oh yes I do."

"You don't, Alice. You can do it for yourself. Take it easy. And remember, whatever it is, it's already happened. The worst is over."

"That's easy for you to say."

"It's true. I'll see you when I get back. OK?"

"OK. Have a lovely time. Don't forget the sunscreen."

When she hung up Alice was still shaken, but she felt lighter. It scared her sometimes that it was so easy for Ruth to bring her back to life. It took so little: a word, a look, a tone of voice. She knew she was fiercely dependent on Ruth and it terrified her. She had fallen in love with the sound of Ruth's voice saying her name, *Alice*, with no blame attached. But now she had gone away. Leaving Alice to cope.

She is as cold and smooth as glass, but she shows nothing. There is nothing for me to hold on to. She slips out of my hands like water when I try to touch her. She is always leaving, on her way out, turning away. She walks as if she has made up her mind already, knows where she is going. Never towards, always away from, me. I watch her go, numb. Through the window she doesn't hear what I try to tell her, already she's too far away. She doesn't look back.

They drove down to the Corrib to stay with Nell, as they'd done every summer and Easter of Holly's life. How long they stayed depended on how much time Alice could afford to take off work. This time she knew it made no difference where she was, she'd get nothing done anyway. But she brought her cameras, in case some miracle happened and her sleeping eye woke up.

Holly loved it at Nell's. She loved the space and the freedom. Nell's youngest daughter, Jenny, was only a year older than her and they got on well together. When they arrived, Holly was shy and stayed close to Alice, but by the end of the first day she was gone and Alice hardly saw her again except at meal times.

Alice took root in the kitchen and did all the things she never did at home. She baked and ironed and made stews and casseroles without complaint. She even enjoyed it. Nell's house was always busy with people coming and going, children's parties, parish fêtes. Alice enjoyed Nell's life from the outside, although she was glad she didn't live it. But she wanted Holly to be part of it, to have the chance to share some kind of family life.

This year everything irritated her. Local gossip bored her to screaming point. She kept checking on Holly, anxious to know where she was, what she was doing.

"What's the matter with you?" Nell asked one night, when the children were in bed and Brendan had gone out.

"I don't know," Alice lied. "I'm just edgy. I'm tired."

"You look terrible."

"I feel terrible."

"Have you seen a doctor?"

"No. Well, not exactly." She gathered her courage. "I'm seeing someone, though. A therapist."

"Oh."

"I've been going to her for nearly a year."

"That long? And you never told me." Nell looked hurt. "Am I allowed to ask why?"

Alice stood up and walked around her chair. She put her hands on the back of it, pulled at the antimacassar, straightened it and smoothed it with her palms.

"OK," she said, as much to herself as to Nell. "I'll tell you."

She wished she'd prepared herself for this. Words slid away from her. She didn't know what to say or how to say it.

"It's about when I was a kid. You know how miserable I was, Nell . . ."

"Oh, here we go again. More of this 'my mother didn't love me' nonsense. Alice, you know my opinion there."

"Only too well. But, Nell, there's more to it than that. There was so much . . . weirdness. I thought I was mad. And other things. Now I know it's more than that."

"More than 'mad'?"

Alice nodded and swallowed. Her hands gripped the chair. "I think . . . I was abused when I was little, Nell." Her voice was distant and quiet and very, very small.

"What? What are you talking about?"

"I was," Alice hunted for words, "molested."

"Oh." Nell studied her nails, her face rigid.

Alice rushed on, trying to get it out before her courage ran out.

"It's like . . . I knew, and didn't know, what it was. I

didn't know there was a name for it, but something was badly wrong. Everyone acted as if there was nothing going on, nothing wrong, but I knew. I had to pretend not to. I cut it off, but sometimes it'd break through the surface and that's when I thought I was mad . . . I'm not explaining it very well, am I?"

Nell made a vague sound that could have meant anything.

"Do you remember when I came to stay with you at your parents' house, that first time?" Alice asked.

Nell stood up suddenly, and faced her. "Yes, I remember. You were such a needy little thing, with your cute blonde hair and your big eyes, following people around, begging everyone to love you. And they did, Alice. They fussed over you and petted you and spoiled you. I remember it very well. So, what's this about?"

Alice felt a rush of blood to her face and then her body went absolutely cold.

"That's what it's about," she said, through stiff lips. "You asked, and I told you. I'm going to bed now."

She left the room without waiting for an answer. She knew she wouldn't get one.

"The next day," she told Ruth at their first session in September, "it was as if that conversation never happened. We stayed a few more days. On the surface everything was fine. But I couldn't wait to get out of there. The awful thing is, I know she's right. In some ways I was a really seductive little kid."

"You mean affectionate."

"No. I mean seductive."

"And how do you think you learned that?"

"I was born that way."

"No, Alice. Little girls are not born seductive."

Alice fidgeted while she considered this. She looked around the room. There was a painting on the wall beside Ruth, but the autumn light shone on the glass so that no matter how hard Alice stared, she couldn't see what was behind it. She bit her trembling lip.

"There's something I have to say, Ruth. And I don't want to say it."

"What is it?" Ruth sounded indulgent.

Alice glared at her. "Don't patronise me!" she snapped. "This isn't easy, you know. Do you think it's easy?"

"I never said that."

"You don't have to. It's the way you look. So . . . tolerant, sometimes."

"What do you want to say, Alice?"

"It's as if this is some kind of game to you."

Ruth straightened.

"No, that's not it. It's more . . ."

"If you don't tell me, Alice, I don't know what you're trying to say."

"It just feels so fucking dangerous. You know?"

"What does?"

"This. You."

"I feel dangerous?"

"Yes."

267

"Why?"

"Because I feel so . . . open. To you. Vulnerable. It's an almost sexual feeling. You could do anything with me." She hung her head, miserable. She wished her hair was long so she could hide behind it. She felt soiled and ashamed.

"Alice. I can promise you that's not going to happen. I'm not playing games with you, and I don't want anything from you."

"But you could, don't you see? That's your choice, not mine. When you went away I felt this, so strongly. I was desperate. I'd do anything to make you stay. And then I realised that I would take whatever I could get from you." She pressed her hands to her mouth, fighting nausea. "No matter what it was." That couldn't be her voice, could it, practically begging Ruth not to hurt her?

When the nausea subsided, she told Ruth what she had done to herself the night before the phone call.

"I feel so stupid," she said. "I couldn't help it. I had completely forgotten, but it's something I used to do when I was small."

All the time, she remembered, shocked.

"Do you know why you did it now?"

Alice twisted the cuffs of her jumper around her fingers and picked at a loose thread. "I wanted to make you see that there was something wrong. I wanted you to notice. And I knew you wouldn't. It would make no difference. It was rage, then, I think. And spite. I thought I'd make you sorry." She laughed bitterly. "Some hope."

"What do you mean?"

Alice scowled at her. "Well, you didn't even see it, did you? I mean, I had to tell you about it. It's pathetic. I'm sorry."

Ruth shrugged. "Why are you apologising to me? The only person you hurt was yourself. That's what self-mutilation is."

Alice stared at her, shocked. "Self-mutilation? What are you talking about?"

"I'm talking about what you did, Alice."

"That's not . . . Christ, you don't think . . . Look, this was something different. It was only *me*. Mutilation, that's with blades and things. People cutting themselves. I don't, didn't, use anything. There's a difference."

"Oh?"

"You know there is."

"In what way?"

Alice glared, furious. "I didn't cut myself, or anything. I'm not one of those . . . "

"I see." Ruth leaned forwards. Her eyes found Alice's and held them. "Well, you just go home and ask Holly what she thinks about the fact that you bite yourself and draw blood, that you bruise yourself, scratch yourself, make marks on your arms and legs. Ask her if she thinks that's OK . . . what is it, Alice?"

A spasm of pain ripped through Alice's belly. She bent double in her chair. "Holly."

She tried to pull away from the impact of Ruth's words but she couldn't. Because suddenly, she saw herself, Holly's age. And younger. And, strangely, on into her teens. Wandering through a fog of silence and locked doors. She saw the old steam pipe in the bathroom. The one she used to hold herself against, raising red weals on her legs. Furious that she couldn't stay there long enough to scorch and sear something slimy and horrible from her skin . . .

I wear a swimsuit in the bath. I don't want them to see me naked. Their cold eyes burn like the scalding water I loosen to my reddening skin, hungry for pain.

I lie down into too-hot water. I have to make myself. There's a knack to it. I get in early, when the bath is still filling with hot and cold water, then turn off the cold, leaving the hot to stream in alone more slowly. Little by little, I can stand the growing heat, until the scalding water falls directly onto my lifted legs. They sting when I force them to the burning metal. The tap-mouth spits directly where I need to scald and scour.

Then I lie back, dizzy with heat, and feel my skin soften and loosen. I could peel myself like fruit now, like an orange, in one unwinding curl. As I swell up I get softer. I drag my nails deep across the surface of my thighs and upper arms, then in under the bathing suit, scraping off strips of skin in the hidden places where the welts will not be seen. By anyone. Not even me. I never look at them again when I am finished and dressed. I know they're there. That's enough.

Like the bites and bruises I give myself, secret gifts.

Between baths, I keep the scarring going. I bring my mouth secretly to my soft upper arm. My lips fasten on the skin. I lift it between my teeth, probe it with my tongue and then work it slowly, dreamily, suck it, pull it deeper into my mouth. The edges of this circle slide across my teeth. I rock and lull myself with the hypnotic pulse of my sucking: gather, loosen, gather; in, out, in, like a breath, slow and rhythmic, like a tide, deeper and deeper. I taste salt as the blood floods in pools under my skin, and the bruise begins. My skin bruises and softens like something rotten before it tears. Then I pull away, the taste of freed blood briny and shocking in my mouth. I do this over and over, rocking, on my upper arms and the soft skin of my shoulder, wherever my mouth can reach that will be hidden by my clothes. A secret cannibal, self-devouring.

They have to stay hidden, these dark bruises, but I like to know that they're there. They prove something, but I don't know what. When they fade, I replace them. They satisfy a need in me that I don't understand or question.

What I most want, and am most afraid of, is that someone else will see. No one must ever see.

Why don't they see?

The anger of my body.

❧

She rocked herself, quietly. "I did it all the time," she told Ruth unevenly. "If Holly . . . I'd know, straight away. I'd want to know why. Why did nobody see? Why did nobody wonder what the hell was going on?"

Every cell in her body was vibrating wildly.

"Just let that trembling happen, Alice, it's OK."

When it was over, she felt completely drained. "I could sleep for a week," she said.

CHAPTER TWENTY

"My parents want to take the kids to the Zoo," Kate said, one Saturday in November. "Let's go for a walk." It was a cold day, but bright and clear. A rare winter sun was shining.

"OK. Where will we go?"

They went through the list, the usual places. The pier. Killiney Hill. Bray Head. Cabinteely Park. The train over to Howth. Finally Kate said, "I know, have you ever been to the South Bull?"

"No."

"Treat in store. It's down near the Pigeon House. Can we go in your car? It's hard to get to otherwise."

Kate rode a bike. On principle, she said. But she only lived three streets away from her shop. She was quick enough to take a lift whenever she needed one.

They set off. It was a cold, clear day. They drove towards town and turned off before Irishtown, then turned again, away from the Tollbridge. "I've never been down here before," said Alice.

The road was deserted. Large buildings loomed silently beside them and litter blew along the road.

"It's like a film set," Alice said uneasily. The lack of traffic and people was bizarre. "It's as if something's happened and everyone knows about it except us."

"That's what I like about it," said Kate. "Hardly anyone ever comes here. If you meet five other people, it's a crowd."

They passed a bus stop. "I can't imagine a bus coming down here," said Alice.

Then they could see the pier. Alice recognised its outline at once. "So this is what you were talking about. Of course I've seen it. I just didn't know it was a pier."

"There's a swimming club half way down," said Kate, irrelevantly. There was a small red car parked in front of them.

"Someone else is here," said Alice, relieved. But when she drove past it to park, she saw that there was a man sitting in there alone, staring at the water. He turned his head and watched them, his face expressionless.

"Are you sure this is OK?" she said nervously to Kate.

"What do you mean, OK?"

"Nothing."

They began to walk on the large, separate slabs of stone that made up the pier. The sea beside them was a cold grey colour, sullen. It rocked and slapped against the stone, white curls of foam breaking the surface. Alice looked back. The car was still there, but there was no sign of the man. She wondered what he was doing. If he was still there. Or if he'd gone off to get his friends. She told herself not to be ridiculous. "How did you find out about this place?"

"Mark used to bring me here. Jake loved it when he was a toddler, it's more exciting than Dun Laoghaire. It used to make me nervous then, in case he'd fall in. But I could see the attraction."

"It makes me nervous now." Alice shivered and looked back again. The car was gone. Her throat tightened. The narrow strip of rock under them and the lowering sky and the cold sea . . . anyone could see them for miles around. Anyone had time to watch them and decide to come down . . . there was nowhere to run to. She stopped.

"What's wrong?" Kate looked back at her.

"I can't do this. I hate it. I'm going back."

"What? OK." Kate shrugged and turned back after her. "Why don't you like it?"

Alice walked furiously, her arms swinging. The sky seemed to lean closer. She moved faster. Kate stopped trying to keep up with her. When she was near the car again Alice broke into a run.

"Alice, what's the matter with you?" Kate called. "Why are you being so weird?"

Alice struggled with the keys. "Come on!" she shouted at the car. She tugged at the door and slid quickly into the seat as if something was behind her. She leaned over quickly to open Kate's door and then waited, gripping the wheel, as Kate got in, puzzled. As soon as the car began to move Alice calmed down, embarrassed.

"Let's go for coffee somewhere," she suggested.

"What was all that about?" Kate demanded when they were settled in a small café. Kate was having orange juice. A mug of coffee steamed in front of Alice.

"Don't you ever get nervous out there?" she asked, lifting packets of brown and white sugar out of a white bowl on the table.

"No. Are you going to use all of those?"

Alice put them back. Then picked one out again and began to fold it into long strips. The paper burst and grains of sugar spilled out onto the red plastic tablecloth. She began to push them around the table with her spoon. "Didn't it bother you that there were so few people about?"

"No."

"Anything could happen, Kate."

"I suppose it could. Do you mean, we could have been mugged or something? I've never thought about it. I don't think that way. For God's sake stop fiddling with that sugar, you're only making it worse!"

"Never?"

"No."

❧

"Kate really upset me," Alice told Ruth.

"Why?"

"She's so different to me. I really saw it for the first time. She's not afraid. I thought everyone was."

She decided to test herself. To go and spend a whole day in town with no particular goal or destination. She'd leave her cameras at home, so there would be nothing for her to hide behind. When she put them between her and other people, buildings, street-life, she felt they made her invisible. Like a character in a fairytale, she vanished and became a sophisticated eye, all-seeing but disembodied.

This time she'd leave her armour behind. She would stroll around and admire the Christmas decorations like a normal person, have coffee on her own. No Holly, no Kate, no camera. Why not?

When the day came, a Saturday, she brought Holly over to her friend Mary's house to play and then went home again to get ready. As a special challenge, she was going to leave the car at home and take the train into town. No quick escapes, no illegal parking right outside the door of where she was going. Normally she preferred to risk the fines rather than walk, exposed, through the streets. She laughed at herself. What was she thinking? This was no big deal. She'd enjoy it.

But what would she wear? Her usual leggings and oversize grey jumper were dull. She'd noticed lately

that everything she owned was either grey or black.
That she dressed in layers, as if arming herself. She
pulled out a charcoal mini-skirt, her only skirt. She'd
worn it twice, with a long jacket, black tights, black
polo neck. Both times she'd gone to a dinner party at
the Kennys'. They were the dressiest clothes she had.

Before she'd had Holly, she'd often gone out
dressed outrageously, emboldened by gin. She'd worn
gold satin trousers and flowing beaded tops. Ringed
her eyes with kohl and worn stilletto heels that made
her legs look ridiculously long and her ankles ache.
She'd dyed her hair red in those days. Kate thought she
should do it again.

"It's trendy now," she'd advised.

"I've earned every single grey strand. I'm proud of
them."

"Well, maybe you're right. It kind of suits you."

"What's that supposed to mean?"

Alice shrugged off the memory of that conversation.
She'd had a similar one with Nell. She didn't care what
they thought. But when she was dressed, she froze. She
knew she couldn't go out looking like that. Into town
alone in a mini-skirt. There would be no Holly holding
her hand, chatting, offering her bright face like a
beacon for Alice to look into so that she didn't have to
see where she was or what dangers surrounded them.

Don't be stupid, she told herself. It's broad daylight
out there.

She went resolutely towards the front door. She picked up her long black coat on the way, thinking it would help. She opened the door, but then slowly shut it again. She went back into her room and sat on the bed, appalled.

I can't do it.

It was the skirt. She'd have to change. Half an hour later her bed was a riot of tumbled clothes and she was encased in black leggings and her usual sweater, the one with distorted cuffs from all the times she'd stretched it down to cover her ravaged hands. It reached almost to her knees.

She pulled her coat on and told herself that at least she'd be warm enough now, but she knew exactly what she'd done, and why. It had nothing to do with the weather.

She avoided looking at anyone on the train. When she got to town she held herself in a tightly huddled, concave shape and walked straight to the cinema, telling herself that she'd be late for the film if she didn't hurry. The darkness in the cinema was a relief. On the screen, figures larger than life played out some drama that meant nothing to her compared with the effort of sitting there and reminding herself to breathe. As soon as it was over, she told herself, There, you've done it.

She walked quickly back to the Dart station to catch a train back home.

❧

"Do you remember asking me if I knew why I was thin?" she asked Ruth.

"Yes."

"I didn't understand what you meant. It was just the way I was built. You should see Nell, she's even worse than me and she's had five kids."

"And?"

"Now I know. What you meant. It's all mixed up with what happened on the pier that time with Kate. It's about being seen. Not wanting to be seen. Not wanting to occupy space at all. Because that makes you a target."

❧

But it wasn't as simple as that. Alice had never noticed before how she avoided mirrors, telling herself she simply couldn't be bothered with all that nonsense. Now, catching sight of herself sometimes in the reflective door of her wardrobe in the mornings, she could see what she was trying to avoid. The fact that she was a woman shocked her.

Her tension was taking a physical toll. She was plagued by aches and pains. When she woke in the mornings from nights of broken sleep her hands and feet ached. A strange growth in her stomach fluttered and pulsed.

❧

"It's like being pregnant," she told Ruth.

❧

She tried to ignore it as they rushed through Christmas.
They spent the day with Kate's parents as they always
did. Holly usually mixed easily with Jake's cousins and
disappeared off to play. But this year she stayed close
to Alice and shook her head when Jake called her to go
and play.

"Can we go now?" she asked, leaning against
Alice's chair.

"Poor lamb," said Kate's mother sympathetically.
"All the excitement, it's probably been too much for
her. She looks exhausted."

Alice had bought Kate a tape of the *Messiah*. After the
Christmas hysteria had died down they spent an
evening in Kate's house, listening to it.

"Remember Miss Sweetman?" Kate asked and
Alice nodded.

She leaned towards the music, not wanting to talk.
An oil burner smoked on the low table in front of them,
releasing a faint, sweet scent into the air. A fire burned
in the grate beside them, beneath a framed poster Alice
had given Kate fifteen years ago. It was the first fish-
eye shot she'd ever seen. A red, leaning, landscape.

"There's something about sacred music," Kate went on, oblivious. "Even if I never set foot inside a church again in my whole life, I think it will always affect me."

"It's all music," Alice said distantly. She reached for her cigarettes and lit one, blowing the smoke towards the fireplace, away from Kate.

Kate frowned. "You're the only person who gets away with smoking in here, do you know that? I wish you'd stop."

"You're as bad as Holly. She's always at me, these days."

"Well, she's right."

"I'll stop if and when I'm ready, Kate."

"It's just a crutch . . ."

Alice narrowed her eyes. "Crutches are useful, if you need them. Right?"

"All right, all right. I give up! I just wish you would, that's all. You know you're killing yourself."

"Do you know," Alice changed the subject, "even ads on TV can get to me. Remember those cigar ads and the *Air for a G String*? I used to feel like there were bass strings inside me being plucked whenever they were on. I miss the choir sometimes."

"Why don't you join one now? You had such an amazing voice."

"Not any more, I wrecked it." She waved her cigarette before stubbing it out. "But maybe, one day, I will."

She braced herself against the erratic bursts of emotion she felt. As she grew more silent, Holly became more watchful. They stalked each other. Holly's deeply shadowed eyes followed Alice everywhere. She trailed around behind Alice from room to room when they were at home.

"Stop doing that!" Alice snapped. "Can't you find something to play with?"

"No."

"Well stop hassling me. Surely you're old enough to find something to do?"

Holly pulled back out of sight. But Alice knew she was just beyond the door, afraid to go too far away, afraid to come too close. She waited for Alice to come back to her. Sooner or later, Alice always softened, sick with guilt. She'd sit on the couch in front of the TV and say, "Come on, Holly, let's see what's on." and Holly would come quickly, as if afraid Alice would change her mind, and cuddle up to her. The flickering images soothed them both.

"Do you ever play with her?" Ruth asked.

"Play? You mean board games and things like that?"

"Any kind of games."

"Sometimes we play these endless games of monopoly and ludo and snakes-and-ladders. I read to her, still. She's been really slow to learn. I don't know why."

"Smart kid. If she did, you'd probably leave her to read to herself."

"That's not fair."

"Isn't it?"

When Holly was in bed and asleep, Alice came and stared down at her sleeping face, aching to smooth the shadows from her skin. She always knew the instant Holly fell asleep. She felt a lightness, as if some weight was lifted, a release of tension. Then she would talk to Holly's sleep, whispering, Forgive me.

CHAPTER TWENTY-ONE

"You should lighten up, Alice. Do you know what? You were more fun when you were drinking." Nell was kneading dough in her kitchen. "How's the counselling going?"

Alice sat across the high counter from her, holding her coffee cup as if it was an anchor. They were making bread, but Alice had stopped working to light a cigarette. She was glad this conversation had opened during the day, if it had to start at all.

Nell was far less predictable at night, when the children were safely in bed and the adults sat in the kitchen under the rack of drying clothes that hung from the ceiling near the Aga. Nell and Tom drank homemade wine, then, made from unlikely sources. Nettles. Dandelions. One year they'd made sloe gin. Alice had been badly tempted to join them, but she hadn't. She hated the way Nell implied she was a killjoy.

"It's hard to trust a non-drinker," Nell explained to her during one of these sessions.

"That's a shitty thing to say."

"Well, there you are. Non-drinkers can remember

every word the next day, they take everything seriously. Drinkers are more relaxed."

"Why can't you just leave well enough alone?" Nell asked now, as she scattered a handful of flour across the wooden counter.

"I know I was abused, Nell. But I can't hold on to it, somehow. It's too . . . elusive. Like what I remember of my father. I can put myself back in a room and I know, exactly, where he is. But when I try to look directly at him, he vanishes. It's all like that. But I'm getting closer all the time. I can feel it."

"What's over is over. You can't change it."

"No. But I want a life."

"You've got a life. What are you talking about?"

"I'm a mess."

"Well, you put up a good front."

"That's all it is, a front."

Nell straightened her back and blew her hair out of her eyes. Her hands and wrists were dusty with flour. Alice reached over and tucked her hair behind her ear.

"Thanks. Look, you've got work you love and you do it well. You've a terrific kid, a nice place to live. What more do you want?"

Alice looked away. "I can't tell you because I don't know. But those things aren't really mine. None of it is me. It never has been. Can you understand that?"

"No."

Alice watched Nell's fists sinking into the dough. Nell's face was red from exertion and she breathed hard as she reached for a knife to divide the ball of dough into two.

"I know it happened." Alice took a deep breath. "It's just . . . I want proof."

Nell dropped the dough heavily into two large bowls. "If you ask me," she said loudly, "you should put it all behind you. What's done is done, Alice. You should get on with your life."

"But it's such a mess. Do you remember how I used to drink?"

"Lots of people drink. I drink. Are you telling me I should stop? Like those reformed smokers who make everyone's life a misery?"

Alice struggled to find words that would convince Nell how serious this was. How damaged she felt. How much it meant to her.

"You never knew how heavily into drugs I was when I was a teenager," she tried again.

"But you got over that. You were wild, but you got over it. There's no need to make a career out of it."

Alice's blood roared and crashed past her ears and silenced her. How could she say anything more to Nell, who stood there with her hip jutting towards her, her floury hands in fists. She felt like a child.

She wanted to scream.

Why won't you listen?

"I'm afraid I'm going mad sometimes. I can't describe it to you, but . . . panic attacks, strange images, nightmares, ideas that won't go away. Maybe I am mad." She laughed bitterly. "Like my mother." Getting back to familiar ground.

"Alice, do you think you could, just once, give your poor mother a break? She wasn't the one who had problems. It was your father who had the breakdown."

She lifted the dough off the wooden block and set it in a bowl, covering it with a teatowel. Then she came and sat opposite Alice, who stared at her.

"How do you know?"

"My mother told me. Years ago. There was an interview in some magazine, with a psychiatrist who was retiring. I can't remember his name, it was something unusual. You did the photos."

"Mendelssohn?"

"Maybe. Anyway, she said, How odd. I wonder if Alice knows that's the man who looked after her father that time."

"How could I have known? Who would have told me? When was this? How old was I?"

A cold, fine sweat fingered the back of Alice's neck. Mendelssohn had specialised in schizophrenia. She remembered him because Brian had asked her to fill in for him at the last minute when his wife had gone in to labour. She couldn't refuse, but she'd hated going to the mental hospital. She smelled fear as soon as she walked through the first of a succession of heavy doors that locked behind her as she was escorted to Mendelssohn's office. The whole time she was there, she was afraid that she'd never get out. That they would recognise and keep her.

Mendelssohn was incongruous in that setting, a small, soft-voiced, pink-faced man with tufts of white hair jutting above his ears and eyes of a wide blue colour that made her think with longing of the sky outside.

"I don't know. Does it matter?"

"It does to me. Why did no one ever tell me?"

Nell shrugged. "You know what their generation was like. The stigma of mental illness and all that."

"But you never told me," Alice accused.

"Don't be so melodramatic, Alice. It was years ago. You were a child. It had nothing to do with you. Let it go."

She wrote to him and asked if he would see her. He was a small, kindly man, silver. His eyes were the same intense blue that she remembered, hard to look at. The walls of the room he showed her into were covered in old black and white prints of the city. Alice looked at a sepia portrait of a woman with steel-framed glasses bridging her nose and a high lace collar, her hair swept back from her face. The woman had heavy brows and a full mouth that curved slightly downwards. The emulsion was damaged. A network of hairline cracks marred the surface and spread across her face. Alice turned away from the direct gaze of her eyes, knowing they would seem to follow her as she crossed the room, if she let them. She suppressed the urge to offer to restore it.

"That's my mother," Mendelssohn remarked. He waved her into an armchair. "What can I do for you, my dear?"

The door opened quietly and his wife carried in a tea tray. Alice had a sense of unreality about the whole experience. She felt like a fraud. Through the rain-spattered windows she could see a small stream at the bottom of the garden, a willow tree. It was like a painting.

He looked at her with one eyebrow raised, expectant.

She wanted to jump up and tell him the whole truth, relieve the pressure of that steady blue weight on her face, make him lift it off her. But she slipped above it, directed herself to smile her warmest smile, to sound tentative, as she accepted a cup from him.

"I'm not sure," she said. "But I recently learned that my father was a patient of yours, years ago. I explained all that in the letter I wrote. The thing is, I'm worried about my daughter. If my father was mentally ill, what is the outlook for her?"

She knew this approach, as a mother, was more likely to work than a direct appeal for information on her own behalf. But she felt ashamed, all the same, as he leaned forward and nodded, his eyebrows drawn together.

"I don't remember your father, obviously," he said. "But I took out his file when I got your letter, and read over the notes. An interesting case. He didn't stay with me for very long, I'm afraid."

"Oh?"

"No. I imposed a condition on his treatment, that he stop drinking. He tried, but was unable to do so. I referred him to a colleague who worked well with alcoholics. There's no point in my telling you his name. He's been dead for years."

Alice sat back, rigid. *Alcoholic.* Like her. The smell she remembered from her childhood. The locked cupboard. What had her mother been trying to control?

"My notes indicate that there was a great deal of domestic trouble. How old would you have been?"

"I was seven when he died."

"It must have been hard for you. No siblings?"

Alice shook her head. She felt uneasy, as if the focus was shifting onto her. She felt the power of this man's look pulling her towards confession, revelation. She stiffened against it. She smiled at him, her professional smile.

"Do you have a diagnosis?"

His manner became more brisk. "It was too early to tell for sure. It would be irresponsible of me to give you an unconfirmed diagnosis. He was severely depressed, with extreme mood swings. He had attempted suicide when he first came to me. He had paranoid tendencies as well. He was an unhappy man, very dark."

"That's true," she said. *Suicide?* Her eyes filmed over.

How could she have been so stupid? Why did she not see it? How could there have been so much. and she knew so little? She remembered her mother's insistence on loyalty, on keeping up the family name. No , for the first time, she wondered, what family name had there been to protect? Her hands shook. She pressed her knees together to control a trembling in her thighs.

"Given to sudden rages?" Dr Mendelssohn's voice rolled calmly over her.

She swallowed. "Yes."

"I can tell you nothing more," he said.

He waited. She gave away nothing. She fought an urge to tell him everything, to ask him, Is this possible? Did you know? Do you have any idea what it was like for me, a child in that house?

The ice floes inside her were cracking, breaking

apart, she was floating into separate pieces. Somehow she had to gather it all up and carry it safely out of here, not splatter her pain all over this tasteful room, not hand herself over to this benign medicine man with the gentle face. She knew he was as hard as steel. She had to get out of there before she bared her throat and handed him the knife.

"Thank you," she said. "You've been very kind."

"It was the strangest experience," she told Ruth. "As soon as he said it, it was as if the surface of my mind went into shock, because it knew that was what was expected of it. But from underneath came this feeling . . . But, of course. I *know* that. I've always known that. So, how did I let myself not-know?"

"He told you a lot," Ruth said. "Most people never get that kind of confirmation."

"It wasn't enough. I wanted more. But that sense of things coming together . . . It was amazing."

"Did you tell Nell what he told you?"

"Yeah, I did."

"What did she say?"

"She said, 'So what? If you go around lifting every rock in sight, you're bound to find something disgusting underneath.' I don't want to talk to her about this any more."

"Why not?"

"I don't trust her." Alice covered her mouth with her hand, but it was too late to catch the thing that had flown out of her mouth and danced in the air in front of her. All along, she'd thought it was herself she couldn't trust. Now it turned out to be Nell.

"Why do you keep going there, Alice?"

"It's where I've always gone."

"It doesn't seem to do you much good."

"That's not fair. I feel disloyal, talking to you about Nell like this. She's always been a good friend to me."

"Is that what you really feel? Yet every time you try to talk to her she shuts you down."

"But what she says makes sense. In a way. That's how she thinks. Maybe she's right?"

Ruth moved her hand impatiently. "It's very interesting to me that every time you make some progress you rush to tell Nell about it, and the same thing always happens. You lose whatever confidence you'd gained. So why do you choose Nell to confide in?"

"I want her to believe me." Alice was hunched and miserable, holding her elbows and rocking.

"Maybe she never will. What then? Will that make it go away, just because Nell dismisses it? Is that what you *want*, Alice?"

Alice shook her head. She didn't look up.

Ruth softened. "Maybe it's time you tried talking to someone else. Someone who might hear you."

❧

That Friday night, Kate and Alice were drinking apricot juice from tall glasses in Kate's kitchen. She had chilled the glasses in her fridge before using them.

293

They were sampling the juice, to see if Kate should stock it or not. They'd already decided that she should. It was delicious, sweet and thick.

It was a lovely room, full of light in the daytime from french windows at one end. There was a large round pine table with heavy slatted chairs in the centre of the room, comfortable to sit around. A pine dresser with plants and herbs and jars of pasta on the shelves leaned against the wall. The kettle was always close to the boil.

Kate believed in herbal tea. She tsked over Alice's coffee drinking, tried to encourage her to eat better, kept her supplied with beans and pulses and organically grown grains from the shop. Alice persisted in buying things that took less than ten minutes to prepare and kept Holly happy. She hadn't the energy for more.

Before she'd come over, Alice had made up her mind to tell Kate what was going on. She looked at her friend, sprawling across two chairs, her long hair pulled back into a ponytail. She still looked as if she'd cross her eyes any second, just to make Alice laugh.

"You know," said Alice, "You look exactly the same as you did twenty years ago."

"Liar."

"I mean it."

"It's the candlelight. Why do you think I like it so much?"

"I'm serious."

Alice swung her glass around, cupped in the palm of her hand, intently watching the patterns the fruit juice made on the sides. It coated the glass, then slid back down, its colour pulling away from the light. Then she tilted it in the other direction. She put the glass down. "Kate?"

"Mmm?"

"There's something I want to tell you."

"What is it?"

"It's not easy to say. I don't know where to start. Will you please hear me out before you say anything?"

Kate straightened up and frowned, then pushed her fringe over to the side of her face, as if to see Alice better.

"It sounds serious."

"It is." Alice took a deep breath. She looked down at the table. She rolled a crumb around under the ball of her index finger. Even in the candlelight she could see how ravaged her fingers looked, the skin around the nails split and cratered. She put her hands down in her lap and held them together, afraid they would fly away if she didn't hold them, they were trembling so violently.

"It's hard to know where to start. I've been in a lot of trouble lately. Emotional trouble. I suppose things came to a head when I stopped drinking. Do you remember? I went into hiding for a while. I didn't see you for ages. I knew I was in trouble before that, but when I stopped everything got really out of hand. I began to have panic attacks, in the street and in the supermarket. Bizarre images . . . it was like a haunting. I thought I was possessed."

She stopped, surprised. "That's it, that's how I feel. Possessed. It goes back a long way. Forever. Back to my parents and the house, being a child. There are things I never told you, Kate. Things you never knew. You're my oldest friend, you know me better than anyone. And you don't know me at all."

She tried to laugh, but the sound came out choked, cut off before it even got started.

"Alice?"

She didn't look up.

"What are you trying to say?"

"I'm afraid you won't believe me."

"Try me."

"Oh God." Alice put her hands up to cover her face, pressed them against her eyes, watched the lights come together and then fade. She couldn't sit like that all night. She pulled her hands down.

"I was abused. Molested." She cleared her throat. "When I was small."

She held her breath.

After a pause, she heard Kate's voice. Hesitant. "Who was it?"

Alice slid her hands into the cuffs of her jumper the way she used to when she was a child, to keep herself warm. Her joined forearms were like a safety bar across her stomach, where a violent pulse beat behind her navel. "I think it was my father."

There, she'd said it. She risked a quick look at Kate, who was staring away from her, looking at the door as if she'd never seen it before.

Oh, God, what have I done? She's disgusted. She'll never speak to me again.

"Tell me about it," Kate said, in a voice that Alice had to strain to hear.

Alice told her everything she could remember. She

talked about Ruth and then about Holly. After she'd
finished she waited a long time for Kate to speak, not
daring to look up, afraid to see that Kate couldn't look
at her.

When she did look up, not able to bear the suspense
any longer, she saw that Kate's eyes were shining
strangely in the light. They wavered, out of focus.
Alice blinked hard and rubbed her own eyes so she
could see more clearly.

"Say something," she pleaded.

"I don't know what to say."

"I could be wrong. I know that."

"I don't think you are."

Alice stared, stunned. She felt her heartbeat
hesitate, then begin to pound.

"What do you mean?" she shouted over the noise in
her ears.

"I'm not sure. But it explains . . . so much.
Everything. The way you . . . Oh God, Alice."

She looked stricken. She stretched her hand across
the table and Alice took it. Kate's hands were broad
and strong.

"I'm sorry," Kate said.

"Why are you sorry?"

"Because you had to go through that. Because I
didn't know. I didn't see."

"How could you have? You were a kid."

"So were you. Jesus, it makes me so angry. The
bastard. How could he?"

Alice winced. A new pain flared, jagged, in her
stomach, where the pulse had been. She pulled away
from Kate and began to hunt in her bag for a tissue.

"Here," Kate said, and tore two strips of kitchen roll off the roller, giving one to Alice and using the other loudly herself.

"Nell doesn't believe me."

"Why the hell not?"

"I don't know." Alice blew her nose again. "To be fair, she's never exactly said that. It's more like, she doesn't want to know. But she makes it sound as if she doesn't believe me."

"Was she there?"

"No . . ."

"Well, then." Kate had a fierce expression on her face.

Alice smiled and stuffed the tissue into her sleeve. "Thanks, Kate. I was so scared of telling anyone, after Nell. Even you. The things she said . . . I think I'd have died if you didn't believe me."

Jake and Holly pushed through the door, looking for something to eat. "Come and see what we made," demanded Jake. They'd been playing with Lego all night, building a space station and bizarre, cubic planets.

The women looked at each other warily. "OK," said Alice, to everyone, and they all went into the other room.

When they got home later, Alice went straight to bed. She lay under the blankets and shivered, the knot in her stomach tightening. The air around her thickened and grew menacing and began to press on her, weighing her down.

She sat up abruptly and turned on the light beside her bed. She stared around the room. Nothing. She got up and made herself some tea, went back to bed and tried to read. But the letters slid blackly around the page, she couldn't follow them. Her head pounded and her stomach turned and heaved.

She ran to the toilet and hunched over it. She retched, but nothing came up. Finally, in despair, she pushed two fingers down to the back of her tongue. She hadn't resorted to this since she'd stopped drinking. She shuddered as she began to vomit. Once she'd started it was as if she would never stop. Everything inside her had to come out and she cried like a kid, the way Holly did when she was sick, as if it was the most heartbreaking thing in the world.

When she'd finished she sat slumped against the toilet bowl. As she began to feel the cold she came back to herself. She moved slowly back towards the bed, pulling on a sweater. Then she sat under the blankets, her teeth chattering.

She was terrified. What had she done that for? The word *Liar* hung in the air. She could almost see it.

She picked up the phone and dialled. "Kate? I'm sorry, I know it's late. Did I wake you?"

"No, it's OK." But Kate's voice was heavy with sleep.

"Listen, Kate. Please don't tell anyone what I told you?"

"Alice, it's after midnight."

"I know. I'm sorry. I just had to ask you. It's important. Please."

"Don't you know me better than that?"

"I just . . . I'm not sure, you know? I feel as if I've done this terrible thing. I shouldn't have said anything. This is really dangerous." She was fighting tears.

"Yeah, OK. All right. Don't worry, I won't tell anyone. I promise," Kate said, and yawned.

"Thanks."

Alice wondered why she didn't feel any better after she'd hung up. It was like when she'd been little and she'd done something dreadful, really bad. She was ashamed and afraid all at once, the whole world ready to fall in around her and it was all her fault.

What have I done?

All night she lay curled into a tight ball near the top of her bed, holding her legs to her chest. Word by word she went over what she'd said to Kate. It was true, all of it. Everything she'd said. It was true about the panic attacks, about drinking, about the phobias when she was younger. Kate already knew most of it. It was true about the strange images that convulsed her mind when she was with Holly. It was true that she believed her father had abused her, although she avoided naming him, even to Ruth, in case she was wrong. She had said over and over again that she could be wrong, that she was trying to find out for sure, to sort out what was real from what might be madness. So why did she feel as if she'd lied?

"I feel as if I'm trapped in quicksand and struggling with every ounce of strength I have, but I'm still sinking," she told Ruth.

"Do you know what you're supposed to do if you get stuck in quicksand?"

"What?"

"Just lie across the top of it and float."

CHAPTER TWENTY-TWO

They found a kitten. One morning they opened the front door and there she was, a scrap of coal-black fur with an insistent cry, as if she'd been waiting all night for them to come and let her in. Holly whooped with delight. She picked up the cat and brought her in for a bowl of milk before Alice could stop her.

"We'll have to try and find out who she belongs to," Alice warned.

"But she likes us!"

"Of course she does, you've just given her milk." The kitten curled up in Holly's lap and fell asleep, purring. The sound made both of them laugh. It was absurdly loud, coming from such a small and scraggy creature.

"Don't get too attached to her, Holly. Someone is probably looking for her right now."

They asked around and put notices in the local shops. Alice even rang the vet, but no one claimed the kitten.

"You may as well bring her down for some shots," the vet advised. By the time she'd paid the bill, Alice knew the cat was there to stay. They decided to call her Tom.

"It's short for Thomasina," she explained apologetically to Dermot. "Are you sure you don't mind?"

"Not at all. She'll be good for Holly. She needs something like this."

"What do you mean?" Alice was touchy these days. On the lookout for criticism.

"Nothing. Just that it's good for kids to have a pet. Isn't that what they say? Didn't you have an enormous dog when you were a kid?"

"Yes. I did."

When Alice played with Tom, running her fingers under a tea towel for the kitten to chase, she saw that the cat took pleasure from her own anger. As she chased the moving towel her tail twitched and she pounced furiously, but her purr got louder.

I could learn from this, thought Alice, envying the cat her pleasure in being herself. She watched the way Tom played with Holly, stalking and pouncing but knowing to keep her claws sheathed. Alice loved the sound of her purr, a round, friendly sound. She liked to rest her hand on Tom's stomach and feel that purr rolling, warm, under her fingers.

She set out to take photographs, but found herself laying the camera aside so that she could touch Tom, her fingers drawn to the warmth of her fur, the sounds of pleasure that burst from the kitten as soon as she made contact.

"You take some pictures, Holly," she suggested.

Holly was thrilled. She'd never been allowed to use Alice's cameras before.

"Use this one," Alice suggested, handing her the Olympus.

Holly took it with respect and listened carefully as Alice explained how to focus, thinking to herself that she would buy Holly a camera of her own for her next birthday.

"See how much she trusts us," Holly said one day, delighted.

"She's no reason not to."

"Alice, come and look at this," said Kate one evening in Alice's kitchen. She was rummaging around in the canvas rucksack she carried instead of a handbag. "I found these photos of us when we were kids."

"That's not me."

"Yes it is."

"Let me see," said Holly, looking up from the game she was playing with the kitten. She stood up and pushed in between them. "Oh look, Mummy. Your hair is so long. And curly."

"I could sit on it," said Alice, remembering.

"And it's so short now. Why don't you grow it again?"

"I don't want to." Alice touched her silver hair. "I like it short. I don't have to think about it."

Kate snorted. "How much do you have to think about hair?" Her own hung in its usual ponytail.

"Not at all, when it's short," said Alice triumphantly. "Where did you find these?"

"Dad gave them to me the other day. There aren't very many of you."

"Do we have any pictures of when you were little, Mummy?"

"No, Holly. I don't think so."

"Why not?"

"I don't know. There just aren't any."

"I want to take loads of photos of Tom while she's still a kitten," said Holly, still proud of her new skill. "She's so cute."

A few days later Alice dropped round to see Kate in the shop.

"I found this," she said diffidently, taking a small black and white snapshot out of her notebook. In it, a small blonde child with shadowed skin sat in a bath, empty of all but a few cold-looking inches of water, and looked warily out of the frame. "It's the only one I have. I found it when I was clearing out the old house for the landlord, after my mother died. I don't know why I kept it. I'd forgotten I had it until after you'd left the other night."

Kate was stocking the shelves. She put down the bags of nuts she was holding and picked up the photo. She looked at it, then at Alice. She shook her head.

"What?" Alice was nervous.

"You look so . . ."

"What? So what?"

"Lost. You look lost. Where'd you get all those bruises?"

"What bruises?"

"Look. You look as if you have a black eye."

Alice looked over her shoulder. "Probably the light."

"I don't think so. Look at your legs. Those marks. Christ, you're so skinny."

"Give it to me." Alice took it back, stuffed it into her pocket. "I don't see any bruises."

❧

"But I did," she told Ruth. "I took it out again later that night and had a good look. I know what she meant." She shrugged. "It was probably dirt. I know I was a grubby little kid. Always being scrubbed." She swallowed hard.

"But I couldn't get it out of my mind. She looked so small and miserable. The kid in the photograph, I mean. Holly loves baths. We pile in bubbles and toys and I have to sit with her and read to her, or she tells me stories. Her favourite thing at the moment is drowning Barbies. She likes to pull their heads off and pretend a shark has got them."

"Who took the photo?"

"It must have been him. There used to be before-and-after photos of the cars he rebuilt, lying around the house. But I don't remember any, you know, family snaps."

"I'd like to see it."

"You can't. I tore it up."

❧

After she'd destroyed the photograph, Alice grew restless. One day, she went into Holly's room when she was at school. She sat on Holly's bed and looked around as if seeing the room for the first time.

There were clothes scattered on the floor, the shelves were crammed with boxes of games and model cars. Soft toys and dolls were piled three deep on the windowsill, while the bed was littered with teddy bears.

Slowly, not sure what she was doing, she gathered up all the dolls she could find. She brought them into her own room and closed the door, as if afraid of interruption. One by one, she removed their clothes and flung the dolls to the floor. Then she took up the Olympus and began to take rapid, unthinking shots of their twisted bodies.

That night, with Holly safely in bed, she worked in the darkroom. When she saw the prints, she felt suddenly sick. She hesitated before she turned on the main light. The dolls' mouths were open in a vacant Oh. Their innocence seemed grotesque when she saw them heaped on the floor, helpless, distorted. Bars of shadow slanted across them. Their silent faces shimmered at her, ghostlike, in the red glow of the safelight. They seemed to call out to her. She turned on the light, took her Stanley knife and slashed them into pieces.

The image from her own photograph came back and haunted her with its straggly hair, its thin, shadowed legs, the eyes that stared out of a wasted face and expected nothing good. The bare, low water and not a toy in sight. Suddenly she wanted it back.

❧

"I'd kept the fragments in a drawer," she told Ruth. "I patched them up, got her back."

"How did you do that?"

Alice leaned towards her, animated. Here was something she could talk about with authority.

"I used Spray Mount to fix the pieces on a sheet of card. Then I got my finest brush, some lampblack . . . The way you do it is, put a dab of gouache on the brush, then spit and lick to get it to the exact shade you want."

She mimed the process, put her index finger to her lips. "Tiny, tiny dots, like this." She dotted the air in front of her. "it's really delicate work. Tiny dots, joining up the gashes, more for the darker bits, pale, pale grey for the face. Lick, lick . . . repainting it, you see? Then you make a new print. And do it all over again, until you get it right."

"Does your mouth get black?"

"My lips do, Holly says. And the tip of my tongue. I don't notice."

"You sound so different when you talk about your work, Alice. It's like seeing a new person."

"Maybe that's because of what happened next. It was a revelation. It seems simple now, so obvious. But I couldn't have seen it before this if you'd hit me over the head with it. It's not information that I'm after. It's her. The kid in that photograph . . . It's me. That's what all this is about. For the first time I can see that what I've done is to dump all the scorn and disgust I feel on to her. It's not exactly self-hatred, because I transferred it all to her and then cut her off. It's as if, to go back to the resistance fantasy I told you about, the double agent . . . her collaboration made my resistance possible. But now that the war is over I've forgotten that, forgotten that we had a pact, and I've blamed her, despised her, for doing the things she had to do, forgetting that what she did allowed me to go on living."

Ruth nodded, encouraging.

"So I really looked at her, this time. Let myself see her. She's all dirty and tear-stained and battered looking. I did something I've wanted to do for her ever since I found the photo. In my . . . our . . . imagination, I filled the bath with lovely, warm, bubbly, fragrant water and loads of toys, ducks and boats and floating coloured balls. I hate baths, myself, but Holly loves them. I don't remember the last time I had one. But this was a fantasy bath. It got bigger and bigger until it was like a small pool, but still warm and safe, not too hot and not too cold. It grew until it blotted out that disgusting, sordid little bathroom. I let her play as long as she wanted, and the water never got cold. Then I lifted her out of the water and wrapped her in a big fluffy towel. I held her until she was dry. But not rubbing. No rubbing. Then I took her out of that house, enough is enough, and put her to bed. In my bed. Beside me. Where she wanted to be. I woke up feeling different. Strong. Alive."

She stopped talking and looked out the window. Even from here she could see the buds swelling on the trees, leaves beginning to unfurl. "I don't know why it took me so long. I think I was ashamed of acknowledging her, or else I was ashamed of her, or of myself for needing her. Do you remember, you told me once that shame is a lie, that it's a denial of self? I didn't understand what you meant, then, but I think I do now. I can't be ashamed of her any more. I know who she is. She's part of me."

"Well done," said Ruth.

❧

Summer came and Alice felt like one raw nerve. She'd gone through the routine with the dolls again, but this time she kept the prints. She chose a doll which seemed more vulnerable than the rest. Patches of its hair were missing from when Holly had left it out in the rain. She shot a sequence of photos of the doll, grotesque and dismembered, superimposed on that single image of herself in the bath. The result made her shiver, but she knew she had done something extraordinary.

"You should show these to Dermot's friend Will," Kate suggested. "He's in some artist's co-op or other. They're putting an exhibition together at the moment. I think you should show these."

"I'm showing them to you."

"I mean properly."

❧

"I agree with her," said Ruth, handing them back to Alice. "They need to be seen."

"I thought you were meant to be non-directive." Alice scowled, trying to hide her delight at Ruth's reaction.

"I still agree with her." Ruth was cheerful. "What has all of this been about if you're going to go on hiding in that darkroom? These are creative and powerful, Alice. You have talent. It's a waste not to use it."

"But I couldn't, until now . . ."

"Maybe not. But now you can. What's stopping you?"

She sent the series to Dermot's friend. A strange excitement built in her. She felt as if she was waking up. Everything looked different to her, with or without her camera. More brightly lit, in clearer focus. Her eyes shrank sometimes from the richness of what they saw around her. The bay filling with summer sails, the rich leaves shining on the trees, the beauty of Holly's dark face.

She was so tired that she ached, with the deep exhaustion that comes after a long struggle. She recognised that even the pain she felt was a gift, because it was part of coming alive.

There was a clothes shop across the road from Kate's, with brightly coloured cotton clothes in the window.

"Like the stuff we used to wear when we were teenagers," Kate said.

"Not me," Alice reminded her. But she was drawn to the shop, all the same. She went in to buy a bangle for Ruth, whose annual break was coming up. There was a long-sleeved dress hanging on the rail in soft cotton, three different shades of red.

"It's beautiful, Mummy," said Holly. "Why don't you try it on?"

Alice looked at it regretfully and shook her head. "When would I ever wear something like that?"

She paid for Ruth's bangle and they left.

One hot day they drove to Brittas, bringing Mary with them. They carried bags full of food, towels, bottles of sunscreen into the dunes. Alice had a blanket folded over her arm. The girls trailed their buckets and spades along behind them, and complained about being hot, sticky and tired after the drive.

But once they had crossed the hot sand and kicked their shoes off, spread themselves out with all their gear, it was worth the effort.

As she lay in the sun, Alice opened one eye lazily to check on Holly and Mary. They were building something in the sand. She caught sight of the curve of her own arm, browning, in front of her. The pleasure she felt in this was new, the warmth of the sun a blessing on her skin.

Why have I never done this before? she wondered.

On the way home, they stopped and bought fresh eggs and fat strawberries from a van at the side of the road. When Alice broke the eggs for an omelette, they were double-yolked and vivid.

It was the best summer ever.

Nell called and asked when they were coming. Alice thought about it. Ruth would be away in August. It would be good to have somewhere to go, but . . .

"I'm not sure, Nell. I've a lot of work to do. I might not be able to get away."

"Could Holly come for a few days, by herself, then?"

"I'll ask her."

Holly nodded at once. She was like a new child. She had turned the colour of toffee over the summer. Her black hair shone. She was getting pudgy. The dimple in her chin had deepened.

"When?" she asked.

"The last week in August, Nell says. That's five weeks away."

Alice slept badly, and in the mean small hours of the morning she suddenly leapt back into wakefulness, not sure who or where she was. Exhaustion crept up on her. After a few weeks of Holly's break from school, the old tensions came back. As Holly grew, Alice could feel herself shrinking. Any sudden noise made her startle and call out. She was grateful all over again for Holly's old nightlight. She was afraid that she could fall through cracks in time and never find her way back without it.

312

I wake up on the stairs. I don't know where I've been or where I'm going. I've been sleepwalking again and I'm cold. The stairs creak and I freeze. No one must know I'm out here in the middle of the night in the silence and the shifting dark. I have to get back to bed before I'm caught. The space between my shoulder blades tingles and I press my back to the wall. I walk upstairs sideways, sliding my back along the stripey wallpaper, so nothing can get me from behind. I run across the landing into my room. Jump over the hungry mouth under the bed and land beside my teddy bear. The sheets are rough and cold, so I've been gone a long time. I wonder where I went. I hold onto my teddy and curl up as tight and small as I can on my pillow. I sleep pressed close to the headboard, legs curled tightly to my chest. I don't like to let my legs fall down the bed. I don't want the thing at the end of my bed to get me. I lie very still, hoping it won't know I'm here.

"And then I can't go back to sleep," she explained to Ruth, "because of the weight."

"What weight?"

"When I relax, begin to drift off, there's this weight that comes . . . I can't explain it."

"Try."

"No. I can't."

"Can't?" asked Ruth. "Or won't?"

"I'm a mess," Alice went on, ignoring this. "It's not

only that I'm not sleeping. But I can't eat. My stomach feels, literally, as if it's tied up in knots. It's so tight."

"I'm not surprised," said Ruth.

"You can't possibly tell me that this is my fault," complained Alice, "that I'm doing it to myself."

"What are you doing to help yourself?"

"What do you mean?"

"Well, look at you. You don't eat. You keep yourself awake. Yes, you do, Alice. You may not know it, but you do. You don't let yourself relax enough to sleep. You're on guard every second. You hold yourself really tightly, you're always tense. No wonder your body aches."

∞

The knot in Alice's stomach grew. Some days it felt so heavy she put her hand over it to support it. The weight of it pulled her down. It invaded her mind. It began to pulse and jump.

∞

"It's like being pregnant!" she told Ruth, again. "What could it be?"

"Whatever it is," Ruth reassured her, "it's only you."

"Well, it's horrible. I don't like it. Stop grinning at me."

"Was I grinning?"

"You know you were."

"Has it occurred to you," Ruth asked her, "that one day you're going to have to let go? That the only thing you're fighting is yourself?"

∽∾

One night she woke suddenly, suffocating in fear. She thought she was dying. A searing pain tore through her pelvis, redhot, her bones ripping apart, the sockets of her hip joint cracking, like a chicken carcass splitting right open. She didn't know where she was. All she knew was that the loud breathing in her ears was not her own.

When she came back to where she wanted to be, in her own bed, now, with Holly asleep across the hall, her pulse slowed to a thick erratic knocking and the only breath she could hear was her own. The fire at the tops of her legs took longer to die down. After that she left the main light on in her room until the birds started singing outside her window.

She was glad that the nights were short. But still, each night, there was that falling towards whatever waited for her, in the dark, below consciousness. Always waking violently, the hot stab of pain and her beating heart.

And then, one night, he caught her.

∽∾

He wants to possess me and he will, it's just a matter of time. He follows me around, stalking me, close but not touching and the tension builds because I know what's going to happen. I know, because it's happened before. I can't get away from him. Everywhere I go he's close beside me. If I try to move away, he gets closer. I'm full of dread. It's choking me.

Then he starts. He takes my right hand and begins to squeeze it, crushing it. The pain is excruciating and, as I try to pull away, it rises up my arm. When I stop fighting, he stops moving and, if the pain doesn't go away, at least it doesn't grow. But it's still there, and it's bad, and after a while I can't stand the tension any more, knowing what comes next. I deliberately move my legs away from him so he will come to it straight away. If it has to happen, just do it, I want it to be over. So I move my legs and he pushes his way inside me and oh, Jesus, the pain is searing and splitting me, it's going to split me in two, my whole body is going to split up the middle like a wishbone when you pull it apart, how can anything be so big and be inside me?

I lie still and wonder how to make it stop, but he's in my mind as well. He knows what I think as soon as I think it. He tells me that he never has to stop, that he can stay like that forever. And I'm bleeding, but I don't have to do anything about it, because if I don't my whole body will bleed away to nothing and then it will be over, I'll belong to him.

Her body was still aching two days later when she had her last session before Ruth's summer break. She walked stiffly into the office and sat carefully on the edge of the chair, leaning on the arm, while she told

Ruth about the dream. She kept her jacket and bag on her lap, as if she'd only dropped in for a minute.

"What's worse, even, than the pain is that it's not new," she said, looking at the floor. The wooden planks were different sizes. There were knots in the wood. She shifted her weight from one side to the other, trying to get comfortable.

"It goes really far back into the past. It was just a dream, but it made me remember something, from the night of the rape. And before. That at some point I did think that, although I never said it. It was in my mind. But I didn't say it out loud."

She began to cough. "This is really hard to say, Ruth. You're going to hate me."

"I'm not going to hate you, Alice. What did you think?"

"Do it then, if you're going to. Don't drag it out. Just get it over with. I couldn't bear the knowing any longer, the dread. I know it's not the same as consent, but it's close enough to make me hate myself."

She was rocking herself, quietly, now. Ruth's form was a blur of colour across from her. "And I did nothing, to help myself. I hate this. I hate myself. Do you want to know what I despise the most?"

"What?"

"The pleading. I can't stand the pleading."

When Ruth spoke she sounded brisk. Impatient. "Maybe it's time for you to forgive yourself," she said. As if this was something Alice should have figured out for herself, and done long ago. "Maybe it's time to start letting go."

Alice stopped rocking as soon as Ruth spoke. She

was angry. This wasn't what she'd expected. She wanted sympathy, comfort, understanding. Not this. "You make it sound as if I've got a choice . . ."

"You do."

Alice glared at her, gathered her things closer to her. "You sound just like Nell," she said.

"There's a difference between suppressing something and letting it go. You know that as well as I do. It won't be easy," Ruth went on firmly. "You're very attached to your pain, Alice."

"What do you mean?" Alice was fighting tears, determined not to give in and cry now. She felt like a scolded child.

No one understands me.

She slouched, sulking. Furious.

"You're used to it. What would you do if it wasn't there any more?"

Alice coughed, to cover the rage she felt.

"I don't know," she admitted.

That night she and Holly went around to Kate for dinner. After they'd eaten, Alice and Kate sat, from long habit, around the kitchen table while Jake and Holly played in the next room.

"The lease on the shop next door to mine is up for renewal," Kate said. "I've been thinking about taking it up."

"You mean, you're expanding the shop?"

"No. Listen, I have this wild idea. Do you remember ages ago I told you I wanted to try a restaurant?"

"Kate! Well done!"

"I haven't done anything yet. I'm still thinking about it. I've just looked at the premises. I have to do a feasibility study before I can apply for a loan. My parents will probably back me. They said they would, if they could, years ago. Karen is a great cook. We could start with lunches. If that goes well, we'd risk opening at night as well. What do you think?"

Alice had stopped listening. For the last couple of minutes she'd been increasingly aware of the noises coming from the next room. The kids were chasing each other around, tussling. She heard Holly protesting, but not what she said. Then there was silence. It made her nervous.

Suddenly, Holly let out a loud wail.

Alice jumped to her feet and ran to the door. She saw Holly lying on the floor on her back while Jake sat on her, straddled across her heaving chest, laughing down at her. Holly was red with rage and frustration, twisting her body away from him.

"Get off me!" she yelled at him, panting.

He went on laughing.

From the pit of Alice's stomach came a sound she had never heard herself make before. It was a roar. "Let her go!"

There was a shocked silence. Kate had come through the door behind her. They all stared at her. Pins and needles burned her face. From a great distance she heard herself shouting, "Can't you hear what she's saying to you? She's telling you, NO! Get off her this minute, you . . ."

"Take it easy, Alice," Kate warned.

Jake had already climbed off Holly.

"I'm sorry, Holly," he said, his face flushed. "I was only playing. I didn't mean . . ."

Alice glared at him, breathing hard. "I was in the other room, Jake, and I heard her. Perfectly. She asked you to stop. She told you no. You should have listened to her." She tried to steady her voice. "Don't ever, don't you ever, do that again. Never." Her hands were bunched tightly against her stomach.

"I've said I'm sorry," Jake muttered again. He put his hands in his pockets and sidled out of the room. Holly got to her feet, looking stunned. She looked over at Alice uncertainly.

"Are you OK?" Alice asked her.

Holly nodded. She crossed the room slowly to the Lego box and picked up a red piece, then a blue one. She looked over at Alice again and then began to build something, intent, sticking her tongue out between her teeth the way she always did when she was concentrating. Her face and neck were flushed pink.

When they were back at home and Holly was settled for the night, Alice let herself down into the fog that gathered around her. She stared at the wall and rocked herself back, felt herself shrink. She felt a groundswell of fear. Her skin tingled, alert and apprehensive. A wild rage built up in her.

Don't laugh, don't fucking laugh at me.

Suddenly she was back there, feeling everything. She heard laughter as hard fingers dug into her skin. She felt the rage of powerlessness, the futility of trying to get away. Her mother laughed that nervous laugh of hers. Her father held her, tickling her.

She didn't want to be tickled.

❧

It's so easy for him to hold me and he laughs. No matter how hard I squirm and wriggle and try to pull away, I can't do it. I can't get away from him. The more I fight the funnier he thinks it is. She's laughing too, as if it's all right. It's not all right. Not ever. She doesn't hear me. She's right there and she doesn't see. She doesn't know that I'm being blown out like a candle.

"Daddy's only playing," she says. "It's a game."

Daddy's only playing.

I hate her for watching and not stopping him. His hard fingers, digging deep, unfriendly. I see the red armchair in the corner, his chair. He pulls me towards it, fingers rushing all over me. Sly. Punishing. Tormenting. He's tormenting me. I don't move my feet but my body drags along behind him. I hate, I hate, oh if only I could smash and break my way out of here, but I can't.

He is cold hard flinty feely hurting rock. Rock hard solid. A wall I can't get past. He holds me with his legs and one arm wrapped around me hard like a chain, leaving one hand free to move around, biting into me, push and poke and prod. My head fogs up. I am weak, worthless good-for-nothing spoilsport. I'm letting it happen to me again. Even though I know my body's hurting and hates what's happening to it, no one else can see.

She's laughing.

I know it's not a game. I try to tell them I need to pee but they don't listen and then I wet my pants and everything, the laughter, the fingers, everything, stops so suddenly I fall to the floor. I can see their disgust. I'm disgusting. Dirty, smelly, wet pathetic messy little thing. She tells me to go and clean myself up. I'm snivelling as well, wet everywhere, eyes streaming nose running mouth wobbling and now wet down there as well, cooling pee seeping through my clothes. A slimy little piece of dirt. Rotting. Rotten.

She shook all over. Her head felt heavy, as if her neck might snap. She leaned over to rest it on the table in front of her.

How many ways can you say rage? she wondered. How many times? How can you show what it feels like?

She reached for some paper and her pen and began to scribble, furiously, as if words could release her. But what came out instead were wild, dark slashes across the page, tearing the paper into shreds.

I give up.

Words fail me.

She wrapped her arms around herself, stunned by the immediacy of what she remembered. She knew that she was feeling the climate of her childhood.

She knew, too, that somewhere, sometime, she had decided that if she didn't fight, he couldn't win. This idea crept into her mind and settled, cautious, in a corner. She let it stay. She let herself know it was there without looking directly at it.

Then she was swept by a wild fit of coughing and retching. She ran to the bathroom and threw up, shuddering and recoiling from the smell of her own bile.

CHAPTER TWENTY-THREE

July slipped into August and Ruth was gone. Alice felt like an unexploded bomb. For the first time in years, she recognised a hunger for speed that nothing else could satisfy.

Why not, the voice in her head insisted. Why the hell not? You know it's what you need. What have you got to lose?

Only my life.

Do you care?

Holly, then.

Maybe she'd be better off without you.

She drove to the death-tree. Its leaves were dusty and speckled brown, poisoned by fumes from passing cars. It looked about ready to give up. Alice wondered if it was tired of waiting for her. Death pulled at her, but she was afraid. Not in the way that she imagined other people were afraid, but because death, for her, was a country where her father waited to claim her.

She drove slowly home. Everything she did these days seemed to be in slow motion.

A thick black weight welled up inside her, seeped through her blood, pressed at the back of her throat, her eyes, her nose, damped her down. Her ears were blocked as if she had driven through mountains. When Holly spoke to her, Alice had to call herself back and force herself to listen. It exhausted her to answer, to say anything more than yes, no, maybe.

She had nothing left to give and no way of giving it if she had.

They stopped going to the beach, because Alice didn't have the energy. She counted the days until Holly would go down to Nell, hoping she could get through them without destruction. She could hardly look at Holly any more without feeling an urge to pick her up and throw her against a wall.

Alice knew it wasn't fair. She had to do something. Maybe if Holly had someone to play with it would be easier for both of them. They invited Mary over for a day.

Holly and Mary dragged out the trunk of old clothes and dressed up in elaborate costumes, ran around from kitchen to bathroom to bedroom, admired their reflections in Holly's mirror. They shrieked with glee, delighted with themselves.

"Alice!" Mary demanded in her high, irritating voice, "Come and tell us who's the prettiest."

"You're both gorgeous," Alice pronounced.

"Yes, but who's the prettiest?"

"I'm telling you, you're both lovely. You're the blondest, Mary. And Holly's the darkest."

"Yes, but who's the best?"

Alice gritted her teeth. "It's a tie," she announced. "Now, I'm going into the darkroom to do some work. You know what that means, Holly."

"Don't open the door under any circumstances," Holly recited. She rolled her eyes and slid a look towards Mary that Alice saw in the mirror.

Brat.

Alice wished she could turn them out into the garden, but there was a fine drizzle outside. Mary's mother was the type who fussed, loudly and at length, over things like wet clothes, white bread, too much sugar. She wouldn't take it lightly if she came back to discover that Mary had been banished to the garden in the rain. More's the pity.

Alice shut herself into the darkroom for an hour. She sat on the three-legged stool and read, trying to ignore the riot going on outside the door. When she finally came out she couldn't see the carpet for all the clothes strewn in a trail leading to Holly's room.

"Holly! Come and pick these up!"

The girls bundled up the clothes and dropped them in a pile on Holly's bed.

"Can we watch a video?" Mary asked.

"Yes," said Alice, and listed all the videos they had.

"I've seen all those," whined Mary. "Can't we rent one?"

God, I hate you, Alice thought.

"No," she said shortly. "Just decide which of those you want to see."

She heard Mary whispering to Holly, "Ask her if we can have popcorn."

"Can we have popcorn?" Holly repeated obediently.

Alice stopped herself before she could say no. "You know where it is," she said wearily. How could she have forgotten that she couldn't stand being around children for more than five minutes? It wore her out.

When Mary had finally left, Alice breathed a sigh of relief. But when she turned back from closing the front door she saw the trail of devastation Mary had left behind her. Alice could cope with Holly's average mess, but this was different. It looked deliberate. Malicious, even. There was at least as much popcorn on the carpet as they'd eaten. Sweet papers and sticky rings on the low table in front of the TV.

Through the open door to Holly's room she could see the pile of clothes on the bed, shoes and soft toys scattered across the floor. They'd dragged out several board games, started and abandoned them. Even from where she stood, Alice could see that she'd be finding Monopoly money all over the house for weeks.

Holly sat at the table, working on a jigsaw puzzle.

"Pick those toys up at once," Elaine said, out of Alice's mouth. "You're disgusting. Pick it all up and then go to your room and clean that. How do you expect me to let you have your friends here when this is the damage they do?"

"It's not much." Holly didn't look up. Her tongue slid out between her teeth. She looked from the piece in her hand to the partial image in front of her. A jungle scene. Trees and bright green leaves, a blue and yellow parrot, a golden monkey.

"What did you say?"

"It's not much. Mess."

"Pick it up, then! Now!"

"I'll do it in a minute, Mummy. I want to finish . . ."

Alice reached over roughly and broke up the picture Holly had formed on the table. She scattered the pieces, not caring that they fell to the floor. "And I want you to pick those toys up right now. Do it!"

Holly's face was sullen. "You knocked over my puzzle." She didn't move.

Watch it. This is getting out of hand.

Even as she warned herself, Alice heard words boil out of her mouth. "Go to your room, Holly," she yelled, "Now. This second. Before I . . ."

Holly shouted back at her, "No!"

Alice's mind broke open and fury poured out of it. She walked right up to Holly, her hands clenched tight, her face distorted. She could feel it twisting and contracting into an ugly mask of anger. But her voice came out low, controlled and full of menace.

"Oh yes you will, you little bitch."

Her hand shot out and hit Holly, full on the shoulder. She pushed her, hard. Holly's mouth was still open with surprise when she fell. There was a loud cracking sound as she knocked her head against the edge of the door. They stared at each other.

Alice, stunned, reached out a hand to help Holly to her feet. But Holly, her face scarlet, swung her own arm around and struck Alice's hand away from her. The force of the blow surprised them both. Holly began to cry.

Alice laughed. She didn't know why. She stood there and laughed.

Holly screamed, "I hate you Mummy, you're mean!"

She ran to her room, threw herself on her bed and started sobbing.

Alice was suddenly afraid.

What if Dermot heard it all, upstairs? Is he there? What if he comes down to find out what's going on? What if she's bruised, or worse? Someone will see, ask questions. She'll tell. She'll be taken away from you. You have to stop her.

She was trembling with fear and anger as she stormed in after Holly and stood beside her bed, looking down at the rigid, small curve of her back, her head buried under a small heap of soft toys.

"You listen to me," Alice said hoarsely. "That was your own fault, do you hear me?"

"You pushed me!" Holly's voice was muffled.

"No, I did not push you! I told you to go to your room and you wouldn't go. How dare you? You get this into your head, Holly. You're not to say things like that. I was only trying to make you do what you should have done at once. You've no one to blame but yourself. You'll do what I tell you to do, do you hear me?"

Elaine's voice echoed back to her, you've no one to blame but yourself.

Alice froze.

Do you hear yourself? Do you see what you're doing? You're making her doubt what happened, to protect yourself. You're pretending she's a liar because the truth is too shameful for you to bear.

Abruptly, she sat down, on the side of Holly's bed. Holly curled herself up even tighter as if to avoid touching her.

Alice saw that movement. She breathed deeply to calm herself, tried to steady her raging pulse, breathe some warmth back into her voice. She wanted to be very sure that she was back to herself before she spoke again. This might be the most important thing she would ever say to Holly. She had to be careful.

"You're right, Holly," she said eventually. "Look, I'm sorry. I lost my temper. I had no right to talk to you like that and I had no right to push you. I did push you. I don't know why I said I didn't. I think because I was scared. I didn't mean to do it. I think I thought that if I said I hadn't done it, it would be true. Do you understand what I'm trying to say to you?" *Please.*

Holly nodded. After a while she turned over and sat up, sniffling. "I feel like that too, sometimes," she said, "and you give out to me for lying. I don't mean to either."

They looked at each other, then both looked away. Alice studied a poster of the night sky, while Holly played with Max's battered ears. At last she edged a little closer to Alice, then cautiously leaned against her arm. Alice put her arms carefully around her daughter, half expecting Holly to pull away. Instead Holly sighed and let her weight settle against Alice's body.

It seemed too much, something undeserved, that Holly could understand and forgive such outrageous treachery so easily. Alice wondered what she could do to match Holly's trust.

"It *is* lying, what I did," she said slowly. "And you were right to stand up for yourself. I think you're great, Holly. You're brave and strong and I'm really proud of you. I'm sorry I hurt you."

"OK. Mummy?"

"Yes?"

"If you ever hit me again, I'm going to hit you back."

Alice stared at her, her fists clenched. She saw that Holly's hands were knotted too. Her breath rose and fell as if she had been running.

"I mean it."

Alice waited, not knowing what to do or say. Her mind was frozen, but under the surface there was a battle raging, between fury and delight.

"You told me to stick up for myself, in school and with Jake. And you were right. I'm going to stick up for myself with you, too."

Delight won.

"Fair enough," was all she managed to say.

She looked at Holly with new respect. How could she ever have seen Holly as a smaller version of herself? How could she not have seen that Holly was someone completely different? Someone new.

The day she brought Holly down to Nell's, Alice woke feeling nervous, apprehensive. Even though it was bright outside, the walls of the house were cold. Flakes of plaster had drifted loose from the wall near her bed overnight and lay like dandruff on the floor. They reminded her of damp, the coming winter. She pulled on a T-shirt, an oversized rugby shirt and a pair of bleached blue jeans. She hadn't worn them for months. She was surprised when she saw how loosely they hung from her waist. In the end she had to borrow a belt of Holly's to keep them up.

Holly had packed her own bag and Alice didn't check it. She was so tense she knew she could snap at any second. She wasn't sure that she could hold herself together long enough to get Holly safely down to Nell. Details were beyond her. Nothing mattered except getting Holly safely away and then coming back here to . . . what?

Now that it had come to it, she wasn't sure that this was such a good idea. She couldn't remember why she had thought a break from Holly might be good for her. Her throat tightened as she saw her daughter sitting quietly near the door, one leg swinging, waiting to go.

"I'll miss you, Holly," she said suddenly. "Will you be all right?"

"I've got Max," said Holly, holding out the stuffed dog, bedraggled and bald from years of love. "Mummy? Why don't you come too?"

"There are things I need to do here, lovey. I'll come for you as soon as I can. Then, maybe, I'll stay for a while, OK?"

"OK."

Holly was unusually quiet in the car. Alice didn't enjoy the drive either. She was jumpy and uncoordinated. She missed gears twice, and once she almost hit a dog that ran out from behind a hedge. After that she drove more slowly, concentrating on everything around her. The muscles in her neck were tight.

When they got to Nell's it was lunch-time and the whole family was already sitting around the table. There were calls of welcome, extra chairs were brought out, and everyone squashed up to make room for them.

During lunch Alice thought she was going to suffocate. As usual, Nell fussed over how little she ate, passed her the basket of bread repeatedly without being asked. The hum of conversation around her didn't reassure her as it usually did. To relieve the pressure she was feeling, she told them all a sanitised version of what had happened between her and Holly.

"The other day we were fighting and I lost my temper," she told them. "I slapped Holly, and do you know what she did?"

"What?" Nell's youngest, Jenny, was eager.

"She turned around and walloped me right back." Alice beamed at them all. Brendan laughed out loud but Nell frowned, puzzled.

"Then she told me that if I ever did it again, so would she," Alice went on. "Don't you think that's great? I think it's great." She got up to go to the kettle, touching Holly's shoulder lightly as she passed her.

Everyone evaporated from the table as she made tea. Nell's children were glad of the chance to escape without having to clear up after themselves. It was understood that whenever Alice came she took over all the basic jobs like washing-up and laundry. Even Holly had slipped off with them, unconcerned about Alice's imminent departure.

"Are you sure you won't stay, too?" Brendan asked. "For at least one night? You could drive back tomorrow."

"No, thanks. I have work to do." Mentally she

crossed her fingers and then uncrossed them, annoyed. She'd lie if she wanted to. To Brendan or anyone else.

"What was all that about?" Nell demanded to know. "That story you told. What were you getting at?"

"Are you two going to fight? Should I leave?" Brendan asked.

He made a face at them. Alice smiled back, willing to be coaxed away from the tension between her and Nell, but Nell ignored him. He took his tea and left.

"It's just a story." Alice reached for a spoon and began to stir her tea.

"I swear to God, Alice, you are getting so weird," Nell said. "You just wait until Holly grows up and starts with all this counselling stuff. Then it will be your turn to get the blame."

"For everything," she added darkly.

"I wanted her to know that it's all right for her to tell the story. That it was a good thing, what happened."

"You can't be serious."

"I am."

"But what about," Nell stirred her tea, watching the leaves spin around the top, "Families? Discipline? I know it's a bit different for you, but you needn't go around giving mine ideas, thanks. Kids have to learn to do what they're told."

"Do they? I wonder. Surely they don't have to put up with being hit. Where does family come into it? She's learning to defend herself, that's all."

"You're exaggerating, as usual," Nell complained. "Family has everything to do with it. It's all very well for you. You can cut yourself off if you want to. It's not that easy for me. There are rules that have to be respected, you know. Roles. Responsibility. Look at all the people I have to keep track of . . ."

"But why don't you just ignore it all?"

"It's not that simple, Alice. Someone has to keep in touch with everyone, send cards, remember birthdays, ring the old people to make sure they're all right."

"Who said it has to be you?"

It suddenly struck Alice that if Nell was any different, she wouldn't be leaving Holly here with her now.

"I'm sorry," she said. "I know you're right. It's just as well for the rest of us that there are people like you around, Nell. And you're so good at it. It's just not my way of doing things." She stood up and cleared their mugs from the table.

"I'd better think about going, as soon as I've done the dishes. I want to get back early tonight, get a good start."

She loaded the dishwasher and washed the salad bowl, put the bread away in the pantry, while Nell told her about Shane's new girlfriend.

"Her nose is pierced, can you imagine?"

"Loads of kids do it, around us. I don't think it's so bad."

"Well, I can't bear to look at it. I think it's horrible!"

Alice drained the sink and wiped it, then turned back to Nell, amused.

"Noses are only the tip of the iceberg, Nell. You'd be surprised where else people pierce themselves. Bellybuttons, nipples . . ."

"Stop! I can't bear it!"

They'd both folded their arms across their breasts, involuntarily, and at the same time. Seeing this, they laughed. Alice crossed the kitchen and hugged Nell with real affection.

"Thanks for taking Holly, Nell. I'll come down in a few days, when I can. OK?"

She went looking for Holly and hugged her lightly, not wanting to make a big drama out of her departure. But when she felt Holly's small body press quickly against hers she felt sudden doubt. Her belly ached, as if the invisible cord between them was being stretched to breaking point.

"Will you be all right, Mummy?"

Alice made her mouth stretch out across her face. "Yes, lovey. I'll be fine. Will you?"

"She'll be grand, won't you, Holly?" Brendan put his arm around her shoulder. "She can come fishing with us this afternoon and then there'll be all those fish to gut."

"Yuk." Holly made a face.

"You do have lifejackets on the boat, don't you?"

"Stop fussing, Alice. She's going to be all right."

"Be careful, Holly."

Alice began to add, *Do what you're told*, but stopped herself. "Have fun. I'll see you soon. I'll ring you tomorrow."

She kissed Holly one last time and left quickly, her face hot, her vision blurred. She felt an empty space behind her in the car where Holly used to be. It was like the feeling she got when Holly fell asleep. A fresh absence.

But by the time she'd turned onto the main road she wasn't thinking about Holly any more. She'd forgotten everything. It was as if someone had pulled a plug in her head and everything had drained out of it. She drove home in a trance. When she pulled up outside the house she felt exhausted. She was shivering. Maybe I'm getting flu, she thought, and went straight to bed, sure that there was a sleepless night ahead of her.

CHAPTER TWENTY-FOUR

She slept heavily. In the morning she was stiff and sore. There was something wrong. The air around her was empty. Holly was gone.

She lay still and listened to the silence, feeling uneasy. What would she do? She'd made this time for herself but now she wasn't sure how to use it.

She swung her legs over the side of the bed and winced as hot needles of pain attacked her lower back. She must have slept in the same position all night, without moving. When she stood up she felt as if she'd left her body behind, still lying on the bed. She moved slowly to the kitchen and turned on the kettle.

I must be getting old, she thought.

Maybe a bath would help. She had an unopened bottle of massage oil in the bathroom cupboard. She'd bought it because she liked the name, Ylang-ylang. She found the plain brown bottle and poured some oil into the bath as it filled. Then she made herself some coffee and put it on the window ledge beside the bath, feeling outrageous and decadent as she stepped into the fragrant, oily water.

She lay back and closed her eyes. She couldn't remember the last time she'd had a bath. The closest she'd come was that imaginary bath she'd given the

child in the photograph. It was something she avoided.
But why?

The image of herself in that old photograph swam
in front of her eyes. Her mind began to stain with
anger. She moved, as if to push it away, but the water
slapped at her skin and she let herself slip further into
the image instead. It shifted, became a memory. She
could remember herself in the bath. Small. She
remembered lying back, wishing she was a mermaid,
with her legs fused into a long, powerful tail. She
remembered holding her breath under the water and
wishing she could stay there forever.

♋

I'm not allowed to lock the bathroom door.

"Something might happen," she says.

Doesn't she know that it does? Does she?

He comes in, looms against the light.

"Are you washing yourself properly?" he asks. He
picks up the washcloth and looks at it closely, not at
me.

"Stand up," he says, "so I can check how clean you
are. Come on, now. Stand up."

I lie back further into the water, hoping he'll think I
can't hear him. Hoping he'll go away. I close my eyes.
A mermaid, swimming away, down under dark rocks
into pools of silence no light has ever touched. The
octopus pulls me, struggling, back to the surface.

"I know you heard me, Miss."

His face is red. The skin around his eyes tightens
and his hands squeeze my shoulders. His nails. His

voice is cold when he says, "You could drown, you know, doing that."

I follow his hands. They lift me towards the ceiling until I am standing, staring away from him at the bubbling light on the window and the darkness behind it as the cloth pushes in between my legs. He hunts for dirt. No matter how deep it's buried, he'll find it.

I hear his voice from far away. His breath is caught, as if he's been running. He's telling me how filthy I am, that I need to be scoured clean.

When he's gone I wrap myself in a towel from the hot rail and sit on the edge of the bath staring at the place where the green wall tiles meet the metal rail. The edges shift and blur. I'm practising. I can make things move by staring at them this way. Lift and waver. No one else can see them shift but me. One day they'll slip enough to let me pass and I'll disappear behind the wall for good.

Maybe they'll be sorry, then.

There's a secret room back there, behind the hot press. There's someone hidden there. I want to know who she is. I know she's small, like me. I know her hair is gold and tangled, like mine. I hear her creeping around when there is no one but me to hear her. I've called out to her, I've put my mouth up close to the wall and whispered, but she won't talk to me. She doesn't trust me.

I've measured the walls and spaces of the house a million times and then run outside to check, counting windows. It doesn't add up. I know this secret space in the wall is there, that it's real. That she is real. I run in and out, looking, measuring. I always hope I'll see a window for her but I never do. She must have no light in there. It must be cramped and dark. I hope she's not afraid of the dark, like me.

∞

The water had gone cold. It was an effort to drag herself out of the bath and wrap a towel around herself when the phone rang.

"Alice? It's Kate. Did Holly get off OK?"

"Yes."

"Do you want to come over for dinner tonight?"

"No. Thanks."

"Are you OK? You sound weird."

"Kate, I'm just not in the mood. I feel wrecked. Like I could sleep forever. I'm going to bed for the day. I'll ring you soon."

She hung up, then lifted the phone off its cradle. There was no one she wanted to talk to, nothing to say. The house above her was empty because Dermot had flown to the States. He'd told her he'd be gone for a week. Knowing this made anything seem possible. She could make any meaningless, violent sound she wanted and go unquestioned.

She lay down again on her bed, still swaddled in the damp towel, and pulled the covers over her head. Moving was a huge effort. She felt as if she was dreaming.

She used Nell's voice to tell herself that, if she chose, she could pull herself out of this languor, get dressed, find something to do.

But why? Ruth was right. Alice knew that this trance was exactly what she had to let happen. It was like letting herself float away. As if her aching mind could no longer hold its heavy, dark curtain in place. It began to slip and, gratefully, she let it fall and fold around her like a shroud.

Behind it there was darkness, a darkness that had nothing to do with the absence of sun. It was in front of her now, a cave she had to enter. She reminded herself that she had already been inside it, had left a part of herself behind. What she was looking for. All her resistance fell through the emptying drain in her head.

The old, familiar creasing started in her brain. Ripples. Like a labour starting in her psyche. She knew that, this time, she couldn't stop it.

When she had given birth to Holly there had been days of warning twinges, sometimes so powerful and consistent that she had begun to time them, to see how regular they were. But when real labour had started, she'd known the difference. Wave had followed wave, relentlessly, with growing force. She had let herself sink into and become part of them until they had cast her and Holly up, separate, on a hospital bed. The force of this was the same, she couldn't fight it. It was too powerful. She rocked herself. She felt herself sinking. Then she was weightless, dreaming darkness and silence. The past closed over her head like water.

Words spun lazily through her emptying mind. Words like Forgotten. Lost. Inevitable. Each twisting free, empty of meaning. She fell into a deep well of silence. She dreamed she was locked in a room. The mirror, dark and filmed with dust, showed nothing. She came back to herself in her mother's house.

❦

This room is heavy and feels dark, even in the daylight.
The air hangs thick, like the blood red curtains that fall
from floor to ceiling. The light from the curtains is a
dull ruby glow. It throbs against the red leather chair in
the corner. His chair. Everything else in the room is
vague. Subdued. Hangs back, wanting to avoid trouble.

When he calls me, I always think, this time I won't, I
won't go. But when the pitch of his voice changes,
hardens, I always do. See? There is nowhere here to hide.

This is not me. You don't see me.

He is watching me. His eyes pass over me like a
touch and I shiver. Something deep inside me curls
even tighter into itself, away from the look, away from
touch, away from him. Away from me. It shrinks. I
don't look at him. I pretend he's not here. I'm not here.
I stare hard at nothing, at a place beyond his reach that
doesn't exist.

Now I'm in my father's room. The darkness sighs
and groans. I'm in the dark. The dusty musty dark. The
smell. The closed curtains, no-light, under heavy
covers smell, trapped in the dark smell, stale no-light
no-breath, cigarettes and shit smell. But the darkness
breathes and moves.

"Your hand."

The blanket moves.

"Give me your hand," he says. "Come here."

I say, "Daddy?" But this is not my Daddy, this is the
bad man who comes. He looks like Daddy, but he's not.

Don't let on, oh don't let on you know, because if

he knows you've caught him he'll be raging and he might not ever let your Daddy come back. Then you'll have to stay with this man forever and he wants to hurt you and punish you because you're bad and dirty. He holds your wrist so tight, squeezing till it wants to break right off your arm and you say, I say, "I want to go now. Please."

He says, "You'll stay right where you are, young lady, until I say you can go."

I'm wriggling now.

His eyes are like stones that glitter and he says, "No, you can't go."

I wish my Daddy would come back now, now, and see what this man does to me. Make him stop.

I wonder where he goes, why he lets the bad man come and take his place. Doesn't he know the things that happen to me? And I wonder why no one else can see that this is a bad man and not Daddy, even though they look the same.

Daddy says I mustn't tell because it's a secret, and if I tell, the bad man will stay forever and not let Daddy come back. That would be my fault. So it has to be our secret. Daddy says the bad man wants to kill me. Eat me up and take me away with him. As long as I don't let on I know, say nothing, that won't happen. You can't kill the bad man because he's already dead. I think he's God and he's out to get me 'cos I'm bad. He sits on the bed I stand beside and holds my arm.

"Where do you think you're going?" he says. "I haven't finished with you yet."

"Please let me go," I say, "I have to go to the toilet."

The tightness down there burns and I'm afraid I'll

wet my pants. Then she'll be angry too. She hates it when it happens. I'm supposed to be able to stop it, but I can't.

He won't let me go. He holds my wrist. I see pyjamas, striped. Glasses, glittering. Teeth. His yellow teeth like a wolf. He moves. His legs. I don't know where I am now, he holds me with his legs, I see his teeth. I hate him. This is not my Daddy.

This is not me. Not me. Not my skin feeling the cold burn of him not touching me. Not my clothes lifting over the not shivering not skin. His teeth get bigger and come closer with his open mouth a cave I will fall into. I can't breathe.

I'm on fire. I'm being crushed. I squeeze out of myself, before it's too late. I shoot up to the ceiling and stay there, watching.

Don't touch me with your dirty eyes I hate you. I can't stop you looking, touching, but that's not me you see, not me you feel. That's a shell and I'm not in it. I've left you far behind. I can escape, I will escape, I have escaped and you're so stupid, carrying on as if I was there when I'm not. That's not me. An empty shell pretending to be a person – no, a thing – for you to paw and prod and suck on. It's not a person, body, you've made it something else, your slave. Your thing. Don't touch me. Don't.

The hand lands somewhere on the not body of the not me and doesn't feel its burning way along the not skin, cold, hot, shrinking. The fingers don't stroke and push into my not body. No. This isn't happening. Not in me, no. I shiver. I am so cold I burn and the eyes pierce me with their not looking at not me. No, not me.

I will run and run until I fly from you, and never ever come back except to punish you.

But I am the punished one here, swallowed by the beast. Down in the deepest cavern where the light will never find me. I lie in a pool of slime. Your slime.

I wander through the house, the air thick with something I can nearly touch but never name. I rock from foot to foot and hold my hands up to blot out this *thing*. My father's face, dark and angry, looms in my mind and then he fades into the slavemaster, harsh but pleased. With me. Urging. That's right, that's right, and all my muscles clench and tighten and explode into a sweetness of creamhoneylight and I pull back red and flailing raw skin burning breath hard heart pounding. I run, then, to the scalding pipe in the bathroom and throw myself against it, crying out with the relief. Pain is what I need.

At night in bed he comes to me and I moan and toss and turn away. No, please go away, please. Don't look at me. I hide and burrow but it's not deep enough and the moving legs come together as I twist and turn and the need starts, the hunger for touch, and I let myself go into it. Hand over hand I let myself down into it, rocking and rocking with it against it into it and falling, again the burst of light, the darts of sweetness, the sting of pain. Over and over again I am nothing but this, this is all I am. And I begin to cry, stop, please, stop. I can't stand it anymore. But it's relentless and never-ending. I'm sore now, destroyed, skin raw, weeping, full of rage and shame and hatred it has to stop please.

It's dark. The heavy dark. The heavy moving dark. The dark gathers, takes shape, moves closer and bends over me. The whole surface of my body sings a warning, alert. Skin raw and bristling. I wait. The voice so far above me starts, hollow. A litany of dirt. The dirt I am, the dirt I must absorb and become until there's nothing else. So that everyone will see what he knows. The filth of me. My skin is crusted with it, with the dirt he has brought to me, covered me with, tries to smother me in. The others struggle and weep and beg and try to get away. I hate them. We rock ourselves in the pool of cooling slime he's left us in. It pools under us. We lie in it. It covers us. We're smeared in it. And the hate words fall from a hate face hitting me like fists. As if I was just like them. Weak and helpless. But I'm not. I'm not.

It's a gutter we lie in, the belly of a whale, like in the bible. There's no way out. Even if I got away he'd find me. I'm marked with his scum. I am his, I belong to him.

He hovers over me in the dark and it comes out. Comes out and hangs. Hangs over me. It touches me and I freeze, everything inside me coiled tight, pulled in. I am drawn in and waiting, afraid to breathe and he puts it between my legs. Close, he says, so close, can you feel how close we are, close together, can you feel it, and he moves, rocking on me. It moves down there, it grows and my skin prickles. He rocks and rocks, and I am out and over him watching him rock and groan red-faced and then his face all knotted and the big veins standing out on his neck and his teeth showing his wolf face and it bursts out, all that stuff slithers

346

over me. He lies on top of me, rocking slowly now, rubbing it into me. More of it. I have no skin anymore not made of this – it's my crust. All I have is my two eyes looking and they don't look from down there but up here, where I escape to watch from somewhere else.

Now I'm choking on it, gagging, the stuff is everywhere. He pulls away and it's in my retching throat, my eyes, my hair, my face. I will drown in it.

The slavemaster keeps coming back. He hovers over me, dark and leaning, bending, harsh. He tells me what I am, *dirty, filthy, slut, evil,* and what to do, *turn over, open your legs, lie still, stop whining.* I can feel his weight and his darkness and the breath from his mouth, his teeth, his sounds grunting, his rubbing against me, and the slime that smears me, covers me, fills me, the slime I am.

It goes on and on. Forever.

Redness everywhere all around me and behind my eyes a sea of red, the dark red of the curtains, and I am crying, sore.

Please, no more, let it stop now, I can't stand it. Please.

But it goes on and on. I rock in it, furious and sore and trapped. There is no beginning and no end, it's my life, it's who and what I am, I'll never escape it because it's everywhere I go, it's in me, I'm lost in it.

It *is* me.

I have to be careful not to make him angry. So I act as if I see nothing, hear nothing, say nothing. I do what he tells me to do. I lie as I am told to lie. I shut my eyes. I shut my eyes.

347

I shut.

He opens his dark clothes, he covers me. His weight. I wait.

Can you feel it, he says, can you feel how close we are. Then he rubs it up against me, rubbing and pushing, grunting, open your legs, and burning and it floods out over me and in me and it's everywhere. It coats me again, another layer, building on the last one. He's making a new skin for me to wear. It's thickening. So thick that soon I won't need clothes at all. I'll walk around in what he's given me, another body. He wants to do it inside me, to relieve himself inside me. I feel him pushing it against me, big and hard it's too big it won't go in and he strains and strains and it bursts all over me again and he's angry. Angry, and then he cries, I can't help it, God forgive me, I can't help myself.

And he's holding me then. Stroking me. I'm his little girl. I stare up into the dark and wonder if I'll ever get away and I know I can't but I have to try. I've learned how to climb out of my body and move around so they don't even know I'm gone. The crust he's made is still there to fool them. They can't see the difference. But I always have to come back. She calls me back.

I look for a way out through the wall but there isn't one. I can leave my body but I can't get out. There are others here, tied like me. I despise them because they cry and beg and plead for release, they haven't learnt yet, they haven't learned to shutup stopcrying beltup like I have. They should learn. It makes it easier.

Babies, crying for a mummy who never comes.

CHAPTER TWENTY-FIVE

She came back cautiously. Little by little, she felt her way back into her stunned body, settled into it. She felt battered and exhausted. She looked around her slowly at the outlines of her room.

One by one, she named everything, so that she would know where she was. Window, curtains, chair. Clothes, thrown over the open door of her wardrobe. Her backpack, loaded with cameras and filters, over in the corner by the ladderback chair. A framed series of the coastline, her own prints, on the walls. Damp stains on the plaster. Bookshelves. A stack of books on the floor beside her bed.

In the faint light coming through the door, she scanned the spines of the books. Gradually, the letters came together and made sense, restoring order. She could remember reading those books. She could remember who she was.

She began to pull away from herself, shamed by what she'd seen and felt. She smelled something alien and sickly. She was shivering. She pulled the quilt around her. She felt dirty. But then she remembered the photograph.

She thought she heard Ruth's voice whisper, "Not dirty. Just a little girl. Hurt."

Hurt.

Bitter tears stormed out of her, until she was empty. Then she rested, quiet, in a stillness she had never known before.

Not dirty, she repeated, and this time the voice was her own.

Something warm stirred inside her. She was shocked to realise that what she felt was love. As she recognised it, it grew. Love for her self, both then and now. Love and a fierce kind of pride. *This is who I am. I survived all that.*

The cat scratched at the window and Alice got up to let her in. Tom wound herself around her legs, purring. Alice poured some dry catfood into a saucer and changed the water in the dish outside the back door. Then she got dressed quickly, pulling on the clothes she'd dropped on the floor. A lifetime ago. It was daylight outside, but it felt early. The light was fresh, the air crisp and clean.

She could hear Ruth's voice as if she was in the room and not on a beach thousands of miles away: Maybe it's time to forgive yourself.

The beach. She'd go to the beach. She looked at the clock. It was nearly seven o'clock. Her favourite time to go down to the sea. There would be enough people around for her to feel safe, but not too many. Out of habit, she picked up her backpack. At the last minute, she decided not to bring a camera, and emptied the bag, except for her cigarettes and disposable plastic lighter.

She drove through empty streets to the tiny harbour

where Holly loved to paddle, near the Forty Foot. On hot days it was packed with people, but now there was no one on the sand. She parked the car. There were already swimmers changing over by the far wall. She walked past them, towards the round tower. She leaned against the wall and looked out over the rocks towards the horizon. Beside her, a worn sign declared that this was a bathing area for men.

Two women passed her, jogging. At the end of the road she could see a man walking his dog. The place was stirring. She could feel it waking up, the city's slow summer easing into wakefulness, unresisted.

The tide was low, the water flat and peaceful. The thought that she could walk out to the edge of the rocks and sit where normally she would be out of her depth in water drew her down towards the shingle. Her mind was empty as she filled her pockets and her backpack with stones. She chose the largest she could carry comfortably. The heaviest. Then, placing her feet carefully on one boulder after another, she walked cautiously out to the farthest rock uncovered by the fallen tide. She looked back once, to see how far she'd come. Land seemed very far behind her.

When she got as far out as she could go, she emptied her pockets and her bag. She arranged the stones in a neat pile and sat beside it. At her feet there was a small hollow, like a basin, with water trapped in it. The sea rocked gently all around her. The air smelled of salt and seaweed. She waited to see what would happen next.

When her mind began to fill with images again her

stomach clenched, but she willed herself not to turn away from them. She breathed carefully but deeply as, once again, she remembered the night of the rape.

She saw herself as she had been that night. How she'd looked. How she'd felt. Hopeful, eager, looking forward to a good time. She let it play itself out all over again.

As she watched, she felt herself shrink, again a child, powerless. This time, she understood everything. She watched it all. What he did. What she did. Ogod.

And then her own younger self took shape in front of her, grey and strangely still, as if she had been cast up, lifeless, by the tide. Alice did for her now what she wished someone had done for her then. She held the ghostlike creature and began to rock her. Strange sounds broke from her throat and formed into words, O my poor love. It's all right. It's over now.

She rocked the cold grey girl and stroked her hair and told her over and over again, it's not your fault, you did nothing wrong.

She dipped her cupped hands into the basin at her feet and lifted cool water and let it fall over her. She washed her, very gently. Then she sat very still, holding her, watching over her as she slept, life and colour slowly coming back into her body. Slowly, she took her back into herself. It was like osmosis. She could see and feel, behind that awkward teenager, the grubby child she'd been in the bath photograph. All of them, coming together. She softened, opened, ready to take anything in to herself.

Behind the love she felt came anger. Molten, it

began to heave in her, then to flow, clear and hot like liquid fire. It drove her to her feet. She picked up a stone and weighed it in her hand, then swung it far out, as far as she could throw. Gulls flew up from the rocks around her, alarmed, and flew out to sea, calling each other.

"Fuck you," she called, past caring who might hear her. "Fuck you!"

One by one she lifted and flung the stones far from her, knowing only that she was shedding something, like an unwanted skin that had weighed on her forever.

"You're dead!" she shrieked at last, "and I'm not!"

She began to laugh then, wildly and carelessly, mouth open, eyes streaming.

He's dead, she thought, and I'm not. I'm alive.

Alive.

She was white hot, luminous. She could feel herself glow with energy. Her blood sang, it was better than any high she'd ever known. Liquid, molten, silver and shining, she was coming together again, like mercury, all the dispersed parts of herself flowing into each other. She held herself ready and let them fill her.

When it was over she felt clear and new. She sat on the rock again until she grew aware of the warming air, the rising water, sounds of traffic in the distance. The sky stretched over her head, but it was only sky. The tide was turning, but slowly. Calmly, she got to her feet and climbed back towards the shore.

When she got home she pulled open the curtains of the living-room. Sunlight struck the windowpanes, showing spots of dirt. Everything was filmed with dust.

The table was grubby. When she lifted the ashtray, fine grey powder spilled over its edges, staining her fingers. She could see rings from old cups of coffee stained into its surface. There was a can of polish at the back of the kitchen cupboard and she brought it out and wiped the table. Then she cleaned the windows, wiping them with old sheets of newspaper. She was full of a strange, restless energy.

Without making a conscious decision to do it, she found herself kneeling on the bathroom floor with a bucket of soapy hot water beside her. She worked slowly and thoroughly, starting at the far corner and using a heavy cloth under a scrubbing brush. The way her mother used to do it. Square by square she cleaned the tiles, leaning her weight on the brush and swinging her body into it.

When she'd finished washing the floor and hoovering the rooms she began to drag the furniture around, making more space. Her hands were crusted and grimy and the skin around her nails throbbed, but she felt satisfied. She carried one of the armchairs back to her own room and threw a blanket over it. A reading chair. Her shoulders ached. She was making a new space for Holly to come home to.

She went to tackle Holly's room, but stopped at the door. Holly could re-arrange it herself. If she wanted to. And what did it matter how messy it was, if no one but Holly and her friends went in there? Alice got out the acrylic paint set. She rinsed the lids until she could twist them off and then, using big strokes and different colours for each letter, she painted "Holly's Room" on the door. It looked crude and garish, but she liked it, because of what it said.

She was driven. She couldn't stop herself. She attacked the kitchen cupboards, emptying them out quickly, sorting the cans on the kitchen table and cleaning the shelves before putting everything back in some kind of order. She looked at what she had. Cans of beans, soup, corn and tuna. Their lazy diet. It occurred to her that there was no reason for her not to cook, not to make bread and biscuits here, the way she did, without thinking, at Nell's house. No reason at all.

She dragged everything out of her wardrobe. It was evening now and she was tired. But once she'd got this far, she couldn't turn her back on the mound of clothes on the floor of her room. She couldn't bear to stop until she'd finished.

One by one she lifted everything out and looked at it critically. Things she hadn't worn for years went into black plastic bags to go to the recycling bins the next day. Kate would approve of that. She folded what was left and put it back. The spare appearance of the shelves pleased her. She could tell at a glance where everything was. It was a good feeling. She closed the wardrobe door and went to bed.

When she woke up, she ached all over, inside and out. She felt fragile. Raw. One minute she was swept by a wild feeling of elation and the next she found herself crying.

But it's all right, she told herself, reassuring. It's going to be all right.

She got into the shower and turned the water on, hard. She folded her arms across her breasts and bent her head, letting the water fall on her curved back. Again, images from her childhood filled her mind and she shivered in the steam. Her knees buckled as if her legs were not strong enough to bear her own weight. She closed her eyes.

"How can I live with this?" she asked out loud. "How?"

The now familiar, horrible, sense of filth rose up in her. She would never be free of it. Never. She imagined saying this to Ruth, and immediately Ruth's brisk voice was there too. Arguing with her.

That filth is not yours. It never was.

But it's where I come from.

It's not you. You don't have to stay there.

She straightened and opened her eyes, relieved to find herself in her own bathroom. She had a sense of instability, as if any minute she could fall through cracks in time and never find her way out again.

Nonsense. You know that can't really happen.

She turned off the shower and dried herself. The weight in her stomach pressed against her diaphragm. There was some sound she needed to make. She coughed, experimentally. Feeling foolish. Nothing happened.

She rang Kate.

"Hi, it's me. Why aren't you at the shop?"

"If you thought I was at the shop, why are you ringing me at home?"

"Habit? I forgot. I'm a bit addled. Why aren't you, though?"

"Karen is working. We weren't busy. I'm doing the books. What have you been up to?"

"Re-arranging furniture."

"Typical! I thought you were going to indulge yourself while Holly was away. Reading, was what you said. Pure escapism, you said you wanted."

"I changed my mind."

"Do you want to come over?"

"No. I have a plan. Are you very busy?"

"I'll be finished in about an hour."

"Will you come down to Bray with me?"

"Why Bray?"

"I want to go on the Ghost Train."

An hour later Alice drove towards Bray with Kate beside her. "Thanks for coming with me," she said.

"You know me, I'll try anything once. At least this isn't likely to get me into much trouble, not like some of the things you've dragged me into in the past. Unless Jake gets to hear about it. He'd probably never speak to me again."

"Rubbish. He'd be proud of you." Alice drove to the end of the promenade and parked outside the arcade. "Here we go."

"Are you going to tell me what this is all about?"

"It's therapy." Alice grinned. The muscles in her face ached. "Don't put on that patient look. I've had an idea. It'll be good for you too."

The noise inside was deafening. They walked past indoor rides, slot machines with their lights flashing. On their left the dodgems spun and crashed and children shrieked. The noise level made Alice's head ache. They climbed the stairs quickly towards the train. No one was waiting.

Alice walked up to the teller. "Could you do me a favour?" she asked. "Could you keep us going round for a few turns?"

"I dunno about that." The young woman behind the glass looked bored. She chewed gum noisily.

"So long as there's no one waiting?" Alice wheedled.

"How many gos did ye want?"

"Four or five? Only if there's no one else waiting," she repeated, waving a ten pound note.

The teller popped a bubble with her tongue, then nodded and took the note. "I'll see what I can do," she said.

"I can't believe you did that," hissed Kate as they climbed into the small car and put the shoulder straps on. "You've been watching too much telly. Bribing people . . . "

"Well, it worked," Alice whispered back. Adrenaline was surging through her system. She knew that whatever she tried to make happen now, she could. The car creaked and moved forward.

"Here we go, Kate!" she shouted, as they pushed through the double doors into total darkness. A phosphorescent skeleton loomed out of the darkness and they both screamed, laughing. The loud shrill sound infected both of them and they carried on screaming until they emerged into the light again, trundled across the track where nobody waited to get on and in through the double doors once more.

The dark closed around them. Alice's throat was open. She was crying and screaming at the same time and she could feel Kate's body solid beside her in the dark and knew she was safe. A steady stream of sound poured out of her. When they rattled across the lit section of track again she covered her face with her hands until they were back in the dark. She howled until there was no sound left inside her. When the car rattled into the light again it creaked to a halt. Shakily, Alice got out, not looking at Kate, and walked away. She walked straight down the stairs, out across the street and down the steps to the beach. She sat on the dirty sand and watched the sea roll in. She heard Kate come up behind her.

"Are you OK?"

She nodded. Then she said, "My throat hurts, after all that yelling," and began to laugh.

"God, so does mine." Kate was laughing too. "How about an ice cream? A ninety-nine?"

Alice nodded and Kate was gone before she could notice that Alice's laughter had turned to tears. They felt the same, part of the same thing. Out of control. But she was too tired to cry for long. She reached into her pocket and pulled out an old scrap of tissue and blew her nose, hard. There. She felt calmer now.

That night Alice curled into the sofa, holding a pillow

and let herself drift. Aftershocks of emotion kept hitting her. First, she felt a wild energy and exhilaration. Then a flood of sadness. Anger quickly followed grief and then she was left feeling a raw tenderness. For herself. Just as, after Holly's birth she had felt both sore and powerful. She felt the same awed respect for herself now.

I survived all that.

A current of power surged through her.

There is nothing, she thought, that I can't do.

She was ravenous. She ate eggs and a whole pan of salted, fried potatoes. She couldn't get enough salt. Then she ate apples, one after the other, the cool juice a relief to her burning tongue. She rummaged in the drawer for her secret stash of chocolate and ate steadily through the evening, barely finishing one thing before she was on her feet rummaging for the next.

The hot relief of letting herself cry, stopping when she was tired and then starting again when she was ready, surprised her. She was exhausted. Drained, as if the plug that had been pulled had caused her to empty out completely.

The question now was, how to fill herself up again?

Then she remembered. She wasn't hollow any more.

CHAPTER TWENTY-SIX

The next day she was wild with impatience to see Holly again. She put some food out for the cat and left the bathroom window ajar, knowing she'd be away for a night. This time, she felt the power of the car surging under her as she drove to collect Holly. She turned the stereo up loud, and rocked her way across the country.

She could feel the way the music fed her heartbeat, affected her mood. Maybe I'll take up dancing, she thought. Or singing again. Find a choir. It might be fun.

The country slid past her in its familiar order, lovely in the sunshine. It occurred to her that there were other roads to take besides this one. That there was no reason why she and Holly shouldn't explore other parts of the country. She wondered how much it would cost to rent a cottage somewhere for a week. If she could manage it. They could try life in the country alone, with no obligation to anyone. The possibilities were endless. Her excitement grew. Underneath she still felt raw, exposed. But it would be all right. She knew it would.

It was hot when she arrived at Nell's. The dying heat of

another summer. Alice parked the car and pushed the front door open.

"Hi, everyone!" she called.

Nell and Holly came out of the kitchen. Holly's face creased into a huge smile when she saw her. Alice picked her up and swung her round, then pulled her in and held her close. She loved the feel of Holly's arms around her neck, the texture of the skin of Holly's cheek against hers. She breathed in Holly's hair, her warm smell.

"God, I missed you, lovey," she whispered.

Holly squeezed her neck and lifted her head, grinning. "I missed you too," she said. "How's Tom? Is Dermot looking after her? You should see the blackberries in the top field, they're huge! Will you come and pick them with me?"

"Let her have a cup of tea first, Holly!" Nell laughed. "She'll need something after the drive."

"No, I'm fine. I'll make one when I come back, if that's OK."

"Of course it is." Nell frowned, as if she was thinking. "There's a clean bucket in the kitchen. You can use that."

"Thanks."

They set out across the fields, warning each other not to pick too close to the ground because of cow-dung. It was a hot day, the air hummed around them. Alice felt lazy and peaceful. Holly chatted about going back to school the following week.

Once they got to the brambles they talked about nothing but the berries, intent on what they were doing.

"How about a blackberry crumble for dinner?" suggested Alice.

The peace of it was hypnotic. They moved around the edges of the field, the cattle edging away from them. Their eyes scanned the defensive brambles, the sweet, rich, creamy pink-white flowers thick with pollen clusters. The defensive undersides of the leaves clung to the skin at the back of their reaching hands. Buried nettles burned and stung their fingers. They stopped to hunt for dock leaves, rubbed the sour green juice deep into the webs between their fingers. They both wore boots and jeans, so their legs were safe. But because Holly was closer to the ground than Alice, she got scratched and stung more often.

Alice loved the spring and yield of the black, glossy berries. Their juice sacs were firm but perfectly ripe, ready to fall into her reaching hands. She loved the colour when they burst and spilled their purple stain on her fingers. The warning buzz of wasps was hypnotic in their ears. They grew dazed from the sun and the hum of insects and stopped to rest on a moss covered stone wall.

They watched dragonflies and talked about fairies.

"Oh, look, Holly!" Alice put her hand on Holly's arm and pointed. They held their breath and watched a damselfly hover over a sloe-bush, her fabulous tortoiseshell face and sparkling segments brilliant in the sun.

"She's beautiful."

A cluster of berries above them caught Holly's eye and she asked Alice to lift her up so she could pick them. As she stood there holding onto the waistband of Holly's jeans so that she wouldn't fall, Alice had a sudden flash of memory, herself, a child, with her father and mother. They had done this together, gone blackberrying. She remembered him lifting her so she could reach further. She remembered sorting the berries later with her mother, hunting for worms.

In her surprise she nearly let Holly fall. "Come on down now, Holly. That's enough." She let go and Holly jumped off the wall, arms waving.

"Lucky there are no cowpats just there," Alice teased, as Holly tumbled onto the grass. They went back to their picking and as they moved along the edges of the field the memory became more and more distinct. That lazy feeling, sticky fingers, the sound of bees, the hot sun on the back of her neck. It had been something good and they had shared it. All three of them. Quiet, intent, doing something together.

How extraordinary.

No, she thought, that couldn't be right.

She had grown so used to seeing her parents as monsters, herself as permanently miserable and threatened, this cosy image didn't fit at all. And yet she knew it was true. Both things were true. It shocked her that there was more to remember. How much she'd lost.

As they went on picking, images flashed through her mind of scenes between her and Holly. The time she had pushed her over and yelled at her and tried to make her believe that it hadn't happened like that. Every word she had spoken to her in a voice cold enough to stop her own heart, never mind Holly's.

Every time she had looked at her, and how she wished it wasn't so, but it was, with absolute hatred.

Yet here they were now, picking blackberries, calm and easy together. There was nowhere she would rather be at that moment, no one she would rather be with than Holly. Given a choice, of course she would prefer if Holly would only remember the times like this, not those other, dark and twisted moments. But would she? There was no guarantee.

They walked down to the lake and watched the wind blow patterns on the surface of the water, stopping on the way back at the ruined tower on the edge of the water.

"Rapunzel," they called up, "Rapunzel! Let down your hair!" They climbed up the steep and crumbling steps with their fine powder of peat dust to the top. They stared down into the empty well of the building and tried to imagine what it had been like to live here hundreds of years ago.

"No TV, Holly," Alice teased. "You'd hate it."

Holly made a face. "It's much better now, I think. I'm glad I live now and not then."

Wise child. Happy with what she'd got. Not hankering after a past she couldn't hope to change.

They turned back towards the house for tea, collected the bucket from where they'd left it on a wall so as not to have to lug it around with them on their walk. They picked their way over limey rocks covered in lichen, trying to step from rock to rock and stay off ground. Once they landed on the same small rock and Holly pushed at Alice, cross.

"Don't get in my way, Mummy."

"I'm trying not to."

They picked hazelnuts and tried to crack them open. Alice had to hit them so hard with a stone that they crumbled, the meat clinging to the undersides of the shell.

"They're not ripe enough yet," she told Holly. "Let's leave them." They wrinkled their noses at the smell of pine martens.

Alice tried to name the flowers for Holly, loving the feel of their names in her mouth. Foxgloves, deadly nightshade, yellow ragweed, michaelmas daisies. Poppies. They picked a handful each and carried them back to Nell along with the blackberries, asking her to identify the flowers they couldn't name. Holly filled a jug with water and put them on the table while Alice began to sort the berries for the crumble.

That night, Alice and Nell sat up late in the drawing-room. Alice sprawled sideways in the comfy, deep armchair, her legs folded over the arm, her head back on the opposite arm. A mug of tea balanced on her stomach, with her fingers laced through the handle.

"You look like a kid, sitting like that," said Nell.

"I feel like a kid." Alice swung her legs. "That was a great dinner, Nell. Thanks. And thanks for having Holly too. The break was really good for me." She stretched luxuriously.

"What did you do with the time?"

"Do you really want to know?"

"Of course I do. I'm asking."

Alice eyed the ceiling.

"OK. I suppose you could say that I let myself have a mini-breakdown."

"Oh. I see. I hope you're not going to make a habit of it."

Alice watched Nell, cautious.

"Well, go on."

"There's not much to tell, in one way. In another way, it could take a lifetime."

"Oh stop hedging. Spit it out, whatever it is. I suppose it's about this counselling business?"

"Yes. But if you're going to be like that . . ."

"I'm sorry. Go ahead. I'll shut up." Nell drained her glass. "Wait a minute," she said and stood up to make herself another drink. "Are you all right there?"

Alice lifted her cup and nodded. Already she was wishing she'd gone to bed sooner, that this conversation hadn't started.

Nell sat down again with a full glass and gestured to Alice to begin as she took a drink, licking her lips. "That's better," she said. "Go on."

"I was remembering things," Alice began. "From when I was small. I thought I was going mad, the last few months. Well, years. My whole life, actually. But there were these flashes of, something, I didn't know what. And by the time Holly came down here, it was taking over. I couldn't handle being around her, having her around. I couldn't look after her and myself . . ."

"You needed a break?"

"Yes, but . . ."

"That happens to all of us, Alice, for God's sake.

There's no need to make a tragedy out of it. And we don't all have somewhere to send our kids, do we?" Nell's face was flushed. She stabbed the ice in her glass furiously with her index finger.

Alice watched the ice bobbing around under Nell's finger. "You're angry," she said, carefully, her heart pounding.

"No, I'm not."

"Yes, you are. Why?"

"It's so self-indulgent, all this stuff you've been doing. When is it ever going to end?"

"Soon. Very soon." Alice was surprised to hear herself say it, but knew it was true. "I've learned most of what I need to know. On the other hand, it will never end. But I'll know how to deal with it, myself."

She took a deep breath. "I know that my father abused me, Nell. I can't pretend to myself that it's not true any more."

"How can you be so sure?"

"Because I remember."

"I thought you didn't know, you didn't remember anything for certain?"

"I did. I just didn't know what it was. I was trying so hard to be sure, you see . . . I thought what I knew was something else, madness, a dream, even a fantasy – anything, so long as it wasn't real. Because no one, ever, allowed it to be real."

Including you.

"How do you know it's true? I read the other day about some crowd in America, something to do with false memories, they're suing their therapists now. They say their therapists decided they'd been abused and then made them believe it."

"Oh well, America."

"I'm serious, Alice."

"So am I." Alice was furious, suddenly. She pulled her legs in under her and sat up. "How dare you? You'd do anything to make me pretend none of this ever happened, wouldn't you? I don't understand why! All my life, you've been the closest thing to family I ever wanted to have. You were like a sister and a mother all rolled into one. You've always been there when I needed you. And yet, you've been trying to pull the ground from under me ever since I started this. Why, Nell? Haven't you listened to anything I've told you? I went to Ruth knowing I'd been abused, for Christ's sake. I told her, not the other way around. I'd always known it. But I'd been taught not to trust what I knew, to believe what I knew was false. So in the end I couldn't tell the difference between what was real and what wasn't. What was me and what wasn't. I literally lost myself. No wonder I didn't know how to live in the world. I couldn't even live in myself! But somewhere inside myself, I always knew. And the first one I could put a name on was your bloody father."

She stopped, panting.

That's it. That's why.

She leaned over and put her mug down on the floor, an excuse to hide her face. Her fingers seemed stuck to the handle, unwilling to let go. She pulled them away with an effort and looked up. Nell's face looked oddly loose, as if it was melting.

"I don't know what you're talking about," she said thickly, sounding suddenly drunk.

"You're going to 'forget' all this tomorrow, aren't you?" Alice said. "You'll pretend we never had this conversation. You'll only remember what you want to. It's like all the other times you've sat there and torn me to shreds and then been all sheepish in the morning, clutching your head and saying 'what happened?' I let you get away with it! And you're the one who went on at me about not hiding behind drunkenness as an excuse! You don't want to know all this, Nell, because of what it might mean about you. That's it, isn't it? Isn't it?"

Nell pressed her glass against her chest. She seemed to be having trouble breathing. Her eyes were hooded.

"You listen to me, Alice." Her voice was low and dangerous when she spoke. "And listen very carefully. Whatever muck you're trying to rake up in your own life, you leave me and my family out of it. Do you hear me?"

But Alice couldn't stop the flood of words from her mouth. "No, you listen to me for a fucking change! No matter what you say, I know what I know. Do you think I *asked* for any of this?"

"Yes! Actually."

Alice stared at her, disbelieving. "You can't mean that."

"I don't know. Maybe you've been manipulated by this therapist of yours. Maybe it did happen, with some stranger, and you're blaming the wrong person." She glared. "People. Blaming all the wrong people. Maybe there's some twisted reason you *need* to believe it. Like the way you stopped drinking."

"What?"

"You made such a bloody fuss, deciding you were an alcoholic and couldn't drink any more. When there was no need . . . you drank no more than I do, for God's sake!" The last three words slurred into each other.

Alice almost laughed out loud. She felt hysterical, elated all of a sudden. It was like seeing Nell, hearing her, for the very first time. She sounded unconvincing. Desperate. There was no need to be afraid of her at all.

"What makes you think you know more about how I felt, how I drank, than I do? How *could* you know? And why the hell does it bother you so much?" she asked.

"I know because I remember you, Alice. Don't forget that. You were this bright, bold little kid, all over everyone, looking for notice. Irresistible, if you must know. Who knows what happened to you? Or why?" Her features were twisted, vicious. "But you sure as hell didn't act afraid, or damaged in any way."

Alice shivered at the suggestion, the naked hatred she saw in Nell's face. But she refused to back down.

"The difference between us is, I know how I felt, and you can't know that," she said, as calmly as she could. "There are a million ways for kids to hide the things that happen. I don't pretend to understand it. I'm just telling you the way it was."

Nell moved suddenly and Alice jumped, startled.

"I get so sick of all this," Nell hissed. "Why can't people just pick themselves up and go on?"

"Surely even you can see that, before you can pick yourself up, you have to let yourself hit the ground?" Alice was impatient now. She didn't care, any more, what Nell thought. "This is my ground, Nell. This is where I begin. It's as simple as that. Do you know, all along, I've been waiting for your approval, without even knowing that's what I wanted. I needed you to tell me, 'Yes, you're right, that's how it was,' before I could believe myself. I wanted you to see it too. I didn't trust myself enough without you to back me up. I don't know why. You weren't even there. Still, that's what I wanted. And you'll never do it. But I don't need that now. Because I *know*. In here." She put one hand on her heart, the other over her gut, her fingers spread wide. "I can even accept that you don't believe me." She wondered if this was true.

"I just wish you'd get on with your life and stop picking old scabs."

"You mean like you, running yourself ragged looking after everyone but yourself?"

"You were glad enough to send Holly here."

"You invited her, remember? I thought you wanted her."

"I did. I didn't mean . . . let's stop this, Alice. Before it goes too far."

Alice did laugh, then. "*Before* it goes too far? Have you any idea what you've said to me, here? How destructive you can be? Of course, you're so bloody perfect, there's no need to look at *you* too closely, is there? But how much of that is surface, Nell? Maybe you have some letting go of your own to do. Have you ever wondered what would happen if you stopped playing the matriarch? Have you?"

"You're such a self-righteous bitch, Alice!"

"And you're not?"

They glared at each other, bristling.

Nell was the first to look away. "Maybe there are things I don't want to look at too closely . . . but isn't that my right? I don't see the point. I've done my best for my kids, to make a *good* family. It's very precious to me."

"I know that," said Alice, astonished. She watched Nell, who was swaying slightly, tilting her head from side to side. She looked lost, fragile, uncertain. As if she could shatter any second. Alice knew the feeling well. She was taken aback to see it, naked and apparent, in someone else. So that's what it looks like, she thought. And then something struck her.

She knows. She knows, and she doesn't want to know.

Alice could certainly identify with that. With each new realisation, she could see Nell more clearly, but from a greater distance. She felt a sense of pity. "I've never questioned that, Nell," she said carefully.

"But you have." Nell still wouldn't look at her.

"You and people like you. With your insistence on challenging everything, turning everything upside down. As if it's all bad. As if the life I live is worth nothing."

"Nell!" Alice was shocked. "I've never . . ."

"No? You've always been so independent. Sometimes I envied you, with your jobs and your funny stories. You could make it all sound wonderful. And then, when you had Holly, I thought you'd need me again. But you didn't."

"But I did, Nell. Don't you see?" Alice was suddenly aware of everything she stood to lose. She wasn't sure if she was ready to let Nell go. She knew she didn't want to hurt her. The ugly things that Nell had said didn't seem to matter as much as understanding why she'd said them. And along with that came the sure and certain knowledge that she was stronger. She could afford to be generous.

"This is where I come to recover, to remind myself of how families can be," she coaxed. "I've learned so many important things from you, that I'd never have known without you. We don't have to agree about everything, do we? We never really have, when you think about it."

"No." Unexpectedly, Nell's face softened. "You were always stubborn, exasperating, opinionated . . ."

This was familiar ground. Nell sounded teasing, but there was an edge to what she said.

Has she *ever* liked me? Alice suddenly wondered. Do I like her? What's happening here?

The furious energy she'd felt earlier left her as abruptly as it had come. She felt empty, sick, afraid. She'd had enough.

"I don't want to lose you, Nell," she said shakily. "But all of this is part of who I am. You've got to stop undermining it, because you're undermining me."

She couldn't be sure Nell was still listening, because her features were set in a mask, an empty half-smile, turned towards the dying fire. She was gone.

"I'm going to bed now," Alice said lamely. She pushed herself awkwardly to her feet and edged towards the door, suddenly desperate to escape the tense atmosphere, her words, Nell's silence. "Thanks again for having Holly. I'll see you tomorrow."

In the morning, Alice took Holly home. Nell said little to Alice before they left. She said nothing about the night before, but she was cool and distant, and Alice knew that she hadn't forgotten it.

"Thanks again, Nell," she offered.

"For nothing," Nell said stiffly, stroking Holly's hair. She didn't look at Alice. "You can come any time you want to, Holly."

"'Bye, Nell. 'Bye, Jenny." Holly kissed Nell and Brendan and waved at Jenny before she got into the car. "See you next time!"

If there is a next time, Alice thought.

"Come back soon," Brendan said to Alice. "Don't worry about Nell. Whatever you're rowing about now, she'll get over it. She always does."

But, will I? Alice wondered. Will I want to come back here? She looked at Brendan's kind face and felt a sense of loss. Everything was changing so fast.

"Thanks, Brendan." Impulsively, she kissed him. "You're a good man, do you know that? A treasure. Thanks for everything."

CHAPTER TWENTY-SEVEN

The sense of exhilaration left her. Now she felt as if she had an emotional flu. With Holly back in school and her scheduled appointment with Ruth looming, the pressure inside Alice built up. She felt as if she was living through an extended panic attack. Her body was too fragile and exhausted to contain her shaking anymore. She was sick of reminding herself to keep breathing, of the pins and needles in her face, of not hearing what Holly said to her.

She forgot what she was doing when she was in the middle of doing it. She was clumsy and awkward, dropped things, walked into walls. The photocopier blew up when she tried to use it.

"It needs to be serviced," Brian said casually, but Alice knew better.

All the clocks in the house stopped except Holly's. Alice had to change the lightbulb in her darkroom three times in one week. Dishes fell and shattered on the kitchen floor. Alice knew she was out of control, but she only became more and more determined.

You can't stop me, she told herself, I'm going to do this.

She had to force herself to take soup when Holly

was eating. Chewing would have been too much to ask.

Her determination to tell Ruth everything exhausted and scared her. The day before her appointment she brought Holly to school and then went straight home again, to bed. She pulled the quilt around her and let herself sink into the lethargy that pulled at her.

But now there was a fresh battle inside her, between the weighted paralysis she felt and all her recent knowledge. She imagined telling Ruth about this depression. She could see Ruth's scepticism, her dismissal.

Well, you can lie there and wallow if you like. Or you can get up. It's up to you.

She sulked for an hour, furious. But she couldn't escape the knowledge that, this time, she had a choice. Finally she threw back the quilt, defeated, and got out of bed.

She went out and bought the red dress, without trying it on. There were limits, after all, to this reluctant energy. But as soon as she got home again she put it on. It was soft and fell almost to her ankles. Its colour warmed her.

"You bought it!" Holly sang out when Alice picked her up from school. "Oh, Mummy, it's lovely! Can I try it on?"

The sleeves flapped foolishly below Holly's wrists, the hem crumpled in folds on the floor.

"You'd better take it off, Holly. It's miles too big for you."

Holly grumbled, but lifted the dress over her head

378

and gave it back. "Will you leave it to me in your will?" she asked, head tilted as she watched Alice put the dress back on.

Alice laughed at her. "The nerve!" she said. "I'm not planning on dying anytime soon. Maybe I'll give it to you when you're bigger. If you still want it."

The next day she wore the dress again, with a sloppy black cardigan over it to make her feel less conspicuous.

"You look good, Alice," Ruth said when she saw her. "Tired, but good. That colour suits you. You were very grey-looking when I left."

Alice nodded. She couldn't speak. She sank into the chair opposite Ruth.

Now that she was here, it was harder than she'd thought it would be to tell Ruth what had happened. Even though she knew what she wanted to say, the words would not come easily, she had to drag them out. Her voice was shaky and kept stopping. Her breath was jagged and rough, making holes for her words to fall into. But she forced herself to go on, to say it all out, to tell.

"In all the time I've been coming to you, I've never told you what it felt like for me, to be a child in that house," she began, shakily. "What really happened. I couldn't. I tried, Ruth. I swear I did, but I couldn't find the way out, for the words. I held it all back and told myself it was nonsense, and gave you hints, hoping you'd name it for me, that you would say what it all meant. I thought, if it came from you, I'd believe it."

"How could I know, Alice? You're the only one who knows. You wouldn't have believed me at all."

"I know that now. I would have fought you as hard as I fought myself. Maybe even harder. But I want to tell you now. I think I can do it. I want you to listen."

"I'm listening." Ruth moved, leaning into her chair as if to make herself more comfortable. Her long legs, tanned again, stretched across the floor towards Alice.

"I have a sense of myself, as a child . . . that I was this smelly, damp little kid. Something rotten . . . I've told you about that . . . thing in my life that I didn't have words for, couldn't explain. The waking nightmare that played itself out over and over again, that I had no control over. Once it started I couldn't stop it. I've told you about it before. But I didn't know what to call it, what it was. What it is."

"What is it?"

Alice swallowed. "Memory. It's a memory. That's what it was all along."

She held her hands in her lap, away from her face, where they wanted to be. Don't hide now, she told herself. Don't.

"I remember," she said, her breathing jagged and uneven. "Remember. It's such a complicated word. Putting it all back together."

She told Ruth what had happened while she was away. What she'd remembered. About her father and being his plaything. About the slime that washed over her, crusting on her skin.

It came out fast, less and less coherent, but it kept coming. She was shocked by how difficult it was to say the words, even now, when she knew what they were. How her throat locked against them. But she made herself continue. Her voice was out of control as she veered wildly around her story, crashing into details and leaving gaps. But telling it. More or less. She felt nothing like the joyful steady relief she'd anticipated. It burned its way out of her.

When she'd finished she felt as if she'd turned to stone. Petrified. The weight of her own body pinned her to the spot, she would never be able to move or speak again. She felt the familiar wash of shame and then anger. She stared at the floor.

"I thought," she forced herself to say it all. "I didn't understand, you see. I thought, I thought my father was using me," she swallowed hard, "as a toilet."

Fear coiled around her throat, trying to clamp it shut, but she held it open and something else squeezed through.

I'm in the outhouse. The musty smell of old air and Jeyes fluid and dead flies, the bare stone floor. Cobwebs in the corners of floor and ceiling. In the far corner a big, fat spider is working on her web. A sudden draught, the door opens and he's there, his breath loud and smelly. He leans over, puts a hand up suddenly against the wall. It stops him falling.

"I want to use that," he says.

"I'll be quick, I'm nearly finished."

"I can't wait." His hand isn't on the wall any more. He's opening his trousers, fumbling. He says something I can't hear. I'm trying to get off, leaning down to pull up my pants but, "You'd better open your legs," he warns.

And then the warm splashing over my bare legs, my hands, my clothes, it's in my hair. His adam's apple shakes when he laughs. The wall beside me is solid as rock. There's no way through. I am the spider, fixing her web, waiting. The smell fills the back of my mouth. I press so far into the wall I can taste stone.

His glasses turn in my direction. He has no eyes. He sees nothing. His voice scrapes me like broken glass when he says, "Look at the state of you. You'd better not let your mother see you like that. You're disgusting."

Then it was all out of her like air from a balloon. She shuddered and subsided. There was nothing left in her, not even disbelief. Ruth's room smelled of urine.

"Alice."

At first she thought it was Elaine's voice, trying to wake her, calling her back from the place she went to when the dream started. She looked around for her mother, but then she saw that it was Ruth, calling her back.

"Yes?"

"I wish you'd stop hurting yourself."

Alice started. She looked down and saw that she

was raking the skin of her forearms with her splintered nails, leaving red tracks swelling on the skin.

"I didn't know. I didn't know I was doing it," she said in wonder. She looked at Ruth again, still confused.

"Where is she?" she whispered.

She lifted her arms towards Ruth, showing her the weals. "I didn't know," she said again. She brought her hands up to cover her face, not able to bear the exposure any longer.

"O God." She screamed into her hands. The sound stretched away from her. The air shook. When it settled she took her hands away from her face.

She wanted more than ever to hide, to shrivel up and die. But she knew that Ruth would ask her to look at her. She knew it was important. So she forced herself to lift her head and look straight into Ruth's warm open face. Ruth's brown eyes seemed larger than usual and they shone. They held her. She felt steadied. The shaking subsided.

"That was very brave, what you've just done."

"I'm exhausted."

"I'm not surprised. There's something I want to ask you. You've talked about 'the others'. Who were they? Do you know?"

"They were all me. One for every filthy time he touched me. Some of them even liking it," she shuddered, "until he hurt them. Us. Me. One of the reasons I couldn't believe that it was real was because of them. I wondered who they could be, how could there be a collection of small children, tied and beaten and crying their eyes out, locked up in the house with no one knowing? Where could they have come from? Now I know. It was me. You see, I've always known. There is nothing I didn't already know, but I didn't believe myself. I invented a million other explanations except the fact that it's true. All of it. Oh God." She was crying while she talked.

"Is there anything you need now, from me?" Ruth asked, when she'd calmed.

Alice took a deep, heavy breath. "I think I just needed to be heard. Thank you."

"What are you feeling?"

"Empty. No, that's not quite right. Volcanic. Do you know what I mean? There's this hatred, deep down, and rage. Ready to erupt and burn its way out of me. I want to learn how to use it. I'll want you to help me. I might even be looking forward to it?"

They smiled at each other, smiles that held all the pain and fear and hope that had passed between them in this room. Then Alice said, slowly, daring herself: "I think I'd like you to hold me."

They met in the centre of the room. Alice felt Ruth's strong arms around her, felt the full length of the other woman's body holding hers. She felt cherished. Her body turned to air and shook like a wind.

"Thank you," she said, when she could trust her voice to work again. "You saved me. You and Holly saved me."

"No, Alice. You saved yourself. You did it."

"Yes, but you heard me. You believed me. You believed in me. I learned how to do it from you."

She sighed, stepped away from Ruth, sat down again. Her knees were still shaking.

She laughed, suddenly, and told Ruth about the Ghost Train.

"It was weird, going with Kate like that. Maybe I should have gone with Holly. But that's different. When I was sitting on the beach waiting for Kate to come back I thought of all the things that are out there for us to do together. Me and Holly, I mean. Besides going to the cinema and for walks. Fun things. I'd better hurry up before she's too old and doesn't want me around anymore."

She shivered. "It's odd. I'll tell you something. I always used to think of my mother as cold and hard, you know? Always rejecting me. But the more I remember, the more it seems to be the other way around. I was the one who couldn't forgive her. I thought she knew, you see."

"And now?"

"I don't know what to think." She hugged herself, because she'd started to shake again. "She can't have known. Because if she knew, she'd have to have done something to stop it. Wouldn't she?" she pleaded.

Ruth spread her hands in front of her, as if to say that anything was possible.

"Instead," Alice went on carefully, "everything she did made it easier for him."

She stopped.

"I'm in trouble, here."

"Why?"

"This feels so dangerous. I don't know if I can

handle it." Her fingers tugged at her lip, slid into her mouth. She took them out again. Fastened the buttons on her cardigan. She'd missed one, so she undid them all and tried again, but her fingers didn't work properly. She linked them together and dug them between her knees.

"I can't bear it," she said distantly.

"What?"

"I feel disgusting. His genes are all mixed up with mine. Embedded in me. He's still inside me." She shuddered.

"That's an evasion, Alice." Ruth sounded dismissive.

Alice shrank from her, hurt and angry. "You don't understand what I'm saying!"

"I understand exactly what you're saying. And why you're saying it. But do you?"

"I don't know what you mean."

"You don't want to deal with the way you feel about your mother, so you're switching to your father. Just as, before, you shifted your hatred to your mother. It was easier to hate her than to take in what he was doing to you."

"She deserved it!" Alice shouted, as if it was Ruth she was angry with. She shrank even further, then, waiting for Ruth's anger to match hers.

Ruth didn't miss a beat.

"Yes, she did. They both deserved all the rage and hatred you felt," she said evenly.

Another knot loosened at the base of Alice's spine. She let herself grow back to her original size.

"I can see that you're right," she said, surprised. "But I didn't know I was doing it. It's like all the other times I've avoided saying things to you because I was so afraid of being wrong, of saying it wrong. So I said something safer instead, and tied myself into more knots than ever. I thought I was being super-truthful, but it was a kind of lying. To myself, if not to you."

Ruth nodded.

"I couldn't see it then, but I can see it now." She yawned, a deep, involuntary yawn. "I'm tired, Ruth. I've had enough. I can't deal with it all at once."

"You don't have to. It won't all change overnight, Alice. How can it? But now you know what you're doing. And you're strong enough to do it."

"Strong? Me?"

"Yes. You."

"I suppose you're right." Alice suddenly felt elated. "But I suppose there are things I'll never know for sure. Like, why he killed himself. Or even if he killed himself? No," she shook her head. "I know that's true. It's funny, I still go through these little pantomimes of accepting and rejecting something. But they're harder to reject as time goes on, you know? The thing is, I know it's not over, but it's different."

"In what way?"

"I'm not sure I can put it into words. I'm not even sure I understand it properly, how I feel. But it's as if, recognising and accepting the parts of myself that I'd lost was like coming into the world other people are born to. Before then, I didn't know what was real and what wasn't. I didn't even know that I was real. Or could be . . . There have been so many turning points. Like taking the image from the photo in, as part of myself. I think the first was that time I . . . marked myself, when you went away, remember?"

"Yes."

"Once I understood what I'd done, and why, it made a difference. Then, when I realised the extent of it when I was younger, how self-destructive I was, I knew I was on the right track . . . The next time I got depressed, I went to do it again but I couldn't. Because this time, I knew what it meant. And because I knew, I'd be choosing to do it. Consciously. Knowing what I knew, how could I? It's like drinking, or speed. It's all the same. I've always known that, if I ever drink again it will be because, somewhere, I'll have made a decision to do it. Knowing I'm responsible for it makes it less likely to happen. Does this make any sense at all? Like yesterday. I really thought I could die, I felt so . . . crushed. But, lying there, I knew it didn't have to be like that. So I got up and went and bought the dress. It's a choice I didn't have before . . ."

"But you have it now."

"Yes, I have it now. It's exhausting, in a way. Taking responsibility for that too. It's like, I'm not a victim any more. I've got to take charge of it all myself. Even though it hurts, and I know there are battles still ahead of me, and I resent that, I think I can remind myself that it's up to me to fight them. What matters is that I survived him . . . in more ways than one. I'm going to make the most of it."

"Living well is the best revenge?"

"Something like that. And there's Holly. I think it will be the same with her. If I recognise when I'm feeling destructive and can remember why, I think it will change. Because it's not about her, at all. I've talked to her. Warned her, in a way. It seems such an enormous burden to put on her."

"She's not you, Alice. She never has been. And you've given her a lot. She wouldn't have stood up to you the way she did if she didn't know, at some level, that it would be safe. Things are better for her than they ever were for you. And she'll make it better for her children too. It may take generations to overcome this, but the important thing is that you've broken the pattern. You've allowed Holly her perception of what's happening. You've even encouraged her to talk about it, to challenge it. And not only to you. That's huge."

Alice nodded, then brightened. "Hey, do you remember the photos I showed you? They've been accepted for that exhibition I told you about, next month. I've decided to join the co-op. They invited me, imagine! There's going to be another show in three months."

"Will you enter the same photos?"

"No. I have a beach series that I like. I'm going to try and pull them together. Shots of rock and driftwood, that kind of thing. There was a herring gull with only one leg. At first I thought he was pathetic. It was a windy day and he fell, more than landed, on the rocks. But then I saw that he was as tough as an old boot. He blustered his way through a battle with other gulls over some pieces of bread that Holly was throwing, and he won, every time. He had some kind of edge over them. Sheer bloody-mindedness. A survivor." She stretched, then stood up. "Like me."

"I'd like to see them."

"OK. I'll bring them next time. I'd better go. I have to pick Holly up from school. We're going to do something to celebrate this." She smiled at Ruth. "My telling you. Finding myself. Finding Holly. All the other stuff can wait. We'll get to it. Won't we?"

"I have no doubts about that." Ruth's whole face was lit by a wide smile. "Well done, Alice. You've come so far. You are barely recognisable as the woman who first came in here, do you know that?"

Alice nodded, delighted.

"What will you do, for this celebration?"

"I haven't decided yet."

Alice stood up, crossed the room to hug Ruth again, and left. She floated out of the room, as light as air. She felt alert, expectant. Ready. She would carry the strength that Ruth had helped her to find away with her and use it. She would always know what she had survived and how. What it had cost her and what it had given her.

When she got to the school, Holly ran to meet her. "What are we going to do, Mummy? You said something fun."

"What would you like to do?"

Holly shrugged and climbed in to the back of the car. She wasn't used to being asked. "I don't mind. I can't think of anything. A surprise. What do *you* want to do?"

The drive to collect Holly had left Alice feeling

exhilarated and restless. The traffic was light and the car hummed easily along. Despite her impatience, she had been sorry when she arrived and had to shut down the engine, turn off the stereo.

"I know," she said slowly. "What about going for a drive?"

"Where to?"

"Anywhere." Alice laughed suddenly. "Anywhere at all, Holly. It's Friday. We don't have to be back for two whole days. Let's just drive until we feel like stopping."

"What will we do then?"

"That depends where we find ourselves, doesn't it?"

"What about Tom?"

"It's going to be a warm night and there's food on her dish outside. We can ring Dermot and ask him to check on her."

Holly tilted her head to one side, considering. "Are we going to Nell's?"

"No. Not this time. We always go there. Let's go somewhere new."

"Where will we sleep?"

Alice laughed. "A Bed & Breakfast. We'll find somewhere."

"What about pyjamas?"

"Holly!" Alice was exasperated. "This is worse than twenty questions! You're so practical! I can see that you're going to boss me around for ever. But just this once let's not worry about all that, OK? It's not the worst thing in the world to travel without a toothbrush. It's called travelling light. Anyway, I'm the one who's supposed to worry about things like that, not you. You're far too serious for your age."

"What do you mean?"

"Never mind."

Alice started the engine and they moved off. They stopped once to fill the car with petrol and buy chocolate and crisps. Holly chose toothbrushes while Alice rang Dermot and asked him to look out for the cat.

As she drove out of the city, she realised that she had passed the kink in the road, her death-tree, without even noticing. She smiled. She knew where it was, part of her personal landscape. But moving out of the foreground now, into the shadows. Behind her.

She turned the car south and headed down the coast. Soon they had left the city behind. An ache of love caught in her chest. The whole country seemed to stretch out in front of them. Limitless. The road was a leafy tunnel and then they burst out into the open again, mountains all around them, the sea shining on their left.

Her foot sank on the pedal and the car surged forwards. She drove faster and faster. A Beatles' tape played on the stereo, and the music throbbed, swelled up through her feet and filled her. She and Holly sang along together, loud. "Take these sunken eyes and learn to see . . . " They smiled widely at each other in the mirror, still singing.

Alice looked at the road ahead. She felt the pressure of happiness build in her until she was sure she would burst, lift off from the ground and soar. Nothing, not even gravity, was strong enough to hold her down. The sky bent over her in a wide blue curve and she flew to meet it.

Strong.

Forgiven.